DANG

The Perfect Family

Rei BiLLi

Copyright © 2022 Rei BiLLi
All rights reserved
First Edition

PAGE PUBLISHING
Conneaut Lake, PA

First originally published by Page Publishing 2022

All rights reserved. This book or any portion thereof may not be reproduced or used in any manner whatsoever without prior written permission except for the use of brief quotations in a book review.

ISBN 978-1-6624-6867-4 (pbk)
ISBN 978-1-6624-6868-1 (digital)

Printed in the United States of America

Also by Rei BiLLi

Children's Science Fiction
In Chadwick's Eyes
Pseudonym—Rae Yung

Shamika, you will always be a part of me.

Fear is similar to the indelible stench of mothballs.

—Rei BiLLi

CHAPTER 1

Alexandria

Alexandria cannonballed through Hammond Sea International Airport. Her parents shuffled to keep up as the blinking monitors flipped to various places worldwide. The terminal rumbled with travelers embracing hellos contrary to tristful goodbyes. Uncontrollable children rioted through the lobby while parents nursed and coddled their infants. She cringed, watching the young boy beside her pluck boogers from the tip of his spindly finger. The snot mirrored a tiny slug slithering down the boy's moistened skin.

Scanning the room, she watched her parents' scrupled faces stuck in the seam between not wanting to let go but needing her to leave. Her father's fluffy beard disappeared amid the rumpus crowd. A few months ago, she had stroked his tufts of hair each morning after breakfast before heading to school. It became a ritual she adhered to because of the significance the whiskers held. It was like his pet. She had her kitten, Bumper, and her dad had his pretentious beard. Her mother stood next to her father with poignant eyes capturing the blinding glare Alexandria threw into space and time. The family's exuberant past played like a sad, apocalyptic song drumming in her heart.

Jolting chest pains jabbed her breastplate. The muscles tightened, rupturing the tissue underneath, releasing her soul through the cracks of it. Staring blindly, her parents were no longer standing in the distance waiting. They'd left, left her to the unknown world she was birthed in. She toppled to the floor next to a pile of luggage, mumbling words no one understood. Indistinct voices echoed in the foreground as necks craned from the background.

"I think she's choking."

"My *god*. Hope it isn't a heart attack."

"Someone call the paramedics!"

"Is it a seizure? She's shaking!"

"I hope she's okay. Her eyes are rolling in the back of her head!"

A tall, willowy man with an athletic build pushed through the crowd kneeled in front of Alexandria, gazing at her. "Excuse me. I'm a doctor. Someone get help!" His words aimed toward the throng of bystanders as she lay there convulsing.

A few people peered at the ceiling, while others looked down to the floor. The doctor examined her from head to toe when a steward snaked his way through the ruckus.

A subtle gasp escaped the steward's mouth as he blurted, "Is she dead?"

"She's had a panic attack." The doctor snatched the mask from the steward's hand. Then, placing two fingers under her jawline, he noticed her chest inflated and caved in the same breath.

A few minutes later, Alexandria sat straight up as though nothing had happened. "Thank you." She grasped the floor searching for her bags. Embarrassed, her cheeks rosy red, she placed her feet on the floor.

"Are you okay?" The doctor shone a gleaming light into her emerald eyes.

Alexandria attempted to block the bright light with her hands. "I'm okay." *I'm not okay. I feel like a freak show. All eyes on me like owls in the night.* She swatted the flashlight from her face. "Thanks."

Stumbling across his shoes, he supported her forearm.

"I said I'm okay!" she squalled before slipping again but this time over her feet.

The doctor caught her in his arms. His hands were soft and firm as she latched on for dear life. "All right." A smile ran across the doctor's face. His thick eyebrows floated above his unfurled eyelashes, and he had no visible body fat. "I'm Agatone." He cleared his throat.

"What?" Alexandria lifted the duffel bag over her shoulder.

"My name is Agatone." He picked up the boarding pass she dropped and placed it in her hand. "If you need me, I'm seven seats in front of you." Then, casually pointing toward the entranceway.

"Cocky 101." Alexandria smiled between her teeth. "Thank you." She staggered over the tarmac, following the scent that lingered behind him.

His biceps protruded with the fling of his leather bag. He caught her ogling him. She ducked, landing in a passenger's lap. "Shit!" Her eyes bulged, and her mouth flew wide open, releasing ignominy.

"Excuse you!" the young woman hissed, holding her breast. She pushed Alexandria to the floor.

"My bad," Alexandria spouted while crawling to her seat. The pilot's monotone voice articulated rehearsed instructions through the speaker. Soon after, the aircraft gained speed. A wad of bubble gum filled her cheek as she blew bubbles, inhaled, then exhaled as the sky cradled the plane into the clouds.

"No smoking!" A woman aimed a fire extinguisher directly at her face.

"What the fuck!" Alexandria's face was covered in water. "Thanks." She snatched the towel from the scowl-faced woman, swiping the substance from her eyelids.

"That was stupid," someone muttered behind Alexandria.

"How'd she get past security?" another person whispered to another.

"*Loca!*"

"Way to go, genius."

"Throw her ass off the plane!"

This day too shall pass. Alexandria's mother's voice resounded, and she slivered down into her seat.

CHAPTER 2

The Weakest Link

Alexandria planted one foot after the other into the deep muddy plain. Her legs trembled as she hopped over barrels, tumbled under bridges, and climbed through wooden fences. Sweat pebbles oozed from her skin with every push-up, chin-up, and sit-up. With limbs weighing flimsily like wet spaghetti strings, she possessed zero advantage in the field. Then unexpectedly, her stomach rumbled. First, she felt faint—then it happened. Breakfast bars, mixed with coffee, expelled from her esophagus through her mouth and rippled down the dirty uniform.

"Go! Let's go, recruit! A thick vein waved across Gunnery Sergeant Belcroft's forehead. "No slowing down, vomit breath!" He grabbed his crotch as if showing authority were linked to his seminal duct.

"I don't think I can…" *I really don't think I can. I feel like I am literally going to die.* Alexandria wiped emesis from her mouth, spitting one last time. "This gear weighs more than I do. My menses are heavy. It's wet, and your breath stinks." *I've been served up a bad breath and stomach cramp mélange.*

"Complaints don't get heard around here, turd!" The gunnery sergeant shoved her along.

Alexandria nose-dived into a mudhole, and muck filled her mouth as she retrieved stolen breaths.

"Up now, turd!" Gunnery Sergeant Belcroft lifted her by the collar.

Alexandria sniffled, attempting to wipe the goop from her face. Her heart pounded as she exhaled deeply, feebly trampling near the tunnel ahead when she collapsed to the ground.

Alexandria arose from an unfamiliar bed, panicking. The lights on the ceiling nearly left her sightless. "Hello, anybody, somebody?" A teeth-chattering chill strong-armed her slender frame.

A man who wore blue scrubs appeared in her peripheral. "You're awake?" His voice was familiar.

She whisked from behind the curtain. "Where am I? My clothes?" Her head rotated like clockwork.

"It's you. You're in medical?" The man walked closer. "No worries. How do you feel?" A shiny stethoscope dangled from his neck.

"You're a marine?" She squinted.

"Navy corpsman, rookie."

"I didn't know."

"What else would I be doing on a plane full of marines?"

"I don't know. I'm a rookie, remember?" Inspirational quotes written in bold, italic letters circled the wall above the entrance. "We have to stop meeting like this," Alexandria mumbled as she scooted back on the bed.

"If you stop having anxiety attacks, we will." He placed the stethoscope on her chest.

She flinched. "Not everyone is a macho feminist." Alexandria shivered. "Not all of us are trying to prove we're equal to you." She cleared her throat, looking away when his eyes fixated on her.

"You're right." He grinned. The dimple in his cheek left a lasting impression.

Blood dripped down her face, one speck at a time. "May I have a mirror, please?" Smearing the blood off her face. "This is going to leave a scar." She rubbed her marred eyebrow.

The doctor snapped his fingers in front of her face. "I am Petty Officer Socorro when the others are around, not Agatone." He took the mirror from her hand. "You're a little troublemaker. Always the small ones, huh?" He chuckled hard.

"It's not that funny, Petty Officer." Alexandria frowned, outlining the bloody blemish once more. "Is that a birthright name, or did you earn it?"

"It's not my fault you've been defiant toward the gunnery sarge twice and smoking on a government plane…" His lips were confident as the judgmental words he spoke.

Shamefaced, Alexandria scrunched her nose. "He spits in my face, and the smoking was an unintentional, habitual mistake." She frowned harder.

"Everyone fucks up." He chuckled more. "Except me."

Alexandria poked his shoulder. "Jesus Christ, Mary, and Joseph made Agatone Socorro perfect. Woo-hoo."

"What do Jesus and his parents have to do with it?" Agatone grabbed her hand, cuffing it into his. "Let me take you on a date?"

"You don't believe in Jesus and his family? God?"

He took a handful of bandages from the shelf above her. "Not particularly."

Alexandria's face turned solemn. *Shit. I'm crushing on Satan.*

"Dinner?"

Alexandria ignored him.

He stared at her without blinking. She hopped off the bed and rushed into the nearest washroom. "Don't forget to stop by the sergeant major's office when you leave here!" he yelled out so she could hear him above the running water.

An unpleasant smell seeped from underneath the sergeant major's door as Alexandria entered. It reeked of stale cigars and leftover food. Wide-eyed, she gnawed at her remnant fingernails, awaiting vulgar demands. The sergeant's face was quizzical as his chin folded and unfolded with every word that projected out his mouth. The furrows in his face resembled the skin of a Shar-Pei. The legs on his chair leaned inward as if they were about to break the longer he reclined back. He licked the corners of his lips, attempting to remove the pale substance hanging in the crevice. Despite the pressure his tongue applied, it remained stuck.

"Private, this is the last straw. One more pull, and you're out." The sergeant major slammed his fist down on the desk. "Try to make it the next few weeks, why don't ya?"

Alexandria remained calm on the outside, unnerved on the inside. "So that's it?" She rubbed the slits of her mouth, hoping the sergeant would follow her lead.

"That's it. You may leave now," he urged.

Alexandria left in a hurry, bypassing the telephone at the end of the hallway that worked occasionally. The sergeant major coggled out of his office when Alexandria ran through the hall, jumping across tables and chairs, landing on Secretary Shultz's desk. Secretary Sucks, the recruits called the secretary after she was caught blowing the sergeant major down in the men's sauna. Some said she had a son by the sergeant major. Neither rumor nor boy proved evident, Alexandria reflected, staring at Secretary Shultz sideways.

"May I help you, Private Paz?"

"No, madame secretary." Alexandria tiptoed across the desk, knocking over her coffee mug, staining a stack of papers. "Have I received any mail this week?" She ignored the mess.

A displeasing wrinkle ran down the center of the sergeant major's forehead. "Alexandria? Are you trying to get a dishonorable discharge?" he yelled.

Alexandria shrugged. *Fuck you.*

Secretary Shultz's face contorted as she pointed to the exit sign above the door. Alexandria gibed and dashed into the hallway.

Swim lessons with intense strength training from Agatone alleviated Alexandria's stress levels and increased her stamina. During her morning run, the wind blew fierce as she sprinted through the wooded area. Her speed slowed when a unique shrub caught her eye. She sat underneath the large tree with branches that hung like an umbrella—the disordered leaves mesmerized her. The sun pried through its spaces as a giant bird looped around a nest directly atop the distinct trunk filled with hatchlings.

God is creative. I guess Agatone does not notice God's creativity since he doesn't particularly believe—the trees, the sun, the birds. If I were a bird, I'd be an ostrich—long necks and fast runners. Alternatively, maybe, I'd be an owl—wise and shit. These little guys don't stand a chance against the wild—it's sad. They can't be brilliant. Maybe it's where the term birdbrain *originated. Perhaps it's why Mrs. Hannah wrote* birdbrain *on Brady's midterm quiz after she had given us the answers prior. After all, if one of those little birdies fell out of the tree, how would the mama retrieve them with her beak? Her tiny stick feet? The little fuckers probably drop to the ground and die,* she thought, pressing her hands together. "Thank you, Jesus, for not making me a member of the bird family or like Brady Stevenson." *Oh no, I sound like my mom.*

A loud noise chimed through the forest. Soon after, the prayer ended, and Alexandria sprinted away. The sound settled after a while. No one was there. Her muscles still, she waited in silence when the footsteps became louder but slower, crushing across the leaves on the ground. A voice sounded. Alexandria darted toward a stream and stumbled right into his arms.

"I knew you'd be here." Gunnery Sergeant Belcroft's debauched mustache waved across his lip. He jerked her aside, forcing his cold chapped lips against hers. She bellowed, stomped his foot, and kneed him in the groin.

"Wait, slow down…can't a sarge have a piece of confectionery?" The sergeant held his throbbing scrotum.

"No! Stay the fuck away from me, you fetishist fuck!"

"Don't make me run after you."

"Perv!" Alexandria ran as fast as she could through the perennial plants.

"I'm the reason you're still here, bitch!" he yelled, limping in the opposite direction.

CHAPTER 3

Rebecca

Alexandria made it back to her room, peeling off her wet clothes, dabbing her bottom lip with her shirt. Her roommate threw a towel at her chest.

"I see you made it back."

"Gunnery Sergeant Asshole sexually harassed me in the woods." Alexandria nervously pulled off her soggy socks.

"What?" Her roommate typed minaciously on her keyboard.

"Nothing. It's not like anyone will believe me. Who'd believe a private over a gunnery sergeant?" She contemplated. "What should I do, Rebecca?" Alexandria sat in the center of the floor, exhibiting deep-breathing exercises. She stretched her limbs, crisscrossing one arm over the other, waiting for Rebecca's response.

"Just ignore it."

"What if I report him? I wish I could teach him a lesson. Asshole!" Alexandria visualized his crooked mustache wavering across his smirky face. The horrid breath of turmoil tortured recruits with every morpheme uttered. "I hate this place." Switching positions, she stretched her legs across the floor.

"Why are you still here?" Rebecca continued to stare at her computer screen.

"My parents." Alexandria rolled her eyes, tying her hair into a bun. "What did your laptop do to you?"

Rebecca laughed. "Emailing Daddy, asking for shit he should've sent me weeks ago."

"I haven't talked to my parents, and I don't want to."

"How demure of you."

Alexandria flopped on top of her twin-size bed sulking.

"A few of us are going to a private party later. You should join us."

"Thanks, but no thanks. There's a culinary instructor coming tomorrow morning."

"Ennui…we'll have you back in time."

"I don't know, Rebecca."

"It's Bec…come on. Be a sport. All you do is practice."

"Have you seen me out there?"

"You're horrible because you think you are."

"I don't know. Gunnery Sergeant Asshole said we're not allowed."

"Please keep talking. I'm always extremely interested when I yawn." Rebecca propped her feet on the desk.

"I don't want to get into any more trouble."

"Beauty without expression…that is a thing."

"What?"

"You're a bore!"

Alexandria took a deep breath. "Okay, you've convinced me. I'm in."

"Are you all in?"

"I said I'm in."

"Say, 'I'm all in, Bec.'"

"I'm in, bitch."

"This is going to be fucking awesome." Rebecca clasped her laptop shut.

"Excited much?"

"I'm just happy you're letting go."

* * *

Everyone had settled down across the camp. Mice scampered through the cafeteria, searching for cheese crumbs or whatever edibles they could find. They weren't the only warm bodies benefiting from the restricted hours. Nearby, Alexandria and Rebecca prepared for their outing with roommates Kristen and Mink.

Kristen scuffled to pull up her rubber catsuit, while Mink applied glittery lip gloss to her plush lips when a loud knock at the door frightened them. The banging interrupted their singing. They shuffled away from the window, scattering like ants. Rebecca jumped on her bed. Alexandria flopped onto a bedsheet that stretched across the floor. Kristen slid into the closet, knocking over a lamp, and Mink fell inside Rebecca's dirty laundry basket.

"Ew, now I have to shower again." Mink pinched her nose. "What the fuck, is this a tampon?" She examined it with her quick reflexes and whirled the stained cotton into the closet next to Kristen. Kristen almost barfed when it landed on her thigh.

"What the fuck are you doing?" Rebecca threw a hairbrush at Alexandria's head.

Alexandria dodged the brush. "What? Are you trying to give me another concussion?"

"Get the door!" Rebecca yelled.

"No! Why me?" Alexandria objected.

"Just answer it!" Rebecca demanded.

Alexandria launched the brush back at Rebecca as she tiptoed to the door. "Satan? What are you doing here?" She stepped outside, rubbing her eyes in restlessness, pulling the door behind her.

Agatone pushed her bangs away from her face. "You are the most beautiful woman I have ever seen."

Alexandria stepped aside. "That's the Irish, Italian, and Black in me," she said sarcastically. "What do you want? I was trying to sleep."

"I can't get your epigrammatic mouth out of my head."

"What are you...forty? Who says *epigrammatic*?"

"Twenty-seven."

The effect she had on him excited her. "We can't talk right now. Where will you be in about ten years?"

"I know you like me." Agatone smirked, grabbing hold of Alexandria's hand.

"No, I don't. I have to go!" She jerked away.

"I've wanted you since the first time I laid my eyes on you at the airport, Alexandria. You killed the Snow White act, by the way."

"We can't do this, Agatone. Training partners only, remember?"

"So you don't like me?" He smiled that dreamy little smile.

Alexandria grinned a little. "Yes. No…I don't know. We can't do this now." Fidgeting her fingers.

"Let me cook dinner for you tomorrow night. If you don't like the food, I'll never ask again."

"I'll think about it, but I'm busy tomorrow." Alexandria reached for the door handle. Agatone's hand covered hers, holding tight. "What now?" she whined.

Agatone gripped her fingers. "My number." He turned her hand over. "Whenever you need me, call me." He slipped the pen back in his pocket.

"Shut up and go." Alexandria snatched her hand away and slammed the door in his face. Mummified, her head rested against the door.

"Well…who was that?" Rebecca shrieked.

Alexandria, nervous, hit her hand against the doorknob. "No one." She screeched, *fuck*, attempting to shake the pain away.

"Just make sure they're gone." Rebecca put two fingers up, creating air quotes.

The jeep bumped sounds of music as it roared through the steep hills. The girls screamed along with the lyrics verbatim. The gales massaged their scalps as their hair blew wild.

"My best friend Aamir's a daredevil!" Alexandria yelled, swiping the bangs against her forehead behind her ears.

"Are we daredevils?" Mink ridiculed as she sped down the crooked road.

"I prefer masters of the universe!" Kristen screamed.

Rebecca scoffed, "More like sycophants."

Ignoring them, Alexandria focused on the long line of trees towering among the clouds. The smaller trees admired the larger ones as the branches swayed from left to right. The forest shadow praised streams of water. Mink slowed down when they came upon a triplex field leading into several directions. She parked the jeep in the center of it. Rebecca pounced out of the back seat as Kristen leaped from the roof, screaming. Mink and Rebecca howled at the moon as if they were summoning a wolf pack. It was dark, and the only visible things in sight were the stars in the sky.

Rebecca, Kristen, and Mink laughed, pumping their fists angrily at the wind, shouting and chanting like they were on a softball field. Alexandria did not believe her eyes or ears. Her friends in San Francisco never made noises like these girls. They didn't burp or fart, and if they did, it was in the sanctuary of their bathrooms.

A cluster of eyeballs floated near them and then disappeared. Alexandria looked around. "What in the…hello?" she called out, shaking in her open-toe sandals. "Where did you guys go?" She walked back to the jeep—animal noises choired in the night. Her heart raced. "Come on, guys! I tend to have panic attacks. You know this." *Why did I come here? Shit. Shit.* She swiveled her phone, aiming the flashlight toward the trees, the ground, and the jeep, then a voice bellowed out. Alexandria's feet ascended from the earth, spinning around in circles. Laughter filled the air. "Put me down, assholes!" Wild-eyed and screaming, veins coursed down the side of her neck. Omega, Rebecca's cousin, placed Alexandria back on the ground. Upset, she stomped away.

"Wait!" Omega ran after her. His friends followed.

"What did you think we were going to do?" Rebecca's pupils dilated as she watched Alexandria. Her eyes glazed as she nodded toward Mink.

"I'm leaving." Alexandria dusted dirt mites from her sandals.

Mink moved closer by Alexandria. "Don't leave, Alex. We have so much planned," she whispered.

Kristen bumped Mink's backside. "Yeah, you can't leave." Her words fumbled out of her mouth.

"Prank playing on my account, not my idea of fun. You can do what you want without me." Alexandria searched through her contacts on her cell.

"Who you gonna call? Ghostbusters?" Omega grinned, showing all his teeth to his friends, and they all started singing the *Ghostbusters* theme song.

The pixilated glare in Rebecca's eyes threatened them, and they all settled down at once. "Please don't go...we were fooling around. Please stay," Rebecca pleaded with Alexandria.

Desperate to leave, she pouted in silence while everyone watched in suspense. Rebecca carefully eased closer to Alexandria, extending her hand, and their fingers interlocked. She led Alexandria deeper into the woods, where strobe lights pierced the ambiance, perforating her eyesight.

In between two eucalyptus trees sat a large cabin. The scenery resembled a painting inside Alexandria's mother's gallery. Pushing the creaky cabin door open, "Thysia," she read the engraving above the door, unsure of the meaning. As they crossed the threshold, she pivoted toward the basement near the stairway. A golden sarcophagus sparkled in the center of the kitchen. Bodies spewed from the stone coffin. Women climbed out with ten-inch heels, bikini bottoms, leather masks, while the men paraded around in sheer nakedness. Alexandria's mouth flung open.

Who are these people? What type of Day of the Dead shit is happening here? My stomach...I feel faint. I need it. Yes, I need this. Alexandria grabbed a red cup from a guy's hand, whose hard-on poked her in the side as she weaved past the crowd of flesh. The thick purple solution coaxed her throat. Breasts greeted her from every angle. A man wearing a lamb's head rushed past, propelling her forward. The quick onward spin reminded her of the days she practiced ballet with Aunt Tippy. *First, learn the basics—stand up straight, position the feet, plie, relevé, saute, turn—and it's pivotal to understand the terminology.*

Tippy was a ballet scholar until she cracked her femur skiing when Alexandria was fifteen. The accident ended her career. Professionally dancing was Tippy's lifeline. Alexandria lost touch with Tippy after she moved away to teach at the Ballet Institute of Chicago. She was embarrassed or sad. After she healed and received help for depression, she accepted the job offer at the prominent school for dancers. Tippy's voice resounded as Alexandria pinched the Fenris's nose, checking for authenticity.

Music flooded the building as alcohol absorbed the room. Alexandria rotated cigarettes one after the other, watching heads bounce up and down, capping the ceiling. A man whose beard swung across his navel stooped in front of her. She tumbled over his back, landing on the shaggy black carpet near the bar. Rebecca stood there, wearing a mischievous grin.

"You'd think by now their hormones would be under control," Alexandria joked as she stood up straight. Her stance imitated a dancer—poise and appropriate. Dancer genes run in their family, according to Tippy.

Rebecca laughed. "I think he's a goat or something." She sipped a mouthful of foam from the rim of her cup.

Alexandria smiled until her cheeks hurt, dancing in circles, allowing the music to control her body.

"Nice moves!" Shouting above the thunderous beat, Rebecca's eyebrow raised as if it had a mind of its own.

"Were you trying to give me a heart attack outside?" Alexandria accepted a shot glass with rainbow swirls from her.

Rebecca laughed. "It was Omega's idea!" she screamed above the music.

"Why were you staring at me like a livid person just now?" Alexandria sipped from the shot glass before tossing it back.

Rebecca moved closer. "I was watching your hips. Is that a crime?" Rebecca placed her hand on the small of Alexandria's back.

Is she flirting with me? Alexandria giggled nervously. "These knock-knees?" She swiped her hair behind her ear.

"The sexiest thing about a woman is when she doesn't know she's sexy as hell." Rebecca kissed her cheek.

Alexandria took another swig from her drink, inhaled, exhaled, and lit another cigarette from the deteriorating nub before throwing it out, not sure if it was Rebecca's hand on her spine, the rainbow shots, or the euphoria-filled room that had her lady parts excited.

"I couldn't wait any longer." Rebecca took the cigarette from Alexandria's lips, inhaled, exhaled, and then placed it back between her pout. "Those fucking early morning jogs." A whiff of smoke escaped her mouth as she spoke. "Watching you stretch, sweat racing down the dip in your back"—Rebecca sipped from another crystal vial—"dripping down your little kiwis." She grabbed the back of Alexandria's neck. Their lips met.

At that moment, the room ceased as their bodies morphed into one. Rebecca's tongue, smooth and slippery, and bitter and sweet drivel slid down the back of Alexandria's throat. Then a glass broke, disrupting the intensity between them.

Alexandria backed away. "I'm…not into girls…" she stuttered.

Rebecca squinted, pulling Alexandria closer to her pelvis. Their lips grazed again. "Sure feels like you're into girls." A mixture of Jolly Ranchers and liquor spilled from her breath—the words parroted inside Alexandria's head.

"I can't…I…just." She staggered against the bar.

Rebecca clutched her hand, blowing smoke in her face. "Come with me. The girls and I have a surprise for you." She intertwined her arm between Alexandria's and guided her down the stairs underneath the cabin floor. It was dark and spooky. Kristen and Mink expected their arrival as they stood in silence, watching their legs tread down the stairway.

"What is going on?" Alexandria pulled out another cigarette, lit it, and that was when she saw him attached to a large wooden cross. "Gunnery Sergeant? What the fuck!"

"You wanted to do something about this asshole, right? Well, here he is. It is time for him to get what he deserves." Rebecca dragged a chair from a worn-down table, placing it in front of him. "Kristen, it looks like Belcroft needs a shave." She laughed aloud.

Kristen dropped a medical bag beside Gunnery Sergeant Belcroft's naked body. She spread plastic on the floor and placed the tools down neatly on top. Mink pulled a wooden stick out of his mouth.

The gunnery sergeant screamed so loud the girls covered their ears. "You're all going to be in deep shit! Do you know who the fuck I am?" He wiggled and squirmed, shaking the wooden cross. The girls could barely hold it in place.

"Yeah, we know who you are, Sergeant Dick?" Rebecca forced a wooden stick between his teeth. "Do you know who I am?" Her voice carried across the room. She picked up a long needle. "I make the demands." She squirted the substance from the syringe before injecting it into his neck. His muscles stopped contracting, stiffening his limbs instantly.

Alexandria's breath deepened. "Guys, we can't do this."

"We are doing this." Rebecca placed a scalpel in Alexandria's hands. "Now, carve both of his balls. Start with the skin first, then the testicles. After that, we'll leave his little dick." Her laugh reminded Alexandria of Ursula's when she took Ariel's voice.

Alexandria did not move. She couldn't believe her eyes were subjected to such atrocity, hate. The sergeant's asshole qualities besieged her, but to kill him was out of her range for revenge.

"I told you she wouldn't go through with it." Mink giggled.

"She's a scary bitch," Kristen snickered. "This asshole treated you like shit, and now you wanna bitch up?"

Rebecca took the blade from Alexandria and gave it to Mink. "Then you do it."

Kristen laughed. "I'll do it. I'm the one in medical school. I'll incise the hell out of his skin and balls and leave the little sweet pickle." The gunnery sergeant's eyes filled with fright.

"He can't move. What did you do to him?" Alexandria asked. At first, she was afraid, but then calmness ensued, intrigued by what was about to occur. The sergeant had made her life a living hell since her first day at camp. The roles had reversed. He was the victim now.

"We gave him a neurotoxin. He's alert, but he can't speak. But he will feel everything." Kristen stooped in front of him, lifted his scrotum, and gently cut the skin from around the pouch. Tears filled the gunnery sergeant's eyes. He hollered, but no one could hear him.

Next, Kristen sliced the veins, and his testicles plopped down into the tub. *Splat*. Alexandria jumped from disgust. Afterward, Mink pinched the testes with plastic tongs and placed them inside a clear jar. Mink and Kristen sat down beside Rebecca. The blood drained from his body like water from a hose. His body was bloodless.

"Now what?" Alexandria panicked.

"Now, Kristen and Mink will dispose of the body, and we'll go back to the party." Rebecca grabbed the jar and took it upstairs.

Alexandria watched as Kristen and Mink disintegrated the body into nothingness.

* * *

The following day, Alexandria awoke with a pounding headache. The room spun, and her stomach turned along with it. Rebecca bounced back and forth across the room like a bushy-tailed, bright-eyed bunny rabbit. She glowered at Rebecca, inspecting the room. It was difficult to remember anything about last night. How and when did they return? She popped a seltzer, along with a mouthful of Diet Coke, while Rebecca pranced around the room gleefully.

A hairpin hung from Rebecca's lips. "You were great last night, Alexandria. So sweet like pineapples." She giggled. Her autumn berry fragrance fumed the room.

"What?" Alexandria was dazed and confused. She curled her knees up to her chest. Foggy thoughts of cigarettes, Jolly Ranchers mixed with swirly shots clouded her brain. She dropped her head between her legs, and a trail of red marks lined her inner thigh.

* * *

The classroom was cold. An icebox couldn't be warmer on the last day of hell camp. Everyone was on pins when the clock struck three. Alexandria rested her head on the hard desk as the class waited for the gunnery sergeant's arrival.

She opened her eyes when a man wearing a sergeant's uniform walked through the doorway. His shiny shoes glistened as if he had polished them before entering the room. The man sprinted near the whiteboard like someone was after him. Master Sergeant Edwards wrote his name with a navy-blue marker. She grabbed her queasy stomach, and suddenly puke spewed out her mouth. It splashed in the private's hair, sitting in front of her. Rebecca smirked from across the room, giving her a thumbs-up.

"Thanks for the warm welcome, Private Paz. Go clean yourself up." Master Sergeant Edwards pointed to the door. "And hurry back. Time waits for no one."

Alexandria passed by the private, whose stringed hair dripped vomit. "I'm so sorry, girl." Alexandria tapped the girl's arm as she ran out the classroom, dashing into the bathroom, her stride laggard when she reached the tarnished row of guck-filled sinks. Water dripped from her face as the reflection in the mirror copied her every move. The scar on her eyebrow was now a trademark. It was nothing like the birthmark that covered half her waistline. The birthmark reminded her of the many countries her mother visited in South America before she birthed Alexandria into the world of the unknown. The eyebrow scar was now a war wound. "I am a woman. Hear me roar," she growled under her breath when the bathroom door swung open. She cleared her throat. An autumn berry fragrance filled the room. *Sweet like pineapples* plagued her mind when Rebecca entered.

"Are you okay?" Rebecca asked. "Do people piss on these floors intentionally, or what?" She rubbed her body against Alexandria's hip.

Frowning, Alexandria wiped her mouth, moving to the last sink by the window. "Yes, I will be okay once I leave this place." Alexandria leaned against the mirror, reapplying her lip gloss.

"I'm sorry I've been MIA, Alexandria. I wish so badly that I could tell you what I've been up to, but it's better that you don't know."

"I don't care." She sliced Rebecca in half with her eyes as she slicked her hair back into a messy bun.

"Talk to me, Alex. Please I adore you so much."

"Says the person that drugged me and did God knows what to me." She wiped the vomit crumbs from her collar. "I never want to see you again!" She slammed Rebecca into a bathroom stall. The toilet water splashed, soaking Rebecca's uniform. Alexandria stood there as Rebecca squirmed her way off the commode filled with excretory product.

CHAPTER 4

Family Affair

After passing the Marine Corps exam, training, and sadistic behaviors at Camp Montz, Alexandria skipped out on the first flight home. She wanted nothing more to do with the marines and anything that came with it, including Agatone. A few weeks in a hotel room was the perfect getaway after everything that happened during infantry camp. It was a great start to leaving the marines behind before mending her relationship with her parents.

Reminiscing, she yearned for their hugs and kisses, planned movie nights, and exotic trips overseas. Margarita nights with her mother after Bible study was most fun, even though she did not understand the correlation. She enjoyed imbibing with her mother, but not as much as she anticipated the exquisite evenings with her father at the cigar lounge. Her father introduced her to the honeysuckle cigar complemented by red whiskey on the rocks. The combination was an acquired taste for some, but it was like heaven in her mouth. The cigar lounge was a secret place that only she and her father visited together—smoke-filled, where the elite made deals, invested, shared business ideas, and got laid. It intrigued her being among the crème de la crème, absorbing all their secrets. Politicians, producers, directors, aristocrats, and actors entered the cigar club on Sunday nights; but their wives were turned around at the door. It wasn't that she had dressed as a man to get inside the lounge, but the owners allowed her inside because they believed her to be her father's mistress—undoubtedly, her father did not evade the misconception.

The chauvinism pissed Alexandria off. Billie Jean King would not tolerate the bigotry, and neither would she. So despite the pact she made with her father to never divulge their secret, unmasking the lounge was her ultimate plan. She attained data for months to present to her journalist friend at the *Times of Now*, a popular news outlet that everybody read.

Little did Alexandria know someone watched her—the same as they'd paid attention to the rest of the doxies in the establishment. The informer notified her father of her eager intentions. The evening that she had arranged to meet with her source, someone had broken into her vehicle that morning and retrieved the cell phone, laptop, and notepad where she kept the information acquired. The planned operation ended since there was no proof. Months later, she found out it was her father that set her up. It spooked her. How could her father side with the misogyny? *Shouldn't I, his firstborn, be a priority?* But she soon realized his power and status overruled her relation to him. She could do nothing during this time, so she promised to never get involved in his affairs again. Family secrets ran through the Paz household, and she knew she could never tell a soul.

Alexandria focused on the park outside of the hotel window. Nostalgia took over when a family of four captured her attention. The wind blew the canary yellow scarf draped around the woman's neck as she filled a glass with lemonade. A tray filled with triangular-shaped sandwiches with no brown edges sat beside it. The woman smiled gleefully while the man, a young chipper fellow, ran behind two toddlers as they played on the sliding board and swings. The visual brought back memories of her mother, when she was more courteous; her father, when he was more energetic; and her brother, Abram, when he was alive. The small boy stayed close by his sister, as Abram had always stayed close to Alexandria.

* * *

Before classes began at San Francisco University, Alexandria spent the summer reconnecting with her mother and father in Malibu like she dreamed of. When they returned home from a relaxing getaway, Agatone sat waiting on her parents' doorstep. Her eyes stuck on him when he stood up. His chest was more prominent than before. She tried not to engage. He held a bouquet in one hand with a large bag of groceries in the other. Alexandria poked the pocket, laughing.

"Introduce us, dear." Mrs. Paz grabbed Agatone's arm leading him into the foyer. "Young man, who are you, and what do you want with my daughter?" She took him to the kitchen, placing her designer bag on the breakfast nook.

Satan.

"I never got my date, ma'am" was Agatone's excuse for being there.

"His persistence is appealing," Alexandria whispered to her mother as they sat at the nook. Agatone took many carrots out of a bag, smiling, shooting his dimples in her direction. "Not even remotely cute enough." She sipped from the wineglass. Then shoving the vase of *Liliums* aside, she noticed his swiftness as he worked his way around the kitchen to the other side.

He pulled his shirt above his head, tossing it on the coatrack near the pantry room. *His chest had grown bulky.* Alexandria's elbow slipped as she leaned out of her chair, almost hitting the floor. She fanned her face.

"Warm, dear?" Her mother poured her a glass of iced green tea. "Maybe this will help you, darling."

A few weeks later, normalcy kicked in. Alexandria's parents were better than ever. Mrs. Paz threw a handful of magazines on her bed. Bumper purred, pouncing to the floor when Alexandria shoved him from underneath her stomach. Fumbling through several papers, a distinct postcard that smelled like Agatone slip through her fingers.

"Aggy for sure. Aggravating 101." A chain with a silver heart dangled from another envelope. She ran her finger over the initials, ATP, engraved on it and clipped the bracelet around her wrist. She giggled a little, crumpled the letter, and tossed it inside her pajama drawer.

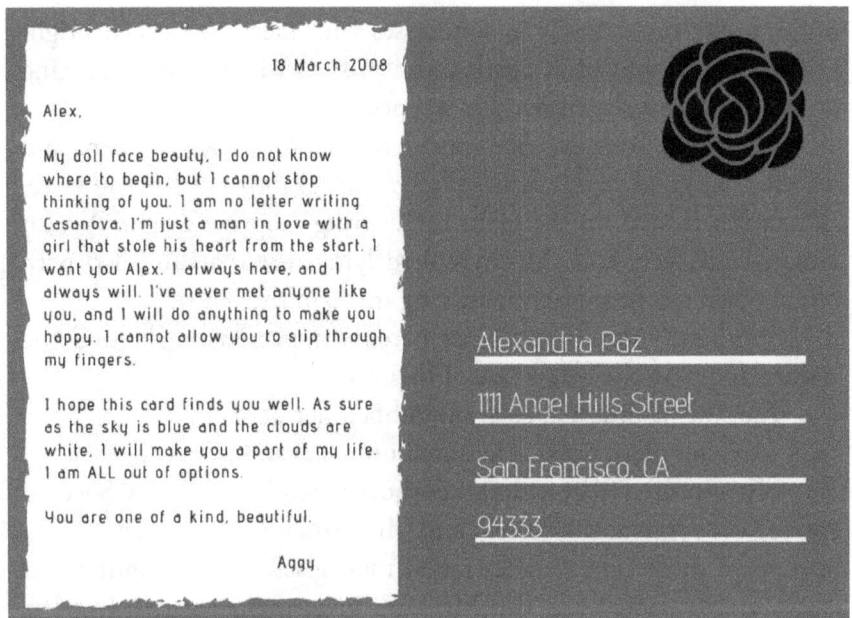

One year later

Mr. and Mrs. Paz invited Alexandria and Agatone to dinner one Friday evening. Mr. Paz created a nineties theme since it was Alexandria's birth year. Her mother dressed as Cher, and her father wore a ukulele around his chest.

"Mom!" Alexandria yelled when she and Agatone entered the vestibule. Agatone grabbed her waist, spinning her around. "What are you doing?" Her hips wavered.

"Kissing you." He planted several kisses on her neck.

Landin stepped inside behind them, holding the door open. "Hi, everyone. Autumn, my wife." He pushed the door wider as his wife struggled inside with a basket of blueberries. "Women and their feminism." He chuckled. "Come on in, angel." He took the basket from her wobbly arms.

As Autumn stepped inside, memories of the first time Alexandria met her flashed in her mind. She was different, unlike any other woman Landon had dated. Her mannerisms were androgenous and nothing like the damsels in sundresses with faces covered in bright yellows, blues, and pink lipstick and prissy social climbers hanging on his arm like a shirtsleeve she was accustomed to meeting.

"Call me, Tummy." She dusted her hands across her jeans and waved. "So good to see you." She gave Alexandria a firm squeeze. Alexandria fixated on the giant rock sitting atop her finger. A flash radiated her face, and she envisioned lying inside a tub filled with blood when she heard her name ring through the hallway.

"Surprise! Alexandria!" Her parents stepped from behind the sliding doors on the other side of the room.

Alexandria jumped. Agatone rubbed her bare arms.

"Are you okay, doll?" He stared into Alexandria's eyes.

She appeared to be in a state of shock when Mr. and Mrs. Socorro entered the room abruptly. Mr. and Mrs. Fancy, the next-door neighbors, were there. The Fancies raised their glasses to Alexandria and Agatone. Mr. Fancy was also Mr. Paz's investment partner. Mr. Paz invested in Mr. Fancy's software business after he was compelled to sell his stainless-steel company. The two men had been inseparable since. The equity allowed Mr. Paz to purchase oil shares in South America. His investments skyrocketed. The placement lotted him a residual income that turned his short-term money long-term. The two men became multimillionaires throughout two years. Their financial breakthrough created opportunities for them to make more money than either of them could count. The men were placed in an elite society so privileged that their wives were out of the loop.

Mr. Paz sold his company's stocks after sending her to the marines. Furniture, jewelry, Mrs. Paz's diamond elephant collection, and many other items were sold; and he was forced to file bankruptcy. They refused to reveal the hardship to Alexandria after her two-year stint in the Marine Corps since everything was better when she returned home. The trips, the fantastic restaurants, new furniture, vacation homes, damn near everything in their home were more decadent than before. Mr. Paz's success led to his wife's indulgence in ostentatious purchases.

Mrs. Paz eagerly revealed to everyone that her new kaleidoscope-stoned elephants in the hallway shot beams of chromatic lights down the hall when natural light hit them. The chromatic elephants reminded her of the days' rainbows lay across the desert sky in Nigeria. "Every morning at dawn, I washed and lathered their dexterous trunks and large floppy ears," she divulged. "One summer when I was ten years old, a terrible thing happened." A tear fell from her eye. "I found Peanut, my favorite elephant, suffering in the pasture. Just a baby. Those damned animal poachers." She held her fist up in anger.

"It's all right, dear." Mr. Paz rubbed her shoulders. "Think about all the good you've done with the Peanut Foundation."

"Did you know your parents would be here?" Alexandria whispered to Agatone.

"No, I'm just as shocked as you." He plastered a smile on his face.

She placed her hand on his cheek. "Do not lie to me, Aggy."

"I do not lie to you, babe."

"You're lying now." Smiling, she loved that Agatone worshipped her. She could feel his protective armor even when he wasn't near.

"Well, aren't you happy to see your family?" Mr. Paz placed his hand on Agatone's shoulder, and he jumped.

"Yes, sir, yes, sir, Mr. Paz." Agatone shook his hand and quickly turned to hug his mother and father. "Why is Gracie here?" he whispered to Mr. Socorro before releasing him.

"Luran is okay with it, so I'd hope you'd be okay with it too, son." Mr. Socorro smiled and held Gracie close.

"Is this true, Mom?" Agatone asked.

"Yes, I am wonderful with Gracie being here, son." Mrs. Socorro stood on her tiptoes, struggling to kiss Agatone's chin. "Look who I brought with me." She pointed toward a skinny boy and an even more petite girl. Both children looked like two cocker spaniel puppies with messy curls.

"Hey, knucklehead." Agatone pulled Orion near him, messing up his shaggy hair. His little sister, Luka, ran circles around his legs and chased Bumper in and out of the room.

"Hey, Luka Lu. Give your big bro a hug." Agatone reached out and caught her by the waist before she scampered past him a third time.

"Whoa! Nice." Orion's eyes ebullient, he elbowed Agatone's thigh, pointing to Alexandria.

"Family, this is the love of my life, Alexandria, the greatest. Alex, this is the family." Agatone's dimples embedded so profoundly they appeared to be permanently indented.

Alexandria wrapped her arms around Agatone's stomach. "Nice to meet you all." She shook Mr. Socorro's and Gracie's hands. When she turned to shake Mrs. Socorro's hand, she threw her body into Alexandria, hugging her until her face turned blue. Orion waved, and Luka picked her nose. "Hi, Havid, Gloria." Alexandria stared at Mrs. Fancy's newest breast implants. The swelling was still visible. Mrs. Fancy revealed that it was her second breast augmentation due to the first messed-up surgery. She warned everyone with flyers and billboard signs to avoid the doctor that ruined her precious breasts. Mr. Fancy seemed satisfied with his wife's new purchase based on his eye-to-breast contact.

"Gloriana," Mrs. Fancy corrected Alexandria.

"Yes, right, how's the growing business, Glo-ri-ana?" Alexandria raised her eyebrows at Mrs. Fancy as emphasis rolled off her tongue.

Mrs. Fancy omitted the question, and everyone began speaking at once.

"Your mother showed us your baby pictures, Alexandria. Beautiful," Mrs. Socorro said.

"Not all of them, honey," Mrs. Paz said.

"Don't let your mother fool you. I think she showed them the entire photo album, sweetheart," Mr. Paz said.

"You and my son will make beautiful babies—exotic. When's the wedding? Aggy used to say he wanted three boys," Mr. Socorro said.

"Dad?" Agatone's voice quaked.

"How long have you two been dating?" Mr. Fancy asked.

"When did you get so tanned, dear? Is that spray?" Mrs. Fancy touched Alexandria's arm, massaging it almost.

"I'm quite pale." Alexandria examined her arms.

"You have any friends, say around nine or ten years old? I like older women." Orion blushed.

"I'm so happy to be here. Where is the cabernet?" Gracie asked.

"Umm…Mom?" Alexandria said.

"I guess you're no longer Daddy's little girl, huh?" Mrs. Fancy giggled.

"Mom, Dad?" Alexandria turned her back to Mrs. Fancy.

"I poo-poo piddle." Luka pointed to the floor where she had defecated next to one of Mrs. Paz's elephants.

"Mom, Dad, a word, please!" Alexandria tugged at her mother's arm. Gracie picked Luka up, carrying her to the nearest powder room. Mr. Socorro threw a wad of paper towels on top of the waste where Luka had left evidence of her existence.

"Sure, honey," Mr. and Mrs. Paz spoke at once, staring at each other as if they were in trouble.

"Make yourselves comfortable. We'll be right back. Appetizers are in the dining area." Mrs. Paz clutched Alexandria's hand, leading her to the study.

"Just follow the *90s baby* banner." Mr. Paz directed.

"What is going on here? My birthday was supposed to be small and intimate. Instead, it looks like my elementary Halloween party!" Alexandria beat the bottom of her cigarette pack.

"Calm down. Agatone wanted to celebrate your first anniversary," Mrs. Paz whispered. "Your father and I wanted to surprise you by inviting his family. What's so wrong with that?" She straightened her skirt.

"What's so wrong? It's my fucking birthday, and he doesn't like his father. And his mother is batshit!"

"Alexandria Talar Paz, lower your voice!" Mrs. Paz demanded while Mr. Paz peeked through the sliding doors.

"They're all in the dining area, honey. It looks like they got the little one's shit off the floor." Mr. Paz snapped up a Cuban cigar from his desk drawer.

"I'm sorry. This was nice of you and Dad, but I can't stay here. I'm not ready for this. Anniversary? Has it even been one year?"

"We only invited his parents because of Aggy." Mrs. Paz said.

"Agatone…" Alexandria corrected her.

"Because Agatone said it was your first anniversary, and you refused to meet his parents."

"So you decided to go behind my back?" Alexandria lit a cigarette.

"Didn't you quit?" Mr. Paz puffed his Cuban.

"Says the pot to the fucking kettle." Mrs. Paz leered at him.

"No, Dad, I did not quit. I'll quit when you quit." Alexandria inhaled.

"Why are you so frustrated about this? You must learn to control your emotions, Alexandria. You will stay, and you will mingle with your boyfriend's family. They flew all the way from Honolulu, Hawaii, or wherever they've come from. Now, pull it together, goddammit!" Mrs. Paz exited the room, leaving Alexandria to blow smoke with her father.

After a while, Mr. and Mrs. Fancy left the family room to check out the renovated deck out back. Luka finally warmed up to everyone and tried to pounce on Bumper numerous times. The cat could not get away from her fast enough. She squatted over him. He made a fricative noise, and Luka ran away. Eventually, Luka's impulsivity created tension between Gracie and Mrs. Socorro, so they sent Luka outside to the koi fishpond.

"Thank you for having me." Gracie burped from the twenty-something glasses of champagne she had downed.

"Oenophile much?" Alexandria whispered to Agatone as they watched Gracie down three more glasses back-to-back. He coughed in between chuckles, trying not to seem obvious.

Now that dinner was over, Mr. and Mrs. Paz's invited their guests into the great room for coffee and tea. Landon and his wife Autumn brought homemade biscuits along with the blueberries. Mrs. Fancy gathered her favorite peanut butter cookies, proudly setting the tray on the coffee table.

Alexandria smacked Agatone's hand when he attempted to grab one of the cookies. Mrs. Paz seized the dish when Mrs. Fancy wasn't looking and rushed them into the kitchen. The last time the Pazes and their friends ate something homemade from Mrs. Fancy, strange things occurred. Some of their guests went skinny-dipping in the pool out back. Mrs. Paz raided the refrigerator without warning. Mr. Paz slept for two days. Tippy laughed all night, even in her sleep, and Alexandria couldn't remember the answers to a test she had the following morning.

"Who knew you were such a cuisinier?" Mr. Socorro held up his coffee mug, nodding toward Mr. Paz.

"He learned from the best," Alexandria boasted.

"She's right." Mr. Paz grinned. "She hated us for sending her to the marines. But she has benefited greatly, right, sweetie?"

"It's getting late." Alexandria pulled a cigarette from her handbag, shaking her leg nonstop.

"Who is that on the picture?" Orion pointed above Alexandria's head.

"That's Alexandria and her twin brother, Abram. Bram, we call him," Mrs. Paz replied, stroking Bumper's fluffy coat. "They were seven-year-olds there."

"Called him." Agitated, Alexandria snagged her handbag abruptly and left the room without warning.

Agatone quickly followed behind her. Searching the backyard, he spotted Mr. and Mrs. Fancy sitting underneath the elephant tree that Mrs. Paz had flown in from Mexico. Suddenly Luka screamed, pointing to the thick curtain of smoke ahead of her.

"That's Alex, the smoke bandit, Luka Lu." Agatone laughed at the fog of smoke. But his smile faltered when he reached Alexandria. "You never told me you had a twin brother, doll."

"Yes," Alexandria answered abruptly.

"Why haven't you mentioned him before?" Agatone scoffed.

"He's not up for discussion. I'm ready to go. Can we leave now?"

"Why can't we talk about him?"

"Because my brother is dead!"

CHAPTER 5

First Time

In between catering gigs, classes at San Francisco University, and Agatone, Alexandria barely had time for mani-pedis and mimosas. Sitting on the steps of her analysis building, waiting for the university's bus to arrive, she read over last-minute notes while smoking a cigarette. "What are you doing here?" she yelled. "When did you get back?" Staring at him with bold eyes, she didn't blink as usual.

"You happy to see me, doll?" He opened the door from the inside, reaching for her hand.

"You have scruff?" Alexandria outlined his mouth and chin with her finger. Has it been that long since we've seen each other?" Alexandria continued to stare at his chin.

"A goatee. I'm trying something new."

"Yes, you are." She lit another cigarette.

Agatone tried to take the cigarette from her, but she immediately turned her head. At times, his eyes filled with judgment. Alexandria disapproved of his notions of her. Does *second-hand smoke kill? Sure it doesn't*. She imagined him saying. They sat in front of the crowded building for a while, admiring each other.

He talked about his recent trip to Dubai while she gushed over catering gigs. He snatched the cigarette hanging from her lips during their conversation and flung it out the window. Displeased, she pulled another from the pack. Her hair flowed as she rested her head back against the seat. "I'll quit one day." She inhaled. "But today is not the day." She exhaled. "Where are we going?" She ran her fingers through his floppy hair, watching as they missed the turn toward her parents' home.

Agatone thumbed gently across her cheek and continued to drive down the coast.

"Where are we?" You have to tell me before I go nuts." She stared at the oversize garage attached to an even larger building.

"Get out. You're not going to go nuts." He lifted her out of the truck and covered her eyes. "I hate covering the glossy greens, doll." He guided her onto the elevator. "But a man's got to do what a man's got to do." He kissed her cheek. As soon as they minced from the elevator, he led her down a long hallway. "Okay, open your eyes."

"What is this?"

"It's for us." Agatone's eyes lit up when he saw her face filled with joy.

Walking around the condominium, she did not say a word. Instead, she lay flat out on the floor. "When did you do all of this?" Waving her arms and legs on the plush carpet like a kid in the winter snow. "Roses and lilies…a sofa, a recliner, a plasma TV, and a cappuccino machine with to-go cups? Oh my!" Her voice squeaked, and she covered her mouth, giggling.

"You like it, Dorothy?" Agatone's pupils twinkled.

"I love it, Glinda." She laughed and ran to the balcony. "I can see the coast from here. Aggy baby! Must've cost a fortune." She slowly kissed his lips. "And I don't have to smell smelly feet in the dorm anymore. I used to think it was only guys who carried dragon feet."

"Nothing is too expensive for you, doll." He picked her up and carried her to the bedroom. "I love it when you ramble. Bring that sweet blackberry ass to me." Agatone planted kisses all over her face down to her stomach.

The sun pierced through the cracks in the blinds. Alexandria gleamed at the sunlight through the window. She stiffened when he climbed on top of her. "I'm still not ready." She scooted against the headboard. A heart dangled from the chain around Agatone's neck, grazing across her breast. "What's that?" She pointed to his chest.

"Can we trade? I give you mine, and you give me yours."

She outlined the initials on the charm. "You want me to give you my heart, and you want me to have yours?"

"Yes, doll, I love you."

Her legs curled to her chest. A single tear fell down her face, and she quickly wiped it away. Flashes of the triplex field ran through her mind. It was as if she'd left her body again, watching herself from the outside.

"Doll…it's been two years. Why are you hesitating? Why are you making me wait so long?" Agatone's hard-on imprinted his jeans.

A stream of tears rushed down her cheeks as if they were trying to catch the first tear that she'd wiped away. "I…I'm a virgin, kind of."

"There's no in the middle. Either you are, or you're not."

"I…umm…I don't know. I don't want to talk about it." *Because I was raped in the Marines by my roommates and now it is difficult to relinquish myself to you—to anyone. You don't believe in Jesus, and I don't know why I'm even dating you.* She screamed underneath her breastplate until her lungs nearly exploded as she stared into his bulging eyes.

"Don't shut me out."

"It's confusing. I can't explain it."

"What about oral?"

"Ew."

"Ew? Come on. Look at me." He unzipped his shorts and bounced his penis up and down. "I've been beating my dick for almost two years, Alexandria!" He stormed out of the bedroom.

She leaped from the foam mattress and followed him. Watching from afar, his hands moved inside his boxer briefs. She continued to stare, wondering how far he would go.

"Aggy baby…" She snuck behind him.

"Don't." He moved her hand away. "I think you need to see a therapist."

"What?" Alexandria backed up.

"Yeah, I think maybe you should."

"Aggy? Okay, I'll have sex with you."

"No, it doesn't work like that, doll."

"I'm not crazy."

"Seeing a therapist does not mean you're insane, doll…but if we're going to make this work, you have to see one." Agatone tried to hide his arousal.

Alexandria liked his vulnerability. The control she had over him excited her. It seemed men were hypnotized by a woman's anatomy, let alone the space between their legs. She never imagined the power her pussy possessed until she graduated high school—first, Sergeant Belcroft, then Rebecca, and now Agatone. She teased him as his boxers hit the ground. She emulated pornography she had watched with the girls at the dorm and cuffed Agatone's balls like in the movie. He moaned as if never touched by a woman. *I must be doing it right.*

A couple next door watched their every move, but she continued to massage Agatone's tender spots. She pressed her breast against his toned back, smelling him, his scent like fresh roses in her mother's garden. She tugged at Agatone's schlong; the blood in his body started to build. "Have your way with me," she whispered in his ear.

Tears trickled down her face from the pain and discomfort she felt while Agatone entered her. *I can do this, I can do this,* she closed her eyes tight, envisioning a happy place.

* * *

Alexandria began to have sessions with Dr. Winters at San Francisco University. The doctor was a world-renowned psychologist with several bestsellers under her belt. Alexandria picked up three books from the coffee table written for the university, *Free Your Mind, Heal the Body: College Crisis,* and *How to Survive Early Adulthood.* The service the doctor rendered was part of the students' college plan. Her counseling style utilized games and different treatment plans from psychoanalytical and psychodynamic to humanistic and feminist approaches. It was difficult for Alexandria to focus on the treatment plan when she wanted meaningful and fun sex before reaching her sexual peak.

"I've been seeing you for a few weeks now, Alexandria. How is the sex between you and Agatone?" Dr. Winters was a neat freak. Her entire office was dust-free, and it smelled like the janitor cleaned it before each session. *Forty looks good on her. Maybe the saying "Black doesn't crack" is true.* Alexandria looked down at her caramelized skin, admiring it, hoping she would look just as good when she'd be older.

"Alexandria?"

Alexandria's face was clammy. "Yes, I'm sorry, Dr. Winters. What were you saying?"

"Where were you just then?"

"In my head, I guess."

"That's the purpose of hypnosis. Share with me." Dr. Winters jotted in her notebook.

"Nah, it's nothing. What did you ask me?"

"Is the sex better with Agatone?"

"I like getting him so hard that he thinks he's going to die without me."

"You like playing games with him?"

"Yes, I suppose I do. It's inexplicable if I climax. I mean, it feels good, but as soon as the feeling is over, I'm sort of disgusted after."

"Disgusted?"

"Not like I want to vomit. I just don't think I enjoy it as much as Agatone does."

"Do you think you're ready for sex?"

"Agatone is ready, and if I don't give it to him…I have to. It's what people do in relationships. They have sex, right?" Alexandria twirled her fingers through her hair.

"Alexandria, it sounds like you're forcing yourself to have sex. That's why you don't enjoy it. A healthy sex life consists of consenting partners. You must be ready, or it's not going to work."

"Relationships are tough. I'd like to end the session now." Alexandria grabbed her handbag and rushed out of the office.

CHAPTER 6

Nial

Alexandria read several books on sexuality, love, and relationships after her last session with Dr. Winters. The crashing waves captured her attention while reading when a phone call interrupted. "Hello. Aamir! Aamir? You're back!" Alexandria screamed, running to the entrance, waiting for Aamir to show his face. As soon as he appeared, she jumped into his arms, knocking his cap to the floor.

"I missed you too." He laughed, carrying Alexandria back through the doorway to the kitchen counter. "Did you miss me, or you just bored?"

"Both." She laughed. "I missed you so much. You know you're my only friend. Everyone is acting strange, Rafe and Kensington. I haven't spoken to anyone else since I've been back from the marines. I've either changed too much or not enough."

"Fuck 'em all. All you need is me."

They both laughed.

"I got some *fire*-ass news." Aamir did the little two-step dance in a circle that he did when he was excited.

"What?" Alexandria filled two glasses with white wine.

"Your boy—Aamir Bahar, son of Sea and Bash Bahar, racer of cars, lover of women—is fucking rich!" he shouted as he towered above her.

"What? Your family's been rich, Aamir. Your people own Hammond Sea International, for Christ's sake." Alexandria continued to sip from her glass.

"No. Me. I. Aamir. I am rich. Not my mom or pop or grandpop's money—my very own."

"What?"

"Yeah! I won my last race. If you watched the sports channel, you'd know. I'm going international, baby!"

"No shit!"

"Shit yeah! Watch out, NASCAR! I'm coming for you."

"Amazing news!" Alexandria grabbed another bottle of wine from the pantry heading into the bedroom.

"Come to my race. No excuses. You're done with classes."

"No, school isn't over, Aamir. I have three more years. I'm far from done." Alexandria changed her clothes, stepped into a black slinky silk dress and red pumps.

"That shouldn't stop you. You're my best friend, my sister from another mister. I want you there."

"Money is tight."

"I said I'm rich! I'll take care of it."

"I can't let you do that." Alexandria poured another glass of wine.

"What is up with you? You used to be a savage." Aamir plopped down on the edge of the sofa.

"I can't let you spend your money like that."

"I won half a million. When I win this next race, I'll sign a multimillion-dollar deal with NASCAR."

"You need an accountant. You really should speak with my dad about investments." Alexandria reached for his keys and placed them in his hand. "Now, let's go. I need a drink."

"We're already drinking." Aamir tore a piece of thread hanging from the knee on his ripped jeans and tucked his button shirt.

"I want to dance and drink. Come on!"

Aamir's vehicle slid up to the Mirage's entrance. "I remember when we first came here in my hooptie, valet wouldn't touch my car. Now they're jumping to park the Gallardo."

"That's money and power," they crooned at the same time, laughing.

"Get out my head. Damn." Alexandria nudged Aamir's side. "Just wait. Women are going to be flocking over you." Alexandria waited for the server to take their order.

"What do you mean? They're all over me now." Aamir's cell phone rang. "See, here's one now." He pointed to his phone.

"You've gotten firmer and tighter." Alexandria squeezed his arm.

"For the ladies." Aamir made an obscene noise while flexing his muscle.

* * *

The moon shone on Agatone's face as he sat in the dark living room. Alexandria staggered through the hallway. She made it to the bedroom successfully after tumbling over his rugged boots. "Fucking Aggy never cleans up behind himself, his shit on the floor." Her words slurred. "Maybe if he were on the floor, I'd sit on his face. But no, it doesn't matter. I won't come anyway."

"Who are you talking to, Alex?" He appeared in the doorway.

"Fuck! You scared me. When did you get here?" Her eyes glossy, she flushed the commode, forgetting to wash her hands. Agatone guided her back to the sink.

"A few hours—long enough to know you weren't here. Where have you been? I was worried out of my mind."

"Aamir's back. We went for drinks." She climbed on top of the sheets. "I want to sit on your face, Aggy baby." She muffled.

"You swear more when you're drunk, doll. You sound like a sailor." He laughed, lying down beside her. "You're my favorite person in the world." He kissed her face. "I think we should get married."

Alexandria was fast asleep.

After a long night's rest, she woke up in bed alone. Her desolate mouth craved caffeine. She took a hot shower, lapping the water from the showerhead. Afterward, she grabbed her favorite blue blanket with the white clouds and bundled up on the recliner with a bagel and coffee. Flipping through *Cater Magazine* pages, page

8 read, "Ten Foods to Help Heal a Broken Heart," and page 10, "How to Survive Sophomore Marriage with Mac 'n' Cheese." She vaguely recalled Agatone mentioning marriage. *Oh, no, no, no, no, no!* She picked up her phone. "Answer. Answer, please, Aamir. Answer. Aamir? He's going to propose!" She paced back and forth across the floor, smoking a cigarette.

"What? Who?"

"Who? Aggy. Agatone."

"What's wrong with that? The guy is crazy about you."

"I'm twenty-two, he's thirty-one. I'm not ready for that."

"Why?"

"Why? I'm just not, okay?"

"Are you leading him on?"

"No, God, no. What the fuck, Aamir!"

"Liar."

"This conversation isn't going the way that I expected. I'll call you later." Alexandria held the phone, waiting for Aamir to speak.

"You're in denial."

"Shut up!" Alexandria hung up.

Almost midnight and several missed calls later, Alexandria didn't return anybody's phone call, not even her parents'. She drove the car her dad loaned her to uncharted places, searching for *liquid* courage. A Seventh Star gas station was nearby. Briskly strutting inside the store, their most excellent wine caught her eye. After filling her arms with boxed wine and snacks, she raced a truck driver to the register.

"That'll be $42.50."

"Thanks." Alexandria grabbed her bag and rushed outside.

She fumbled inside her handbag for a cigarette when she realized the pack was empty. She ran back up the steps, but the cashier had placed the Closed sign on the door. Alexandria ignored the warning as she rushed back inside like a lost puppy. "Cigarettes?" She gave a hand signal to the cashier.

"Up at the counter." He glowered. "We're closing!"

"Three packs of Camel, please." She threw a twenty on the counter, waiting for him to give her the cigarettes. "Thanks," she scoffed before sprinting out the door.

Fumbling with the package, she lit the cigarette. The store had officially closed. The parking lot was dark and empty. She was alone, scrambling near the vehicle when a hard blow weighed on her like a ton of bricks. She fell to the pavement. Her head made a cracking sound. She crawled, reaching for the keys when her feet scrubbed the pavement as she was pulled in the opposite direction.

"Give me the bag, bitch!" a deep voice shouted, kicking her keys away, pressing her face to the ground. The man ripped her shirt off, exposing her under the streetlight. Her nose scraped the gravel. Tiny pieces of rock and glass pierced her delicate skin.

"Please don't kill me," she cried. "Please." *God, please don't let me die tonight.*

Blood seeped from her mouth as she tried to move forward. Her legs and arms grazed the concrete, leaving traces of blood behind. Alexandria, unsure of what to say or do to save her life, kicked and bellowed, "I have HIV!" She closed her eyes tight, waiting for the nightmare to be over.

"Nasty cunt" were the last words she heard. She attempted to pull a shred of clothing over her but was too weak to move.

Moments passed as she lay on the cold hard surface. Her nose tingled from the pitter-patter of tiny insects swarming her face. She tried to blink them away, but they overpowered her. The rain splattered, hitting against her bruised skin. Unable to swallow, her throat closed as a wet sensation oozed from her nose. Those days in the marines falling into mud pits and sand holes did not compare to the pain and humiliation she experienced lying beside the malodorous dumpster, naked for the world to see.

Several hours later, a black Mercedes pulled into the Seventh Star. A tall woman stepped out of the vehicle, hurling several bags into the dumpster when she noticed Alexandria's shadow. The woman panicked and ran back to her car. She sat there for a moment, then jumped out again.

"What is that?" the woman in the passenger seat asked.

"I think it is a dead body." The woman had a thick French accent. Her *T*s were pronounced as *Z*s, her *V*s like *F*s, and she often said, "Uh."

"Heavy"—she contemplated getting back into her car, driving away—"as fuck!"

"Let's go."

"We cannot leave this person." The woman pulled her vehicle closer to Alexandria. "She appears to be breathing. Can I get a little assistance, Taiyo?"

"No, no, it's raining." Taiyo rolled up her window and readjusted the stick in her hair bun.

The woman leaned toward Alexandria's chest. "Hello, anybody in there? Hello?"

Alexandria yowled.

"I am Nial. I will take you to the hospital. So happy you are tiny." She pulled off her trench coat, draping it around Alexandria as she muscled to the passenger side of her car.

Taiyo reluctantly moved over. "She's bleeding everywhere, and you're going to put her here?" she griped.

"Scoot. Scoot. I will put the girl here. Now!" Nial placed Alexandria next to Taiyo. At the brink of every speed hump, inaudible moans escaped Alexandria's mouth. Nial sped to the nearest hospital. Alexandria attempted to look around, but her head hurt. And her vision was hazy.

Nial sped into the ambulance bay, honking, alarming security. "I found her by the dumpster at Seventh Star on the West Bay Street." Nial's words jumbled. "I think that maybe she was mugged."

"I'll take it from here. Thank you, miss." The security guard wheeled Alexandria inside, and Nial sped away.

* * *

The next day, Agatone arrived home from a twenty-four-hour shift. His boots were in the center of the floor, and his scrubs straddled across the bed. He had not received an early-morning text from Alexandria, reminding him to empty the trash. After exhausting all his possibilities, scratching his head in silence was his only option. He pondered unpleasant thoughts and grabbed a beer from the refrigerator. "This is unlike her." He tossed his Crocs inside the coat closet, grabbed his sneakers, put on black joggers and a tee, and jetted out the door.

The darkness caught up with him as he drove around the city for hours. She was not at the university, and Aamir's driveway was vacant. Her parents' home on the other side of town was his last option. The truck tires ran up the curb with the door left wide open. He jumped the gate. "Hello, hello!" Beating on the door until his knuckles turned purple, there was no answer. So he hopped over the privacy fence to the backyard. "Hello! Hello! Mr. Paz! Mrs. Paz!"

"Get away from here before I call the police!" a woman shouted, holding a cat in one hand and a baseball bat in the other.

He raced back to his truck when his phone rang. "Yeah," he answered. "Yes, I know Alex. Who is this?" He listened attentively. "North Coast. Seventh floor. Susan Buck," he repeated. "On my way." Dodging in and out of traffic, he passed every vehicle on the road.

* * *

Alexandria opened her eyes. Agatone was sound asleep, drooling to the left of her. At her right sat a gorgeous woman wearing black high-waisted pants, a red cropped blazer, a pearl necklace, and black six-inch stilettos. Her hair was black as night and her skin creamy as milk. She had a presence about herself, a solemnity of command as she sat poised in the chair with one leg crossed over the other. "Hello." Her French accent was familiar.

"Hi." Alexandria covered her swollen mouth.

The woman stood over her, filling the cup on the table stand with water. "I am Nial." She placed the straw to Alexandria's lips. "You are beautiful even with bumps and bruises." She smiled.

Alexandria grabbed the back of her head, muttering.

"I'll get the nurse." Nial left to find Susan Buck, and a nurse came quickly.

"That's the first time I have ever seen nurses move that fast," Agatone joked as he watched Nial's every move. He stared at her strangely as though he had seen a ghost.

"It is because I am responsible for the bill." Nial leaned over to shake his hand.

"You don't have to do that." He left her hand hanging in midair.

Nial smirked. "It is done." She sat on the bed beside Alexandria. "Can you speak, beautiful?"

Alexandria nodded slightly. "Thank you," she whispered, holding her mouth.

"You are welcome. Rest." Nial sat back in the chair beside her, watching as she dozed off.

CHAPTER 7

I Love Him

Doctors, nurses, and other staff weaved in and out of patient rooms as they managed their daily schedules. The hallways were chaotic as Mr. and Mrs. Paz waited for the elevator.

"Going my way?" Aamir nodded toward Mr. and Mrs. Paz when the elevator door opened.

"Aamir," the Pazes spoke in accordance.

When they reached Alexandria's room, her face flushed red as she giggled like a kea. "Oh, Mom, Dad. You finally made it back with my Greek salad? I'm starving." She snatched the bag from her mother. "Great, you have my books. Nial, these are my parents and my best friend, Aamir. Mom, Dad, Aamir, meet Nial Paul, the woman who saved my life."

"That is not accurate. It was the doctors. I'm just the carrier." Nial and Alexandria laughed.

"Inside joke," Alexandria revealed, snorting.

Her parents paused, and Aamir ambled to a chair near the back of the room, freakishly staring at Alexandria and Nial as the two ladies conversed. Their chemistry was unlike anything Aamir had ever witnessed between Alexandria and another human. They were like two of the same people except different as they completed each other's sentences like they had known each other for years.

"It was my pleasure finally meeting all of you, but I must be going. I will check on you later." Nial gently tapped Alexandria's nose. She draped a long white trench jacket around her arms. A boy brought a purple box with a giant pink bow inside the room before she left. Nial pointed, and he placed the package on Alexandria's bedside table. Nial winked at her and exited the room.

"Who was that woman, and where did she come from? She is Sexy 110. I'd go to class." Aamir hopped on Alexandria's bed and lay beside her. His feet hung off the foot of the rail.

"Rude 108? What is wrong with you people?" Alexandria rested her head against the pillows. "She found me lying beside a dumpster—a foul-smelling dumpster! The least you could do is thank her."

"I'm sorry. Hottie in the trench made me forget why we were here. Are you okay, my sister from another mister?"

"Yes, I'm fine, Aamir. Thanks for coming." Alexandria rolled her eyes.

"I still don't understand why you were at the Seventh Star at twelve o'clock at night, dear?" Her father sipped his coffee.

"Dad, I told you it was Agatone. He was going to propose. I tried to avoid him, and this is my karma. He is so sweet and loving, and I...I..." *I once thought that he was Lucifer reincarnate; but he's nice: nice hair, nice smile, nice smell, nicely caring even if he doesn't believe in a higher power. I suppose I should not judge his morals because they do not align with mine.*

"Like girls," Aamir blurted out.

"What?" Tea spilled from Mrs. Paz's mouth, and Mr. Paz dropped his plate.

"What the fuck, Aamir!" Alexandria screamed.

"I'm sorry, Mr. and Mrs. P. I was trying to lighten the mood."

"Bad idea, Aamir." Mr. Paz's face loomed.

"Now I see where Alex gets the resemblance, Mr. P. Oscar the Grouch," Aamir mocked. "You know? Sesame Street? The green guy? Trash can? Too soon?"

"Yes!" they all shouted at once.

* * *

San Francisco University had its annual festival for entrepreneur's week before spring break. The campus police rode their bikes throughout the property, checking for fake badges and illegal drugs. Students covered the campus ground, searching for fashion deals, ways to acquire accessible health care, the newest software inventions from the technology squad, and food for the students who strived on scholarships alone.

Alexandria and Aamir attended the event. People were coming and going, shouting and buying food and drinks from food stations all around them. The aroma from the barbecue and greasy foods streamed the air. Booths were all around the campus for student alumni who graduated at the top of their class. Young business owners offered gift cards, prize giveaways, accessible free tutoring, and legal services to individuals who purchased over twenty-five dollars or more. Alexandria took advantage of the food-truck services in the parking area. Aamir pulled out a flask that resembled a cell phone, took a quick swig, and placed it back in his pocket. "How do you stay so thin? You eat more than I do." Aamir burped.

"How do you stay sober?"

"Voyeur."

"Takes one to know one." Alexandria scrunched her nose, giggling. "Delicious. Want some?" She teased Aamir with her double cheeseburger. "I don't care what my mother says. These trucks have the best cuisines."

"You mean fast food. If it's not seafood and vegetables, I don't want it." Aamir laughed. "Check out the DJ..." He bumped Alexandria's arm. "Sexy 103?"

"Sexy 0. Fuck you very much. Why are you always trying to get me to rate women? Is there a secret fetish you're not telling me about?" Alexandria licked ketchup from her fingertips, dining her eyes on the fashion designer's booth in the distance. "NPD..." she read the banner. Her mouth hung open. *What the fuck is she doing here? Nah, it can't be her. It just cannot be*, she thought. It was her, tall as a statue, standing on top of a booth, wearing dark oversize sunglasses, a low-rise miniskirt, and a crop top showing off her diamond-encrusted belly ring atop her firm abs.

"Hottie in the trench?" Aamir laughed. "You holding out on me?"

"No, I swear."

"She is your type."

"How do you know my type?" *Is she my type?*

"Because I am all-knowing." Aamir chuckled, taking another swig from his flask.

"Well, we can't just stand here. Let's speak." Alexandria pulled Aamir along.

Students overcrowded the stage.

"I wonder..." Aamir tossed a piece of mint gum in his mouth.

"What, Aamir? What do you wonder?" Alexandria continued to hold Aamir's arm as they pressed through the group of students.

"If hottie is into men or women. I'd tap that—give her all twelve inches of this muscle freak."

"Yuck, Aamir. I don't know...I think she's sweet. Besides, she..."

"Saved your life," Aamir mocked. "I know."

They walked closer toward the DJ booth when Nial shouted, "Beauty in the red sundress and handsome in the tight jeans! Nial Paul summons you NOW!" she called them out, and everyone screamed above the music.

Aamir looked down at his jeans and back at Nial. Alexandria pointed to him and looked back at Nial. Nial gleamed directly into their eyes, nodding her head up and down. The mob made way for them to walk through. Security assisted Nial down from the booth before she leaped off. She prowled in their direction as if she was on the runway.

"What up?" Aamir nodded.

"Aamir, luff your shirt. NASCAR? Cool. What are you, seven feet?" She gave him a thumbs-up and held her hand out for him to shake.

"Six foot three." Aamir smirked.

"Beautiful." Nial quickly turned to Alexandria, pushing her sunglasses above her head, staring into her unfaltering eyes.

"I guess that answers my question." Aamir breathed.

"Hi." Alexandria smiled, elbowing Aamir in the side. "What are you doing here?" She stared at Nial.

"Nial Paul Designs." She tapped the podium with confidence. "Let's go someplace we do not have to yell. Excuse us, Aamir. My assistant, Zoe." Nial pointed to Zoe standing next to security. "She thinks you are hot." She gripped Alexandria's hand, avoiding the crowd.

Aamir grabbed an NPD luxury sweatshirt from the table and strolled to Zoe. "Me zinks she is hot too." He mimicked Nial's accent.

Nial and Alexandria found a quiet place underneath a sequoia tree. "Give me luff." She air-kissed Alexandria's cheeks. "I am proud that you are feeling much better. You are the most beautiful woman I have ever seen." Nial gazed with excitement in her eyes. It was as if she could see directly to Alexandria's soul.

Alexandria speechless, her feet were cemented to the grass. She did not imagine her day would lead to seeing Nial again. Her daily tasks had been planned before sunrise—the last follow-up visit with her orthopedic doctor, breakfast with her parents, and Bumper's playdate at the Fat Kat Kitten Farm with Guinevere. Later, Aamir would swing by her and Agatone's place, annoying the neighbors with his sound system giving her the cue to come downstairs.

Like the sunset, she had no idea she'd be listening to Nial talk about her childhood in France, the countryside where she raised and trained horses at the age of fifteen, her travels across the continent, and the five languages she spoke—French, English, Spanish, Russian, and Japonic. Her voice filled with confidence and assurance. Alexandria forgot about the other intimate connections she had ever encountered. Nial's accent flowed from her tongue like Alexandria's favorite candle scent: pineapple papaya. *Is this what love at first sight feels like?* she wondered. She could sit inside an empty room with Nial watching paint dry on a rainy afternoon, and boredom would not show its dull face. "I...I'm not gay." *Stupid. Why did I say that?* Her face glowed.

"Neither am I."

They both laughed.

"I know you have the boyfriend. But that does not stop me from finding you attractive, Alexandria." The wind blew their hair wild. "I want to know more about you." She moved closer to her.

Her smile is contagious. There could be a million people in a room, and I wouldn't take my eyes off her. Alexandria cleared her throat as if her thoughts spewed out of her ears. Her face flushed. "I'm sorry. Excuse me." She turned her back, taking slow deep breaths, pulling a cigarette from its pack. *Shit. She is my type.*

"Ma chérie?" Nial whispered. "I'm sorry if I offended you. It was not my intention."

"Why are you here, Nial?" Alexandria turned back around to face her.

Inching closer, Nial wiped Alexandria's tears away. "You know why I am here."

"I have never seen you on campus before."

"Uh…maybe you never looked…I graduated two years ago. I created this festival for for-profit and exposure three years ago. It began as my final project for my dissertation in couture art—high recognition, dean's award—and now it is a part of the university plan to help students build entrepreneurship skills, etcetera." Nial smiled with her eyes proudly.

"I'm impressed. You created all of this from a project?" Alexandria looked around. "That's huge." *Can she be any more charming and intelligent?* She swooned. "We can be friends, but nothing more. I love my boyfriend." She backed away.

"Then we will be great friends." Nial tucked Alexandria's hair behind her ear, tethered together, purging memories from the past and talks of attainable dreams when the disc jockey strutted in their direction.

"What are you doing with her?" The DJ scorned.

"What?" Alexandria cut her laugh short.

"Not you." The DJ pointed to Nial.

Nial glared. "Alex, this is Taiyo, my girlfriend."

Alexandria stared for a moment before backing away. Nial watched as she ran to the main building. Taiyo pointed fingers, poking and prodding Nial's shoulders. Nial continued to stare at the footprints Alexandria left behind.

Alexandria charged through the double doors toward the administration area. Dr. Winters placed her briefcase on her desk when Alexandria barged into her office. Tears rushed down her face, but she did not mumble a word.

"Come, come. Sit down." Dr. Winters took her hand.

"I'm quite sure I have a problem."

"I have fifteen minutes, Alexandria. I'm on my way to my son's recital. So tell me, what's going on?" Dr. Winters relaxed in her ergonomic chair.

"I'm sorry. I came unannounced."

"Alexandria? It's okay. You have my undivided attention."

"She looks at me like I'm an angel, past my flaws. But I cannot love her. Is this normal? I love Agatone." Tears plopped against the windowsill as Alexandria gleamed outside. "It's an evil act, and my parents would not stand for it. Come. Look at her." She pulled Dr. Winters up from her chair. "That's her, near the giant sequoia tree."

"Hmm…I see."

"You see? What does that mean?"

"I shouldn't say this, but stay away from Ms. Paul, Alexandria."

"What?"

"I've grown fond of you over the years. But I need you to stay away from Ms. Paul."

"Why?" Alexandria's face turned redder.

"Enjoy Agatone. He's a good man."

"What!" Alexandria raised her voice. "What the fuck, Dr. Winters?"

"I've had other girls come to me concerning Ms. Paul. Unfortunately, one of them committed suicide." Dr. Winters closed the blinds in Alexandria's face. "I must get to my son's recital. Meet me here tomorrow around noon." She escorted her out the office and scurried down the stairs.

Alexandria sat alone in the shadows of the hallway, surrounded by lingering voices from the past. Students who left their problems behind roamed free, judging her. Crouching to the floor, she sat against Dr. Winters's office door. Jack, the janitor, stared at her with his mouth tooted.

"Don't worry. I won't mess up your waxed floor." She held her middle finger up when he turned his back.

CHAPTER 8

Earth Life

Agatone took Alexandria on a surprise vacation to visit his parents in Brazil. They toured the tropical rain forest. The tour guide was a scrawny man with bifocals. His badge read Real-Life Scientist in bold letters. First, the guide explained the adaptation of plant and animal life using molded food. Then he created holograms of land and water animals in front of the crowd. Agatone ignited with excitement as he handled the computer-generated backpack, while Alexandria mocked the lack of authenticity.

During the two-day tour, they visited Cloning Caves, where they kept nearly every extinct animals. Orion and Luka went along to enjoy the festivities.

"You would make a brilliant teacher." Agatone admired Alexandria as she read to Orion and Luka.

"Aggy babe, you're sweet, but I am going to make a brilliant senior marketing agent someday."

"You're right, doll."

"Whoa! Mom, Dad, and Gracie should have come!" Orion yelled. "What kind of bird is that, Aggy?" Orion tried to climb inside the cage.

"A dodo bird." Agatone pulled him down.

"Why are they cloning dodo birds?" Alexandria read the biography.

"So they can be eaten again in case there is a food shortage—the Apocalypse, world hunger, government shutdown, a pandemic. Who knows?" Agatone revealed.

"Clone it to kill it again? That makes sense," Alexandria scoffed.

"Luka piddle." Luka pointed to the trash can in the corner.

"No, honey, that's not the ladies' room. Come with me." Alexandria took Luka by the hand. "I'll take her. We girls have to stick together."

Agatone laughed.

The Cloning Cave's restaurant mimicked natural caves back in the Stone Age. After eating dinner, Alexandria and Luka ventured out independently, while Agatone and Orion waited for them to return. Suddenly Alexandria whisked from around the corner with Luka, dumbfounded. "They cloned the woolly mammoth? I just saw a fucking woolly mammoth. Excuse my expression, Luka."

"I have more to show you." Agatone guided them to a cave where the facility kept leopards, giraffes, African rhinos, lemurs, and woodpeckers.

Luka walked closer to the mirror and touched the glass. "No more dolphy, Aggy?" Her face gloomy, she plopped down on the floor.

Agatone sat down beside her and placed her in his lap. "Sweet pea, they will soon become extinct. That's why they're making more, so there will be more. Do you understand?" He held her tight.

Luka grasped his cheeks. "I think so, so there will be more dolphy?" She stared, bug-eyed.

"Yes, Luka Lu, there will be more dolphy." He smiled. "Now, who wants ice cream?" Agatone asked.

"This is depressing. Can we go home and get ice cream?" Orion asked.

"I was thinking the same thing, kiddo." Alexandria ran her hands through Orion's messy hair.

* * *

DANG

The trees blew slightly in the wind as the clouds hovered, pondering rain. Alexandria lay out on the oceanfront, watching the boats pass when her phone buzzed. "Hello," she answered, slurping wine from a glass.

"Ma chérie?"

"Nial?" Alexandria became straight-faced. "Hi." Coughing, she almost choked.

"I am sitting in my Jacuzzi, imagining you naked."

Complete silence took over. Alexandria dropped her cell phone and picked it up quickly. "I will not play this game with you." She hung up.

Nial called right back.

"Propitious much," Alexandria answered.

"Did I do something wrong, Ma chérie?"

"Flirting."

"Forgive me. Friends do not flirt?"

"No."

"You are accurate. I am sorry. Can we have dinner, my friend?"

"I'm in Brazil."

"How long?"

"Another week."

"That is a long time."

"I'm sure Tahoe will keep you occupied."

Nial laughed aloud. "Are you jealous of Taiyo?"

"What? No." *Why would I be jealous of a presumptuous bitch?*

Nial continued to laugh. "It is cute."

"I have to go." Alexandria rushed, wondering if Nial could hear her thoughts.

"Dinner when you return. Promise me."

"Demand much?"

"No, a request."

"I'll call you, bye."

"You first."

"No, you hang up."

"No, you first. I want to hear your last breath."

Silenced engrossed as Alexandria and Nial listened to their eupnea's converse.

"Alex! Alex!" Luka shouted, petrifying Alexandria.

"Hi, I see you guys made it back. I'm starved."

"Alex, darling, dinner is ready!" Gracie yelled.

"Where's Aggy?" Alexandria questioned.

"Aggy got Alex a present," Luka revealed.

"Luka!" Orion screamed. "Bigmouth, go to the ladies' room as Mommy said."

Orion and Luka ran back inside, and Alexandria whispered into the phone, "Hello."

"You first," Nial whispered back.

"Hanging up now." Alexandria hung up, and a text message chimed through.

"Dinner. Promise me?"

"..."

"?"

"Promise."

Alexandria ran inside and grabbed a few mangos from the bowl on the countertop. She pulled the fruit apart as she became lost in her thoughts. *The stupid accent is in my head.* She turned her earbuds on, hoping the music would erase the salacity that stimulated her mind.

The moonlight shone through the bay window as the stars relaxed the night. Luka had fallen asleep, hiding from Orion underneath the bed where Alexandria and Agatone lay.

"Wake up, sleepyhead." He pulled Luka by her dumpling legs quietly. Soon after, he rushed back and hopped on the bed, pouncing on Alexandria, but she did not say anything. "You good, doll?"

"Yes, enjoying the sounds of the waves. It's so peaceful and calming." She kissed his cheek.

"My folks love it."

"Your parents and Gracie Gray love it, you mean?"

He took a deep breath. "I need to tell you something, Alex."

"What? Your parents are polygamists?" She rubbed his face. "Just making sure there's no stubble," she quipped.

"Not exactly."

"What? I was joking," she said when he didn't smile.

"Mom isn't Orion and Luka's mommy."

"What?" She sat up, facing him head-on.

"Gracie's their real mom, but Orion and Luka think Mom is their mommy."

"Oh my god, Aggy! Why?"

"Mom wanted more kids and couldn't have them. Dad fell in love with Gracie during the process."

"With Gracie Gray?"

"Gracie took them away before, and Mom cracked. That's why she was in the rehab clinic before we met."

"So Gracie lives here?"

"Yes, that is the agreement."

"What about Orion and Luka? Will they ever tell them?"

"Probably not."

"Will you?"

"No, it isn't my place." Agatone reached underneath his pillow and pulled out a long, slim box.

"Aggy? What is this?"

"Open it."

"I'm scared to open it. What is it?"

"It's not what you think."

She slowly unraveled the bow and pulled out a diamond necklace. "Aggy, I don't know what to say. Thank you." She curled into his chest, and he fastened the chain around her neck.

"I hope one day you'll marry me."

"Maybe…" She groaned and fell fast asleep.

The next afternoon, Mr. and Mrs. Socorro set the table for brunch while Gracie made the mimosas and cachaças. The housekeeper assisted Luka and Orion with their hand-washing before they devoured their food. Everyone finally settled down and prepared to eat, while Alexandria entertained herself on social media.

"Aggy? Is everything okay?" Gracie sipped her mimosa.

"I suppose no time is better than the present," he spoke softly.

"What?" Alexandria placed her phone on the table.

"I've been selected for deployment," he said in one breath.

Alexandria sighed. "Again?"

"Agatone," Mrs. Socorro said.

"Son," Mr. Socorro said.

"How long?" Alexandria asked.

"Two years," Agatone answered.

"What? Two years?" Orion shrieked. "What's *deployment?*"

"What is it, Aggy?" Luka climbed out her chair and walked toward him.

"Deployment, Luka Lu, it is a purpose that I must fulfill for the government."

"No, tell them no," Gracie repeated.

"I can't. I took an oath I must honor."

Luka slowly ate Agatone's fried rice balls from his plate while no one paid her attention.

"We'll get through it, babe." Alexandria rubbed her hands through his hair. "When are they requesting you?"

"They're giving me time to get my affairs in order, so in about two months."

"I can think of a lot of things we can do in two months." Alexandria hugged him around his neck.

"Yes, honey, don't be sad. We'll be okay, and so will you." Mrs. Socorro sipped some of Mr. Socorro's cachaça.

Luka climbed onto Agatone's lap and hugged him tight. "Don't be sad." She kissed his cheek. "Luka Lu will be okay."

"Okay, baby girl." He gave her his dimpled smile.

Luka grabbed another one of Agatone's fried rice balls and ran back to her chair. "Aggy will be okay too!" She held up her sippy cup as a shout of encouragement.

* * *

In San Francisco, Alexandria and Aamir had dinner plans at Parliament Park on Northeast Avenue and ended up at a bar on Sixth Street. The bar was smothering inside, but it was just what the doctor ordered. Aamir invited Zoe to join him and Alexandria. They ordered salads and cocktails, awaiting Zoe's arrival.

"So you and Zoe?" Alexandria waited for Aamir to swallow his spicy shrimp.

"She's fire."

"Fire?"

"I laid down the law a few times."

"Something's different." Alexandria stared at him. "What did you do?" Her eyes were stern focused on him, the way she did when trying to gain information.

"What makes you think I did something?" He stuffed his mouth.

"Waiting."

"Damn you." He took a swig of beer. "I went down under."

"What!" Alexandria pulled a cigarette from her handbag. "I'm listening."

"I deep dived in Lake Zoe."

"You're okay with that now?"

"Yep, finally did it."

"I'm shocked, Aamir. You must really like Zoe. I cannot believe you ate her cream pie. How long did it take? The first or the second date?"

"After she took all this muscle freak." He laughed aloud. "She's a beast. When I say all, I mean *all*. Deep Throat Debby."

"No way…not Deep Throat Debby. From high school Debby?" Alexandria hollered. She could not contain her laughter.

Before he disclosed more details, Zoe twitched her hips inside the bar. Her silver, black, and white plaid button-down stopped right below her vagina; and a slim blue belt hugged her waist, matching her royal-blue eight-inch heels. Alexandria's eyes followed her every move. The bartender spilled a drink on the bar while taking Zoe's order. Her breast leaned toward him as she took the beer from his trembling hand.

"Zoe is beautiful, Aamir." Alexandria paused.

"I agree. She is *fire*." Aamir bit his fist, lusting over Zoe.

"Hey, boo." Zoe wrapped her arms around Aamir's neck when she reached their table. "I'm not wearing any underwear," she whispered in his ear, then turned toward Alexandria to shake her hand.

"Yes, we caught that when you leaned over the bar," Alexandria revealed.

"Great minds think alike." Aamir grinned, lifting his shirt slightly, pulling his pants down, revealing the pubic hairs that touched his navel.

Zoe kissed his lips. "Isn't he handsome? I can't wait to get you back to my place so I can climb that pole."

Alexandria cleared her throat repeatedly. "Get a room."

"Let's order before I start a fire in this joint. Who chose this place? Aamir?" Zoe winked at him.

"That would be correct." Alexandria chuckled.

"Wait, whose side are you on? The food is blazing." Aamir clumped lettuce into his mouth.

"So where is Ms. Paul?" Alexandria inquired.

"I love the way you slipped that in." Aamir laughed.

Alexandria scrunched her nose.

"I think they're in France visiting her mom." Zoe hesitated a little to reveal Nial's whereabouts.

"They?" Alexandria questioned.

"Taiyo is with her. Nial's mom is a famous photographer. She takes pictures of Nial's models and sends them to her rich friends."

"Nice." Alexandria inhaled her cigarette when a waiter came over with a box for her to discard. She scrunched her nose, dumped the burning ash, and put the cigarette back in its pack.

"Yes, it's great. Nial became the youngest millionaire in the fashion world last year. Look her up. She's hot stuff in Europe." Zoe sipped her drink and filled her mouth with biscuit crumbs.

Alexandria slyly took her phone out and searched Nial Paul Designs in Europe.

CHAPTER 9

Surprise

Agatone pulled in front of the Paz residence to pick Alexandria up after a long exhausting shift at work. He blew the horn, but no one came outside. He parked and jumped out of his truck and rang the doorbell. Nobody answered. Wiggling the door handle, he stepped inside.

"Surprise!" The lights flashed on, and his friends jumped out into the foyer.

"What is this?" He looked around.

"Surprise, baby." Alexandria jumped around his waist. "Are you in shock?" She kissed his lips.

"Of course, what is this?" Agatone uttered.

"I wanted to do something special for you. I have a surprise waiting for you upstairs, then you can come back down to mingle." Alexandria led the way.

Once he reached the top of the stairs, three women greeted him.

"What is this?" Agatone eyes popped. The women wore a bathrobe with nothing underneath. One of the women held an oversize towel in one hand and edible oil in the other. Another lady stepped in front of him to unbutton his shirt while the other woman slowly unbuckled his belt, prying her hand inside his khaki pants. His penis swung out of his boxers, hitting against his thigh. He cuffed it so the ladies wouldn't notice his erection.

"They are going to relax you, Aggy. I'll be right here to make sure you behave accordingly." Alexandria sat in the chair across from the bathroom.

"No freaking way, doll."

"Yes freaking way. Now go."

Agatone did not hesitate to step into the open bath after the three women undressed him. They bathed him in every place. Finally, one of them buried her face underwater. "Babe." Agatone squirmed. "This cannot be happening." His voice quaked.

"It's your day." Alexandria nodded. "Let her take you."

Agatone tried to resist the pleasure bestowed upon his erogenous zones. His head fell back against the tub. He groaned uncontrollably. "Babe, are you recording this shit?"

"Aggy, of course not. Don't close your eyes. Look at me," Alexandria demanded.

"What is happening?" Agatone could not keep his eyes open.

"They are professionals."

"Like prostitutes?"

"No, Aggy, massage therapists." Alexandria moved closer to him, kissing his lips as though doing him a favor. He had been working tirelessly at the medical center, and since she hadn't been giving him sex, she granted the favor. The excitement on his face made her feel powerful, in control. The way they touched him turned her on.

"Would you like to join?" one of the women asked Alexandria.

"No, thank you. This is for him, not me." *Did she read my mind?*

"Babe, come on," Agatone pleaded. "Sit on my face."

"I want to watch you have fun with these beautiful ladies." Alexandria leaned back in the recliner, watching him have his way with the women. He flipped one of the women over roughly as he entered her from behind. Pounding her insides as if there were no tomorrow, the woman screeched and screamed. Her cries escaped through the cracks of the door, and the lead woman stuffed her mouth, tying a silk scarf behind her head. Agatone commanded every position imaginable. The masseuse took him inside her mouth one last time before his penis fell limp, shriveled like a prune. He stared into the ceiling with eyes half-open, unable to speak a single word. Alexandria exited the room when he fell fast asleep inside the tub.

After the session ended, Agatone found Alexandria sitting out back, smoking a cigarette. She was alone, talking on the phone when he sat next to her, smiling. "Doll? I cannot believe you did that for me."

Alexandria quickly hung up the phone. "Did you enjoy your celebration?" she asked. "You practically slept the entire time."

"Yes, I did enjoy it…thank you. Is everything all right, doll? You said it was cool. We are cool, right?" Agatone's voice trembled.

"Yes, but…"

"What?" Agatone moved closer to her.

"We're over, Aggy."

"You're joking, right?" He laughed.

"No, you're leaving in a few weeks. I can't be with you while you are away for two years."

"Alex?"

"I'm sorry." *I'm ashamed to face him. His eyes are so still almost like death arose inside them.*

"Are you seeing someone else?"

"No."

"Then why are you doing this? I love you."

"I can't promise you that I'm going to wait for you. It was so easy for you to sleep with those ladies. How can I trust you after that?"

"Alex! You said it was okay. Don't do this. I'll have a break in between and…no…no. I don't want that." Staring at the dangling locket, he pushed her hand away. "Keep it."

"It's not going to work. I'm sorry. I'll come by the condo to pick up my things later."

Agatone stormed out of the backyard, hopping over the gate. Alexandria listened to his truck roar away. Bumper, close by, crawled onto her lap. Nudging with his head, he placed his paw on her arm. She rubbed his furry head and kissed him. His intelligence never ceased to astonish her. He never snubbed her, even when she pushed him off the bed in the middle of the night. It was as though he had a seventh sense.

Bumper was tiny and scared when Tippy brought him home from the shelter. He had been the only kitten to survive the flood in the animal shop. Afraid and curled up in Alexandria's arms, she fed him from a bottle. She didn't realize that she needed the cat just as much as he needed her. Every time Tippy ran over a speed bump, his little claws clenched Alexandria's shirt, and from that day forward, she called him Bumper.

Alexandria's eyes were red and watery. She was hysterical when Aamir showed up.

"Are you okay?" He sat down beside her, resting his feet in the pool.

"No, that was one of the hardest things I've ever had to do in my life—worse than the marines, I think." Alexandria laid her head on Aamir's chest.

"Maybe you guys will get back together."

"I'm pretty sure he'll hate me."

"The guy couldn't have expected you to wait, Alex."

"Yes, he did."

"You love him?"

"Yes, I do, but I don't want to break his heart."

The night had fallen, and the sun rose. The janitorial services had come to clean the Paz residence as they did every Saturday. Cigarettes, confetti, bottles of wine, and kitty litter were strewn across the entire yard. The housekeeper trailed around Alexandria and Aamir, stuffing paper cups and cigarette nubs inside a giant trash bag, tiptoeing over their taut bodies as they lay on the lawn in a comatose-like sleep.

* * *

Is she awake?
She is, but she's shit-faced.
We must complete the initiation.
How do you know she is a virgin?

She said so.
Do we have everything?
Yes.
The knife? The stones? The plants?
Yes, yes, yes.
"Alexandria?"
"Yes, Dr. Winters?"
"Where did you go this time?"
"I don't think we should do the hypnosis anymore. Some weird stuff is happening in my dreams." Alexandria sat up quickly.
"They're not dreams, Alexandria. It's your reality." Dr. Winters gave her a bottle of water.

* * *

The humidity swept across San Francisco like a vortex. While stuffing two large suitcases inside his trunk, sweat pellets rolled off Aamir's forehead, neck, and back. He guzzled two bottles of water to fight off the stifling heat underneath the parking deck.

While Aamir waited, Alexandria roamed around the apartment, rubbing her hands across the furniture she once lay on, the kitchen she cooked in, the memories that she anticipated leaving behind. A tear fell from her eye, realizing how elegiac she'd made Agatone when she told him it was over. Sadness engrossed his face. His favorite sweatshirt straddled the countertop; she couldn't resist smelling his fresh scent one last time as she picked up the shirt to take a whiff.

"Alex?" Agatone said her name calmly.

She turned around, clumsily bumping into his bulging chest. His ripped jeans hung from his waist. Frozen, she didn't move. "Hi." She hesitated.

He paused. "You got everything?" He walked around the living area, searching for items she could have left behind.

"I think so." She held a pair of stilettos in her hand.

"So we're doing this, huh?" He moved closer.

She backed away. "Yes."

"Why are we doing this? I thought you said you'd wait for me."

"Aggy…" she said right before he kissed her lips. She tried to resist, but it was difficult to refuse his touch. It was the second day after her period ended, and she'd been horny since. Her body melted like putty in his hands, and she quickly unbuttoned his jeans. Rippling surges shot through his veins. He snatched her panties down.

"I can't let you go, Alex," he muttered as he laid inside her. "Never."

"I love you, Aggy, but I can't." She cried out until he released on top of her stomach. She grabbed her panties, wiping what was left of him from her stomach as they lay in silence. He tried to touch her, but she moved his hand away. "I have to go." She sat up quickly. "Aamir is waiting for me." She straightened her dress, forgetting her panties beside him.

"I love you," he said when the door slammed behind her.

CHAPTER 10

Her

Alexandria concentrated on classes while pursuing a second major in culinary arts since Agatone left for deployment. Her catering gigs increased after her culinary arts professor referred her to his colleagues. Some days she'd hire an assistant to help with significant events. Bumper played with a yarn ball at the foot of the bed while she was organizing upcoming events in her calendar. *Aamir's in Tampa. Dad is with Mom at her fundraiser benefit. Rafe and Kensington,* she contemplated before calling them.

Moments later, they pealed the doorbell. Rafe rushed inside the guesthouse as if he had to pee badly, his hands filled with designer bags. Kensington stepped high behind him with Guinevere beside her. Bumper ran behind the recliner, scowling at Guinevere as usual.

"Antisocial feline!" Kensington yelled at Bumper.

"Your cat is on a leash." Alexandria rolled her eyes.

"Where's Aamir, the golden Greek *god*?" Rafe smacked his lips, looking around the room as if Aamir was tucked away inside a cabinet or underneath the sofa pillows.

"Working." Alexandria pulled out a cigarette. "Aamir hates it when you call him that."

"Too bad. Maybe if the Greek god stops bragging about the muscle freak between his legs, I'll stop calling him that. Who knew Arabic men had big dicks. I've seen his dick before."

Alexandria coughed smoke from her mouth, and Kensington stopped and stared in awe. "What!" they both yelped at the same time.

"In the locker room. Remember, we were in Bitch Face Dazzle's class. It swung out of Mir's boxers, took both hands for him to put it back. I could've just gotten on my knees and praised him. Damn. It should be a crime." Rafe rolled his eyes and tooted his butt up, twirling it around. "Anyway, fuck, Aamir. Let's get drunk." He placed his bags down and scurried into the kitchen, giggling for no apparent reason. "Kensington's pregnant, by the way, but the bitch is still drinking."

"What?" Alexandria's mouth flew open, releasing smoke.

"I'm not keeping it." Kensington sipped from the glass Rafe gave her. "It was a mistake. I didn't make Benjamin wear a condom, and apparently, his pullout game is weak. I told him I'd swallow, but the fucker came before I got it in my mouth."

"I bought swim trunks. Let's go swimming in your parents' pool." Rafe pulled his polo shirt above his head, stepped out of his jeans, standing naked in the middle of the floor. His penis dangled as he tussled with the tag on his swim trunks and slid dark sunglasses over his eyes. "I'm ready." He grabbed a few champagne glasses and skipped outside.

"I cannot believe you're going to abort your baby. It's not like you were raped." Alexandria frowned at Kensington as they sat around the pool, smoking and drinking.

"So, bitch? It is my body."

Alexandria twiddled her thumbs, wondering why she invited them over since they hardly engaged with one another anymore. Since returning home from the marines, she was out of touch with them and several other classmates she'd graduated high school with, except Aamir.

Their interests didn't interest her anymore, or perhaps her interests didn't engage them any longer. Either way, she needed some new friends. She lay back on the patio sofa, scanning old text messages from Agatone, deleting them. Rafe was in his own world, relaxing on the rubber ducky, sipping from a bottle of champagne. Kensington sunbathed as she took selfies of herself and Guinevere from every angle. Alexandria pondered before calling Nial. "Fuck it," she said right before dialing her number.

"Hi, Nial?" Alexandria hesitated as she watched Rafe eyeing her underneath his shades.

"This is Zoe, her assistant."

"This is Alexandria. Nial around?"

"Sure, one moment."

"This is Nial."

"Hi, it's Alex. Alexandria."

"Umm…I can call you back, yes?"

"Okay." Alexandria hung up.

Waiting for Nial's call, she deleted old pictures of Agatone from her social media accounts and scrolled through to locate Nial's profile. Most of Nial's images were black-and-white with no captions. Other pictures focused on specific body parts, her "legs for days," as many followers commented below the leg pictures; her freshly manicured toes; her smoky eyes; her toned arms; her red lips, which were sketched by a famous artist she'd tagged; and, most of all, artistic photos of famous models and images with people she didn't know but people liked a lot, based on the comment section.

After Rafe and Kensington left, Alexandria lay on the floor in her parents' living room, roaming through an old photo album she found inside a wicker shelf in Abram's bedroom, the only place in the house she vowed to never enter again.

Today was different when she walked past the room. Abram's peewee soccer uniform and softball cleats were out on the shelf. His money bank, shaped like a football, was filled to the top with silver and gold coins Mr. Paz procured from a vintage shop in Italy. The money bank sat waiting for his return, she hoped, denying his death. The duvet on his bed smelled like baby soap that Mrs. Paz still used when she felt it was time to rewash it.

It isn't strange at all that Mom still uses baby soap to wash garments that haven't been used in years, Alexandria thought as she sniffed the freshly scented blanket. His sensitive skin afforded him luxuries that other preschoolers dreamed of, including her. She ran her fingers across an old picture of Abram underneath his bookshelf. She glared at it. His plaid pants and black suspenders matched his paperboy hat. He reminded her of a wise old man inside a child's body. She dozed off on top of his bed unknowingly until her phone buzzed.

"Ma chérie?"

"Yes." Alexandria's voice raspy, she cleared her throat.

"Dinner?"

Alexandria hesitated. "Sure, when?"

"Seven o'clock tonight?"

"Sure, I'm in North Village."

"I will be there."

Alexandria hung up, bewildered. She jumped from Abram's bed and ran to her bedroom closet. Checking the time, she searched through her reds, whites, blues, and blacks when finally, she came across the perfect black, gold, and white plunging wrap dress with sparkling gold heels.

By the time she finished showering and washing her hair, the doorbell resonated. She checked her teeth in the oversize mirror inside the foyer. She opened the door. And Nial's body dripped in a slim black open-back body dress, silver stilettos, and her voice was smooth as butter.

"Beautiful does not describe how gorgeous you look." She stared at Alexandria, extending her hand to hold.

"You look great." Alexandria ogled.

"Thank you." Nial laughed. "How hard was it for you to say that?"

Alexandria sneered.

The driver opened the door, and Nial offered Alexandria a glass of champagne. The partition instantly went up, and Alexandria sat upright in a quiet position. "Are you nervous?" Nial placed her hand on Alexandria's jumping knee.

"Mind if I smoke?"

"Yes." Nial grabbed a stick of gum from her silver clutch.

"Seriously?" Alexandria pouted and tossed the gum in her mouth.

"Hold that thought, please." Nial held up her finger as her phone rang. "Uhh…yes. No, yes. Okay." She paused for a moment. "We must postpone dinner. There is an emergency at my office building. Join me." She paused, waiting for a response. "Or my driver can take you home?"

"I'm with you." Alexandria shrugged.

They pulled into the parking area near the flashing lights. Once parked, the driver quickly opened the door. Nial and Alexandria strutted near the building. Their heels clacked the ground in accordance. "I am Nial Paul. What the fuck happened?" She stared at the smoke.

"Ma'am, do you have any idea how this could've happened?" the fire chief asked.

"No, I do not! You're the fire marshal, goddamnit!" Nial walked closer toward the building. "I must see for myself."

"Usually we don't allow it, but it's at your risk."

"I WANT TO SEE!" Nial demanded.

"You'll need this." The fire chief handed her and Alexandria a mask and led the way.

The office was cloudy, and debris rained down on the tables and tile, creating a puddle of ash across the floors. Nial coughed, maneuvering through the rubbish while entering her office. Alexandria was close behind. The officer stood in the doorway. "Can I help?" Alexandria laid a hand on her back.

"Yes, move the desk over." Nial struggled as she tried to push the desk forward. She pulled a giant blade from her clutch and stripped the carpet where the desk sat. There was a large briefcase in a safe underneath the floor. "Thank you, Alexandria."

Alexandria never heard Nial's voice so dispiriting. She rubbed her hands across Nial's naked back. "You're going to bounce back from this like the boss that you are." Alexandria winked at her.

Nial smiled, gripping her hand. "You are accurate," she said as they quickly left the room.

* * *

Nial purchased another high-rise building in the heart of the city. She and Alexandria began spending more time together since the night of the fire. "I never had quinoa and pulao before. It is delicious." Nial sipped from the ladle.

"Hey, you're supposed to wait." Alexandria poured another glass of wine.

"Your parents have a luffely place. I luff the open space inside your cozy little home." Nial stood beside Alexandria, watching her mix the spices into the boiling pot. "I want to kiss you."

Alexandria walked away from Nial toward the patio, looking out at the koi fishpond. "We broke up," she confessed.

"You did not tell me?" Nial sat on the edge of the mustard-color sofa. "Come to me."

"I'm enjoying our friendship. I do not want to mess things up." Alexandria went back into the kitchen to check on dinner.

"Things can only get better." Nial got up from the sofa, prancing near the kitchen sink, where Alexandria chopped scallions. She brushed against her hand, and a sudden rush raced through Alexandria's femur—a feeling she had never felt before. It wasn't butterflies. It was more intense.

"I asked you to come," Nial repeated. Her lips lightly touched the back of Alexandria's neck. Heat rose from her body like a furnace.

"More wine," Alexandria cleared her throat as she poured another glass of wine. She shied away.

"Are you afraid of me?"

"No, I'm just not into the girl-on-girl thing."

"Is that so? I do not believe you."

Oops, watch her head, you idiots. We're not trying to kill her.
Are we ready to proceed?
Yes.
Bloodroot?
Check.
Wormwood?
Check.
Burn the oats.
She'll notice the incision?

It's small, and the oil will numb it. No one will notice.
All we need is a little of her blood.

"Alexandria!" Nial raised her voice.

Alexandria spilled the wine on the countertop. "You scared the shit out of me." She quickly placed a paper napkin on the messy spill.

"I had to go full mummy mode. What just happened?" Nial asked.

"Nothing."

"Yes, you blanked out. Is there a problem?"

"No…I…I…had a thought." Alexandria sat down on an oversize beanbag on the living-room floor. Her heart raced as she lay flat on her back, taking deep breaths.

"And you are not into women, accurate?"

"I'm not sure if I'm into women, but I have feelings for you." Alexandria's head sunk back into the beanbag. She covered her eyes.

Nial sat next to her. "I have strong feelings for you, Alexandria, stronger than any other human."

"Even Taiyo?"

Nial leaned over, kissing her cheek. "Stronger." She smoothed her finger across Alexandria's pinky, latching on.

I want to give myself to her. How can I do that? I'm not a lesbian or gay or queer or whatever word they use for same-sex intimacy. She makes me want to experience life above and beyond anything I could think of or even imagine. She makes me feel like the world really is my oyster. How does she do that? Is it her confidence? Her beauty? If she lost everything—her money, beauty, voice, style, personality, and sense of humor—I would still want her just as much as I do now. Well, maybe not because if all those things were stripped away from her, she wouldn't be Nial. She'd be someone else, and I don't want someone else. I want her. I don't understand. Am I gay? Alexandria questioned as she lay in silence next to Nial. She soaked up the smell of her, basking in it like her favorite scent.

"Sweetheart!" Mrs. Paz sprinted inside the guest home where her daughter resided.

"Mom! What are you doing here?" Alexandria sat up, pulling down her dress.

Mrs. Paz's mouth dropped open. "What is going on here?" Her eyes shifted to the kitchen stove, the sink, wine bottles spilled on the floor, and Nial next to her daughter.

Nial quickly stood to her feet. "It is nothing." She backed up, holding her hands in the air as if she was under arrest.

"Get out!" Mrs. Paz's voice quivered. Her hands shook as she shouted, "Get out now!"

"Mom, it's not what you think."

"I know this looks bad. Well, I do not know what it looks like. What does it look like?" Nial asked.

"I said leave now!" Mrs. Paz threw a glass at Nial, then a plate, a bowl, and eventually picked up the bottle of wine from the countertop until Nial was out of her sight. "And stay away from my daughter!" she yelled, breathing deeply, grabbing her chest. Her head hung low. "Alexandria, what is going on?" She shook her head, crying frantically. "No!" She screamed. "You will be cursed for this sinful act, Alexandria. No one can outrun sin. No one."

"Mom! Mom!" Alexandria called out, but Mrs. Paz ignored her.

"I cannot speak with you right now, Alexandria. I want you to leave as well." Her mother continued to cry. "I did not raise you to be this way."

"But, Mom…I wasn't doing anything. Nial is only a friend."

"Gather your things and go now!" Mrs. Paz beseeched.

"Mom, please. I don't have any place to go. I'll be a homeless kid over a misunderstanding. Mom!" Alexandria screamed, fighting tears as she gathered her things, Bumper, and exited the sliding doors. Mrs. Paz immediately locked the door behind her daughter.

CHAPTER 11

Lady Lovin'

There was no place for Alexandria to go after her mother kicked her out of the guesthouse. Aamir was on tour, and Rafe and Kensington's mansion was the last place she wanted to stay. So the driver drove around the city until Alexandria decided on a designated location. She was nervous as she watched homes on display decorated with ghosts and goblins in one of the swanky neighborhoods. "Stop here." Alexandria gazed out the window before stepping out of the vehicle.

"Should I grab your bags?" the driver asked.

Alexandria nodded, and he placed her bags beside her on the sidewalk. She gazed at the door with Bumper in her arms until she gathered the nerves to ring the doorbell. Then suddenly the door flew open. Nial pulled her inside, grabbing her tight.

A carved pumpkin in the windowsill glowed as if smiling at her. Pine cones and cedar oak with a hint of pumpkin spice greeted Alexandria as she entered the artistic space. She had never been to Nial's home before. It was large and modernistic. Nial led the way, grabbing Alexandria's luggage, placing them in a nearby room.

The first floor exhibited black-and-white mixed patterns of polka dots, stripes, and plaids, with butterfly decor matching the color scheme that feathered up the wall. The vivid colors on the second floor matched sky-blue butterflies leading the lepidoptera from downstairs. Alexandria admired the orchid-shaped chandelier hanging on the high ceiling. An eclectic painting of Nial crying with mascara running down her face faced the large window inside the kitchen a few feet away. The royal blue complemented the soft white Italian leather furniture in the living area. Finally, the ladies reached the third level, where brown butterflies circled the ceiling, as the ladies stepped onto the deck.

The fireplace crackled as a woman and two men lounged on the chairs, taking in the view from the city while listening to music. Alexandria had never heard old-school alternative before. Nial introduced Pierre, a music executive who spoke to Alexandria cursorily, then turned toward Lance, speaking in another language. Lance, a savvy tech entrepreneur and model, worked for Nial on special occasions.

"Madeline," Alexandria heard Pierre say her name twice as she puffed on a doobie. Then Madeline chunked two fingers up like her mouth had been wired shut and proceeded to tap the buttons on her cell phone.

"I'm exhausted. I need a bath." Alexandria leaned over, whispering in Nial's ear.

"Mi casa es su casa." Nial kissed her cheek.

"Thank you."

"Bienvenue." Nial winked at Alexandria before she disappeared downstairs.

* * *

Months had passed since Alexandria showed up at Nial's home. She and Nial were running wild like teenagers after high school graduation as they explored together. Body painting was the first lark they embarked on. A beige canvas was their playground as they rolled around on the flat surface, creating bright images of their naked bodies. After the paint dried, the paintings fit perfectly inside Nial's theater room.

Nial picked titillating novels from her booklist. Alexandria chose poetic literature, and soon after, they'd switch reads. Most erotic books, Alexandria refused to read because she became aroused by them, so she'd secretly take the reader back to the bookshelf. Nial noticed and dared Alexandria to read the ecstasies aloud. Furtively Alexandria loved it when Nial watched her read the exotic books. It was an unverbalized sex game for them. On other days, they molded pottery on the rooftop. Neither one of them was good at it, but the cold clay was like therapy as it soothed.

One starry evening while Alexandria prepared dinner, Nial equipped the roof deck for an intimate massage beside the fireplace. After dinner and a long hot bath, Alexandria anticipated game night. When she reached the top floor, a whiff of her favorite scent filled the room. She followed the aroma to the roof, where Nial waited. Her red floor-length negligee looked as though someone had poured blood down her frame. A table stretched across the floor. White towels and an oil bottle sat atop the table. Nial smiled with her eyes as she reached for Alexandria's hand, leading her near the spitting fireplace. Alexandria jumped as if she'd get burned.

"It is all right." Nial removed Alexandria's robe from her shoulders and tapped the table for her to climb on.

"What is this?"

"It is called an erotic massage. I promise to only use my hands." Nial stepped away momentarily to turn on Alexandria's favorite melodic sounds.

Alexandria hesitated.

"Come." Nial assisted her onto the table facedown. She covered Alexandria's back with a large towel, dabbed the warm oil on the bottom of her feet—first, the left, then the right. Next, she poured oil on the back of her legs, gently rubbing both legs at once, paying particular attention to her thighs, moving in circular motions. She grasped her soft twin cheeks firmly. The closer she became to her emotional spot, Alexandria's breath deepened, turning into whispering moans. Nial squeezed more oil between her legs, massaging and gripping. Her fingers were gliding in and out of Alexandria while lightly rubbing across her rosebud. She squirmed and wailed uncontrollably, flinching and trembling as her flower swelled. Nial removed the towel from Alexandria's back, touching her waist, the nape of her neck, her arms, hands, and fingers. She caressed.

"Are you all right?" Nial asked Alexandria, but she was speechless. "Turn over." Her voice, in unison with the music, aroused Alexandria even more. She carefully assisted her onto her back. This time, Alexandria's feet were flat on the table, her legs spread far apart. Nial slowly pushed them wider, as wide as the butterfly wings posted alongside the wall.

Alexandria covered her eyes in disbelief. Her heart raced. Nial squeezed more oil between her legs, massaging, letting her fingers slide across her papaya, pacifying yearns. She continued with ease, moving in and out of Alexandria with tenacity. Her hands propelled with speed. Alexandria dripped wet, squirming, unable to resist the fluttery warmth that poured from her yoni when she spurted all over the table, soaking Nial's hand. It was like a pipeline had erupted, but Nial didn't stop. She proceeded to dip her fingers in and out of Alexandria, fondling and tapping her pink pearl faster as she squirted all over the table again until there was nothing left. Shaking, Alexandria's body recoiled. "I think I had a panic attack." Her voice was mechanical.

"You had an orgasm, bébé." Nial kissed her forehead and dried her off.

In that moment, Alexandria knew that her body had been slaked for the absolute first time. *My frame is the foundation of the love she has for me. Her love is art. It is red whiskey coaxing my palate. Her love is the sunlight strengthening the crops and trees, the bluest sky, the green grass beneath my feet. Her love is paintings of portraits that stare you down and follow you around, rousing poetry deep inside, outside, and through me. She is my haven, the place I go to escape the pain of angers past and existential hurts. And in an indefinite time to come, she will be my bliss. She is Eden.*

After a shower, Nial sat near the fireplace with a bottle of wine and a joint in her mouth. The breeze outside swept through the glass door. "Bébé?" She held a clear vial up when Alexandria entered the room.

Alexandria slowly took the vial, examining it. "I don't usually…"

"Sit." Nial patted the seat beside her and dabbed the white substance onto her tongue. She pried Alexandria's lips apart with her thumb, sticking her tongue inside her mouth, leaving traces of the white content on her lips.

Encapsulated by her thoughts, Alexandria's tongue was numb as the white powder dissolved—it was bitter like it could be what poison might taste like. She gleamed into Nial's glossy eyes. *I wonder if she wants me to make love to her, touch her the way she moves me. Or perhaps she expects me to take her in my arms and give her praiseworthy orgasms.*

"Did I do something wrong?" Nial scraped the powder into a thin line before sniffing it in one breath.

"What are we doing?"

"Enjoying each other."

"So we aren't a couple?"

"What is that eyebrow thing that you do? It is sexy." Nial giggled.

"Don't change the subject." Alexandria sipped from her wineglass.

"I...think you can luff, make luff, and have compassion for more than one person."

"You don't believe in monogamy?"

"I find it perplexing and cumbersome."

"Can you be with only me?"

"I am with you only."

"That is not what I mean."

"Your questions make me unhappy."

"Are you and Taiyo still together? What about the other women you bring here? Madeline? Shai? Do you give them erotic massages when I'm away? Are you just friends, or is it more?"

"Yes, I want to be with you and Taiyo only. You are the only person I give an erotic massage."

"I will not do this again if I cannot be the only one."

"Yes, you will."

"What?"

"Yes, you will." Nial moved closer to Alexandria.

"No...I...no...stop."

"You want me."

"No, I do not."

"Yes, you do. I can feel your pulse racing."

* * *

In Miami, Florida, Aamir attended his first NASCAR tournament. Alexandria flew in late to watch the event after completing a catering job. Once she made it inside, she followed the directions he gave her and sat in private box seating. An oversize summer hat and dark shades covered her face. She popped popcorn kernels in her mouth when a pair of stilettos caught her attention. "Hi." Alexandria tapped Zoe's shoulder.

"Oh, hi, Alex, Aamir said you'd be joining me." Zoe chugged her beer. "Want one? There's wine also and water."

"Beer is fine."

"How are you? How are classes going?"

"Good. One more year and I'll be a boss." Alexandria cheered.

"That's awesome. I'll be right back. Have to take this call." Zoe looked down at her phone, speeding away.

"Okay." Alexandria scoped out the cars racing against Aamir. He was in the lead. She applauded and screamed when Aamir marked the finish line. "Woohoo!" she shouted when he accepted his trophy. Alexandria searched for Zoe so that they could congratulate Aamir together. Zoe's bright-green dress caught her interest as she stood in another private box across the way. Alexandria squinted through her binoculars, glaring at Zoe. She strolled in Zoe's direction. "Excuse me. Excuse me." She meandered through the crowd, nearing Zoe's location on the opposite side of the dome. Alexandria peeked inside the private room, watching Zoe converse with Nial. She pressed her ear against the door, covering half her face with the brim of the hat.

"Why are you here?" Nial asked Zoe. Her hand gestures and eye contact looked familiar, firm but intimate.

"Supporting Aamir." Zoe became submissive.

"Why are you still here, Zoe?" Nial arrested Zoe's arm behind her back.

"Please stop."

"Zoe?"

"You want me to leave?"

"Yes, now."

Alexandria's eyes watered thinking of Nial's fingerprints stamped across Zoe's body. She felt betrayed. The woman she trusted, fell in love with, lived with, eaten from her mouth like a baby birthed from its mother's womb allowed her to do all things that one could not imagine another human would do. She could not bear it any longer as she burst through the door, screaming uncontrollably, "What are you doing?"

"Hi, bébé, I need to speak with Zoe." Nial pranced toward Alexandria, tight-lipped as if nothing had transpired.

"When I left you earlier, you never said you were coming to Miami."

"Must I say?" Nial kissed her cheek. "Gorgeous, I planned to be home in time for you."

"Nial does what she wants. You're no exception," Zoe scoffed. The muscles in Nial's face contracted and her eyes turned red. Before she knew it, she'd slapped Zoe facedown to the floor. "Ask her about the office fire." Zoe whimpered, holding her bruised face.

"Zoe!" Nial yelled. "Stop!"

"Ask her, Alex."

"Who burned the office down?" Snot dripped from Alexandria's nose.

Nial moved closer to Alexandria, grasping her hand. "Alex, do not do this."

"Who!"

"I did."

"Why?"

"I was blackmailed..."

"That doesn't make sense. Blackmailed? By who? Wait. You were with me that night." Alexandria exhaled deeply.

"I did it for her," Zoe admitted.

"Oh my god! Dr. Winters was right," Alexandria revealed. "You are a sociopath."

"Dr. Winters? What is her role?" Nial's demeanor changed.

Alexandria had never seen this side of her—a look of hatred. It was intimidating, to say the least. "She said I should stay away from you. She was right." She snatched her arm away from Nial's grip.

"I should've never gone along with this plan," Zoe cried. "I'm sorry, Alexandria. You are a great person."

"Plan?" They all turned around to see Aamir standing there.

"Let's go, Aamir." Alexandria sniffled, her face red and clammy.

"What is going on?" he asked.

"I'll tell you later." Alexandria wiped her eyes.

"No, tell me now."

"They are fucking. Nial and Zoe are fucking!" Alexandria screamed.

Aamir's eyes rotated back and forth between Zoe and Nial. "Wow. Smooth, Zoe."

"Aamir, please…" Zoe was teary-eyed. "It's not what you think."

"Alex, we should leave." Aamir pulled Alexandria by the arm, and they left Nial and Zoe standing alone.

CHAPTER 12

The Unexpected

Alexandria read Agatone's emails repeatedly until her eyes crossed. Her office was small, cozy, and well worth the internship at Mercury-Venus Company. After graduating from San Francisco University, she immediately obtained an invitation to work for a high-profile company. She kept busy, and everything fell in line according to her vision board. It wasn't until her six-month anniversary at the organization that things began to go awry. She was the firm's top-selling intern, and everyone was flabbergasted over her talents. The harder she worked, the less recognition she received in the male-dominated association.

"I hear you are doing remarkably here," a familiar voice spoke as Alexandria made a fresh cup of coffee inside the break room. She turned, and Rebecca Weinberg stood behind her. Alexandria dropped her mug, and it cracked all over the floor. "What's wrong? You look like you've seen a ghost." Rebecca laughed aloud.

Alexandria scattered to pick the glass off the floor and refilled the coffee maker in silence as Rebecca's eyes stabbed her in the back. Afterward, she poured herself a fresh cup of coffee and left Rebecca standing near the refrigerator.

Alexandria's office neared a basement on a secluded floor where mostly the mail carriers hung around. She did not mind because she could smoke as much as she liked, and no one would care. The humidifier and the small open window evacuated the smoke, so it wouldn't smolder her clothes. *Why can't I get away from her? Is she purposely torturing me?* Alexandria's computer froze. She looked up to see Rebecca standing in the doorway.

"You do know that you work for me?" Rebecca smirked.

Alexandria did not say a word.

"I hired you. You are part of the girls' club, and we protect our own. Don't you remember, or have you forgotten, *Thysia?*" Rebecca asked.

"What do you want from me?" Alexandria did not want to cause a scene. Although it was her first internship, she refused to allow Rebecca to ruin it for her. It took every fiber in her being to overcome utter hate with equanimity.

"Your friendship?"

"I work for you. Isn't that enough?"

"I want more, Alexandria, or I will make your life miserable." Rebecca sneered and exited the office.

* * *

After work, Alexandria visited Aamir at his new home. She unlocked the door and made herself comfortable inside the billiard room, her favorite place inside the mansion.

"Honey, I'm home!" Aamir shouted as he tossed his blue blazer across the coat stand next to the doorway, unbuttoned his yellow long-sleeved shirt, and slipped out of his blue oxford shoes. "Has Mimi been here yet?" He rushed past each room when he noticed the light inside his poolroom was on. "Wake up." He rubbed Alexandria's forehead.

"I'm awake. I'm awake." Alexandria sat up quickly.

"What's up? How was work? See any sexy ladies or men today?" He opened his large bay window.

"No, but I did see the bitch from the marines." Alexandria lit a cigarette.

Aamir turned on the ceiling fan above the pool table and sat across from her. "What bitch?" He grabbed the cigarette from her hand, puffing it twice.

"Yes, that shrewish bitch!" Alexandria frowned.

"Fuck." He filled a glass with red whiskey.

"Pour me a shot while you're pouring." Alexandria inhaled. "Make it two shots." She exhaled. "She's one of the supervisors. I've gotta get the fuck out of there. She's already threatening me." Alexandria stressed.

"We have to do something about her." Aamir sipped from his glass.

"There's nothing we can do. Jarvis Weinberg, the billionaire, is her father." Alexandria dropped her head.

"So what?"

"So I need to find another internship." Alexandria inhaled and exhaled again. "How was your business meeting?"

"I'm officially a real-estate investor. I own Morgan Hill." Aamir smiled.

"Wow. *The* Morgan Hill Estate?"

"Yes!" A goofy happy expression took over his face.

Alexandria jumped into his arms. "I'm so happy and proud of you. I know you've been through a lot in your life with your parents and everything." She held him tight.

"I want to gift you one of the condos," he mentioned.

"Wait, what?" Alexandria sat up straight.

"Yes, there are over fifty condominiums on Morgan Hill, and I have one that is completely furnished and waiting for you. I know you're not happy back with your parents. There are no stipulations. The place is yours."

Tears filled Alexandria's eyes. "Wow, Aamir. It's a five-million-dollar condo."

"Yes, it is a graduation present. You're my best friend, Alex. I'll do anything for you."

Alexandria was speechless. She held him tighter.

"Hold on…wait. Wait. No sentimentalisms allowed. Everything is going to be okay." Aamir wiped Alexandria's tears away.

"I've been in contact with Agatone," Alexandria murmured.
"Why are you whispering?" He laughed.
Alexandria shrugged. "He's coming back."

* * *

Alexandria settled in Morgan Hill Estate. She enjoyed the condominium's intelligent applications and other amenities offered. The estate's housekeepers, security, and maintenance staff operated around the clock to ensure the tenants' satisfaction. She enjoyed the landscape as she sunbathed by the poolside. The dark sunglasses protected her eyes from the piercing rays when a shadow hovered, blocking the sun from her entire body. She jumped, pushing the shades above her head, squinting. "Aggy?"

"You look amazing. You still have those unwavering doll eyes." He laughed.

Alexandria stared at his buzz cut, and the scruffiness on his chin had returned thicker and longer. "Thanks." She giggled. "Sit down. I have a few minutes left in the sun."

A few of Alexandria's neighbors swam while others lay by the pool slide. "Are these guys always around?" Agatone inquired.

"What do you mean, Aggy?" Alexandria puzzled.

"Brooding over you?" he asked, watching their every move.

"They're not." Alexandria hopped up. "Jealous much?" She draped a sheet towel around her shoulders. "Let's go inside." She took him by the hand. "When did you get back?"

"A few days ago." Agatone's eyes gleamed when Alexandria opened the door. "Woah, you make how much as an intern?" He walked around the spacious room.

"Seriously?" Alexandria stepped out of her two-piece.

Agatone was close behind. "It's just…wow. I'm proud of you, doll. Did the French chick put you up?" He pried.

Alexandria was stunned. "What did you say?"

"The French broad. Your mother called me when you moved out, said you turned into a dyke. Did you? That's why you left me, right?" Agatone continued.

"Agatone? What the fuck is wrong with you? Insulting me?" Alexandria rushed into the bathroom to shower. After her bath, the aroma of sweet spices and ginger filled the corridor when she walked into the kitchen. "Aggy, can we talk?" She slowly neared him and sat on the barstool.

"Sure." He smiled.

"You are the only person I'm dating, and I'd like to keep it that way. But you must respect my feelings and not include our past in our present."

"Okay, doll, sure."

"Thank you for cooking dinner. It smells delicious."

* * *

The sun shone bright as the clouds peeked through the blue sky. Alexandria skipped into work with a massive smile on her face until she noticed everyone glaring at her. She slowed her pace, spoke to security and a few people on the management team. Some engaged, while others leered. "What is going on?" she asked the attendee at the front desk. He shrugged his shoulders, continuing to push a cart of envelopes in the opposite direction. She hurried into the ladies' room. *Okay, my period did not sneak up on me. My makeup is still neat. My outfit is crimped, no underarm sweat. My hair is entirely blown out,* she pondered, running her finger across the scar embedded in her eyebrow. She had begun to fixate on the blight after Nial swooned over it in bed when they first made love. She flew out of the restroom, and a security guard grasped her by the arm. He escorted her upstairs to the main lobby. "What is going on?" she asked the security officer, but he did not speak a word.

"Sit here and do not move," another officer demanded.

The cubicles were empty, and no one was around when a handful of board members suddenly spread out of a spacious office. "Ms. Paz, you may enter." Bill Brant, Mercury-Venus's lead supervisor, summoned her into his office. Alexandria picked up her briefcase, watching her surroundings. "Close the door behind you." His voice was stern and grave.

Yes, Mr. Brant, what can I do for you, sir?" Alexandria sat back in her seat.

His hands were clasped together on top of a manila folder. "Do you know what's in here?" he asked.

Alexandria, uncertain, cleared her throat. "Umm...no, sir, I can't say that I do." Her eyes were full and round. *How the fuck would I know what you're holding.*

"Secrets."

"Secrets?" Alexandria repeated.

"Yes, Mercury-Venus secrets that someone leaked to another firm from your computer."

"What?" Alexandria was astonished. *What the fuck!*

"Ms. Paz, did you leak the board's information to our competitors?" he inquired.

"No, sir, why would I do that? I love my job."

"Apparently not enough."

"This has to be a mistake, sir."

"Your supervisor, Ms. Weinberg, brought this to our attention. Why would a supervisor lie? Tell me why, Ms. Paz?"

"I honestly have no idea, sir."

"We're going to make sure you never work in another firm as long as you live. OUR STOCKS HAVE PLUMMETED IN THE LAST TWELVE HOURS BECAUSE OF YOU." He raised his voice, straightened his tie, and cleared his throat. "We would've gone out of business if Ms. Weinberg hadn't involved her father. Ms. Paz, pack your things. Leave immediately, or security will escort you out." He turned his back to her, facing the window.

The city bus pulled up to Mercury-Venus, and Alexandria hopped on board. There was a horrific smell streaming the air as she sat beside a woman with white hair that seeped from underneath a violet scarf. The distressed skirt hung to the floor, floating above the worn open-toe sandals. It seemed everyone had someplace to go except for Alexandria and the woman as the driver continued down the long road.

Alexandria eyed the woman, waiting for her to get off at one of the stops, but she never moved. Then finally, the sun began to fade, and Alexandria realized that they'd both ridden the bus for nine hours. Yet for some reason, she had not provided the bus driver with a location, and neither had the weathered woman. "Why aren't you getting off?" she asked the woman.

"Why aren't you?" the woman spoke softly and slowly.

"I lost my job. No one is home waiting for me." A tear fell from Alexandria's eye, and she wiped it away.

"I don't have a home. The bus is my home."

Alexandria placed her hand on the woman's withered arm. "What is your name?" Alexandria inquired.

"Goether, Goether Mack." She smiled and looked ahead.

"Come home with me, Goether." Alexandria smiled.

"No, no, you don't have to do that, child. Besides, you're outta work. You may be homeless soon." Goether chuckled.

"I own my place. Please let me cook you a hot meal and wash your clothes." Alexandria smiled. She grabbed Goether's trash bag, and they stepped off the bus at the next stop.

"You altruistic, child." Goether's smile flushed.

As soon as Alexandria reached her condominium, she ran Goether a warm bath, providing her with clean towels, and washed her laundry. Afterward, while Goether enjoyed a hot bath inside the large Jacuzzi tub, Alexandria called Aamir to tell him the news.

"She's sweet, Aamir. I told her about Rebecca, and she said I should've kicked her ass." Alexandria and Aamir laughed aloud.

CHAPTER 13

Je t'aime

As time passed, Goether and Alexandria became the best of friends. She took on the mother role—helping Alexandria with catering jobs and supporting her hopes and dreams. She exaggerated Bible stories as they'd gather around the fireplace. Alexandria sat on her beanbag, and Goether sat with her legs folded like a pretzel on the floor next to her. But most of all, Goether imparted what it meant to have irrepressibility. The more time Alexandria spent with Goether, she fell in love with her.

Agatone waited downstairs for Alexandria to join him. "Hi, doll." He opened the door for her.

She smiled and kissed his cheek. "Goether is sweet." Alexandria put her feet on the dashboard, watching Goether wave goodbye from the window.

"You mean creepy." Agatone chuckled. "I bet she's a witch."

Alexandria did not laugh at his joke. "She's a brilliant woman. She thinks I should sue Mercury-Venus for firing me without proof. They didn't do an investigation. They just let me go."

Agatone drove in silence.

"Do you not agree?" Alexandria asked him.

"I think it's over, doll. Move on."

Alexandria lit a cigarette while turning the radio volume up.

Agatone pulled into valet parking at a popular restaurant near Morgan Hill Estate called the Red. The bricks on the building were candy-apple red with cherry-red shingles, and the windows were tinted dark black with a high-rise roof deck. No one could see inside, but everyone could see outside. Agatone held Alexandria's hand as they entered the building. The barista checked their reservation and seated them near a window in the corner of the room.

"I have to pee, Aggy. I'll be back." Alexandria got up from the table, rushing toward the ladies' room. Meanwhile, Agatone ordered champagne and twelve diamond-encrusted red roses that the restaurant was famous for.

Alexandria washed her hands and checked her makeup. Smearing the pink shadow above her eyelid, she poked her pupil. *Shit.* When she looked up, Nial stood behind her with an alluring smile. "Still a beautiful faux pas." She smiled with her eyes as always.

Alexandria yelped. "What are you doing here?"

"Did you receive my gift?" Nial fixated on her.

The restroom attendant exited the room, quickly placing an occupied sign on the outside of the door. Alexandria sneered as she reached for a hand towel in the willow basket next to the faucet.

"Yes, I trashed it."

"I do not believe you."

"Still smug."

"Je t'aime, Alex. I need to explain."

"Explain?" Alexandria fleered. "Didn't think explanations were your thing."

"I am an idiot." Nial blocked the door as Alexandria attempted to leave.

"Didn't take you for the uncouth type. Then again, yes, I did." Alexandria tried to pry Nial's hand away from the handle until her fingers turned purple.

"Five minutes." Nial breathed.

She smells so damn good. She doesn't have to speak a word. Her mere presence captivates me. Why! Why do I let her do this to me? Why can't I resist her? Alexandria questioned. "It's been three years. I've moved on."

"You play in my head like my favorite song all those years. You are salubrious for me. You never change. I am drawn to your heart, blatant honesty, and most of all, your will to luff others before yourself. You are a goddamn maverick, Alex. I luff everything that is the existence of you."

Her insides turned into mush, listening to Nial speak. It took everything in her not to dissolve in her arms like sugar. "Poetic," Alexandria ridiculed. "Dr. Winters left the university. Was that you?"

"No."

"No?"

Nial swept her primmed hair behind her ears. Sadness circled her eyes. She forcibly took Alexandria in her arms. "I want you, Alexandria Talar Paz. Tell me you do not luff me, and I will walk away—forever." She breathed deeply.

"No, I do not. I'm with Agatone. I love him."

"No, you luff me." Nial kissed her lips, and at that moment, time froze. The longer they kissed, she became liquified as wetness oozed down her leg. Nial kneeled in front of Alexandria, palming her twin cheeks, sliding her panties to the side with her teeth, sipping until she drained Alexandria's body. Her knees shook as if they would disconnect from under her. "I am in luff with you, Alexandria. We belong together." Nial continued to hold on to her hips, gazing at her. She stood up.

"I hate you." Her lips gently grazed Nial's lips.

"You luff me. I luff you, bébé."

"You always do this to me, and then you fuck up." Alexandria straightened her skirt. "I have to go." She looked at her watch.

"I will release the door if you promise to contact me soon." Nial continued to hold the door.

"Nial?"

"Meet me at my office tomorrow, 3333 Broadway Avenue. It's the tallest building on the corner block, the twenty-fifth floor. I will expect you around noon."

"Okay, now let me out of here." Alexandria tugged at the door. Nervous, sweat poured down her face. Discombobulated, it had been thirty minutes since she entered the ladies' room and two minutes since the intense rupture.

Agatone was on the brink of entering the restroom when he rushed by a befuddled Alexandria. "Alex," he called.

She turned around quickly.

"Oh, Aggy, I'm so sorry. I got my period. We need to leave."

"Sure thing, doll. You get the truck." He gave her the keys. "I'll grab the food." Agatone waited for the server to bring their bags when Nial pressed past him. He did a double take. "Hey!" he yelled out, but Nial bolted forward, ignoring him.

When Agatone and Alexandria reached Morgan Hill Estate, Alexandria hopped out and ran upstairs, leaving Agatone to park his truck. Goether was sound asleep in the guest room. Alexandria scuttled into her bedroom, shut the door, and locked it. She sat on her bed, breathing heavily. She lit a cigarette as Goether's words replayed in her head.

Alexandria, you are a confident child. Everyone is human and bleeds the same blood. Don't you be afraid. You are the strong woman the Lord created you to be, sturdy and fearless.

Agatone knocked at the door. She wiped the tears trickling down her chin.

"You okay? What happened?"

"Nothing, I just got my period. I was embarrassed."

CHAPTER 14

SOS

The following morning, Alexandria prepared breakfast for herself and Goether. Goether looked like a new person—her skin smoother with no smudges on her face—and she smelled like fresh gardenia since she lived with Alexandria. She'd met Aamir, and he fell in love with her just as much as Alexandria did. They found a hairdresser to style her soft white hair and bought her new clothes that fit. Goether refused to wear new clothes. She'd wait until Alexandria wasn't around to slip back on her old worn dresses and sweaters.

"Don't forget you have a doctor's appointment this evening, Goether," Alexandria reminded her. "And wear that new bra I got you. That old one makes your boobs look like they're sad." Alexandria giggled.

"Child, I haven't seen a doctor in years. Why start now?" Goether filled her mouth with grits and eggs. "Ain't no doctor scoping for these old saddlebags." Goether snickered.

"That's why you need to go. I'll be right there cheering you on." Alexandria sipped her coffee.

"I don't need cheering on. Where you off to?" Goether pried.

"I'm going to meet Nial, but if Aggy calls or comes…"

"Child, I don't know where you're off to."

"Good deal. See you soon, Goether." Alexandria kissed her on the cheek and fled.

* * *

Broadway Avenue crawled with pedestrians. Alexandria hopped out of a cab, ambled into the gold-and-silver building, and passed security straight to the twenty-fifth floor. The entire building belonged to Nial. For now, she was the only person occupying the vast space. It seemed she enjoyed working alone, based on the vacant offices.

As soon as Alexandria stepped toward the doorway, Nial's legs crossed in the light of day as she anticipated Alexandria's arrival. She stood quickly, greeting her with open arms. Her smile bright as the sunshine's light, Nial reached for Alexandria's hand, leading her into another room toward the back of her office. She took Alexandria in her arms, holding her tight, nudging her neck. She rubbed her nose against her cheeks, kissing her lips, speaking softly, "Voilà. I made you dinner."

"I never took you for a romantic."

"I am not usually. You bring something different out of me." Nial took the lid off the entrée, and the aroma seduced Alexandria's nose.

"Smells amazing." Alexandria bit a small piece of the roasted pickle.

"Tell me about life without me in it? I want to know it all."

"No, no, first, I want to know what your intentions with me are." Alexandria continued to fill her mouth with the roasted carrots and pickles.

"Zoe is no longer my assistant if that is what you wonder."

"And Taiyo?" Alexandria's eyebrows lifted, almost touching her hairline.

"No Taiyo. There is no one that I luff. You have my heart. I apologize deeply for hurting you. I am afraid if you know the real me, you will run away."

"I want to know the real you. I am in love with you, Nial."

"Promise me you will never leave me."

"I promise. But I have had some challenges in my life."

"Difficulties?" Nial asked.

"Yes, I lost my internship. Someone had it out for me. I got fired…" Alexandria sipped the red wine from her glass.

"What? Who is this person?" Nial scowled.

"Rebecca Weinberg. Short with freckles, black hair sort of neck-length—it seems to be her signature style. We were in the marines together. She's a horrible person. I cannot describe the extent of her cruelty."

"Hmm…Weinberg? I am familiar with a Jarvis Weinberg."

"He's her father. So now I'm blackballed from every firm in the state."

Nial got up from the chair and kneeled in front of Alexandria. "I will take care of it. No worries." She kissed her forehead.

"What? How?" Alexandria inquired.

"Do not worry your beautiful face. I will take care of it. Trust me."

"Okay, I think."

"Alexandria, I need you to do me a favor." Nial sipped from her glass.

"A favor?"

"Get rid of the man," Nial demanded.

"What man?"

"The man who has been leaving traces of his presence on you, inside of you. I want all of you to myself now and forever." Nial cleaned up the table and prepared a carryout box for Alexandria. "I need to make a few phone calls. I want to take you dancing tonight, yes?" Nial gave her the leftovers.

"I have to take care of something with my friend, Goether, but yes, I love dancing."

Nial held Alexandria's hand and walked her to the elevator. "Come to my office whenever you desire." Nial planted a lengthy kiss on Alexandria's lips, patting her ass before the elevator took her downstairs to the lobby.

That evening, Goether and Alexandria sat in the lobby, waiting for the doctor to call her back when Alexandra received a text message.

"Doll!"

"?"

"Where are you?"

"With Goether…?"

"I need to see you."

"I'll call you later."

"Wru? Wyd?"

"???"

"I need to see you. I'm coming there."

"It can't wait?"

"No!"

"Text me. I'll come down."

Forty-five minutes later, Alexandria received a text message from Agatone, and she went downstairs while Goether received a thorough checkup.

"Come to the inside deck."

"OMW."

Alexandria hurried to the dark parking deck and hopped inside Agatone's truck. "What is the urgency?" She pulled a cigarette from the pack and lit it. Agatone's face was dismayed, and he did not say a word. "Aggy, what the fuck!" She dropped the cigarette between her legs, deathly quiet from the gun aimed at her stomach.

"You've been lying to me. You are seeing that French bitch!"

"What? Aggy—"

"Stop! Stop calling me that. You don't mean it!" Agatone's voice carried. "You are a fraud, and Rebecca should have killed you!" he screamed like a mad person.

"Aggy, Agatone, what are you saying?" Alexandria tried to open the door, but he had placed the child lock on it.

Mucus dripped from his nose as tears ran down his face. "My ex-wife, Rebecca!"

"Rebecca? Ex-wife? What the fuck! Aggy, please."

"'Aggy, please' what?" he mocked her. His breath smelled of cow manure. The bulging vein in his eyeball popped. Everything about him at that moment was distasteful. The vibration of his voice resembled frightening thunder. The protruding biceps that he used for comfort now terrified her. The more he shouted, it was evident that his adoration for her had evolved into arrant hatred. He pulled a brown pouch from underneath the seat and untied it. Alexandria's eyes nearly popped out of her head at the sight of Bumper lying there stretched out, stiff and lifeless. She screamed, and he slapped her in the mouth. "Shut up! You loved that fucking cat more than you loved me. Kiss him now!" Agatone grabbed Bumper by the fur, forcing him in Alexandria's face. She turned her head away, and he dumped Bumper on her lap. Blood oozed down her legs from the bloody sack. She cried out until her voice went numb.

He is the devil. "Okay, okay." Alexandria was drenched in sweat. "What do you want from me? How could you do this to Bumper? Oh God! Jesus Christ!" Alexandria screamed out.

"Leave him out of it. I'm so tired of you bitches lying."

"I did not lie." Her legs shook as if they were about to fall off.

"I've been following you. You have been seeing that French bitch. You went to see her, and she was at the Red. Stop lying!"

"Okay, I did see her." Alexandria's body shivered, and her voice trembled. "It was not planned. I swear!" Alexandria's phone rang. Agatone tried to knock it out of her hand. She resisted, and he jabbed her between the eyes with a closed fist this time. The back of her head pound against the passenger window as blood ebbed from her nose.

"Give me the phone, Alex!" He snatched the phone, answering it. "Hello."

"Alex, I'm ready," Goether spoke soft and slow.

"You old, oafish Black bitch. Call a bus." Agatone hung up on her.

Alexandria sprayed his face with a small bottle of car fragrance that he kept in the cupholder. With blurred vision, she lit the hairs on his chin with her lighter, quickly rolled down the window, crawled out, and fell to the ground while Agatone beat the fire from his torched beard. Alexandria's knees scraped the concrete. He fired a shot at her head as she darted away. She rushed back inside the building, where Goether waited. Goether got up and took gradual steps toward her. Hysterical, Alexandria mumbled as blood streamed down her knees. A nurse came running in their direction and assisted her in one of the vacant rooms nearby.

* * *

Nial visited a high-profile mental-health rehabilitation center. The eminent center was on San Diego's outskirts, surrounded by ample water and green grasslands. Dr. Winters relocated to the mental-health facility after she left San Francisco University. The doctor earned a position as the lead psychiatrist after winning a literary award for her bestseller, *How the Mind Heals—Heart and Body*.

Nial entered Dr. Winters's office, tossing a beige envelope on her desk. "We need to talk." She sat in a chair across from the doctor and crossed her legs.

Frenzied, Dr. Winters leaped from the chair. "I have a client, Ms. Paul. How did you get past security?" She looked out the door. "Where is my secretary?"

"Tell your client to leave!" Nial demanded.

"He is in a hypnotic state. I cannot wake him instantly. It will harm his process. He cannot hear us. You may speak freely." Dr. Winters placed her hand on her hip.

Nial lingered near Dr. Winters's client. The client had a computer-based machine covering the top of his head. She waved her hands across his face, snapping her fingers beside each ear, but he did not respond. "Alex needs your help. You are the only person that she trusts."

"First, you threaten me to stay away from Alexandria. Now you need my help?" Dr. Winters scoffed. "Make up your mind."

"THIS IS NOT ABOUT ME! Alex needs you!"

"Clearly." Dr. Winters grabbed a Kleenex box from the countertop, handing it to Nial.

"Don't patronize me." She knocked the box out of the doctor's hand. "Alex encountered a traumatic experience. Her parents admitted her to the hospital in San Francisco. Unfortunately, the hospital is not helpful. She is unlike herself. I need her to be herself."

"No. No, Ms. Paul, I simply cannot. I will not. Please leave this facility at once." Dr. Winters pointed to the door.

"No, if you do not do this, I will be forced to take action against you."

"Action against me? I have done nothing wrong, Ms. Paul. I cannot involve myself with you and Alexandria's affairs. I don't trust you."

"Open the envelope on your desk. If you do not help Alex, I will be forced to give the files to the board of doctors." Nial propped her feet on Dr. Winters's desk.

Dr. Winters slowly grabbed the files from the envelope and flipped through the papers. Sweat seeped through her thin blouse, saturating her chest and back. Her face turned green, and she ripped the files and pictures into tiny pieces. "How…how dare you blackmail me? It is unethical and illegal."

"What you are doing in the pictures is unethical and illegal. The girl was a student, a minor, to be exact."

"That is behind me now, and I'd like to keep it that way."

"To encourage you, I have donated five hundred thousand dollars to your charity." Nial threw her long trench around her shoulders. "One hundred thousand for Alexandria's admission, room, board, and treatment. Buy yourself some nice shoes." Nial winked, placing a check down on Dr. Winters's desk. "I expect you will take the proper channels to have Alex transferred immediately. If you do not do as I ask, my threat back in San Francisco will no longer be a threat in San Diego." Nial rushed out the door.

The client woke from his hypnotic state screaming. Dr. Winters raced over toward him. "Her admission is two hundred thousand," the doctor mumbled as the door slammed shut. "Bitch."

CHAPTER 15

Newness

The doctors in San Francisco transferred Alexandria to the San Diego rehabilitation center without her parents' permission. In the beginning, Alexandria struggled to follow the rules at the recovery center under Dr. Winters's care. At first, she refused to eat, drink, or participate in activities and treatment plans. Finally, the doctor ordered tube feedings due to her depleted weight.

Alexandria pulled the tube from her nose repeatedly, which was when Nial contacted Tippy for reinforcement. Tippy left the ballet school right away. She assisted Alexandria with morning showers and, eventually, morning fruit to start her daily regimen. Tippy anticipated Alexandria's health increase as she posted daily quotes all around the room.

The wall crawled with ballet images, symbols of love, and banners of encouragement. Each day she'd pin new sayings in decorated letters and shapes around Alexandria's room. Nial did not like the images and quotes; so she ripped them from the wall, prowling inside the room each visit, aiming directly toward the bright notes, and snatching them away from the windowpane. Alexandria found Nial's displeasure humorous until she overheard her telling Tippy that the images were weak. Soon after, Tippy insisted on taking Alexandria back to Milan with her, but Nial objected, which caused a wedge between Alexandria and Tippy. Tippy, unsettled by Nial's need to control the situation, left the hospital immediately, leaving Nial to attend to Alexandria independently.

Mr. and Mrs. Paz refused to visit their daughter once Tippy called to notify them of what happened. They became angrier after realizing they had no power over the high-profile facility. Their money and power were no match for Nial. Meanwhile, Nial ordered uniquely made recipes created by world-class chefs to comfort Alexandria during her stay at the center. Eventually, Alexandria began to feel like she was on vacation instead of a patient at a psychotherapy hospital. Nial rented a suite nearby to be closer to her. Some nights, she'd pay the mental-health workers a small stipend to permit her an overnight stay. When Alexandria reached the forty-fifth day at the facility, her diagnosis had changed. Dr. Winters's forty-five-day method approach for trauma on the mind healing the body was a huge success. After Alexandria's post-assessments proved successful, Dr. Winters released her from the facility on the fiftieth day.

* * *

Back in San Francisco, the leaves changed colors as they swiveled far and between the breezy wind. Finally, Nial pulled up to a French-inspired estate surrounded by acres of land. The sun shone on their path leading the way to the entrance. Elated, Nial blurted out, "I purchased a home"—she paused—"for us."

"What?" Alexandria readjusted her seat, sat straight up, and veered her head around. It was a three-story with a large tennis court attached to its side and a guesthouse almost as big as her condo at Morgan Hill Estate.

"I luff you, Alexandria. I want you to be my wife." Nial's face beamed brightly.

"I can't help you pay for this."

"Bébé, no worries. I have a surprise for you." Nial pressed the button to the garage door and drove her Lexus RX 450 Sport inside next to five other vehicles. "Take your pick! A foreign for each day if you like." She pointed to the line of luxury vehicles.

"The Porsche perhaps." Alexandria blushed.

Nial held the door open for Alexandria as they stepped into their new home. Aamir; his godmother, Mimi; and Goether waited for them inside the grand foyer.

A line of tears rolled down Alexandria's cheeks when she saw everyone. They all surrounded her with love.

"Don't you ever leave me again." Aamir held up his shot glass. "Drink?" He hesitated to pass Alexandria a glass filled with champagne.

"Yes, please." Alexandria took a sip and placed the glass down on a nearby table next to the flower vase.

"I cooked a huge meal, all of your favorite dishes." Mimi gave her another hug.

"Child, I missed you," Goether spoke slowly with a contagious smile plastered on her face.

"Thank you. It's so great to see all of you. Excuse me. I have to pee." Alexandria giggled.

Nial followed Alexandria into the hallway, watching as she peeped inside each room when suddenly she came upon a dance studio.

"How did you know?" She turned to Nial, planting a wet kiss on her lips.

"What?" Nial's eyes pierced.

"Ballet. How did you know? Did you speak with Tippy?" Tears flooded down Alexandria's cheeks. "I'm crying too much. Namaste." She breathed deeply.

"I may or may not have overheard Tippy boasting about your dancing."

"You are so sneaky."

Nial grabbed her arm, intertwining her fingers in between Alexandria's. "I make it my business to know everything about you. I luff you. Come. Les toilettes are this way." She led the way into an ocean-blue and canary yellow bedroom with a large vase filled with sunflowers in the large window. A California king-size bed sat in the middle of the floor surrounded by vintage wall masks and paintings of images that jumped out of the frames. "This is our bedroom." Nial sat on the sofa in front of the footboard.

Alexandria sat beside Nial and laid her head on her shoulder. "I cannot believe you did this shit." She laughed aloud.

"Believe it. Your studio at Morgan Hill is still available to you." Nial kissed her forehead.

"Goether will live there. I don't want her back on the streets or the fucking bus." Alexandria continued to relax her head on Nial.

"It is settled, then." Nial planted another kiss on Alexandria's cheek.

"I love you so much." Alexandria entangled her arm in between Nial's.

Alexandria sipped coffee from a mug that read Mrs. VIP engraved on the side. She stuffed her mouth with pieces of toffee apple tarts while Nial held her close. The women and Aamir discussed everything from entertainment, food, art, and politics to updating Alexandria on the latest fashion. Alexandria's mind drifted in and out of conversations until she heard Rebecca's name.

"I read Jarvis Weinberg's daughter doesn't have long to live." Mimi filled her mouth with green spinach topped with paneer and peppers.

"Hmm, lost everything. Went complete bankrupt." Goether flipped through the newspaper.

"Bankrupt?" Alexandria reached for her cell phone, searching the headline. "Fraud? Conspiracy? Oh my god!"

Aamir, damn near drunk, propped his feet on the table in front of him. "Serves them right for firing my fucking friend." He laughed in intervals.

"Someone becomes a bit feminine when he drinks, yes?" Nial laughed, winking at Aamir.

"Go to hell, bitch." Aamir tossed his whiskey back.

"Touché." Nial laughed harder.

Mimi ignored the two bickering back and forth as she stared at Alexandria with an estranged look on her face. "Karma is a bitch."

"Tell me about it." Alexandria held her mug up. "Here, here to that," she scoffed.

Aamir, Mimi, and Goether left after they overate and drank themselves drunk. Alexandria continued to lie outside on the patio sofa in front of the fireplace.

"Are you all right?" Nial sat beside her, rubbing her legs.

"I can't get Rebecca out of my head."

"It's late. We should go to bed." Nial covered the fireplace. She reached her fingers toward Alexandria, helping her up from the seat, and they went inside. "Rebecca is no longer a factor."

Alexandria waited in the home office upstairs for Dr. Winters's video call. They had fourteen weekly follow-up sessions since Alexandria left the mental-health hospital, and today was their final session. Dr. Winters explained their Televideo session's final process when suddenly Alexandria vomited all over the laptop keys and screen.

Dr. Winters patiently waited for her to finish puking. "Are you okay?" She anticipated a response as bile dripped down the camera lens while a wet wipe sprinted across the screen like windshield wipers.

"Yes, it must be something I ate." She continued, "I cooked a light breakfast for Nial and myself this morning."

"You're not pregnant, are you, sweetie?" Dr. Winters moved closer to the screen, squinting under her glass frames while Alexandria sat in wonder.

"Well, I didn't have a period while incarcerated."

"You weren't held against your will, Alexandria. Instead, you received help to cope with your life's stressors."

"Shit! Doc, what if I am pregnant? I start my new job next month. Nial? Agatone's seed, ugh!" Alexandria screamed.

"You can handle it. If you are carrying, your child will have your gentle, warm spirit. Speak with your primary doctor. Call me. And speak with your girlfriend, Alex."

* * *

Alexandria bit her nails while waiting inside a small coffeehouse. She laid her hands across her stomach, eyeing the people around the café. A man and a little girl sat across from her. The little mole-faced girl kicked the man's leg with every word he spoke. It was as if the man's leg was numb to the little girl's antics. He didn't flinch a muscle.

A woman and a small obese boy sat at the table beside her. The little boy stuffed his mouth with doughnuts and a mountain of whipped cream, chasing it with strawberry soda. The woman next to him continued to peck the keypad in front of her. Alexandria focused on the adults and the children in the room, rubbing her belly.

Nial rushed through the door. "Bébé." She kissed her cheek. "What is the emergency?" Her eyes zoomed in on Alexandria's mouth.

It's now or never. "I'm pregnant." Alexandria's voice vibrated, and her legs shook the table. Fidgeting, she tugged a cigarette from her handbag.

Nial scooted next to her, snatched the pack of cigarettes, crumpling it. "We have a bébé?" Her face was bright with a wide smile. She wrapped her arms around Alexandria's shoulders, holding tight. "Wait?" Nial slid her chair backward. "What do you mean a bébé? How is this possible?" Nial began to babble in French. "It was not I that made the pregnancy possible."

"I am pregnant, Nial. I slept with Agatone before the incident. You're the only person I want now. You do know that?"

Nial did not utter a word.

Tears stood still in Alexandria's eyes as she waited for a response. "I hate him. How will I love this baby?"

"This bébé will be ours. I will love this bébé. I will adopt this bébé, and it will be Alex and Nial's bébé." Nial planted a long passionate kiss on Alexandria's lips. "In the words of you, okay?"

"I had a noninvasive prenatal test performed this morning to check for chromosomal conditions. It's two babies. I'm pregnant with twins, Nial."

"Two? You will eat for our bébé. Thanksgiving and every day after." Nial laughed aloud. "I luff you, Alexandria Talar Paz. I want to make you Mrs. Paul, Mrs. Alexandria Talar Paul, my wife—right now." Nial got up from the table and clutched Alexandria's hand, leaving their beverages behind.

DANG

The young obese boy swiped the drinks from their table, filling each cup with whip cream.

Nial's vehicle waited outside the café as they slid into the back seat. The driver drove a few miles before they reached the court district. Nial and Alexandria ran up the stairs. Mayor Salem Biggs stood in the doorway, conversing with a security officer when Nial rushed past her, almost knocking her over.

"Ms. Paul!" the mayor shouted.

"Shit! Mayor SB, the bitch I am looking for."

"You asshole, where have you been?" The mayor kissed Nial's cheek.

"Why, Mayor SB, watch your language. Meet my future wife and the mother of my children, Alexandria."

"Hello, the future Mrs. Paul." Mayor Salem Biggs stretched her hand toward Alexandria.

Alexandria shook the mayor's hand gently and smiled. "So you know each other?" she inquired.

"Yesss, my luff, we go way back. Officiate? You don't look busy," Nial blurted.

"Off to pull the plug on some unwanted functions in the city, but come to my office. This will not take long."

* * *

Crusade Marketing & Consulting Firm hired Alexandria as an analyst to help them make informed decisions. After being fired from Mercury-Venus, the company's lawyer sent her a hefty settlement for defamation of character and ruined credibility. However, Crusade Marketing & Consulting Firm had their ears to the ground. Once they heard of Alexandria's excellent work morale at Mercury-Venus, they reached out to hire her. Alexandria's office at Crusade Marketing & Consulting Firm was more extensive and more beautiful than the office space at Mercury-Venus.

"Hello, Mrs. Paul," her secretary spoke enthusiastically. "Today is the day you introduce your new informed plan." He organized a stack of papers.

"Yes, excited much, Ivan." Alexandria giggled. "I'll be the youngest analyst in the room." Alexandria held her belly.

"Looks like those twins are ready to pop." Ivan handed Alexandria a bundle of paper.

"They can pop at any time as long as it's not during this presentation." Alexandria scurried into her office when her phone resonated. She picked up before her assistant answered when she saw it was Aamir calling.

"Alex, I'm downstairs. I'm coming up."

"Aamir?" Alexandria stood up. "You can't be serious?" She chortled right before he rushed through her office door.

"Sit down?"

"No, I just stood up. What's going on?" Alexandria rubbed her stomach as she paced the floor, flicking papers.

"I need you to sit down." He pushed the door, closing it in Ivan's face.

"No, what?"

"There was a fire at Morgan Hill Estate, and the majority of the condominiums burned down," Aamir continued.

"Wait, what the fuck did you say?"

"There were many casualties."

"Oh my god!" Alexandria yelled.

"Yes." He took a deep breath. "Alex? Goether was in the fire. The authorities are saying the explosion was inside your place," he blubbered.

The papers in Alexandria's hand fell to the floor, landing in a slush pile, and so did she. Aamir picked her up and placed her on the sofa.

* * *

"Agatone set fire to Morgan Hill Estate and killed Goether. He had to be waiting around, watching," a voice murmured.

"What about the twins? Are they okay?" another voice inquired.

"Yes, they're perfect. Nial has security around the clock. But wait. Be quiet." Mimi said quietly. "Hi, darling, how are you feeling?" She rubbed Alexandria's hands.

Alexandria rubbed her stomach. "Where are my bunnies? Where are my bunnies?" Finally, she attempted to get out of bed.

"A nurse is coming to calm her." Nial hurried inside the room.

"Where are the cameras?" Aamir maneuvered his head around the room when he saw Nial burst through the door.

"Over there, there, and there." Nial pointed upward in the corners of the room and above the door. "I will keep a close eye on my wife and my bébés until someone catches the sick fuck." Nial sat beside Alexandria while the nurse gave her a calming agent.

"Where are the twins?" Alexandria spoke softly.

"They're safe," Aamir spoke.

"The nurse will get them." Nial pressed the call button. "Can you bring the Paul bébés?" she requested.

A nurse quickly brought two babies into Alexandria's room and placed them in her arms. Alexandria stared at the tiny humans with wide eyes, and tears trickled down her face. "My tummy is sore. When did I deliver them?" Alexandria sat upright as she held the baby girl close to her chest.

"You had a C-section. Your blood pressure was elevated, but you are doing great, mon amour," Nial spoke softly, cuffing the baby boy into her arms.

"They were early but healthy. Fly little ones. The doc is keeping a close watch on their lung development," Aamir explained.

Alexandria scanned over the babies. "They are identical. We will name this beautiful one Abella Rose. Her hair is red as mines." She kissed the baby girl's tiny hand.

"Fire, no pun intended." Aamir saluted Alexandria.

"I will call him Nathaniel." Nial laughed. She ran her pinky across the boy's dark shaggy hair.

"My love, I think Nathaniel is a beautiful name." Alexandria puckered her lips, and Nial kissed them gently. "Is Goether really dead?" She looked at Mimi, Aamir, and Nial as they eyeballed one another.

"Goether did not make it. I'm sorry." Mimi leaned over and kissed Alexandria's forehead.

"It was Agatone, and I will not rest until he is put away." Nial rubbed Nathaniel's thick hair once more.

Alexandria did not make a sound as she playfully intertwined Abella Rose's hands in between her fingers. It was as if she had fallen into a daze.

* * *

A blossoming spring followed a shy winter, and there was no sign of Agatone. The detectives labored to locate information about the bomb's properties. It was as if Agatone had disappeared from the face of the earth, taking traces of his DNA with him. No signs were pointing toward him ever being at Morgan Hill Estate. Without evidence, there was no way authorities could acquire a warrant for his arrest.

Nial grew restless of the constant misleads and inefficiencies, which led to taking matters into her hands. She flew her private security team from France to the United States to protect Alexandria and the twins. Alexandria grew tired of the officers following her around ubiquitously to scheduled appointments, doctor visits, her job, and with their nanny.

One beautiful evening, she prepared a decoy after the twin's twelve-month checkup. The emollient sun shone bright, and the weather was perfect for a time at the park happily, with no worries of armed guards standing nearby, ready to obliterate the first person they saw. First, she tied a bonnet around the twins' head to block the sunlight. Then after smothering them with hugs and kisses, she laid a yellow and blue blanket on the soft grass and placed the twins down with a few of their favorite toys. Then she joyfully rolled around in the honeysuckle, allowing the green foliage to embrace them.

"Are those babies mine?" A deep voice vibrated behind Alexandria.

She jumped. "Agg…" Alexandria exhaled deeply. "Agatone?" Distressed, she quickly scooped Abella Rose and Nathaniel into her arms.

"Why didn't you tell me? I know those are my seeds. They look just like me, their dimples. I want to hold them." Agatone's face was disfigured, and his words were indistinct.

Alexandria reached for her phone, quickly pressing numbers to notify the security team of her location. "They're not yours. They are mine." She held the twins tighter.

"You and that French bitch!" he yelled.

"Please, Aggy," Alexandria cried.

"I'm going to kill both of you just like she killed Rebecca."

"What? No, Rebecca fell ill."

"Yes, Rebecca had a debilitating disease. Do not believe everything you read in the headlines, DOLL."

"No, you're lying." Alexandria looked around for security, but they were nowhere in sight. "You killed Goether." Her face saddened.

"The fossil was going to die soon anyway." Agatone threw a magazine at Alexandria.

"No, stop!" Alexandria covered the twins' ears.

The louder Agatone's voice became, the more spit flew out of his mouth. "Page 8!" He shoved the magazine close to her face. "The model right there in the middle was seen with Rebecca the night before she mysteriously became sick. Rebecca told me the model injected her with a dirty needle with noxious antibodies. Her skin began to disintegrate, falling from her body. And that…that woman in the picture is wearing NPD clothing—the same bitch that was seen with Rebecca at the Rockery Club." Agatone snatched the booklet from Alexandria when suddenly blood splashed all over her face.

The twins were soaked in blood from their bonnets to their bootees, and Agatone's body stretched out across the yellow-and-blue blanket. Security rushed to Alexandria, swooping her and the twins away, leaving their things behind.

"I'm sorry, ma'am, but the boss told us to kill on sight," the lead guard spoke as he carried Alexandria to a black Cadillac SUV with dark tinted windows. She trembled as she held the twins close to her heart. Tears dripped down her face. They sped away. Alexandria cried until they reached the private deck underneath Nial's office building.

Nial ran out to the truck and hopped inside. "Are you okay?" Alexandria stared at her, speechless.

CHAPTER 16

Darkest Secrets

Nial stared from the penthouse terrace rooftop as raindrops bounced off the glass, striking her face. *It is a beautiful rainy night. The streets are foggy, and the cars are crawling. The moon sang to the sky as the clouds cry.* A shot of brown whiskey coaxed Nial's throat as she gazed into the night when there was a knock. Her eyes blurry, she stumbled inside the room to open the door. "Bonsoir," she greeted.

"What took you so long?" A man carrying a large brown duffel bag entered the room.

"The cars look like tiny, little insects passing in the night. The longer you watch, the more interesting they become." Nial's words slurred.

"What!" The man was confused. He placed the bag down, and it made a clonking sound.

"What?" Nial stumbled over a pair of stilettos.

"You really need to lay off the snow."

"I had to do something while waiting for you, slowpoke."

"Where's the situation you got yourself in?"

"In the corner." She casually pointed.

"You need to leave. I'll take care of it." The man draped a plastic bag over the dead girl's body before spraying a strange liquid around her bleeding head. The liquid absorbed the blood, leaving no residue.

"Wait…what will you do with her?"

"I know what I'm not going to do with her."

"So what does this mean? I do not know what happened…one moment we were talking, and the next—"

"Spare me the details. The less I know the better. Just leave. I'll take care of it."

"How?"

"Don't worry. I'll take care of it…but you owe me big!"

"Whatever you desire."

"I mean it! Now get out of here."

What was I thinking? Expeditiously, Nial gathered her oversize NPD bag with her stilettos in hand. She hurried down the stairwell to her matte black Lotus Eterne. Fumbling the key fob, she tossed her heels into the back seat as the engine sounded. Her lipstick had been smeared across her face, she noticed as she glared into the rearview mirror. She pressed the gas, forcing the vehicle to speed out of the garage onto the slippery highway.

Her eyes glazed over, and suddenly the Eterne spun out of control. The car revolved in circles, hitting a curb dead-on, tumbling into a ditch. Her lips were raw and busted. Blood oozed down the bridge of her nose, dripping onto her trench coat. She attempted to pry the seat belt off, but it was stuck.

* * *

It feels like fires beneath our bed, flames rising, crawling on my skin. It's excruciating, but I love the pain as it moves slowly from my toes to my head. My blood boils, and I cannot do anything about it. Of all the countless irrevocable acts of provocations I could pursue…when my heart consists of luffing only you. Nial fixated on Alexandria's naked body as the sun beamed through the skylight above their bed. *Libidinous spirits haunt my soul. Why am I so ungovernable? You are an aesthetically ethereal being.*

Alexandria moaned as she rolled over into Nial's arms. "Are you okay?" Then she noticed the estranged look in her wife's eyes. "You scared me last night."

"I'm sorry, but it was not my fault. I had no control."

"Were you inebriated?" Alexandria sneered.

"I can handle my controlled substances. But I will be sure to stay away from the dark ditches at night from this moment on."

"My love, it's not funny. You could've been hurt really bad, or worse."

"Yes, bébé. But I was not—"

"I love you." Alexandria laid her head on Nial's breast.

"I luff you."

"I think you should attend church services with the twins and me. Father Mason would be thrilled to see you."

"Sorry, but I am not interested." Nial arose from bed.

"No…wait. Listen…" Alexandria pulled Nial back on the bed.

"Yes…"

"I love waking up with you. I don't know what I would do if something ever happened to you."

"And…uhh…you think if I go to the church services, that will protect me from the umm…big bad boogeyman, yes?"

"Yes."

"No! I don't think so…" She tapped the tip of Alexandria's nose.

"Don't you want to wake up next to me safe and in peace?"

"I luff waking up next to you, but I really must go. I have an early flight."

"So what?"

"I have to go." Nial planted a kiss on Alexandria's lips.

"Are you sure? That's a pretty ugly bump." Alexandria rubbed the lump on Nial's face.

"Nothing a little foundation won't satisfy." Nial removed Alexandria's hand away from her face and grabbed her cell phone.

"But?"

"I'm fine. Drop it? Better yet…pray for me while I am away."

"I always do."

"Did you remember to pick up Nate's medication?"

"Yes, of course."

"Perfect."

"I want to make love before you leave."

"Luff?"

"Yes."

"Bébé, I...I must go. It is six thirty. My flight leaves in a few hours."

"I need you," Alexandria whined. "It's been two whole weeks. What am I supposed to do?"

"It is not my problem you were away for two weeks."

"It's not my fault either, but I'm willing to make up for my absence."

"Really?"

"Yes, my love. Really." Alexandria seduced her, gently kissing the sensitive points around her earlobe and underneath her chin.

"Bébé..." Nial could not resist the pleasures of her wife.

"I want you," Alexandria moaned against her lips.

Nial placed her phone back on the nightstand, slowly climbing on top of Alexandria. She spread her legs apart, nudging her way to her neck. "Maybe I can make a little time." She traced her fingers around Alexandria's erect nipples before devouring them inside her mouth.

"I'm so in love with you, Nial," Alexandria whispered as she gripped Nial's hair, placing more kisses on her bruised lips.

"I luff you, Alexandria Talar Paul." Nial stroked Alexandria's passionflower before entering her paradise. Nial's long fingers laid powerful thrusts inside her emotional spot.

"I want your fingers in my mouth," Alexandria moaned. "Choke me." Nial joined in, sucking Alexandria's tongue right out of her mouth, wrapping her hand around her throat, squeezing. Slowly she made her way down to Alexandria's delicate sugarplum. She raised her hips off the mattress, clutching her twin cheeks, pushing herself into Nial's warm mouth. Every drop of Alexandria fell onto Nial's tongue as she plunged like there was no tomorrow. Holding tight, they vociferated as one, culminating from pleasure.

Suddenly they heard yelling. "Mommy! Mama! We're ready for our third day of school!" Alexandria took a deep sigh before slowly removing herself from Nial's grip. She slid on her robe and galloped into the bathroom.

"One moment, bunnies!" Alexandria smiled until she noticed a disgruntled look on Nial's face. "Earth to Nial? Are you okay, my love?"

Nial lay there quiet, staring into space, lost in her thoughts. *Looking at you, I wonder why I do the things I do. You are intelligent, sexy, classy, exotic, erotic, and so much more…damn.*

"You seem distracted?" Alexandria pinned her hair into a messy bun.

"I cannot be late."

"You say that, but you're not moving at all."

"I'm moving now. See…" Nial's feet flopped to the floor.

"I'll make breakfast for the twins."

"Be right there. I'll have a cup of coffee, s'il te plaît!" Nial yelled, watching Alexandria exit the room.

Rushing into the kitchen, Alexandria spotted the twins sitting at the breakfast nook. "Mommy? We take photographs today," Abella Rose reminded her.

"Yes, sweetie, I remember…Lea picked the perfect outfits. You look gorgeous."

"Ella and I take twinning pictures." Nathaniel jumped down from his chair and ran around the kitchen.

"Twinning? What's that?" Alexandria joked.

"It's a special category, Mommy. They like to show us twins off," Abella Rose said while eating a bowl of yogurt, oats, and berries.

Nial carried her luggage into the vestibule.

"Mama!" Nathaniel screamed for Nial. "Can we go to da water park when you come back? Every kid in da kindergarten is going, but girls cannot go!"

"Young man…what do you mean girls cannot go?"

"Girls can go…besides, Mama's a girl too!" Abella Rose screamed.

"Mama's not a girl, are you, Mama?" Nathaniel asked Nial, still holding on to her legs.

"Now, now…do not be hasty. Of course, I am a female." Nial winked at Alexandria as they stared at each other.

"I'm not hasty, Mama. You are a girl…an adult girl," Nathaniel continued.

"Just so you know, sweetie, adult girls are women, and adult boys are men. This is the correct way when referring to adults—men and women, woman and man." Alexandria placed the dirty dishes inside the dishwasher.

"I know, Mommy…I know Mama's a woman." Nathaniel wiped his eyes.

"But…but what about the men that wear girls' clothes and the women that wear boys' clothes? My friend Kiki's dad wears girls' clothes and fingernail polish with glitter," Abella Rose pondered.

"Well, honey, some adults are happier wearing the opposite sex's clothing." Alexandria did not expect a conversation such as this, this early in the twin's life. "I cannot explain the feelings of other adults, sweetie, but your mama and I try not to judge a person's happy place. Understand?"

"Yes, Mommy. But sex? Yuck. I don't want to talk about sex, Mommy." Abella Rose covered her ears, humming, attempting to drown the word out of her ears.

"Ella is a drama queen!"

"No, because you are, you are a drama king and a crybaby!"

"Stop it right now, you two!" Alexandria demanded.

"Well…only boys and their mommies are going, and da next time Ella can go." Nathaniel carried on.

"And Kiki's dad," Abella chuckled. "I don't want to go. Water parks are stupid. I want to go to Crayola World," Abella Rose whined.

"You are stupid! Kiki's dad can't go unless he change clothes. We can color here at home," Nathaniel suggested.

"Nate?" Alexandria scowled.

"Sorry, Mommy," he apologized.

"That's right, Mommy. Give him the death stare."

"Nooo! Mommy isn't giving me da death stare! She's giving you da death stare…aren't you, Mommy?"

"Both of you…be nice," Nial said firmly.

"I am nice. It's just...girls really can't go, only boys. My teacher said it, not me. Ask Tyler and Taylor's mom. She knows," Nathaniel continued to speak.

"We'll see about that when I return, mister." Nial walked closer to Alexandria, brushing her hips against her thigh.

"I'll ask his teacher." Alexandria passed Nial a baguette along with her coffee.

"For future reference, little boys who are mean to their sisters don't get the opportunities to go to fun places. Understand, young man?" Nial winked at Nathaniel.

Nathaniel's eyes filled with tears, glaring at Alexandria. "But, Mommy?"

"No buts! You heard your mama."

"Mama? Why are you always away, leaving us alone?" Abella Rose asked Nial.

"Sweetie, my schedule is demanding...I must make plenty of money so I can purchase your collector's dolls and Nate's spinners, not to mention the artwork your mommy requests." Nial gently tapped Alexandria's bottom.

"Requests?" Alexandria reiterated.

"Yes..." Nial laughed, pointing at the painting of a naked woman near the entranceway. "Come give Mama kisses." Nial kneeled, stretching her arms wide. Abella Rose darted into her arms, while Nathaniel planted his feet on the floor. "Come, young man. Give me a kiss. What is your problem?" Nial asked.

"I don't have a problem."

"It appears that something is wrong. Did you take your vitamins this morning?"

"Yes, I chewed my vitamins." Nathaniel continued to pout. "I chew them every day," he mumbled under his breath.

"Nate, come," Nial pleaded.

"I'm not in da mood for hugs and kisses this morning, Mama," he refused.

"That usually means he's mad. He's an idiot."

"Do not call your brother an idiot ever again. Do you understand?" Alexandria glowered.

"Yes, Mommy, I understand." Abella Rose sat down against the wall.

"Nate, you have the right to be upset, but not today!" Nial continued.

Nathaniel slowly dragged his feet across the marble floors toward Nial. "When can we talk about the water park?" he whispered in her ear.

"Sweetie…we will discuss the water park when I get to France," Nial whispered back.

"Muah!" Nathaniel gave her a quick peck on the cheek as he continued to pout.

Soon after, Alexandria walked Nial to the door. "Hurry back."

"I luff you, bébé! I promise when I return, we will have lots of luff time."

"I love the sound of that."

"I want to lock you in a secret place where there is no way out. I will tie you up and have my way with you in my secret hideaway. Then you will only feel the movements of my body on your silky skin," Nial whispered. "I must stop before I miss my flight. Why are you so damn sexy, Alexandria?" Nial planted a passionate kiss on her wife's lips before walking away.

Nathaniel ran behind her before she exited the door, wrapping his arms around her long legs. She picked him up in her arms, kissing him all over his face and neck. He giggled so hard he almost peed his pants.

Crusade Marketing & Consulting Firm

What is taking Alex so long to join us? Georgia Gonzales, Alexandria's boss, twiddled her thumbs. "Okay, let's proceed. Our lead analyst Alexandria is running behind, but I have copies of all the documents. I will brief you on the basics."

"I have a question, Georgia."

"Yes, Chairman Jim?"

"Alexandria is the senior executive?"

"Yes, she is."

"Is the position too much for her to handle? Considering she is running late…maybe we should consider a stronger punctual-type for the position…hmm…" Chairperson Phillips intervened.

"This isn't a man-versus-truck competition, Chairman. Alexandria is great at what she does. That's why she is the lead. She surpassed analysts her first year at the company."

"We only want to make sure we are in the green and on the same page, Georgia," Chairperson Jim chimed in.

"We are past the green, chairmen."

"Okay…" the chairmen spoke at once.

"Don't worry, Jim. I can assure you CMCF is safe. Now, if we can begin?"

"Carry on." Chairperson Jim tossed his hand up briefly.

"We will be taking over New York and LA. Alexandria will be the senior advisor, and Robert will be assisting her."

Robert stood to address the chair members when Alexandria treaded through the door. "My apologies, Georgia, ladies and gentlemen, chairmen and board members. Shall we begin?"

"Thank you, Alexandria." One of the chairpersons sighed.

Alexandria passed out new files she had prepared and began representation right away. "Digital marketing is the evolution of today's era. Moving sales in between San Francisco, New York, and Los Angeles is the plan for this year."

"How are we going to expand in two places in one year?" Chairperson Lucinda interrupted.

"All due respect, Lucinda, but I'm just that good. Shall I carry on?" Alexandria waited for another question.

"Yes, please," Georgia urged.

"An international expansion is the move that will place CMCF at the top of VIP lists—billionaire status. We will be ahead of our competitors by light-years. With this specific program, we will be the only firm with legal access to satellites worldwide. Digital implants, these antibodies as I like to call them, will provide a faster, more efficient, and more effective layout. This will be a lucrative move. So we will now view the slides, and you can see for yourself." Alexandria clicked the button on her mini-pad. "One more thing, I am the only person with these codes. They are strategically aligned and locked inside a cyber vault. Therefore, no one can access them besides me."

"Why is this?" Chairperson Jim worried.

"Because if these codes get into the wrong hands, someone will try to take them, and we can't afford the risk," Alexandria explained.

"I agree. The only organization with satellite clearance is NASA. It took Alexandria a great deal to get this thing to go through," Georgia iterated.

"But aren't the codes patented?" board member Billiton asked.

"That does not stop anyone from making an imitation or accessing the satellites. We do not want this chip in the hands of our competitors—essential point."

"Thank you, Alexandria. Shall we continue, please!" Georgia exclaimed.

"Sure," Alexandria continued.

After the meeting ended, Alexandria sat inside her office, going over proposals. Then there was a knock on the door. "It's open!" She continued to flip through folders.

"How's everything going?" Georgia sat down on the brown-and-white sofa that complemented Alexandria's paintings on the wall.

"Fine." Alexandria continued to focus on her files.

"I love the plan you laid out. I would have never thought that we could do so much with just a click of a button."

"Well, we have remarkable engineers that make that happen."

"Yes, we do, and your brilliance doesn't hurt either…might I add."

"Is everything okay, Georgia?"

"Yes."

"Then what do you want? I would like to finish here before the twins reach home from school."

"There is one thing that concerns me."

"What is it?"

"The board members are concerned about your reliability."

"Really?"

"It's no concern of mine, but…"

"Then why are we having this discussion? Isn't this your company? I thought the board members were just a bunch of old farts that invested into the organization."

"They are…"

"So why are we having this conversation?"

"Because I promised Jim that I would speak with you."

"Aha…Jim?"

"Listen, Alex…you are my star player, and Jim is just looking out for the firm."

"Tell your husband the next time he decides to throw a soiree for a fifty-million-dollar deal that I closed, do not celebrate by flirting with my wife. I've made this company multiple millions in the last five years with one late show. How dare he question my work ethic. I can't believe you are seriously married to that man."

"You know why I married him. He is the reason I am a legal citizen."

"Are we done here? I have to get going." Alexandria filled her briefcase and grabbed her *NPD* blazer.

"Yes, Alex, we're done. Kiss those lovely twins for me."

"Sure thing, G." Alexandria exited her office. Quickly striding down the hallway, staring at her watch, she caught the elevator before it closed.

"Hello, Alexandria."

"Oh…hi, Alberto. I didn't see you standing there."

"I heard you won the board over once again. Too bad the company doesn't pay you for your worth."

"What does that mean?"

"Oh, I didn't mean anything by it. It's just Gavin works as Bill's assistant in the creative department, and he makes the same as you."

"Good for Gavin." Alexandria shook her head, waiting anxiously for the elevator door to open.

"But don't worry. I hear you're one step closer to being chief around here—Georgia's right-hand man or, shall I say, woman. Congratulations! Hard work does pay off." Alberto smirked.

"Have a good night, Alberto." Alexandria quickly hopped off the elevator, walking to her car.

CHAPTER 17

What Happens in Paris

Nial conducted business in Paris during fashion week. Extracurricular activities followed as she hit the night scene. She threw herself an elaborate party at Le'melle, a hot new private nightclub hosted by John, the prince of Paris. Nial and John attended an etiquette school together when she lived in the South of France. The two kept in contact over the years exchanging world secrets—anything she wanted to know, John provided.

As soon as he opened the new nightclub, Nial was the first person on his VIP list. "Ma chérie?" John walked up to Nial and kissed her cheeks. "You haven't changed a bit."

"Mon chéri, it's been a long time, my friend." Nial sipped champagne from a glass.

"You always know how to throw a party. Who's ze toy?" John pointed to the woman whose arm was attached to Nial's waist as if it were glued there.

"You don't waste time, do you?" Nial smirked.

"No need for chitchat, darling. I want ze goods."

"John, Mia. Mia, this is John, the prince of Paris…"

"Mia! Ooooh, I love your brows, honey. Where are you from?" John eyed the long-legged beauty.

"She is quite diffident," Nial said firmly.

"So tell her to speak, dammit!"

"You are no good." Nial laughed.

"I fucks wiz you, my lady. I will see you backstage tomorrow. We have business to discuss, yes?"

"Yes."

"Come with me. I have something for you," Mia whispered into Nial's ear.

"One moment…" Nial held her finger up while flirting with another woman opposite Mia. The rest of the night, Nial dealt playfully with countless counterparts, drank champagne, indulging in euphorias. After working the crowded room, she made her way to the DJ's booth. "Everyone! Everyone!" she shouted into the microphone. "My new clothing line is the most diaphanous line of fabrics created. Thank you for coming out tonight! Tomorrow's show is going to kick ass!" she screamed. The entire room clapped, yelping as they serenaded her with praise.

After the party ended, Nial was intoxicated, forgetting about her limo driver. Instead, she jumped into the passenger seat of a red Ferrari, leaving Mia behind.

A few hours later, Mia stormed into Nial's room and lay on the bed beside her.

"Ouch! Why'd you do that?" Nial rubbed her arm.

"Because you deserve it. You are disrespectful." Mia frowned, placing her things down on the floor.

"Disrespectful?"

"Yes, you are very disrespectful."

"I am confused about your behavior."

"You left me! It was supposed to be you and me here together. Why must you fuck everyone?"

"It is you and me here—no one else. Look around." Nial sat up, staring at Mia.

"What were you doing in the car with Zorana?"

"You are absolutely accurate. I was with Zorana, but she is no longer. So that should not stop you from sitting on my face," Nial whispered as her hands crawled across Mia's stomach.

"I can't keep up with you."

"Excuse me?" Nial pulled a vial from her bra.

"This, what we are doing now." Mia moaned as Nial pulled her panties down with her teeth.

"So what exactly are you saying? I'm just a little confused." Nial looked up at her.

"I cannot see you anymore, Nial."

"No?" Playfully, Nial continued to rub against Mia's abdomen.

"Is that all you say? No?"

"Well, I don't know what you want me to say. You are upset, yes?"

"I'm leaving tonight." Mia pulled her panties up.

"Leaving? Don't leave me lonely and naked. No."

"You may be left naked and alone, but I'm sure you will not be lonely."

"I want to make luff."

"Make love? You make love to your wife, remember? At least that's what you told me, two years ago to be exact," Mia scoffed.

Nial wrapped her arms around Mia. "Don't leave me tonight. How can you leave me like this?" Nial grabbed Mia's hand, placing it in between her creamy thighs. She moaned as she continued to guide Mia's fingers inside of her.

"You expect us to fuck all night and forget about me in the morning? Please," Mia scoffed, snatching her hand away.

"Well, no…I don't think I'll last all night."

"You are a piece of work. Fuck you!"

"Fine! Get out! I will not beg for what I can purchase!"

"What is this nonsense you speak? You flew me here—"

"I flew everyone here…"

"You are selfish, Nial!"

"No, I am naked and horny."

"You should've been a man."

"You are correct. We should not see each other again. I cannot give you what you want, and what I want, you cannot give."

"How fucking heartless are you?"

"I will speak with an associate and with my recommendation."

"Don't do me any favors."

"Okay, but we can no longer work like this. This is clear?"

"Crystal!"

"I'll pay you for your time."

"I'm a big girl! I don't need your charity!" Mia stormed out of the room.

* * *

Nial received recognition backstage after her fashion show ended. "Today's fashion extravaganza, a huge success! I appreciate your dedication. Check your emails. I will see you back in the States. Good job and good night." Nial surged out of the room soon after her speech ended. Everyone applauded until she was no longer visible.

Nial dashed into a limousine out back. Darkness hovered as the stars laughed at the sky. The driver dropped her off at a brown 1970 Oldsmobile Cutlass parked near an abandoned lot. She carried a pearl duffel bag and tossed it in the trunk, waiting for the driver to leave. Speeding down a long dirt path, she inhaled from the tiny vial, blasting the radio, singing along with a French guy that wailed every word. Soon she came upon a cave and drove through it.

Moments later, the car sank underground. A set of doors opened, and she stepped into a large room with golden stones embedded in the wall. Whiskey glasses and bottles of liquor stood on the bar. She sparked a joint. "I am back. I hope I was not gone too long. It is funny what news comes when one does not search for it. I suppose you did not think that I would find out what you were up to." Nial scraped her hands across Taiyo's bruised nipples. "Don't you realize that I am indefatigable?"

Taiyo's mouth was dry, and her body was exposed like the day she was born. She was in handcuffs and foot shackles that linked to a steel rod. The rod pressed against her back, making it impossible for her to move. "Please let me go." Taiyo tried to balance herself as she wobbled from side to side on the wooden box.

Nial examined her. The black-and-white pin-striped pantsuit matched the undergarments that she so eloquently stepped out of. "You talk too much, but that is what your kind does, accurate? No?" She snorted another whiff from the vial, commencing to stuff her panties inside Taiyo's mouth. Taiyo grunted. "Keep squirming. I think that you are turned on. Am I correct?" She pinched and twisted Taiyo's nipples until they turned purple. "You wanted to expose me? Now you are exposed."

Slobber dribbled down the sides of Taiyo's mouth. "I'm so sorry." Taiyo's eyes faltered as she mumbled.

"Do not apologize." A hidden door opened, and three women walked out wearing red rubber catsuits. The three women got on all fours in accord, bowing in front of Nial. "Ladies, Taiyo. Taiyo, ladies. Now we are familiar." Nial released Taiyo from the steel rod, unlocked the shackles on her feet, and guided her to a nearby glass shower in the center of the floor. "You stink." Nial pushed her inside the open shower as the ladies waited patiently.

The water was so cold Taiyo's breast ascended as she shivered like a quivering leaf. After Nial thoroughly lathered and rinsed every inch of her body, she dried her off and grabbed a thick rope from the shelf, passing the rope front to back and around Taiyo's body as she interwove the line down her frame.

Afterward, she shoved Taiyo facedown on the bed, grasped a shiny black paddle that hung on the wall near a host of other objects, and spanked her bottom. The first hit was rigid and slow. The harder she beat, the louder Taiyo yelled. The muscles in her butt cheeks contracted until numbness occurred. Nial tightened the ropes between her legs, turning Taiyo's body over to face her. Nial summoned the three ladies, and they climbed on top of her, Taiyo forced to watch them engage in lewd acts of pleasure. Nial relished in the lasciviousness as the three women immersed themselves in her favorable conditions.

A few hours later, Taiyo had fallen asleep, and when she awoke, no one was around. Light shone through the crack underneath one of the walls. Her hands were free from bondage, so she slowly got up from the bed, silently sneaking through the room. She followed the speck of light, trying to find the hidden passage where the three ladies had come from, but there was nothing. There were no door handles or windows to look out of. There was a visible touch pad on the wall near the ice machine, but the passcode was unknown.

DANG

A water pitcher sat by a curtain. She picked it up, released the top, gulping until she couldn't drink anymore. She pressed her ear against the stones to gain a more precise understanding when she heard voices coming from the cracks in the wall.

"The deal was that you pay me one hundred million for finding all the girls. I have the girls now. I want my *dinero*. Tell Catalina she is the head of your organization. Is she not? I keep my promises, and I expect she is a woman of her word," Nial pronounced as she downed another shot of whiskey.

Taiyo covered her mouth as she continued to listen.

"Sí, Señorita Nial. Your dinero will be transferred through an online offshore account," a man spoke.

"No, no offshore accounts, no cryptocurrency. Send it to BAN Pro. Catalina is aware. She is investing in my new production company. We have discussed this," Nial demanded.

"Sí, sí, I will contact Catalina," another voice spoke. "Sí, Catalina." The man began speaking in Spanish.

Taiyo continued to press her ear firmly against the wall.

"Thank you," Nial said, happily watching the funds transfer into her account. She closed her notebook and slid it underneath a steel safe and locked it.

Taiyo continued to press against the wall until she felt it cave inward. She fell through onto the floor, naked. The men instantly pulled their guns, pointing them at her.

"What are you doing?" Nial bolted toward Taiyo.

"Please." Taiyo trembled.

"Wait, wait. It is not what you think." Nial looked at the men and then back at Taiyo. "Please lower your weapons. I keep her for myself, but she can go with you since she is a hardheaded ass—for free!" Nial snatched Taiyo by the hair, dragging her in their direction. "Let Catalina know that her generosity is favored."

"Please don't do this, Nial. Please don't send me with them. I will do anything."

Nial slapped blood from Taiyo's mouth before she could finish speaking. "It is your fault. I untied you. Why didn't you stay put?

It is too late. You must go." Nial nodded her head, giving the men permission to take Taiyo.

"Catalina will never forget this, señorita." The man smirked.

One of the walls lifted like a garage door, and a van backed up. One by one, each girl, chained to the next, came out of a nearby room, wearing elegant gowns. Nial threw a dress at Taiyo for her to put on. One of the men linked her to the last girl exiting the room. Nial gleamed at the van as it pulled away from the decadent cellar.

CHAPTER 18

Misconceptions

Alexandria's phone rang. "Okay, okay!" She ran through the hallway to find her NPD handbag, searching for her cell phone. "Hello." She paused, listened carefully, and quickly dashed out the door.

Moments later, Alexandria pulled into valet parking at the emergency center. She hopped out of her car. Searching for the green room, she entered through a set of double doors. Several people crowded the hospital floors. As soon as she stepped off the elevator and entered the green room, her name reigned from afar.

"Ms. Paz?"

Alexandria turned around, a woman with smooth mocha skin, wearing dark aviators, a black slim-fitted suit; and a gun posted on her hip stood behind her.

"I am Mrs. Paul. My mother is Mrs. Paz," she corrected the woman.

"I'm Detective Jennifer Hallow. Come with me." The detective pulled her neck-length hair back into a ponytail as she hurried down the hall, leaving Alexandria to catch up.

"What is going on here? Where is my father?" Alexandria asked frantically.

"Ms. Paz?"

"Mrs. Paul. I'm no longer a Paz, I told you." Alexandria gleamed at the detective.

"Mrs. Paul?" the detective reiterated.

"Call me Alex, please."

"Alex, this is a very complicated matter. We have your mother in custody. A 911 call was placed—" The detective held the door open for Alexandria.

"Who are you again?" Alexandria disgorge dismayed thoughts onto the stripped floor.

The detective placed a small wastebasket in front of her, watching puke erupt from her mouth like molten lava. She continued to speak, "My name is Jennifer Hallow." She passed Alexandria a roll of paper towels. "I am the detective assigned to this case."

"This case?" Alexandria wiped her mouth.

"Yes, when the ambulance arrived, your father was already deceased. Your mother is being held for questioning."

"Questioning?"

"When there is a suspected murder, the spouse is always held for questioning."

"Murder?" Alexandria repeated. "My mother wouldn't hurt anyone. She loves my father…well…loved him!"

"Your father was poisoned, Alexandria. There were traces of ricin found in his bloodstream."

"Ricin?" Alexandria repeated in a state of delusion.

"The toxin can take up to three days to cause terminal damage. During the first few days, a person may experience abdominal pain, diarrhea, and vomiting, then eventually die if not treated. Unfortunately, this is what has happened to your father. Therefore, your mother is being held for questioning."

"Can I see my mother?"

"Usually we don't allow it. But I'll check with the lead investigator to make sure it's okay."

Meanwhile, Alexandria sat quietly, thinking about her parents and the life she assumed they led. Her parents were firm believers of the Catholic and Christian Church. *This must be a mistake… they went to church every Sunday and Saturday and made sure that I attended.*

Soon after, Detective Hallow entered the room after locating Alexandria's mother.

"Why is she here?" Alexandria's mom asked. "I have nothing to say to her, not one word. Escort me out of here."

"Mom, please…this is very hard for me. I cannot express to you the feelings I feel right now."

"Alex Paz! The day you married that woman was the day I lost you! I have no words for you! Now…if you will excuse me…Ms. Interrogating Person, will you escort me out of this hideous painted room? This paint reeks right along with the sight of my daughter!"

"How can you call yourself a woman of God when you can't forgive your own daughter? You're not a woman of God! I am more woman of God than you are!"

"Don't make me laugh, Alexandria. You wouldn't know God if he was standing in front of you."

"I'm trying, Mom. I'm really trying." Tears dropped from Alexandria's eyes.

"You shamed me…you don't deserve any more of my time."

"Maybe you are guilty. Maybe you did kill my father! You're an evil person."

"I'm sorry, Alex," the detective said before escorting Mrs. Paz out of the room.

Alexandria basked in her tears. After a while of waiting, she left before the detective returned.

Alexandria parked in front of the church she visited periodically. Sitting there, she pulled the small Bible her father had given her from the armrest. Flipping through the pages, attempting to find a verse that fit the moment, was difficult for her. *Thou shalt not…* the words ran through her brain repeatedly as she tried to decipher the meanings. Her face flushed red, as her eyes and nose dripped heartache and tumultuous pain. She finally got out of the car when a homeless person approached her on the front steps.

"Spare some change?" The man held out a silver can.

"Sure," she said, placing a one-hundred-dollar bill inside the can.

"God bless you, ma'am." The man's eyes never faltered, no matter how weak they appeared.

"God bless you." Alexandria stepped on the ramp beside him.

"Thank you."

"You're welcome," Alexandria said to the man before she entered the building, staring at the angels on the wall. The confession booth was locked. "Father Mason?" she called out.

"Alexandria?" A gray-bearded fellow appeared out of nowhere. His eyes were youthful, but his build was mature. Alexandria was unsure of Father Mason's age. He looked her age but sounded much older.

"Yes, Father Mason. May I have a moment of your time?"

"Yes, come with me." Father Mason led the way to his office.

"Father, I have not sinned, but I think I may be a sinner."

"I don't quite follow."

"My mother always called me a sinner. Now she's the one suspected of killing my father. It doesn't get any more sinister than that." Alexandria sobbed. "Now I'm rambling…I feel so disgusted…ugh."

"My condolences, Alexandria."

"Is this conversation private?"

"Yes, always." Father Mason gave her a napkin to wipe her face.

"I'm married to a woman, Father Mason." Alexandria blotted her cheekbone.

"Yes."

"Does that make me a sinner?"

"Is this about your mother and father or your sexuality, Alexandria?"

"Yes, no, both, I don't know…I have been having these scary dreams haunting me…keeping me awake at night. I don't talk about it…not to my best friend, not to Nial. Now this thing with my father…each day I try to hide my feelings, but I think it's starting to get the best of me."

"Everyone is a sinner, Alexandria. However, God loves us all."

"I understand. God loves us all, but a murderer? That's a huge sin. Doesn't compare to my sexuality."

"It does not matter what the sin is. A sin is a sin. Having sinful desires and acting on them are two different things. As I said, God loves us all, and he is the judge of all judges."

"Father, this isn't helping me." Alexandria sat there for a moment, quiet.

"I'm sorry, but I don't know what you want me to say."

"I want you to tell me that I can live my life without fear—fear of catching a fatal disease because I am a lesbian, fear of losing my twins, fear of living a life filled with punishment. I want you to tell me that my nightmare of demons with treacherous scaley horns and burned skin ripping my skin apart is a figment of my imagination. I want you to tell me that my mother is not a killer, and I can love whomever I want."

"I cannot speak on those things in honesty, for it will be a lie."

"Huh?"

"I cannot answer those questions without contradiction."

"I guess you're not a sinner."

"I try not to act on sinful desires."

"Okay, this is ineffective. I would probably have more luck with the homeless guy outside your steps."

"There are no homeless people nearby."

"You'd better check again because I just gave him some change."

"There haven't been any homeless people around this church for many years."

"Well, someone better tell the person outside with the huge trash bag because he didn't get the memo."

"Alexandria, it is illegal. Come with me." The priest led her outside the church.

"All homeless persons will be extracted and confined." Father Mason read the sign.

"Since when?"

"For almost five years."

"What if they do come around and someone sees them?"

"The police will take them away, no questions asked."

"Well, that's horrible."

"I don't make the rules, Alexandria."

"I have to go. This day just became weirder, and I didn't think that was possible."

"Okay, well, come visit anytime. I'll be praying for you."

Alexandria waved her hand in the air, before sitting inside her vehicle.

* * *

Mrs. Paz exited the emergency center right as Annette Hall entered. Mrs. Paz turned around, following Annette. She ducked behind a wall when Annette looked around as if she were searching for someone. "Jennifer!" Mrs. Paz screeched as she strutted into the detective's office.

"Yes, Mrs. Paz, I thought you were gone."

"Yes, I was. But Annette, Annette Hall, is in the building. I just saw her step into the elevator with a large hat flopping off her head." Mrs. Paz gasped for breath.

"Annette Hall?"

"Yes, yes! Annette Hall, my husband's ex-lover. It was her. I know she killed the bastard. I mean my husband."

Detective Hallow arose from her seat to take notice. "I'll handle this, Mrs. Paz. Thank you." She quickly headed in the direction that Mrs. Paz mentioned, holding the picture of Annette in her hand. "Ms. Hall? Ms. Hall!" she called out.

"Yes?" Annette's flip-flops smacked the hard cemented floor when she turned around.

"Can you come with me, please?"

"You? Why!"

"I am working on Mr. Paz's case. I need you to come with me."

"No, not until I see him." Tears filled Annette's eyes.

The detective slowly grabbed her by the arm and forced her into a secluded room.

"What in the hell are you doing!"

Detective Hallow squeezed Annette's wrist. "What am I doing? What the fuck are you doing?"

She popped her gum, attempting to get away from the detective. "I want to see my boyfriend. Now let…me go!" She finally snatched her arm away from Detective Hallow's grip.

"No! I have to take you in for questioning, and now I've jeopardized things because the Annette Hall that is possibly suspected of murder is my crazy-ass mother!"

CHAPTER 19

Bryn

Nighttime approached as Alexandria drove around the city, trying to clear her head of perturbation. Finally, she pulled up to the Mirage and called her nanny. "Lea?"

"Hello! Alex, are you okay? I haven't heard from you all day."

"I need you to stay with the twins later than I anticipated. If you need anything, there is money in the cookie jar inside the pantry. Kiss the twins for me. Tell them I'll see them in the morning."

"Okay, Alex."

Alexandria contemplated going inside the Mirage, watching men in their three-piece suits and women in their six-inch heels wearing skimpy dresses enter the nightclub, making their way inside while others exited the building. She set the alarm on her Porsche and rushed past the bouncer toward the restroom behind the bar.

Washing her hands, staring at herself in the mirror, outlining the permanent scar staring back at her, usually she'd go to the Mirage with Aamir for drinks or with Nial when Nial was in the mood for a salacious experience. The Mirage was filled with down-low men and women, pimps, players, and hustlers. The club was raunchy, entertaining, and anything but exclusive.

"Are you okay?" A young woman noticed Alexandria standing at the sink.

"Yes, I'm fine. Long day…" Alexandria dabbed her lipstick.

"You are beautiful. Are you a model?" the woman inquired as she added more eyeliner to her bottom lid.

Alexandria stared at the girl's reflection through the mirror. "No, I'm not a model."

"You sure look like one. Come home with me tonight."

Alexandria smiled slightly. "I'm not a prostitute either," she said before excusing herself with her head held high.

"Hello, miss, how can I serve you this evening?" The bartender showed off his pearly-white teeth.

"I would like two shots of red whiskey, please, and keep them coming," Alexandria demanded. "Brand name, not the watered-down version." She laid a one-hundred-dollar bill on the bar.

"I'll have what she's having. Hi, I'm Dade." A short man with a bulging belly struggled to sit on the barstool next to her.

"Hi, Dade." Alexandria giggled as she watched him scuffle onto the chair.

"Do you have a name?" Dade asked.

"Alex."

"Can I buy you another drink, Alex?"

"No, thanks."

"Come on. Let me buy you a drink. There are no strings attached. Promise."

"If you insist."

"What's an attractive woman like you doing here all alone?"

"I thought you said no strings attached?"

"Does talking count?"

"Yes, I'm not in the mood to talk."

"Why not?"

"Because I only want to drink."

"Okay...keep 'em coming, bartender. Give the lady what she came for." Dade held up a wad of cash.

Alexandria turned away several men and women as thoughts of her father danced around in her head. She tried getting her emotions intact while Dade continued to buy her drinks and jabber nonstop when her cell phone rang.

"Halleur." Alexandria covered her ear, trying to mute the background noise.

"Alex, are you drunk?" Aamir asked.

"Nope."

"Yes, you are drunk. Your words are slumped. Where are you? I just left your place."

"I'm at the Mirage, sad, alone, and disgusted!"

"Give me ten minutes," Aamir said.

Less than ten minutes later, he arrived at The Mirage. Valet parked his shiny red Viper. As he entered through the sliding doors, an intriguing woman with slanted eyes grabbed his attention. The woman's fluffy, curly hair sparkled like someone had sprinkled golden stars through it. The jeans she wore hugged her thighs perfectly. Her waist was tiny, and her breast sat up high and plush with a series of moles running down the middle of her chest. She wrote inside a journal fiercely—unaware of Aamir's existence. He flipped his cap backward, swiped his floppy bangs away from his face that fell through the hole of the hat. "Hi, I'm Aamir. Are you alone?"

"Yes." The young woman stopped writing and looked up at him.

"What's your name?" Aamir smiled.

"Bryn, but I'm not here to meet anyone, sorry." Her hazel eyes locked in on him.

"I do not want to offend you, but you're gorgeous. Your skin is so beautiful."

"Black people aren't supposed to have nice skin? Is this really how you pick up women?" Bryn smirked, and a dimple entrenched her chin. She continued to write, ignoring him.

"No, that's not what I meant. You're Black?"

"Smart-ass." Bryn blushed, shaking her head.

"I can't help it—your body. I mean, your beauty makes me… Bryn, this is me swooning over you." He motioned to sit down beside her. "You smell so damn good."

"Swooning? Stop. You're making me dizzy." Bryn laughed.

"Hurt my feelings, why don't you. I just call it as I see it."

"I'm just saying next time, try something smoother, like 'Pardon my excessive staring like a mad person, but I can't keep my eyes off you, miss.'" Bryn smiled. "It wouldn't be a lie."

"Okay, okay, I'll give you that one. Thanks, but I'm praying after tonight, I won't have to use any more pickup lines on anyone."

"Praying? What a unique choice of words." Bryn smiled more.

"Yes, I try to choose my words carefully." Aamir swayed his head back, moving his long flowy bangs from his eyes.

"You need to stop while you are ahead."

"The more you smile, the more mesmerized I become. So if you stop smiling, maybe I'll stop staring."

"You're crazy."

"I'm serious, Bryn. Your smile is absolutely breathtaking."

"Okay, I believe you. I think."

"What are you doing in this place? It's nothing but a bunch of perverted people wandering around."

"I needed to get away, different scenery."

"A change in scenery?"

"Yes, something like that."

"Is everything okay?"

"Yes, everything is fine."

"You sound the opposite of fine."

"I have writer's block."

"So your favorite subject was literature?"

"Actually, I failed English in high school. It wasn't until college that I started to do well."

"I think it's great that you have writer's block."

"Why is that great?"

"If you weren't, we wouldn't be fulfilling our fate."

"Our fate?"

"Yes, our fate. Now can I have your number, please?" Aamir placed his cell phone beside Bryn's notebook.

Shortly after, Bryn reached for the phone and programmed her number into the contacts. "Done."

"Thank you."

"Thank you for being a sweetheart."

"I'm going to call you sooner than you think."

"Sure, you will…"

"I have a friend sitting at the bar. I don't want to keep her waiting much longer." Aamir pointed toward the bar.

"You have indeed amused me for the night. So I'm going back to my place to write."

"Glad I could be your muse for the night. Sounds like I'm bringing good luck to you already."

"So it seems."

"I'll walk you to your car."

Bryn agreed, and they walked outside the building together. Valet pulled up in a white BMW. Aamir grabbed her hand, kissing it. "Good night, Bryn."

"Oooh…oh…okay." Bryn's voice trembled. "That was unexpected."

"Expect my call."

"Good night." Bryn waved.

Aamir watched as Bryn drove away before he walked back inside the club.

Alexandria drank shot after shot before he reached her.

"Hey! Sexy lady?" Aamir tapped Alexandria's shoulder.

"Ouchhh!" Alexandria jumped.

"That didn't hurt."

"It did hurt. You know I like it gentle."

"Not from what I've heard."

"What have you heard?"

"I heard Nial doesn't do gentle."

"Whatever…Nial knows the real deal."

"Okay." He side-eyed her.

"What took you so long? I have been sitting here filling my gut with tequila shots, and only God knows the amount of red whiskey I've had. But I think the bartender started watering down my drinks." Alexandria hiccupped in his face. He fanned the smell of bourbon away. "They don't taste the same anymore." Alexandria belted out a long rambunctious giggle. "I think that bartender thinks I'm druunnnnkk! Will you tell him I am not druuuuunk, bestie?"

"Yes, you are drunk, and we're getting out of here." Aamir held his hand up, notifying the bartender. "You've been here long enough. Let's get you home. We will come back tomorrow for your car. I'll let the manager know so you don't have a bitch fit about Porsha."

* * *

Ticking sounds came from Bryn's deceased grandmother's typewriter as she pecked maniacally. The strikers ignited her with each stroke that hit the paper. She sat inside a melodramatic room with the lights down low. The authentic wood around the wall trimming and high ceilings bounced off the cream-colored walls eloquently. A fireplace embedded inside the wall, an Italian handcrafted desk chair, a desk with divided compartments to store her writing material complemented the distinctive room. There were two forty-two-inch monitors installed along with the desk's platform. Her herbal tea and wireless charger sat next to a bonsai tree located on a nearby table stand when she received a message. She read the voice mail transcript that pinged through, grabbed her keys, and hurried out the door when her phone rang again. She picked up this time. "I'm in the middle of dealing with a fourteen-year-old misfit. So if you will, leave your message at the beep. Beeeeep!" She paused, waiting for the person to leave a message.

"Looks like I called at the perfect time."

"I guess my fake voice setup didn't work this time. To whom am I speaking?"

"Aamir. How are you, gorgeous? My timing is awesome."

"Actually, your timing couldn't be worse."

"I've been thinking of you since last night. I know this is sudden. But will you have breakfast, lunch, and dinner with me?"

"I cannot have breakfast, lunch, and dinner with a total stranger. So how about dinner, and we'll discuss breakfast and lunch?"

"So yes to my invite? My place this evening with a couple of friends?"

"Aamir, you are a sweetie, but I'm not looking for love."

"Okay, so what about dinner?"

"Your persistence precedes you."

"So dinner it is, then."

"Fine, dinner it is. Send me your information. I'll call you later."

"Later!"

When a text chimed through from Aamir, Bryn scrolled through her email as she waited in the lobby to see her brother. *I'm almost ashamed that I can't stop thinking of him. It is only one dinner*, she contemplated.

"Ms. Michaels?"

"Yes?" Bryn quickly placed her phone in her bag, attentively listening.

"Are you, Ms. Michaels?"

"Yes, I'm Bryn Michaels."

"I'm Jerry. I called about your brother. Come with me. I'll take you to him."

Moments later, they reached Seary's room. He jumped from his bunk when he saw his sister. "Hey, sis, I swear on my life and yours! I did not do what they said I did. It wasn't me. But that jerk didn't believe me."

Bryn quickly threw her hand up. "Seary! Not another word until we fix this."

"But, sis…"

"Jerry, can you please explain to me what is going on?"

"Ms. Michaels, one of our officers noticed a group of kids stealing a car in the upper side of town."

"I'm sorry. I don't follow."

"Three young boys were spotted in the Pinnacles getting into a Maserati, and the officer caught one of them, which was your brother."

"I'll call my lawyer. Let me get this straight. One of your officers witnessed a couple of young boys getting into a car he assumed was not theirs? How does he know the car didn't belong to them?" Bryn questioned while dialing her lawyer's number.

"'Cause I'm Black as fuck. That's why!" Seary yelled.

"Shut up, Seary!" Bryn screamed back.

"It's true," Seary mumbled quietly, sitting back down on the bunk.

"Hi, Jane, this is Bryn calling. I need you to meet me at the detention center near Stanford. Seary has been accused of stealing a Maserati in the Pinnacle." Bryn's hands shook while speaking with her lawyer.

"Bryn?"

"Yes, Jane?"

"Listen to me. Breathe. I know you are upset. However, Seary is a minor, and he is already in the detention center's possession. I would like to speak with the judge first so that we can initiate a deposition. Therefore, he will have to stay there until then. Do you understand this?"

"I'm not really following you, Jane."

"If I come to the detention center before Seary sees the judge or before I get a chance to speak with the judge, it could compromise our chances of having the deposition."

"I'm sorry, Jane, but what in the hell is a deposition? You are speaking as if I am familiar with these terms."

"A deposition is considered when I conduct research on the case. And once the facts have been discovered by the detention center and me, we will then have the deposition, which means the opposing parties will meet before the trial date is set. And if all goes well… there may not be a trial to endure."

"Okay, so how long does that take? Why are they keeping him? Can I not bond him out?"

"There is a new law about these types of matters. So he has to stay there for now. If we are lucky…we will settle during the deposition, and then you can take your brother home. And there doesn't have to be a trial. But…if your brother is negligent in the matter, then he must suffer the consequences. Do you follow me now?"

"Yes, I follow. But how long does all of this take?"

"It depends…"

"On what?"

"It depends on the information collected. It depends on a few things. But we will resolve this. Don't worry."

"I'm not worried. It's just a little scary leaving him here alone."

"He has to stay until we can find the underlying cause of this. I'm sorry."

"I trust you."

"We'll speak soon."

"Bye."

CHAPTER 20

My Favorite Things

Alexandria walked into the kitchen wearing a pink silk pajama top with laced hip huggers. She opened the pantry door, searching for a snack. Finally, after prying the head off a jar of pickles, she took a heavenly bite.

"Alex! Alexandria!" Nial yelled.

Alexandria dropped the jar on the floor. "Shit!" she screamed when the glass shattered near her foot.

"Bébé, where are you?" Nial yelled after hearing the loud noise.

After cleaning the spill, Alexandria heeded Nial's voice. "My love."

"Beautiful, I missed you." Nial threw her bags on the floor and graced her wife with an enormous hug. She palmed her ass as if it were a basketball. "Oh, bébé, are you okay? I called several times to apologize, but you never answered. Forgive me."

Alexandria placed her finger above Nial's lips. "You're home now. That's all that matters to me." She kissed her long and fervently.

Nial licked the smudge of lip gloss that Alexandria left on her lips. "Where are my bébés?" She looked around.

"Lea took them out."

"So that means you can show me luff?"

"Of course."

"But first, are you sure that you are okay?"

"I was upset last night, but I'm better now that you're here."

"I need to freshen up. I'll be right back. Do not move a muscle." Nial entered their master suite when her phone resonated. "Yes, this is Nial," she answered while stepping out of her pantsuit. "This is not a good time!" She raised her voice. "You do not threaten me." Nial tossed her bra on the bathroom floor. "I'll get you the money." She hung up.

Alexandria waited on the stairway with her legs wide open. "I found a movie."

"A movie? I thought you were going to show me you luff me." Nial's hair was still wet from the shower, and one of her nipples stuck out of the thin shirt.

"Our very own movie."

"I thought you were bailing on me."

"Never."

Nial placed her fingertips on Alexandria's lips, shushing her. "Sounds fun." She pulled her closer, kissing her neck softly, peck after peck.

Alexandria moaned as their lips touched. Their hands were glued to each other's bodies. Alexandria slid her hands around Nial's stomach while guiding her down to the edge of the stairway.

Nial lay beside her, producing loud moans. "I have a surprise for you." She pulled her tank top above her head, throwing it to the floor.

"A new toy? I like it." Alexandria's sensual moans reverberated through Nial.

Nial's hands moved up Alexandria's thighs, ripping her panties off. "Why don't you come closer and see if you luff it," she whispered, nibbling her wife's inner thigh before slowly wrapping her lips around her emotional spot as she slithered her fingers deep inside her, coercing the vibrator between Alexandria's legs.

Kissing, moans filled the room as they moved in sync with ease. Fluttery warmth spilled from both their bodies as they culminated. Afterward, Alexandria pulled Nial closer, holding her tight.

Moments of intense pleasure ensued. Alexandria kneeled on all fours, gently kissing the bottom of Nial's feet, her toes around her ankles, her knees up to her ass cheeks. Then she shoved the dildo inside her from behind. Nial let out an inarticulate moan. "More! Give me more!" she screamed. "Faster, bébé," she wailed.

Alexandria threw the harness aside and lay on top of Nial, allowing their seeds to align. The faster Alexandria moved, the tighter Nial held on to her. The stimulation was exhilarating. Nial could not resist biting her wife's neck until she punctured it. Blood seeped from the skin underneath her chin, but she refused to stop as she sucked the blood. The unyielding pleasure between them was magnetic. Nial panted as streams of wetness flooded Alexandria's pudenda.

* * *

"Mommy! Mama!" the twins yelled as the credits rolled down the TV screen while Alexandria and Nial cuddled on the sectional in the great room.

"My bébés," Nial expressed as the twins ran to her with open arms. "I missed you *so* much." She squeezed them.

"You think we can go to da water park? We never went, Mama."

"Mama! I missed you. Lea took us for yogurt since Mommy said no ice cream and cookies!" Abella Rose exclaimed. "And...we rode ponies on our field trip. You should go, Mama. I will show you how to mount a pony. I'm an expert now."

"We will see, honey. And yes, Nate, we will go to the water park."

"What about the Crayola factory? I wasn't joking. I really want to go there too." Abella Rose pouted.

"Listen, we will go to both places, but for now, I have a surprise for you. Come."

"Go on. Your mama has something special for you!" Alexandria playfully spanked their bottom.

"Come along." Nial led them into their playroom. "I have a surprise for both of you. Now close your eyes and count to five."

"One, two, three, four, five!" the twins shouted.

"Okay, now open!" Nial's eyes brightened.

"Wow, thanks, Mama! I've always wanted a super spinner! It goes around really fast. But the website said they sold out," Nathaniel said.

"I got it from another website."

"Thanks, Mama."

"Thank you, Mama, but I do not want a super spinner." Abella Rose stuck out her bottom lip. "I'm happy for Nate because he talks about them all the damn time!"

"Ella, sweetie, calm down. I have something else for you." Nial smiled as she watched Abella Rose's eyes light up.

"I'm sorry, Mama. Oooooh! A painter set. Wow! Just like the one you had. Yay! I thought they didn't make these anymore? It is vintage, right, Mama?"

"You are accurate. I found it at a vintage shop in France especially for you." Nial tapped her tiny nose.

The twins ran into the great room where Alexandria had dozed off. Abella Rose held the painter set in the air. "Look what I have!" She chuckled.

"That's wonderful, bunny. Just like your mama used to have." Alexandria attempted to clear her raspy voice.

"I know, right!" Abella Rose giggled.

Nathaniel interrupted, "It's not out in the States, Mama said."

"Yes, I know, bunny. Your mama is an amazing woman." Alexandria winked at Nial.

"Yay! Come on, Lea. Let's go play with our new toys!" the twins screamed when they saw Lea enter the great room.

"Okay, okay! Let me get my things out of the car first." Lea left the room.

"I could not forget about mummy." Nial walked from the foyer with a perfectly wrapped box.

"What is it?" Alexandria asked.

"Open it, Mommy!" the twins yelled.

"Okay." Alexandria grabbed the knife from Nial's hand to slice the tape from around the large box.

"Be careful." Nial fretted.

Alexandria ripped through the gifting paper. "My love, it's the *Kermes Oak Tree* painting! Goes perfectly with my Kermes collection."

"Voilà!" Nial's arms stretched wide.

"Thank you, I love it."

"Where will you put it, Mommy?" Abella Rose asked.

"I'll add it to the collection in my office."

"Cool, Mommy." Nathaniel jumped up and down on the sofa.

"So you like your present?" Nial winked at Alexandria.

"Yes, of course, I love it—two presents in one day."

"What do you mean?"

"The last time you bought me a collector's piece like this, it was after Aamir's first NASCAR race." Alexandria lifted her eyebrow in suspicion.

"It is nothing. I know how much you wanted this piece." Nial smirked. "You luffed the pieces I give you, no?"

"Yes, I love every piece you give me."

"Say thank you, and I'll give you more pieces tonight, s'il vous plaît."

"Thank you. I love it." Alexandria kissed Nial's lips.

"Are we still talking about presents?" Abella Rose looked up at her moms, standing between them.

"Ella, go play with your new painter set." Alexandria chuckled. "Hurry along."

Nial smiled brightly. "That is more like it. Come bring me more of you." She grabbed Alexandria closer, kissing her lips.

CHAPTER 21

Showtime

Aamir's godmother and personal chef, Mimi, helped him add the dinner party's final additions. He went over the checklist thoroughly. "Mimi, first, we will start the evening with a bottle of Dom Xavier Monnot Pommard, and then we will end the night with a breath of freshness, Dom Marsannay."

"Check."

"What else?" Aamir nibbled his nails.

"Aamir? What do you know about this girl?" Mimi asked.

"She's an author, has a brother. And she's Black, sexy, and wealthy."

"Are you crazy, boy? You've only met her once, and now you're inviting her here? What if she's crazy?"

"She's not. I googled her."

"You could've taken her out for dinner."

"I appreciate your concern, Mom, but let's get back to the menu, okay?"

"Okay, Aamir. The wines are checked, and Nial is bringing the Chateau Margaux. Now moving on to the appetizers." Mimi side-eyed him as she checked off the list.

"Welsh rarebit with Worcestershire sauce, potato wedges with curry sauce, and warm butterscotch dippers to top it off with dessert."

"Check, but we have two different sauces?"

"Yes, Bryn may not like the curry sauce."

"Okay."

"Moving on to the entrée, we have a slow-roasted shoulder of pork with spiced shrimp, lobster, apple relish parmesan roasted potatoes, butternut, macaroni and cheese, asparagus spears, and delicious Rosetta rolls."

"Check."

"Now, for the dessert menu, we have toffee, apple cookies, along with homemade, churned vanilla ice cream, toffee, apple pudding, and my favorite platinum Blondies. We have the full menu checked, candles on the terrace, rose petals in the pool. Let's see what I'm missing, hmmm…oh yes, me and my sexy."

"Your sexy?" Mimi laughed.

"Yes, my sexy. Bryn won't be able to keep her hands off me."

"Boy, go get yourself dressed."

* * *

Aamir waited on the barstool inside the kitchen, drinking a beer when finally, the gate buzzed. "Showtime!" He grabbed the remote to open the gate before rushing outside the entryway.

"Hi!" he spoke. "Queens!" he exclaimed, watching Alexandria and Nial strut through the entrance, praising the women.

Alexandria nodded. "Thank you, now where is the mystery woman?"

"Yes, where is she? We are anxious to meet this person." Nial passed Aamir three bottles of Margaux.

"We're all waiting for her. But while we expect, the wine and appetizers are ready."

"Do you have a picture of her?" Alexandria pried.

"Yes, I took it from her bio page, but you have to wait to see her in person." Aamir straightened his shirt.

"You're stealing her pictures? Smooth. I'm really anticipating meeting her now." Alexandria laughed aloud.

"Of course, we are. That's why we came." Nial stuffed her mouth with hors d'oeuvres.

"She should be here soon." Aamir sipped whiskey from a glass.

"Also, I want to thank you for helping Alex the other night."

"Sure thing." Aamir led them into his candlelit room. "Welcome to my serenity room where the Zen is contagious." He clapped his hands together. "Namaste."

The gate alarmed, and the three of them looked at one another. Nial grabbed a jewel from her garter.

"Fuck!" Aamir yelped, staring out the window. "I'm in the middle of something!" He rushed outside.

"I missed you too. I would not have stopped by, but I couldn't resist seeing your cute ass."

"It's over." Aamir stepped onto the gravel.

"Over?"

"Completely."

Nial and Alexandria heard the commotion.

"Is everything okay?" Nial asked him.

"Nial? Is that you, the woman's woman? You and Nial got something going on, Aamir?" the woman inquired.

"What!" Aamir asked.

"Fuck you, Francesca!" Nial screamed.

"What is she talking about?" Alexandria grabbed Nial's hand.

"Bébé, she is psychotic, delusional, yes?"

Francesca repeated herself, "You heard me! Does your wife know you give it to all your models—men, women, dog?" She laughed so hard she started to wheeze. "Well, maybe dogs are an exception. She'll only make them lick your pussy. Just add a little peanut butter, right, sicko?"

Alexandria tried to hold Nial's hand tighter, but Nial let go. She tossed her dangling diamonds off her ear as she stepped out of her heels. "You're a lonely bitch! I will fucking kill you! You belong in a mental asylum because you are fucking insane!"

"If I'm so mental…why are you so mad? Extremely mad it seems."

Nial was enraged at this point. She pushed past Aamir and stood in front of Francesca.

"Get out of my face." Francesca took a step back.

Nial bopped her in the chin with her fist. Aamir quickly intervened, trying to hold Nial back. But she continued to kick and squirm until she almost wiggled out of his arms. "Leave, Francesca, before I release her," he said, holding Nial by the waist, her feet dangling in the air.

"Call the cops," Alexandria interrupted.

"You, my dear, need to get a fucking clue!" Francesca screamed as she backed away.

"You will regret this, Nial." Francesca jumped into her Camaro.

"What was that about?" Alexandria rubbed Nial's back.

"I fucked her once—once." Aamir tugged at his manhood, adjusting it.

"So she came to collect?" Alexandria giggled.

"She walked the runway for my summer collection two years ago," Nial recalled.

"That's the Francesca…the clingy one?" Alexandria asked.

"Yes, she sabotaged my charity event at the Fairmont Hotel, the one NASCAR sponsored."

"Yes, she is insane." Alexandria laughed as they walked inside.

"Crazy…with a capital *C*," Aamir concurred.

"I remember Nial fired her because she was so unprofessional," Alexandria recollected.

"I recommended that no one else hire her. So maybe that's why she is upset with me." Nial dabbed her forehead with a paper towel.

Aamir released a loud sigh. "Yep! That's her."

As time passed, they sipped wine inside the serenity room when they noticed more lights flashed outside but no sign of Bryn.

"Maybe something came up," Alexandria said.

"Maybe," Nial cosigned.

"Or maybe she stood me up." Aamir downed another beer.

Alexandria grabbed the controller to the music system.

"Let's eat. Mimi prepared such a lovely meal. We can't let it go to waste." Alexandria tapped Aamir's shoulder.

"I will finish the rest of the Chateau Margaux first." Aamir held his empty glass up.

Forgetting about Bryn after several glasses of alcohol, they laughed and talked about Francesca's abnormal behavior when the gate buzzed. Aamir peaked outside before pressing the button on the remote. His vision blurry. He couldn't make out the driver.

"It isn't Francesca again, is it?" Alexandria stood beside Aamir. "She must want my wife to punch her in the face again." She laughed.

"I'll check it out. I'll let you know if I need my pit bull. Aamir stepped outside and plopped on top of his Viper. The SUV drove closer. He called Alexandria's phone. "It's Bryn."

"It's Bryn," Alexandria repeated to Nial.

"Yes, Bryn!" Aamir straightened his clothes, almost sliding off the car. "Shit!"

"What happened?" Alexandria asked.

"Nothing."

"What's going on now?"

He laid his phone facedown on top of the Hennessy Venom GT next to his Viper. Bryn pulled alongside the pavement next to Nial's Mercedes. She stepped out of her BMW and walked closer, gazing into Aamir's eyes. "Hi, Aamir."

"Why did you come here, Bryn? The food's cold. The wine is warm. And I've damn near drunk all of it. There's none left for you." He poked Bryn's arm.

"Please just listen to me?" Bryn moved closer.

"I'm not sure I want to listen." He pouted.

"Please…" Bryn's hazel eyes twinkled.

"Fine, go on." Aamir's eyes glazed over as he embraced every word that came through Bryn's glossy lips.

"I think you are wonderful. I do not know you very well, but I think we have a connection. I'll admit it took me so many hours to come because I was afraid to have dinner with you."

"Afraid?"

"I was afraid I might like you, Aamir." Bryn walked closer, so close that he could feel her breathe.

"What changed your mind? Why'd you come?" he asked.

"You changed my mind. I listened to the voice mail you left, and you sound so sincere and thoughtful—unlike any man I've ever met. You deserved an explanation. I'm a moron."

"Yes, you are a moron."

"I'm really, really sorry." Bryn grabbed him by the collar, pulling him closer as she stood on the tip of her toes.

He became lost in her voice, her breath, her eyes, her smell. Every word melted his heart little by little. "I forgive you, but I'm going to be completely honest with you. Your brown skin reminds me of the silky smooth chocolate milk my mom gave me when I was a kid. I wanted you the first night I laid eyes on you. Silly me for thinking you and I are meant to be."

"I think you're charmingly beautiful, and obsessed with my skin tone." Bryn squinted indifferently.

"No, not obsessed. Extremely attracted."

"Sure you are."

"Can we seal our friendship with a kiss at least?"

"Aamir?"

"I am joking. Don't be uptight."

"I'm not uptight."

"If you were any tighter, you'd stop breathing. You would literally squeeze yourself into nonexistence."

"Aamir! Can we go inside?"

"Can I have a kiss first?"

"A peck." Bryn caved.

"A peck is a good start."

"A peck on my cheek."

Aamir pulled Bryn close and planted a gentle kiss on her lips instead. He sniffed her face from her cheek to earlobe. "Yum, chocolate milk," he whispered.

"Stop." Bryn stood there for a moment in a daze. "There's this one thing."

"Yes?" Aamir asked nervously.

"I invited a friend. In fact, that's her pulling up now."

"What did you think I would do to you?" Aamir laughed at the Audi R8 pulling up.

"I don't know you like that. I couldn't show up alone at a stranger's home. You don't mind, do you?"

"Of course not."

A pale-faced woman neared Aamir and Bryn, wearing a lightweight rain jacket that matched her stylish rain boots with a phone to her ear. Bryn and Aamir conversed, waiting for the woman to hang up her phone. The woman's face was firm, and she did not crack a smile. Her neck was long, and her torso was even longer. "Hi, I'm Jane Woodell." She shook Aamir's hand.

"I'm Aamir. Let's go inside?" He took Bryn by the hand, leading the way.

"You have a lovely home, Aamir." Jane admired every corner and ceiling, stepping out of her left boot. Her well-manicured toes matched her fingernails. "You don't mind if I take off my shoes, do you, Aamir? It's a habit." Jane motioned before taking off the other shoe.

"Make yourself comfortable." Aamir hung Jane's coat in the closet.

"Rain is in the forecast?" Bryn asked.

"Yes, it is. It is supposed to be severe winds. Don't be scared."

"Scared?" Aamir mocked Bryn.

"More like terrified. Like a little terrified puppy when it rains." Jane giggled.

"I'd rather not discuss it. Can we eat, please?" Bryn shoved Aamir forward.

Alexandria and Nial quickly took a position inside the kitchen before Aamir, Bryn, and Jane entered the room.

"Hello," Alexandria spoke when she became face-to-face with the two women. "How about we grab a bite of this wonderful dinner? I'm starved," she said as she filled her mouth with butterscotch dippers, staring at Jane and Bryn.

Aamir smiled as he took more wineglasses from the cabinet. "Alex, Nial, this is Bryn, and this is Bryn's friend, Jane. Bryn thought I was a serial killer, so she brought backup."

"That's not true. I brought Jane because she's my lawyer, and anything you say will be used against you."

"I like you already." Alexandria laughed. "So do you prefer red or white?" Alexandria held up two different bottles.

"I don't drink. I'll have a glass of water, please," Jane said.

"White for me, please." Bryn smiled.

"What is your poison?" Nial sipped from her glass, side-eying Jane.

"Excuse me?" Jane looked over at Bryn briefly, then back at Nial, vexed.

"Well, you don't drink, so what do you do? Coke, heroin, pills, marijuana, sex?"

"Not everyone has an addiction," Aamir interrupted.

"Yes, darling, they do. Everyone is addicted to something. But I'll let you believe the world is this big wholesome place with no shit stains."

"You don't hold back, do you?" Jane said to Nial.

"Hold back for what? The only thing I hold back is my wife's hair when she's giving me that beautiful redhead of hers."

"Hey, okay, someone has had a little more wine than expected. Can we eat?" Alexandria placed the rest of the appetizers on the table.

"What! I was going to say—"

"Babe, I'm pressing the censor button on your mouth right now!" Alexandria grabbed Nial's chin and kissed her lips.

"You are accurate, bébé. I have so much *vin* inside my tummy. I need solid sustenance to soak it up."

"Yep, you do," Aamir agreed.

Alexandria placed the roasted potatoes on the table.

"Excuse me, where is your powder room?" Bryn asked.

Aamir stood up from the table and led the way. He walked beside her, admiring her beauty. "I'll wait for you outside the door. The towels are above your head."

"I love this powder room."

"Thank you, Jerome Wilds designs."

"Jerome Wilds? Nice. I actually met him once."

"What are the odds of that? He's a good friend of mine."

"Are you about to bring up the destiny thing?"

"He's a good friend. That's all I'm saying."

"Well, he's very famous for his European designs. I love his work."

"Yeah, he's great."

Nial and Alexandria waited for Aamir and Bryn to rejoin them at the dinner table. Jane's phone rang. She hopped up from her chair, dashing to the patio out back.

"Bébé, Bryn looks familiar," Nial mentioned after Jane left the table.

"Okay?" Alexandria waited for Nial to go on.

"College…I think."

"I wonder if she remembers you. I'll ask her."

"Ask her what!" Nial sipped more wine.

"If she remembers you, if she's going to be dating Aamir, there should be no secrets, and God forbid any misunderstandings occur between us."

"Clandestine?"

"Did you sleep with her, Nial?"

"No."

"Did you try to sleep with her?"

"No."

"I don't believe you."

"Am I incapable?"

"In college, I would say yes, you were incapable. Besides, Bryn is a beautiful woman, so why wouldn't you?"

"She is not my type."

"What's your type?"

"Ten years and you do not know my type? You are my type. Now eat."

"Why is she not your type?"

"Have you seen her ass?"

"You think she's fat?"

"No, she is not fat. Her ass is fat—jiggly, wiggly."

"I cannot believe you said that."

"Can I have a preference and an opinion? I prefer your little ass, petite and sweet like peaches and berries." Nial stuck her tongue out her mouth, dipping it past her chin and back in. "Yummy."

"Stop. I never imagined you were so shallow."

"I luff you, bébé. That is all that matters." Nial winked at Alexandria, licking her lips once more.

Aamir entered the dining area where Alexandria and Nial sat. "What's with the dumb look on your faces?"

"I think…ummm…" Alexandria spoke.

"My apologies, I'm ready now. Shall we eat?" Bryn interrupted as she entered the room. "Where's Jane?" she asked.

"She's taking a call," Alexandria continued.

"You think what, Alex?" Aamir asked.

"I think that…"

"Excuse me, but do we know each other?" Bryn interrupted.

"Umm…I believe so. I was speaking to my beautiful wife about it."

"You know each other?" Aamir asked.

"Yes," Nial replied, "uhh…I think it was at CCA during undergrad. We met at a party."

"Yes, we sure did."

"We kissed…" Nial confessed.

"Yes, we sure did…" Bryn's voice trembled. "Who knew we'd ever cross paths again?"

"You did what?" Aamir frowned.

"You kissed?" Alexandria repeated.

"Yes." Nial sipped more wine from her glass.

"What in the hell just happened here?" Aamir inquired.

"I recall meeting at a party. Things were a little chaotic, and somehow, we managed to kiss. And after that, I was so embarrassed that I never attended another campus party again. Nor did I ever see Nial again," Bryn stated.

"What happened to you? It seems you disappeared," Nial asked.

"I moved back to Thailand to take care of my brother after my parents died. I finished the remainder of my program there. Then after I graduated, I moved to San Francisco with my little brother."

"I see we have a lot in common." Alexandria filled her mouth with macaroni and cheese.

"How so?" Bryn inquired.

"We are extremely adored, and I was in Thailand a few years back."

"Nothing else happened?" Aamir interrupted.

"Yes, Aamir, that is correct. It is no big deal. Nothing else happened." Nial rolled her eyes.

"It is a big deal. Try to keep it in your pants for once."

"No, it is not a big deal. Bryn is not my type!" Nial blurted.

"But, you kissed her…" Alexandria was confused.

"I was drunk, and she was smaller then. I do not like big girls."

"What the fuck did you say?" Aamir stood up.

"Big girls? I didn't realize I was a big girl. I thought I was just a girl."

"What are you going to do, Aamir Bahar? Beat my ass?" Nial snarled as she sniffed from the small vial she kept close.

"You're not a big girl, Bryn. You are gorgeous. Forgive my intoxicated wife. When she imbibes too much, her mouth becomes a little untamed."

"That was many years ago. Don't be hasty. But of course, you don't want to be hasty now, do you, Aamir?" Nial sneered.

"This isn't hasty," Aamir retorted.

"You guys, come on…" Alexandria voiced.

"Aamir, we shouldn't make this bigger than it is," Bryn said.

"Yes, Aamir, your concern is bigger than the actual kiss," Nial revealed.

"It's not about the kiss. It's about your fucking endless disrespect."

"What's going on? The tension is fogging up the patio window." Jane scurried back inside. "I need to get back to my firm." She gleamed at everyone, and Bryn got up from the table to assist her to the door. "Will you be okay?" Jane asked Bryn.

"Yes, thank you for coming." Bryn kissed Jane on the cheek and closed the door behind her.

"Don't be an asshole, Aamir," Alexandria said.

"Funny. I was thinking the same thing about your wife."

"That was mean." Alexandria wiped curry sauce from her lips.

"You're right. Forget about it. Let's eat." Aamir waited for Bryn to sit down at the table.

"Good, I'm starving." Nial chomped a piece of an asparagus spear.

"Nial?" Aamir's voice deepened.

"Aamir?" Nial rolled her eyes.

"If you ever disrespect Bryn again…I will kick the accent out your fucking mouth."

"It was not my intent, Aamir." Nial held her hands up high, surrendering.

"Babe? Let it go." Alexandria drank more wine.

CHAPTER 22

What's Love

After a long inconspicuous night at Aamir's place, the ladies gathered their things, preparing to leave. Bryn tossed her bag over her shoulder when she felt a sudden tug on her jeans. Aamir's large hands pulled her backward so Alexandria and Nial could walk in front of her.

"Thanks for coming over to help break the ice." Aamir chuckled as he continued to hold on to Bryn. Nial patted his shoulder as she walked past him. "We're cool," he said to her.

"I'll call you tomorrow," Alexandria slid on her eight-inch pumps quickly before they exited the grand foyer.

"You smell so good." Aamir pulled Bryn closer, grabbing her around the waist, his nose buried in her neck.

"Thanks." Bryn sighed. "Is that your arm?"

"What?"

"Poking me."

"No, it's not." Aamir cleared his throat.

"Don't back away from me."

"You feel some type of way?"

"Surprised."

"Is that a good surprise?"

"Unexpected surprise."

"You excite me."

Bryn's cheeks flushed. "Your bulge? Is that why you're single? Because…um…your dick is huge, son?"

"I hadn't met the perfect one until now."

"The one?" Bryn blushed. "You think I'm the one, huh?"

"No, not really." He laughed. "Yes, you. You, Bryn Michaels, are perfect for me. Come join me on the terrace." He grabbed a batch of toffee, apple cookies, and a pint of ice cream. Bryn carried the bowls, and they made their way onto the platform.

Bryn lay back in Aamir's arms, watching the calm sky. "You lay flower petals out for all your dates?"

"No, only for you, my queen." The night was cool, calm, and the breeze was just right. "Will you have breakfast with me in the morning?" he asked. "You practically know my life story, so it's only fair you stay for breakfast."

"I'm not sure if I should stay. You may try to take advantage of me."

"I take advantage of you? That's funny. You've been drooling at the sight of me all night."

Bryn giggled. "Right." She scooped a cherry nut in her mouth with a spoonful of ice cream.

"Will you stay with me tonight? I don't want you to leave."

"How can I resist your charm? Where did you get it?"

"Probably my mom. She could get me to do anything when I was a kid."

"Could?"

"Yes, she passed away when I was in middle school."

"Oh, I see. I'm so sorry."

"You see?"

"Well, yes, you do not resemble Mimi at all. She's pure Caucasian. No offense."

"I'm not offended. Mimi was our chef when my mom and pop came to the States from Saudi. She adopted me after my mom died and my pop went to prison."

"I'm so sorry, Aamir. Your father?"

"It's okay."

"Tell me, what does your name mean?"

"*Aamir* means 'a true spirit.' *Bahar* means 'youth.'"

"It is a beautiful name."

"I wanted to change my name to Charleston River Brooks, but…"

Bryn laughed aloud. "Charleston is a White boy's name."

Aamir chuckled along with her. "It is, but it's a cool name, you have to admit."

"Not as cool and sexy as Aamir Bahar." Bryn's tongue rolled in her mouth, attempting an Arabian accent.

"My mom's name, the coolest, Sea Bahar." Aamir's smile was warm and gentle.

"I didn't know Sea, but I'm sure she'd want you to keep your name."

"Only you, Bryn Michaels. Only your sexy ass."

Bryn lay back and cozied next to him as the wind blew stronger.

* * *

Alexandria laid her hand on the clutch while Nial jerked the stick back and forth, switching lanes into the night. Their hair blew wild. "Bébé, I have to leave for a photoshoot." Nial glanced at her wife.

"Photoshoot? What about the water park? The Crayola factory? No, that's not going to work. Cancel it."

"Cancel the photoshoot? I cannot do that."

"I will be leaving for New York soon. The agency is expanding. We'll be away from the twins at the same time." Alexandria pushed her hair behind her ears as if swiping Nial's remark away.

"We must find a solution. Canceling the shoot is out of the question."

"I hate your schedule."

"I will spend time with the twins. I made a promise, and I will affirm it. Ella and Nate are everything to me, ma chérie." Nial drove onto their property. Alexandria quickly jumped out of the E-Class. Nial contemplated. Finally, after thirty minutes of thinking, she ambled inside.

"Hey," Lea screeched.

"*Merde!* I thought you were sleeping, Lea."

"The twins are sleeping." Lea laughed. "Someone called," she mentioned before Nial left the room.

"Did they leave a message?" Nial yawned.

"No, the person hung up before I asked." Lea put her earbuds back in and turned around.

"Hmph." Nial crept to the twin's bedroom, kissed Abella Rose on her forehead and Nathaniel on his cheek. Then she went into the bathroom, stepped into the shower behind Alexandria. "I'm sorry, bébé. I do not like it when you make me feel less than a wife or parent. I luff you. You, the twins are my everything."

Alexandria held on to Nial's torso tightly. "I love you, my love. I just hate that you stay away so much—weeks at a time. I know it's your job, but the sad part is sometimes I feel like a single parent. And it leaves room for—"

"It leaves room for what?" Nial stepped back.

"Vulnerability."

"I'm not going to let that happen. I'll make sure you are satisfied before I leave."

"It's not about sex. We miss you being here. I'm having those dreams again."

"I am always away, but it's how we live like this." She looked around the room.

Alexandria paused for a moment when Nial snatched her arm, leading her out the bathroom. Nial laid Alexandria facedown on the floor, planting kisses all over her backside to her emotional spot. Alexandria quickly rolled over, seizing Nial's face. "Are you cheating on me?" She stared into Nial's eyes.

"Do not ask me that again." Nial pulled Alexandria up on the bed and tucked her in. "Let's sleep. It has been a long night."

Alexandria crawled underneath the cover, kissed Nial's lips as they held each other until they drifted to sleep.

* * *

Aamir and Bryn were still awake on the terrace. "Have you ever dated a man before, Aamir?"

"What? No."

"Why not? Do you not like them?"

"I'm 100 percent hetero, babe."

"I had to ask. It's not uncommon."

"I love women—a woman's erogenous zones, her lips when you kiss them, her scent, her soft skin." Aamir rubbed his fingers up and down Bryn's arms, whispering in her neck. "A guy cannot compare."

"You cuddle with all your friends, Aamir?"

"No." He chuckled softly.

"What are we doing?"

"Enjoying each other."

"I agree with that."

"That's what I like to hear."

"Aamir?"

"Yes, Bryn."

"Thank you for inviting me to dinner. I'm happy I came."

"Me too, gorgeous."

Bryn bit her bottom lip as chills poured down her spine. The candlelight dissipated at once. She jumped, holding on to Aamir's shirt. They ran inside, closing the door behind them. Aamir guided Bryn into his open bedroom and lit the fireplace. "You enjoy living alone?" she asked him.

"Before I met you, I did." He passed her a glass of white wine.

"Thank you."

"Get comfortable. I won't bite unless you ask me to." Aamir undressed. Bryn turned her head away.

"PJs?" Bryn slowly grasped the cotton pajamas from Aamir's hand. His body was long and firm. His muscles bulged. There was a giant tattoo of a woman covering his chest. It was a portrait of a beautiful woman that resembled him. Bryn was curious, so she went for the juggler. "Lovely artwork."

"It's my mom. I keep her close to my heart."

"You're beautiful, just like her." Bryn neared him. "You keep pajamas for all your guests?"

"Thanks, and only the special guests."

Sweet, Bryn thought as she lay underneath the duvet. The rain drenched the balcony outside the bedroom. She eyed a photo inside a rusted frame of a young boy standing beside a toy car half his size. "Is that you, handsome?" She pointed to the photo. She screeched when she realized the rain was pouring outside. "It's raining so hard."

"It's not, really." Aamir jumped on the bed. "Lay in my arms and tell me all about the big bad boogey rain."

"The real reason I don't like rain…" She scooted closer to him.

"I'm listening." Aamir paid close attention, trying to contain his arousal.

"I had a bad childhood experience when I was in Kikori, Papua, with my parents. There was a horrible storm that started in light rain. The boat toppled, and my parents and I almost died in that river."

"Well, you're safe now. There is no ocean, and we're not in New Guinea."

"You're poking me again."

"Does that bother you?"

"I like that I turn you on."

"Yesss. I'm almost out of the friend zone," he cheered.

"Not so fast." Bryn pushed him away. He inched closer and held her tighter.

CHAPTER 23

Free Bird Fly

Sweat ran down the detention center walls, and the rooms were stuffy. The floors cracked, and dust mites fell from the musty vents. "Hey, man! When can I call my sister? I've been sitting here waiting for fuckin' ever!" Seary yelled. "You mufuckas suck, man! I cannot wait to get outta this place. You can't keep people locked up like caged monkeys. I see why the caged bird sang because that bitch wanted to be free!"

"Shut up, dumbass!" one of the delinquents yelled.

"I didn't do anything!"

"Screaming and insulting these coppers like you're crazy ain't gonna get you out faster. You're just making them give you a long wait. You better shut the fuck up before you end up with a noose around your neck," the delinquent continued.

Seary slammed his body against the wall and beat the rail with his fists. Security quickly entered his room, snatching him by the collar. "Now, you listen, you little punk! You keep acting like a monkey, and I'll show you how zoo animals are treated. Nobody is getting you out of this mess. Either you wait your turn like the rest of 'em, or you'll get no chance at all. *Comprende?*" The guard released Seary, dropping him to the floor. Seary's elbow hit the rail of the bunk bed.

"You asshole! I'm no fuckin' Mexican, man. Let me call my sister! You country cow!" Seary rubbed the lump on his elbow.

"That's it! No call time for you. You can call your sister Monday."

"I'm gonna get all of you fired. It's going against my rights as a citizen of this state, not letting me get my phone call. You people think just because you carry big black flashlights around that you have some authority. Well, I'm here to tell you, you don't! My sister has more authority in her pinky than you'll ever have."

Officer Jerry overheard Seary shouting. "Seary, calm down. We are not here to harm you. We are here to help. But as Officer Hemp said, you're not making this any easier for yourself. Now, I'll give you one more chance to use the phone, but only if you remain calm. Agreed?"

"Yeah, man, sure, I'll do it. I'll calm down."

* * *

Bryn finally made it home. Relaxing inside her bungalow, she worked on her autobiography. Then the phone rang, interrupting her writing. "Hello, this is Bryn."

"Bry, it's your brother Seary."

"I only have one brother, boy. What's wrong?"

"I'm ready to get out of this place. It's cold, and it smells like shit! The guards are rude, and they didn't want me to use the phone. Can you call that lawyer lady and see when I'm getting out of here?"

"She can't do anything until next week. They must gather evidence or something. Why are you whispering?"

"Because I don't want anyone to hear me."

"Boy, please." Bryn laughed.

"It's not funny, Bry."

"Kid, sit tight and try not to get into any more mischief… please. I'll see you soon. I promise." After hanging up the phone with her brother, she referred to her writing when the phone rang again. "Hi, Aamir! How are you?" she answered.

"I'm great. I needed to hear your voice before the race. When you left my place, you seemed a little…"

"Horny? Excited? Afraid? Yes! I was all the above. I just needed some time to embrace the feelings I'm having about us. It's new to me."

"You have nothing to worry about, Bryn. If you want me, I'm all yours because I want you. I gotta go. I'm up next. If you're not busy, tune in to WGN. Talk soon, queen." Aamir hung up.

Bryn blushed while writing down notes that she planned to implement in her autobiography. Then lost in her feelings, she began to jot down things about Aamir she admired.

* * *

Alexandria and Nial prepared for the water park, and the twins could not contain their excitement.

Lea pulled into the garage. "Sorry I'm late! Where are the twins?" she yelled as she entered the grand living area.

"Waiting for you," Nial said as she rushed by with a handful of snacks.

"I reserved a hotel room at the park in case we're too tired to drive back. I love staying in hotels—no responsibility, no cleaning, no cooking, no laundry." Alexandria grabbed the treats from Nial and placed them inside a colorful duffel bag.

Nial scoffed.

"I cook for you and the twins all the time."

"Yes, that is accurate." Nial pondered while Alexandria rechecked their bags.

Lea walked away, leaving Alexandria and Nial to mock each other. The twins ran out of their playroom directly into Lea's arms. "Yay! You made it! We thought you weren't coming with us!" Nathaniel screamed.

"You are late," Abella Rose voiced.

"Yes, but I wouldn't miss hanging with you guys for anything in the world." Lea embraced the twins in her arms.

"Is Jones coming too?" Nathaniel asked.

"Who is Jones?" Alexandria sat on the barstool, paying close attention.

"It's Lea's new boyfriend, Mommy," Abella Rose revealed.

"Lea has a boyfriend?" Alexandria inquired.

"Yes, Mommy," Nathaniel disclosed.

"Really? So why haven't we met this young man, Lea?"

"Well, it's not serious."

"It's serious enough. Nate and Ella know about him. Have they seen him before?"

"Yes. No," the twins spoke at the same time.

"No." Nathaniel retracted his statement.

"Which one is it? Yes or no? You know I don't like it when you lie to Mommy."

"Yes and no is the truth, Alex. They saw him once when I took them to the yogurt spot on Twenty-Third Avenue. Besides, I know how you and Nial feel about that sort of thing. So I was going to wait to introduce all of you at once. I respect you."

Nial walked into the hallway entrance. "Viens, viens, laisse aller! Mettons-nous en route. N'êtes-vous pas les gars excités?" She rushed the twins along.

The children ran out the house and jumped into Alexandria's Lexus LX truck while Lea placed her bags in the trunk. The twins sat in their favorite seats, positioned in the very back row to watch their favorite movies.

"I wonder what's taking da parents so long?" Nathaniel asked impatiently.

"They're making sure we have wipes and paper towels for hands and faces, he-he." Abella Rose giggled.

"I'm sorry, my bunnies!" Alexandria jumped into the driver's seat. "I know you've been waiting, but we're here now and ready to go."

"No, you're not ready. Where's da other mama?" Nathaniel squirmed in his seat.

"She's coming, big baby!" Abella Rose teased.

"Stop it, you two! Quiet!" Alexandria shouted.

The twins quickly placed their fingers over their mouths and silenced themselves.

"Yay! They are coming. *Boom, boom*, we ready! We ready! We going to the w-a-t-e-r paarrkk!" The twins began to chant when Nial and Lea opened the door.

Nial took her seat when her phone rang repeatedly. "Hello. Yes, this is Nial. I'm so sorry. I must take this," she whispered to Alexandria.

Alexandria interrupted, "Is everything okay?"

"Yes, bébé." She held up her finger, listening carefully. "What exactly is your position?" Nial asked. "Who is your uncle, Elizabeth? Daniel Durkanov is gay?"

"Olly, olly oxen free. Olly, olly, oxen freeeeeeee!" the children loudly chanted.

"One moment please, Elizabeth. Mama's almost done, then we will play games."

"Okayyyyyy!" the twins yelled.

"Elizabeth, are you there? Great! Your uncle was at my first fashion show in Russia. Isn't this a coincidence? Elizabeth Durkanov? I'm on an outing with my family. We will speak Monday, yes?"

"Business?" Alexandria questioned as she drove onto the interstate.

"Yes, bébé, the Durknovs are one of Russia's wealthiest families, and this is great for business," Nial voiced as she placed the steaming cup of tea to her lips.

"The water park is an hour and a half away, so we'll be there shortly, bunnies." Alexandria shifted her focus to the twins.

* * *

Bryn sped directly to the detention center after she met with the new book publishers. She and her attorney, Jane, reached the detention center simultaneously, scurrying into the building. They sat inside the lobby, waiting patiently.

"How long do these things take?" Bryn's legs shook.

"It depends…" Jane placed her hand on Bryn's knee. "Calm down. It'll be okay."

"You always say that."

"I always mean it. This will not take long to win."

"My fingers are crossed."

"So are mine."

"What?"

"I'm kidding. Lighten up a little." Jane chuckled with a snort.

"Soo...I guess it's safe to chat about your love life while we wait." Bryn pried.

"Love life? Please. Love does not live here anymore."

"What happened to Jason?"

"Jason? Please. He stayed in the mirror more than me."

"I thought you two made a cute couple. Jason was smart, fun, and he worshipped you."

"Yes, but he was also narcissistic, conceited, disrespectful to his mother, not to mention rude to others."

"You like conceited men. Every guy you've ever been with has been egotistical, and you know it."

"What can I say? I like confident men."

As time passed, Bryn and Jane looked at their watches, tapping their feet in a synchronized motion.

"We've been waiting over an hour."

"I'll see what's taking so long." Jane walked toward the front desk. "Excuse me, sir. Hello, my name is Jane Woodell, attorney at law. I'm waiting to have a pretrial. Are you familiar with this process, or can you point me in the right direction?"

"I'm the opposing attorney for the detention center. We will begin shortly. I'll show you and your party to the conference room." The gentleman eyed Jane.

Jane scurried back to where Bryn sat. "Bryn, I've found where we're supposed to be. Come with me." Jane pointed down the hallway. The opposing attorney waited as the two women entered the long hall.

"I'm sorry. How rude of me. My name is Phillip Goode, attorney at law. I failed to introduce myself."

"Yes, I noticed," Jane said.

"I've never seen you before. What firm do you work for?"

"I didn't realize all attorneys knew one another?"

"Ha…not all attorneys know one another, but I have bumped into a few."

"I see. Woodell Associates." Jane handed Phillip a business card.

"Now we're getting somewhere. I'm familiar with the building. Your office is in the tall glass building off Broadway Street. Nice firm, Jane!"

"Yes, so I've been told."

"You are feisty. I hope we bump into each other again," Phillip said before he walked away.

"Ehm…excuse me, Jane…were the two of you flirting?" Bryn asked.

"No, Bryn, it's called law humor."

"Yeah…sure…I know a flirt when I see one."

"Can we just get this over with, please?"

Bryn toured the room and spotted her brother in the corner. "He's not a criminal! Why is he in handcuffs?"

"It's the procedure, Bryn. Calm down," Jane said right before the officer detached the handcuffs from Seary's wrists.

Soon after, Seary ran to Bryn, yelling, "Sis!" Seary gave her a massive hug.

"Seary, I'm not in the mood for your shit today. After this is over, there are going to be some changes, mister!"

The deposition

> JUDGE FORD WASHINGTON. Okay, shall we begin? It is noted this deposition is being taken according to the usual stipulations.
>
> JANE WOODELL. No, Your Honor, the usual stipulations do not apply to this particular deposition. It does not in any way pertain to this case.
>
> PHILLIP GOODE. Agreed.
>
> JUDGE WASHINGTON. You, Seary Ross, swear to tell the truth and nothing but the truth so help you God?

SEARY ROSS. I do…

JANE WOODELL. Seary, I am going to ask you a series of preliminary questions, which are questions to ensure you understand what is happening here. Afterward, the opposing attorney, Phillip Goode, will follow up with a series of questions. Do you understand?

SEARY ROSS. Yes.

JANE WOODELL. Have you ever been involved in a deposition before?

SEARY ROSS. No.

JANE WOODELL. You understand you are under oath?

SEARY ROSS. Yes.

JANE WOODELL. Yes, you understand that this means sworn to tell the truth?

SEARY ROSS. Yes.

JANE WOODELL. Even though we are in an informal setting, your answers have the same effect as if we were in a courtroom with a jury.

SEARY ROSS. I understand.

JANE WOODELL. Are you prepared to answer my questions today?

SEARY ROSS. Yes, I am and then some.

JANE WOODELL. Seary, just stick to the questions asked. Now back to the questions at hand. There is nothing that will prevent you from giving me your full attention?

SEARY ROSS. No.

JANE WOODELL. If you don't understand one of my questions, will you let me know?

SEARY ROSS. Yes, I will.

JANE WOODELL. If you need to take a break at any time, tell me, and we will take a break. Okay?

Seary Ross. I understand.

Jane Woodell. On August 2, 2017, did you get inside of a yellow Maserati?

Seary Ross. Yeah, but…

Jane Woodell. These are yes and no questions, Seary.

Seary Ross. Yeah, I did, but I was at the mall, and…

Jane Woodell. Seary, specifically answer the questions accordingly. If you do not, I will decline this deposition, and you will sit here in this detention center until you receive a court hearing. Is that understood?

Seary Ross. Yes.

Judge Washington. Shall we continue?

Jane Woodell. On August 2, 2017, the Maserati, I'm sorry, the yellow Maserati that you got into, who was the driver?

Seary Ross. Ummm…I'm not sure who the driver was.

Jane Woodell. Seary, you are under oath. Who drove the yellow Maserati?

Seary Ross. It was my friend's brother, but I don't know him.

Jane Woodell. So you were not driving the vehicle?

Seary Ross. No.

Jane Woodell. How old are you, Seary?

Seary Ross. I'm fourteen.

Jane placed a folder in front of the judge. "The officer on duty, August 2, 2017, said that Seary was driving the vehicle. Also, he said that he caught Seary coming out of The Pinnacles and followed him into the mall. I have photographs. *Exhibit A*, this is a photograph of Seary getting into the yellow Maserati at the Scottsburg Mall. I obtained this photograph from the Scottsburg Mall's security cameras." Jane passed the photos to the judge. "I had security rewind the tapes back so we could see activity at the start of the day, and it showed *exhibit B*, Seary getting off the Red Line train going into the mall at approximately twelve o'clock noon. So there is no way Seary could have stolen the yellow Maserati."

Seary jumped up out of his seat, screaming, "Yesssssss!"

Bryn grabbed his shirt, pulling him back to his seat. The judge obtained and observed the photographs. "There is no way Seary could have stolen this vehicle. The evidence shows that Seary was an accomplice but not the driver."

Jane Woodell said, "Yes, it does. But it does not make him guilty. Seary was an incognizant accomplice."

Phillip Goode asked, "So where are the other two boys? Why weren't they held in custody? And why was Seary sitting in the vehicle if he wasn't aware of what had taken place?"

"Counselor Goode, you are indeed on the opposing side. Shouldn't you have this information?" the judge stated.

"Why did he sit in the Maserati? I suppose he needed a lift home. Wouldn't you say, Phillip? This case is solely about Seary committing the crime, and evidence proved he did not steal the vehicle. Furthermore, the guilty party is the brother of Seary's friend. His friend's brother, Frederick, is now being held at the jail because that very same day that he stole the Maserati, he burglarized one of the local shopping centers near Scottsburg Mall that night using the same yellow Maserati," Jane revealed. "I know this because one of the officers at the mall patrolled the area. As far as Seary's friend, he obviously got away."

The judge negotiated, "Seary will be on a probationary sentence for twelve months. In addition, he must complete community service every Saturday for the next six months until further notice. Seary, your attorney will notify you of the locations your community service will take place. This deposition is now closed. Ms. Michaels, you may take your brother home."

The judge summoned the two counselors near. "Counselor Woodell, I will notify you of the times and location of Seary's duties. His assignment is jurisdiction 7, helping the inmates. That's the verdict."

The two attorneys exited the conference room. Bryn and Seary waited in the hallway.

"All right, you guys, we are good to go!" Jane said.

Seary was ecstatic that they succeeded. "Awesome! Damn! Ms. Woodell, you're the best lawyer ever!" Seary said as they walked out of the building.

"Thank you, Seary."

"But, Ms. Woodell?"

"Yes, Seary?"

"You already knew I wasn't guilty…why didn't you just tell the judge?"

"Because I wanted to make the opposing attorney look like an ass."

"That's cold, Ms. Woodell."

"I'm joking, Seary. But seriously, even if we, as attorneys, are aware that our client is innocent, we still have to present a solid case to the judge—proof of your innocence."

"Cool."

"Speaking of asses, someone's checking yours out." Bryn noticed Phillip walking briskly behind them.

"Excuse me, Jane. You did a wonderful job in there. Congratulations." Sweat pebbles oozed from Philip's forehead.

"Thank you, Phillip. I would congratulate you, but you didn't do anything."

"Are you single, Jane?"

"I don't date lawyers."

"Ouch! Hurt my feelings, why don't you? Well, you ladies have a good evening." Phillip walked away with his head down.

"Why didn't you just tell the man that you like short men?" Bryn chuckled.

"How dare you? I am simply exploring my options, thank you very much. Enough about me. Let's talk about this young man standing next to us."

Seary smashed into Jane's stomach, squeezing around her waist. "Thank you, Ms. Woodell. You are the best! I'm so happy my sister has you as her lawyer friend."

"No problem, Seary. However, you must get your act together and stop associating yourself with no-good people. You are a brilliant, handsome young man. You should be doing something productive. Don't waste your time hanging out with deadbeats. Remember, you are what you eat."

"I am what I eat?"

"Never mind, just be careful of the company you keep, Seary."

After Jane finished her speech, Seary walked away. He opened the door to Bryn's BMW, bumping his head on the rooftop as he sat. Tall, slouching to fit perfectly in the seat, he turned the radio to his favorite station, watching his sister converse with Jane.

"Jane, you were amazing in there. The nerve of those people, placing the blame on an innocent fourteen-year-old."

"You act as if you've never seen me in action before, Bryn."

"I have…but you never cease to amaze me. I'm proud to have you as my friend and my attorney."

"Just remember, I'll be sending you my bill," Jane said before getting into her vehicle.

"So glad that is over with." Bryn pounced in her seat next to Seary.

"I'm glad it's over with too! I'm starving! The food was atrocious, not to mention it smelled like Cheetos every day in that place. The bathrooms had piss and shit all over the floors." Seary smelled his underarm pits.

"Yes, you smell, kid! And you should've learned a valuable lesson. What would Mom and Dad think? You wouldn't dare if they were still alive."

"Yeah, well, if Mom and Dad were still alive, I'd still be in Thailand, and you'd be elsewhere."

"I love you, kid. And you're with me now. We are family. We must stick together. Jane was right. It would be good if you did something productive with your life. You will be graduating in a few years, and you don't want to be like your friends committing crimes and in jail. People work hard for what they have, and they don't need little punks like you and what's his face taking their things from them."

"I know, Bry. I understand, and I promise I'll do better."

"Great! Because I only want what's best for you." Bryn rubbed her hand across his soft sandy brown dreadlocks. "Also, I have something I would like to share with you," she said as they continued their ride home. "I met someone I really like! And he really likes me too!"

"Who is he?" Seary paused.

"His name is Aamir Bahar."

"Bahar? I've heard that name before from somewhere. So what does he do?"

"He's a professional race-car driver."

"Aamir, the roadmaster?" Seary's eyes widened as he stared at his sister in shock.

"You heard of him?"

"No shit! I've heard of him! He's like one of the best drivers there fucking is. He mastered the short-track races and superspeedway. In my opinion, the only reason he lost that one race to Sam the Ghost Rider was because his tire blew out!"

"Wow! Seary, you obviously know more about him than I do. Besides the racing stuff, how do you feel about us dating?"

"If you like him, that's great! Just be careful. Celebrities are groupie magnets if you know what I mean."

"Well, thanks, onion head. He's too kind for that."

"Yeah, well, sis, I hate to break it to you, but kind people have groupies too." He laid his hand on her shoulder.

"I appreciate your input, Seary." Bryn tooted her nose up at him.

They finally pulled into the garage, and Seary quickly jumped out the vehicle. Bryn walked inside the house before sending Aamir a text message. "I miss you."

"Hey, gorgeous."

"How are you?"

"Missing you. These Tokyo players are giving me a run for my money."

"You got this." She sent the muscle arm emoji.

"[heart eyes]"

"Get some rest. Talk soon."

"Soon, soon."

CHAPTER 24

Communicate

Inside the dance studio, rays of light gleamed through the bay window. Music streamed from the room, meeting the silence expelling from other areas in the warm spacious home. Alexandria's feet faced opposite directions as she slid one foot in front of the other, and then her legs flew across the air, landing on her toes. The sinuous motion of her arms resembled the movements of a snake. She stared into the oversize mirror at her stance as she reminisced about the times she danced alongside Abram and Tippy at the ballet school.

Alexandria stumbled across the room to grab her phone when it rang nonstop. "Hello, hello." She breathed deeply, lightly stroking her forehead and chest with a large towel. "Sure." Alexandria gulped a bottle of water as she walked upstairs. "Mistress! My father had a mistress?"

Nial overheard Alexandria talking and stopped typing on her keypad.

"Jennifer, where exactly is this leading? I had no clue my father had a mistress. Find them? That sounds a little crazy. How could they just disappear? I was under the impression they wouldn't be permitted to leave the state. Why from me? What can that identify? What?" Alexandria stared at Nial with her mouth wide open, listening to the detective.

"Where are you going?" Nial took Alexandria's phone from her hand, placing it on the desk.

"My love, I need to meet the detective. She needs a sample of my blood for the case." Alexandria scuffled to remove herself from Nial's grip.

"I need a sample of you." Nial moved Alexandria's panties to the side.

"I'll give you all of me when I return. Promise." Alexandria pushed Nial's hand back. "I'll stop by the deli and grab some of those sandwiches you and the twins love."

"Great, bébé. Just great." Nial threw her hands up and turned her chair around.

Alexandria quickly left the estate, while Nial continued to strike her keys.

As time passed, Nial anticipated Alexandria's return when the door opened. "What happened?" Nial scurried downstairs to meet Alexandria. "We are supposed to discuss the details of the charity tonight."

"Hold on, my love." Alexandria continued to address the person on the phone, "Sure, first thing tomorrow, I'll check on it. Okay, thanks, Georgia."

"Well?" Nial asked.

"I am so sorry I'm late. I met Jennifer at her office to give her the sample she needed."

"Jennifer?" Nial asked. "So you are on a first-name basis?" Nial followed Alexandria to the kitchen. "You were away four fucking hours, Alex! Did you forget about the charity?" She raised her voice.

"Somebody has her panties in a ruffle. What is wrong with you? The charity event isn't until next week. I'm off to take a soak in the bath." Alexandria left Nial standing in the kitchen alone. Nial flipped through the calendar, checking the dates when she realized Alexandria was correct. It was her who had the dates mixed up.

Alexandria kissed the twins good night, grabbed a bottle of wine from their wine cellar, relaxed in the tub, and pondered her thoughts. *What is Nial's issue?* After a bottle of wine and hours of soaking, she stepped out of the bathtub. Her body had shriveled like a prune from sitting so long. She wrapped a large towel around her slender freckled frame. She smiled a little, dried off before slipping into a pair of her favorite panties, and crawled underneath the sheet close to her wife.

The following day, Nial woke up late. After a hot shower, she searched through their home for Alexandria. "Alexxxx, where are you, bébé!"

"Upstairs!"

"Alex? I'm sorry." Nial stood in the doorway.

"You should really work on whatever's going on with you."

"Work on what?"

"I don't know, whatever your issue is. You sometimes forget that I'm easy to talk to. And raising your tone doesn't help get your point across. It actually presses the mute button inside my ear."

"I was thinking reckless, and I don't know why I assumed the worst."

"You think I'm having an affair?"

"No…no…of course not. I know how you feel about adultery. I was drinking. And one hour passed, then two, three, and the next moment, it was four hours later. You didn't bring le sandwich."

"You're right. I did not bring dinner, but you should have cooked or ordered if you and the twins were starving. Yesterday was a strange long evening. The only thing I wanted to do was come home and fuck until we fell asleep, but you fucked that up." Alexandria persisted.

"We can fuck now." Nial kissed the nape of her neck.

"I love you, Nial. I would never do anything to jeopardize our family." Alexandria stared into her eyes. Nial grabbed her arm and pulled her close. They hugged, and Nial kissed her forehead. And Alexandria quickly removed herself from Nial's grip.

"Why not?" Nial begged.

"Because I'm aware where this is leading, and I need to go to the market before the twins arrive. I'll return in a few hours, and I'm all yours." Alexandria glared.

"Only a few hours?"

"Yes, see you soon, my love." Alexandria eyed Nial as she seductively swayed her hips out the office.

* * *

Alexandria returned home from the farmers market. "Splendid! Robert, I am so excited about this. One more thing, don't worry about the LA office right now. Only concern yourself with New York. Once you've faxed over the documents, make sure they send confirmation. You are the best! Thank you." Alexandria placed her bags on top of the counter and sat the frozen goods inside the cooling system. "Eeeek! You startled me! What the fuck, Nial!"

"We need to talk."

"Must you be so cryptic?"

"I'm serious."

"Okay, can I have a kiss first?" Alexandria extended her arms. "Your lack of enthusiasm is so sexy, my love."

"Sit down, please! I do not like to be upset with you, mon amour."

"Upset about? I want to cook dinner before the twins arrive. Talk to me, baby." Alexandria stored the empty bags away. She grasped Nial's hand. "Baby, you are scaring me."

"The detective called while you were out. She apologized. An intimate dinner?" Nial scowled.

"Love, it's nothing. I didn't have time to speak with you about it. You and I had just made up...I couldn't go into another stressful conversation."

"Alex, that is not feasible. I knew there was something strange about her buying you a salad."

"A salad?" Alexandria scoffed. "Listen, I am honest with you. When I say the words, I do! I meant every fucking word. And I have never backed out on those words for anyone." Alexandria sliced the tomatoes as if they had done something horrible to her.

Nial slid her hands around Alexandria's neck, squeezing tight. "I don't know why I get so angry," she whispered as her lips gently caressed Alexandria's ear.

"Because you're a jealous, bitch. That's why." Alexandria shoved the fruit bowl to the floor. Fruit and vegetables were scattered everywhere.

Nial picked Alexandria up and placed her on the counter. She ripped Alexandria's bra and panties off before nuzzling her face in between her thighs. Alexandria pulled her closer, lying back on the countertop, purring.

"Tell me you luff it?" Nial grabbed her throat as she glazed her body down, French-kissing every inch of her. "I luff you, bébé." She wrapped her lips around Alexandria's emotional spot, teasing light as a feather nonstop. Alexandria constricted her legs around Nial's head. Her hips vibrated with boundless passion.

"Baby!" She panted. "I love it!" Alexandria screamed, climaxing all over the Cristallo quartzite.

"Damn. You are delicious," Nial muttered as she creamed on herself.

Alexandria slowly unclenched her legs. Then she and Nial slithered down to the floor, laughing aloud.

CHAPTER 25

Trick or Treat

Alexandria and Nial shopped for Halloween costumes for the Children Nephrology Foundation Charity. Photographers ambushed them when they entered the mall. Cameras flashed from every angle. Staff members and customers ran toward the flashing lights.

"Nial, is it true you're opening a new store in Russia and Tokyo?" a reporter yelled.

"What about the new fabric you're producing? Are you and your wife still together? Asking for a friend." Another reporter crammed his recorder in Nial's face.

"Yes, it is possible I will open a store in many places. The rest, you must wait for." Nial placed her finger up to her lips. "Please, I'm trying to have private time with my wife. Hope that answers your question." She placed her hand in between Alexandria's as they broke through the chaotic crowd.

"She is famous. Get her to sign my chest." A teenage boy pulled his shirt above his head. Nial bypassed the boy, almost knocking him over.

Another reporter shoved his microphone in her face before she could squeeze by the crowd of people. "When are you going to come out with a gentlemen's line?" he asked.

"Pick up the next *Cozmag*, and you will find out." Nial held on tight to Alexandria as they scurried through checkout and quickly left through the side door. The photographers followed them through the revolving doors, taking pictures until they hopped in their car, and Nial drove away. *The life I lead,* Nial thought when a text message chimed her cell phone, but she ignored it. Alexandria turned the radio up as they sped down the highway. Nial laid her hand on her thigh.

* * *

Lights bounced off the colorful stoned wall. The National Children's Museum was monumental for having opulent events for children and their families. The Halloween decorations were flawless. A robotic mummy hovered above the building as if it were about to devour the people inside. Abella Rose and Nathaniel were overwhelmed with joy that their moms attained tickets for their classmates to attend.

Alexandria was also overjoyed with the Children Nephrology Foundation's focus on small children and young adults born and diagnosed with chronic kidney disease. "Felix would be super proud."

Abella Rose zoomed in on the pictures inside their first-grade yearbook as they reached the front of the building.

"Halloween was Felix's favorite holiday, Mommy."

"Yes, sweetie, we will honor Felix and many others tonight that suffer from CKD." Alexandria eyed Nathaniel from the side-view mirror.

"What is CKD again, Mommy? I forgot," Abella Rose questioned.

"It is when a person has too many kidney beans, and they cannot use the le toilet. Right, Mama?" Nathaniel explained. "Felix's mom read a book to us about it."

"It's not beans. It's an organ, and some people can use the le toilet. Right, Mama?" Abella Rose frowned.

"Yes, that is correct, Ella. Let's go raise some money for those people." Alexandria reached for the yearbook.

"The turnout is fantastic. Mummy did a great job with her foundation." Nial held Alexandria's hand as she attempted to bring a bit of joie de vivre to the experience.

Valet waited patiently outside the big black truck before opening their door. Nial climbed out first before assisting Alexandria and the twins to the orange carpet.

The inside of the museum was like a fantasy playhouse but scarier. Everyone wore costumes, and everyone that was someone attended. The punch resembled a bowl of blood with eyeballs floating on top. Spiderwebs hung from the ceiling with tiny electronic spiders crawling throughout. Candy, cookies, and fruit resembled bats and vampire teeth. Brownies oozed red icing. Fake slime covered the backdrop, and edible insects were passed around the room. Finally, the champagne glasses were smoked, filled, and served to the adults.

Nial danced around in circles on the dance floor with Abella Rose and Nathaniel, while Alexandria sat at the table with Aamir, Bryn, Sammy, and a woman that Alexandria had not seen before. Seary roamed the building with a few friends from his new school.

"So *The Addams Family*?" The unfamiliar woman laughed aloud. "Whose idea was that?" She smirked.

"Nate's." Alexandria pointed to Nathaniel, attempting the moonwalk on the dance floor while Abella Rose showed off the ballet moves that Alexandria taught her.

"Cute." The woman was vibrant and funny, and she fit in like she had known them for a lifetime.

"Right, Alex, this is Cari Phillips. Cari raced alongside Sammy and me in Italy during the Gender Equality Summit. Now she is US-bound," Aamir interrupted.

"You're never too late, Aamir. Nice to meet you, Cari." Alexandria smiled as Cari reached over to shake her hand.

"My pleasure." Cari's face lit up as she smiled brightly.

"Ella agreed?" Bryn asked.

"I think she feels sad for Nate. She's been abnormally nice to him since Felix died." Alexandria straightened her necktie.

"I must say, Alex. You make a handsome Gomez Addams." Cari winked her eye.

"Who are you supposed to be, Pokémon?" Alexandria asked Cari.

"More like poke-her-mon." Cari laughed.

"Are you flirting with me, Cari Phillips?" Alexandria's eyebrows waved up and down.

Before she could finish her sentence, a woman dressed as Elvira appeared at their table.

"Zoe?" Alexandria squinted.

"Hi, Alexandria, Aamir. I saw you and—"

"You thought it would be wise to come to speak?" Alexandria's nose crumpled.

"Yes, Nial invited me. Didn't she tell you?" Zoe smirked more. "Do not worry. It's business."

"Is there a problem?" Bryn stared at Aamir and Alexandria.

Nial glanced in their direction and prowled to the table when she noticed Zoe standing nearby. The twins followed behind her. "Hi, Zoe. You made it?" Nial hugged Zoe.

Alexandria swiped a bottle of wine from the table and left.

Bryn stared at Aamir, waiting for him to say something, anything. "What's happening right now?" she asked.

"Typical Nial, that's what's happening." Aamir sipped from his champagne glass, ignoring Zoe.

"Oh?"

Nial took the twins to the playroom, where a chaperone supervised the children whose parents were too intoxicated to function.

"Why didn't you tell them I would be here?" Zoe stood at the bar beside Nial, drinking a glass of champagne. "You promised me I'd always have a place at your company."

"My intentions did not go as planned. I will speak with Alex." Nial threw back a shot of whiskey and left Zoe standing alone. She searched around the museum and found Alexandria on the balcony next to Cari. She stood afar, listening before approaching. "What is this?"

"What is what?" Alexandria turned around.

"We are leaving." Nial grabbed Alexandria's arm. "I need to explain."

"No, I'm having a conversation with Cari." She pulled away. "Go back inside and talk to Zoe." She turned her back and continued to converse with Cari.

"Alex is my wife, Cari, in case Aamir did not warn you."

"Our conversation is harmless. You're welcome to stay and chat with us," Cari said snidely.

Steam appeared to stream from Nial's ears. Her face turned beet red. Nial bumped Cari's arm as if she wanted to shove her off the balcony. "Don't fuck with me, Cari."

"Go back inside." Alexandria waved her off, grabbed Cari's arm, and left Nial standing there. A group of teenagers watched nearby. Nial did not want to make a scene, so she swayed away.

* * *

Weeks had passed since Alexandria's first annual charity ball. Finally, she had begun to make progress toward plausibility within her organization. The firm's recognition came days after she closed five major deals with high-profile international corporations. This made her the youngest, the highest-paid analytical marketer in California and New York City combined. Twenty-five million dollars was deposited into her bank account after the merger. The goal was to make Crusade Marketing the headquarters for all marketing and communication firms worldwide.

A significant presentation underway would put her in the driver's seat as chief of all eight organizations' marketing and consulting departments. Alexandria waited inside a pizza gallery in New York City for Georgia to arrive. As soon as she ordered a latte, Georgia came rushing through the revolving doors. She placed an envelope on the table in front of Alexandria.

"What is this?" Alexandria quickly grabbed the envelope.

"Open it."

"What? Georgia!" she screamed under her breath. "Fifty-million-dollar bonus?"

"I want you to be my partner, Alexandria. You've made Crusade Marketing a billion-dollar firm. I could not have done that without you. Before you, my company was a small unknown consulting firm. Now we are rolling higher than the biggest wigs in marketing, consulting, and communications. You made this company, Alex. I cannot repay you enough."

"Wow, Georgia."

"That's not all. There's more." Georgia's eyes gleamed as she held her hand up to her mouth, clasped together as if praying.

Alexandria slowly placed her hand in the fawn envelope and pulled out a tinier jacket. Her eyes wide, she inhaled and exhaled. "You gave me 50 percent of the company? I'm speechless."

"Say yes, Alexandria. Be my business partner. Sign."

"YES, Georgia! I'll be your business partner!" She laughed aloud. Teary-eyed, she read over the fine print. "Wait…why does it have 'in case of death'? I? Me? The sole owner of the company and have complete control?"

"Alex, I do not have any family. My husband doesn't count. He's getting his nine shares, so he doesn't give a shit."

Alexandria's eyes were blurry. She could barely see where to sign. Her hand shook. "Wow." She signed and slid the documents back to Georgia.

"Okay, now let's go be great." Georgia stood up.

Alexandria walked next to Georgia to their parked car. The vision board on her wall had become a reality as she lived and breathed through the collages and images of lavish living. From the moment her toddler feet hit the ground without her parents' assistance, the dream of helping people fulfill their needs started with her brother. Abram followed in her footsteps. As she walked, he crawled, and as she ran, he walked. He was never as fast as her, but she was determined to ensure he was close. They were attached like tendons to muscles. If he fell, she was there to pick him up. Her phone resonated as the driver opened the door.

"Hello," Alexandria answered as she sat down, buckling her seat belt.

"How's it going?" Cari asked.

"Hi, Cari, things are great. How are you? Or shall I say, did you recover from the whiskey sours?" Alexandria laughed.

"I hoped you'd forgotten about that. Since you brought it up…I'm at the hospital. I may have alcohol poisoning. Your company may get sued, dude."

"Get the fuck out! I'm so sorry, Cari. Why didn't you…I haven't heard anything. It's been weeks!"

"That's because I'm shitting you." Cari chuckled.

"You suck. You really suck, Jesus! I'm sitting here next to my boss."

"Ehm, business partner," Georgia intervened.

"My business partner and…damn, Cari. Don't ever scare me like that again."

"What scared you most? The fact that you'd never talk to me again or getting sued?"

"Ha-ha, still not funny. I'm on my way to a meeting. I'll call you later."

"Are you sure wifey won't mind?"

"You and I are only friends, Cari. Nial will be fine. Talk soon, jerk."

"I look forward to it."

CHAPTER 26

Wild Russian

Meanwhile, Nial awaited Elizabeth's arrival soon after she got off the plane. She sat inside one of Samara's little cafés, sipping a Christmas mint tea, one of her favorite drinks in Russia. Suddenly a tall dark-haired woman with thigh-high boots and a fur coat dashed through the door. Nial could not verify her face.

"Excuse me, Nial?" The woman leaned over, whispering in her ear.

"Yes, I am Nial." She focused on the woman.

"I am Elizabeth. Let's get out of here."

"Tea?" Nial held up two cups.

"Bring it. I want to show you something."

The ladies walked outside into the smoldering cold. The snow was almost six inches high. Elizabeth slid her hand in between Nial's arm and held on to her tight. "My driver's here." Elizabeth pointed across the road.

"Where are we going?" Nial inquired.

"My uncle's and then paradise. Or maybe paradise first and then my uncle's." Elizabeth let up the partition. Wasting no time, she placed her hand inside Nial's blouse. Her fingertips massaged Nial's breast, examining them with her tongue. Finally, she locked her lips around Nial's nipple while squeezing the other firmly.

Nial moaned. Her lips slightly grazed Elizabeth's earlobe. The more Elizabeth engaged, the wetter Nial became. Finally, she grabbed Nial's hand and placed it between her thighs. "You don't have any panties on," Nial whispered.

"No." Elizabeth gripped Nial's neck with her teeth and sucked harder.

Breathing heavy, Elizabeth gave her undeniable pleasure. Spreading her legs apart, she placed her head between Nial's legs. After sixty seconds of extensive attention, Nial creamed all over the limousine seat.

Nial belted out inaudible moans.

Elizabeth held a feminine wipe. "Allow me the pleasure." Nial's legs opened wide. The driver drove into the gated entryway and released the window.

"It's Elizabeth. Open up!" she spoke to the intercom system.

"I did not bring designs with me," Nial whispered.

"Don't worry. I have it covered. I saw your exclusives online. My cousin wants that entire Milan winter collection. I have them saved on my uncle's computer. You will be centered in the hottest magazines soon."

The driver parked the limousine in front of the mansion's entrance. He opened the door. Elizabeth giggled as she focused on Nial's legs treading up the steps.

"We should take the elevator. My uncle is on the terrace upstairs." Elizabeth held Nial's hand.

"You should have warned me."

"Do you plan everything?" Elizabeth giggled.

"Not everything."

"Do not worry. My uncle does as I ask."

Once they made it onto the terrace, Chef Daniel scuffled as he played a game of ice hockey. Elizabeth waved her hand in the air, trying to gain her uncle's attention. "Uncle!" she yelled.

"I'll be right there!" The chef held his hockey stick in the air, acknowledging Elizabeth.

One of Chef Daniel's assistants met Elizabeth and Nial at the players' box, where they waited. "Hello, ladies, Mr. Durkanov has to freshen up. He'll be right with you. If you will follow me."

"I'm famished. I have encountered many extracurricular activities this evening." Elizabeth picked up a fruit tart from one of the trays. "Tastes almost as good as you, Nial." She stuffed a lemon tart in between her lips, licking the custard slowly from around the rim of her mouth. "Have your way with anything you want, including me." Elizabeth sauntered past Nial's body, rubbing against her legs.

"Thanks, I'll save my delicacies for later." She winked at Elizabeth.

Elizabeth laughed. "Oops! Hi, uncle. Muah, muah. I didn't see you standing behind me."

"To whom do I owe the pleasure?" Chef Daniel inquired.

"Uncle Daniel, this is Nial Paul, founder, editor, and chief of Nial Paul Designs. You remember Nial, don't you, uncle?"

"Yes, I remember Mrs. Paul. Your designs are exquisite. I have been trying to find you. You are a hard person to position. Elizabeth tells me you are a fashion conglomerate. And my daughter adores your designs."

"Merci."

"I have everything we need. I went over the photographs with Lindsey, and she wants them all." Elizabeth swiped through the designs on her notebook that Lindsey chose. "I figured we propose an offer to Nial. Between the two shows, there are twenty collections from the Milan and Moroccan shows, twenty thousand for each set." Elizabeth pointed to the hats and scarves to the boots and jackets. "What do you think, Nial?"

"Perfect. Daniel?"

"No price is too steep for my Lindsey. Lindsey wants all of your newest pieces."

"Yes, she raves about your styles in her interviews."

Nial's phone rang. "Excuse me, I must take this call. Hi, taking a meeting with Daniel. Is everything all right?" She paused, listening to the joyful screaming screeching through the phone. "Alex, that is great news. Umm…my schedule is uncertain. I will call you." Nial hung up the phone quickly. "My apologies, where were we?" Nial sipped more champagne.

"We were wrapping up." Elizabeth coughed.

"I would love you to have *uzhin* with my family. Lindsey would be obliged to meet you." Chef Daniel ambled toward the custards on the table.

"I luff that. When is the uzhin?"

"Tomorrow evening. I'll send a car." Daniel got up from the table.

"There's no need, uncle. I will escort Mrs. Paul for the remainder of her stay. Besides, we have a lot of catching up to do." Elizabeth rubbed Nial's shoulder.

"Okay, I will see you tomorrow, Nial." The chef exited the room.

"Yes, tomorrow." Nial smiled.

After their meeting was over, Elizabeth said her goodbyes to the rest of the family and met Nial downstairs.

"Nial, there is a spectacular nightclub I want you to see. It is secluded." Elizabeth dialed the number to her driver. The driver bolted to the inside gate.

* * *

Club Exotica's name did not do it justice. The ambiance enticed everyone inside, with an orgy taking place in every corner of the room. Nial and Elizabeth danced until morning, touching and fondling each other to every song. The people on the dance floor admired the flirty pair. Nial kissed and hugged Elizabeth all night.

"Come with me," Elizabeth insisted, whispering sweet words of seduction in Nial's ear. "I want to introduce you to a special place." Elizabeth did not let Nial's hand go, leading the way. A long dark hallway appeared in the distance as they came upon a flight of stairs.

"Where are you taking me?" Nial asked as they made their way through a tunnel.

"Through sliding glass doors."

Nial stood close to Elizabeth as they entered a dark room. The vast space was inside a loft with eclectic furniture and a lot of art decor. "What is this room? You cannot hear the music from the club. Where are we?" Nial's eyes zoomed in on Elizabeth.

"Welcome to my abode!" Elizabeth smacked Nial's ass. "I live here when I'm in town." Elizabeth continued to lead Nial to a more secluded area where there were red strobe lights. "Come meet my furry little friend." Elizabeth pointed to a nearby cage.

Nial tiptoed near. "What is that?" she screeched.

"It's my kitty cat." Elizabeth uncovered the cage. "This is my baby. Hi, my big boy." Elizabeth pacified him.

"He is no kitty. You have a fucking white tiger!" Nial's eyes widened.

"Yes, he's here to protect me."

"Ever heard of a security system?" Nial scoffed.

"Come with me. I have one more kitten to show you." Elizabeth pulled Nial to the back of the loft.

"I think I've seen enough pussy for one evening."

"Are you sure you've seen enough because I think you can stand one or two more?" Elizabeth undressed.

"Maybe I can stand to see one more. Whose club is it downstairs?"

"I own the club." Elizabeth sat down.

"You are full of surprises," Nial uttered.

"This is Katiah. Katiah would like to meet you." Elizabeth's legs widened as the lounge door slid open. Nial dropped her dress to the floor and strutted toward Elizabeth.

Rolling out of bed the next day, Nial reached for her cell phone while Elizabeth and Katiah remained asleep. She kept a close eye on the cub as she grabbed a bag of food from the delivery guy. "What are you going to do with him when he gets bigger?" Nial asked Elizabeth.

"Maximus is my baby," Elizabeth stretched her legs out of bed.

"Maximus? I have heard stories of tigers attacking their owners. How safe is that?" Nial filled her mouth with spicy noodles.

"Not my Maximus. Come here, big boy. Yes, Mommy loves you." Elizabeth summoned the cub near. She rubbed his soft mane and kissed him all over his furry face. The cub licked her cheek, leaving a trail of slobber behind. "Now sit!" Elizabeth demanded. The small tiger sat instantly, laying his short thick body across the fox-fur rug beside her.

"What does he eat?" Nial could not take her eyes off the cub.

"He drinks milk for now, but soon he'll require a healthier feast." Elizabeth tossed one of the cub's toys at him.

"Like what? People?"

"No."

"What?"

"Frogs, lizards, fish, snakes, antelope."

"People."

"Yes…Maximus will scare the shit out of anyone that fucks with me." Elizabeth laughed.

Nial sipped her wine, still staring at Maximus.

CHAPTER 27

Yes!

Several months passed since Aamir and Bryn had been together as a couple. Bryn picked him up from a business meeting in the city. His bright smile appeared in the glass window as the escalator carried him from the building's top floor. Bryn hopped out of the driver's seat to hold the passenger door ajar for him. "Hi, sexy." Bryn waved her hand, winking at him.

"Hello, gorgeous. Thank you." Aamir slobbered her down, instantly giving her no room to respire.

"I love it when you kiss me like you miss me." Bryn licked her lips.

"There are a few other places I'd like to kiss you."

"You're not funny, Aamir."

"I'm not laughing."

"You have no idea how grateful I am that you're considering architecture again. You look so cute drawing on your little drawing board. Those classes are really paying off, huh? How was your day today?"

"Today was good. There's something I want to show you. Turn left." Aamir placed his hand on Bryn's leg as she drove.

"Okay." Bryn's face curious, she made a sharp turn.

"Turn right toward Lotus Park. I have a surprise for you."

Bryn stopped in front of the distinctive park.

"Pull over." Aamir pointed.

"You mean on the side of the road? How will we get inside?" Bryn asked.

"I'll show you. Take the entrance to the right over where those two security officers are standing." He continued to point. "They'll lead the way."

Bryn drove near the two officers. Aamir held up two fingers, and the officers pointed in the direction they needed to go. Bryn looked at the officers, and then she looked at Aamir. "What is going on?"

Aamir placed his finger over Bryn's lips. "Drive to the gazebo straight ahead. Turn right at the yield sign. And drive under the bypass, and then stop."

Bryn honored his request and sat quietly. Then a man wearing a suit and tie tapped the window. Bryn jumped.

"Roll the window down, beautiful," Aamir insisted.

"Hello, ma'am, sir," the man spoke. "If you will leave your vehicle and come with me, please?"

They stepped out of the vehicle. "Now what?" Bryn asked right before the elevator door opened. Pink and white rose petals fell at their feet. "What is this?"

Aamir placed his finger on Bryn's lips again. "We're almost there." He smiled. Four white horses and a carriage were at the end of the breezeway. There was another person dressed in white waiting beside the carriage. The man paused, waiting to assist Bryn onto the wagon. Once inside, there lay two dozen red roses with a note.

"What's this?" Bryn smiled, the roses in one hand and the tiny envelope in the other.

"Maybe it's courtesy." Aamir hunched his shoulders.

> Open carefully. I'm fragile.

Bryn continued to read, side-eying Aamir. "Let's see now. It says, 'To Bryn.' That's me!"

Dear Bryn,

You are the love of my life. I want nothing more than to spend the rest of my life with you and Seary.

Bryn became confused. "Aww, Aamir."

"It isn't over yet." He smiled. The horse and carriage carried them to a beautiful grassy plain with pink roses and white lilies along the terrace's rims with a picnic cloth and a large collapsible basket sitting next to an oversize beanbag.

"Come with me." Aamir extended his hand and led the way. They both sat down on the beanbag, and Aamir passed her a pink piece of paper.

My queen,

You mean so much to me. You taught me the true meaning of family and what it means to love unconditionally. I am honored to be your man, baby. I knew from the start that you were the her to my him, the she to my he, better yet, the Mrs. to my Mr. I brought you here today to ask you if you'd do me the honor and be my wife. Marry ya boy!

Bryn laughed. "Wait…what?"

"I miss you when I am not with you. I don't want to be apart from you anymore. I want to marry you, Bryn." Aamir's face flushed, and he began to perspire. "Will you please do me the honor and be my wife?"

She jumped on his lap. "Yes, yes, baby! I'll marry you." She kissed Aamir all over his face.

"Fucking yes!" he cheered. "I was trying to take baby steps, but I just couldn't. You have made me the happiest man in the world, Bryn." He inhaled, then exhaled.

Bryn wrapped her arms around his neck, hugging him tightly. They kissed long and hard for a few minutes, unaware that Mimi stood nearby.

"Ehm...excuse me, but your meal is now being served." Mimi grinned, waving her hand in the air. She summoned the waiters over.

"Mimi was in on this too? You two are a piece of work. I am so fucking happy!"

"So why didn't you ask me?" Aamir inquired while the waiter filled their glasses with champagne.

"Ask you what?"

"To marry you?"

"I was trying to be patient."

"Ha...patient...sure you were, Bryn."

"Seary will be psyched when he finds out about this!" Bryn exclaimed.

"Seary is already psyched, my love. He knows about all of this. He told me yellow roses are your favorite. Also, I want to give you this."

"A ring?" Bryn slapped Aamir's shoulder, shoving him over. "Is this what I think it is?" Bryn asked excitedly.

"Yes, it's an engagement ring."

"Look how fucking huge it is, and it has yellow stones encrusted! You have really outdone yourself, Aamir."

"Thank you. I have another ring that is being flown in from New Castle." Aamir could not contain his excitement.

Bryn blushed as she stared into his eyes. "Yes, my king, yes, a million times yes!"

After dinner, the carriage carried them to a cabin located in the back of the park. "How'd my car get here?" Bryn wondered.

"I had it relocated so we wouldn't have to circle the park to find it."

"This place is beautiful! A cabin, baby, really? How'd you—"

"Don't cry. This is our moment, and I thought it would be nice to stay here for the evening. We'll leave tomorrow or whenever you're ready." Aamir wiped Bryn's tears. He walked up to the cabin door and opened it.

Bryn extended her hand so they would assist each other inside. A fresh sea breeze aroma swept across Bryn's nose as soon as the door opened. The fireplace blazed. Magnolia blankets lay across the sofa, and an ottoman sat in front of a rocking chair—the kitchen filled with fresh fruits and sparkling water. The bedroom complemented the hallway, covered in yellow rose petals that flowed onto the bed.

"Aamir, I don't know what to say." Bryn cried.

"Don't cry."

"You put so much thought and effort into everything you do. And your efforts not only concern me but Seary as well. I wish my parents were here to witness my happiness. No one has ever made me feel so special, Aamir—no one." She hugged him tightly.

"You make me happy. It is the perfect reason why we should spend the rest of our lives together." He held up his pinky finger.

"Agreed, my king." Bryn wrapped her finger in between his pinky. "What about Seary? He'll need a ride home from soccer practice."

"I've taken care of that. Seary can drive himself."

"Seary can't drive. He's only fifteen." Bryn reached for her cell phone.

Aamir grabbed her hand. "Bryn, I hope this doesn't offend you, but while you were on your book tour, I gave Seary driving lessons. His birthday is near, so I took him to get his driver's license."

"You did what? I have officially died and gone to paradise. Thank you. But whose car is he driving?"

"My old Beetle. It's small, and it's something he can handle. He's a swift learner. You should be proud of him."

Aamir and Bryn could barely keep their hands off each other. They enjoyed the rest of the evening as the fireplace sputtered. Then suddenly Bryn slipped out of her dress and straddled Aamir.

"Beautiful, let's wait until our wedding night. We've waited this long. We can wait a little longer." Aamir sat up, hiding his bulging penis.

"What? No, I'm horny. I need you inside me." Bryn pushed him back on the plush rug.

Aamir began to sweat through his clothes. "I don't want to hurt you."

"What?"

"I'm gifted, and I do not want to hurt you."

"That's why you've been holding out on me? You will not hurt me. I trust you." She rubbed him gently, and he became even more aroused. His dick hung halfway to his knees, and Bryn's eyes widened as she slipped her panties off. Leaning over, she grabbed the night bag that he had packed for her. She turned the volume up on her cell phone, and sweet melodies surrounded them. Bryn removed his shoes and unbuttoned his shirt. Aamir cupped her face into his hands, kissing her lips softly.

Bryn breathed heavily, staring into his eyes. "I love you, Aamir Bahar." She laid kisses across his neck down to his chest.

He pulled her on top of his face, kissing between her creamy thighs, making love to Bryn for the first time. The excitement rushed Aamir's reproductive organs like a waterfall as the blood coerced the veins in his schlong. He eased between Bryn's hips slowly, her mouth gaping wide and gasping for air, breath after breath. She breathed deeply. With every stroke, she spurted nonstop, scratching his back and gripping his side. In that moment, they'd found a forever love, a love that would last until the end of time.

* * *

A few hours passed. Lea and the twins were huddled on the shaggy beige carpet, watching movies and eating ice cream when suddenly the front gate opened.

"I think that's Mama. So let's pretend we don't hear her," Abella Rose whispered.

"Why? I missed Mama. No! I'm not doing that." Nathaniel jumped up. "Mama! I missed you!" He ran into Nial's arms, almost knocking her to the floor.

"I missed you too, my luffly boy. Let Mama place her things down and get out of these fabrics." Nial went into the bedroom and pulled off her clothes. She stared at herself in the mirror as if she didn't recognize herself. "I'm exhausted," she uttered.

"You should be." Alexandria stood behind her, watching.

"I didn't see you standing there."

"It's a movie night. Are you coming to join us?"

"I'm drained, bébé. I would like to take a nap."

You should be you smell like a distillery. "The twins are not going to like that."

"I'll watch one movie, then I will nap."

"Good choice." Alexandria left the room before ordering sushi for dinner.

"What is Mama doing?" Nathaniel asked.

"She'll be here shortly. Go pick another movie before she comes." Alexandria laid a blanket on the floor for the twins to eat on.

Nial walked into the theater room, bopped down on the sectional, and put her feet up. "Hi, Lea, Ella." Nial stared at Abella Rose. "Ella? Ella bunny? Abella! Hi, bébé." Nial did not take her eyes off her. "I should not have to call your name more than once, young lady."

"Mama?" Abella Rose said facetiously.

"Hi, Nial, how was your flight?" Lea asked.

"It was long and exhausting, Lea...Ella? Come." Nial patted the seat next to her.

"Yes, Mama?" Abella Rose slowly crawled toward her. "I want a glass of wine," she blurted out.

"What?" Nial, Alexandria, and Nathaniel said at the same time.

"Wine, I want a glass," Abella Rose repeated.

"We need to change this conversation fast. Ella, what is going on?" Nial sat up straight, waiting for a response.

"I'm joking, Mama!" Abella Rose exclaimed sarcastically.

"Did you miss me?" Nial inquired as she held her hand.

"Yes, I missed you. Did you miss me?"

"Yes, of course, I did, but...you are behaving strangely, Ella."

"No, I'm not behaving strangely. I'm upset. I need a glass of wine. It will help calm me like it does for you and Mommy."

"Out of the question, young lady," Alexandria interrupted.

"Okay, Mommy. No wine this time."

"No wine, no time." Alexandria frowned.

"You are upset with me?" Nial raised her eyebrow.

"Yes, Mama. I am upset." Abella Rose kicked Nial.

"Ella, I'm sorry. Mama had a lot of business to take care of in Russia. Someday you'll be traveling too because you'll work for Mama. But I am here now, and you can have me all to yourself."

Abella Rose laid her head on her lap. "Okay, Mama."

Nial leaned over, whispering in Abella Rose's ear, "If you ever kick me again, you will fucking regret it. Now give me luff."

"Okay, Mama," Abella Rose whispered back. "But…Mama?"

"Yes, sweetie?"

"I don't want to work in fashion because I like spending time with our family."

"Me too!" Nathaniel yelled before getting up from the blanket.

Nial gleamed at Alexandria, and she stared back at Nial as they listened to Abella Rose express herself. Nathaniel climbed onto Nial's lap and laid his head against her chest.

"So what do you want to do, Ella?"

"I want to work with people who do not have a home, like Mommy did for the old lady with too much sugar in her belly."

"You can do whatever you choose, Ella." Nial winked.

"Shhhh! Can we watch a movie?" Nathaniel frowned. "I don't care what you do when you grow up. Just hush for now." He grabbed Nial's arm, wrapping it around his stomach.

"Yes, sweetie." Nial planted kisses all over his face and neck, and he giggled loudly.

"The sushi's here." Alexandria ran to the door.

"Give me kisses, Ella. Mama missed you, sweetie." Nial held on to Abella Rose, planting kisses on her cheek.

Abella Rose grinned a little and whispered in her ear, pulling Nial closer. "Don't stay away so long anymore, Mama, and I'll never have to kick you again." She kissed her cheek.

"Don't play with me, Ella."

"Okay, Mama."

"I'll help you, Alex." Lea ran into the kitchen to get the plates and napkins while the twins stretched out on Nial as if she was the sofa.

Afterward, they continued to watch movies and eat. Nial ate a bite of sushi and dozed off soon after.

The wedding shower

As soon as Alexandria and Nial pulled onto the gated lot, Nial noticed a jet out back, two limousines parked in front, and a motorcycle. "Alex, what have you done?"

"Okay, I'll tell you this…I did fly in a couple of girls and guys from Saudi Arabia. We have a caterer and a live DJ."

"Bébé, you did not."

"Yes, I did. Do you have any idea how much Aamir loves Brazilian women? I think that's why he loves Bryn so much because she looks Brazilian." Alexandria excitedly jumped out of the limousine when she saw Aamir and Bryn pull up to the lot. Sammy landed in his helicopter. Cari pulled up in a new Bugatti with the top down. Nial snarled a little when Cari stepped out of her car.

"You invited, Cari? Why?"

"Because she's close friends with Aamir, and I like her. She's sweet." Alexandria kissed Nial's lips.

"Ayo!" Cari yelled out. Her yellow sunglasses matched her half-buttoned shirt. Her chest was bare. A small gold chain dangled from her neck. The sun beamed against her skin, and her hair was pulled into a giant ball.

As soon as they stepped inside the building, Nial, Aamir, and Bryn noticed there were dancer poles, food, a stage, and a live DJ in tow. The music played loud, and the lights were perfect. It was like their own personal nightclub. Bryn looked at Aamir. Aamir looked at Cari and Sammy, and they could not contain their laughter.

"Alex, what is this?" Bryn asked.

"It's your wedding shower. I invited a few people, not too many. Come so I can introduce you to everyone." Alexandria made her way around the room. "I made sure everyone signed NDAs, so you don't have to worry."

Once Alexandria introduced everyone, the party began. When they entered the building, a stack of presents piled to the ceiling sat in the corner of the room. Balloons filled with confetti floated on the ceiling top. A DJ played the hottest songs, and the caterers catered to everybody's needs. There was wine, vodka, Hennessey, uppers, downers. You name it, they had it. Alexandria and Nial danced all evening. Aamir and Bryn sat close until one of the Brazilian models sat between them.

"You two are getting married, right?" Syd, one of the dancers, pried. The glitter on her body rubbed off on Aamir's shirt as he sipped from a bottle of whiskey.

"Yes, we are," Bryn interrupted.

"You guys ready to have some fun with us tonight?" Syd screamed.

"Well, Syd, that depends on what the fun is," Bryn said.

"Come on, it's your party. Anything goes." She shook her boobs and snatched her bikini off.

Alexandria was already drunk. She and Nial kissed and flirted on the dance floor. They were so affectionate, it was contagious. Cari and Sammy played a drinking game with two of the dancers.

Karma, another one of the dancers, walked up to Nial and started dancing on the pole beside her. Alexandria sat back on the couch, watching. Aroused by the movement in her wife's hips, she reached in her bag, pulled out bundles of cash, and tossed the bills at the dancer. She sipped her wine, watching as Nial danced with the woman.

"Wow!" Bryn said.

"What's up with that?" Cari plopped down beside Aamir.

"Typical behavior." Aamir kissed Bryn's hand.

"Let's dance." Bryn kissed his neck.

"Come on, beautiful." Aamir pulled Bryn by the hand, leading her to the dance floor. He wrapped his arms around her waist as they moved with the sounds of music.

Cari watched as Nial pulled the dancer and Alexandria close. "Bébé." She gave Alexandria a seductive eye and kissed her lips softly. Karma grabbed them both by the hand and led them to a room with a large Jacuzzi. The room had a California king-size bed and a fireplace with a bar installed inside the wall.

Karma kissed Alexandria on her neck, and Nial watched as she undressed. Nial inched behind Alexandria while Karma paid extensive attention to her frontal frame. Nial leaned over Alexandria's shoulder and stuck her tongue inside Karma's mouth. "Bébé, are you sure you're okay with this?" Nial asked before proceeding.

"Shut up and kiss me." Alexandria pulled Nial down on the bed, and Karma climbed on top of Nial's back, licking her between her cheeks from behind. Nial grabbed Karma's head and pulled it closer as she hummed into Alexandria's emotional spot, sucking softly but fast. Karma licked every inch of Nial until she released all over her face. When Nial whipped all over the bed, Alexandria let out an inarticulate moan, grabbing Nial's head, pulling her closer, squirting everywhere.

"I luff you, bébé!" Nial creamed again until she could no longer keep her body afloat.

* * *

Cari and Bryn enjoyed their drinks as they watched Syd give Aamir a lap dance. Syd fed him strawberries and revealed her life story all at once.

"Are you okay?" Cari asked Bryn.

"Yes…I'm having fun."

"Good."

"Where's Alex and Nial?" Cari wondered.

"I'm not sure. Maybe in the back."

"In the back?"

"In the back with Karma."

"Threesome?"

"Sometimes, not all the time, at least that's what Aamir said. Who knows?" Bryn shrugged. "I'm not into threesomes, though!" she yelled above the music so that Aamir would get an earful.

"Aamir?" Cari sipped from her beer, watching the dancers closely as they came near her.

"Yep, they have an understanding but don't allow each other to have sex outside of the relationship," Aamir interrupted Bryn and Cari's conversation.

"I don't do threesomes, my love."

"I hear you loud and clear. Neither do I, beautiful."

"I love you, king."

"I love you, my beautiful queen."

Karma walked from the back and started dancing again. A few minutes later, Nial and Alexandria returned with a fresh face and new clothes.

"Are you guys okay?" Alexandria asked.

"Yes, we're good. Are you?" Bryn asked.

"Yes, we're druuuunk!" Alexandria laughed aloud.

"Would you guys like to stay here tonight? Nial and I are staying."

"Sure!" Cari held up her glass.

"Yea, I'm not driving back," Aamir agreed.

"Sounds like a winner." Sammy tried to hide his hard-on.

The following day, Alexandria woke up early and washed the night before off her face. The living room was quiet, but Cari was there. Her shirt was off, and her small, firm breast seeped from under the sheet. She slept peacefully with one arm covering her eyes. Her stomach was toned, and her legs were stiff as she lay stretched across the sofa. Alexandria tapped her on the shoulder. Cari quickly grabbed her tank top from the floor, sliding it over her head. "Are you awake?" Alexandria sat down beside her.

"I woke up early." Cari held up the mug and sipped from it.

"I see you had a good time last night. You seem to have missed the bedroom. Did you sleep out here?"

"Yes, I did. Thank you for inviting me."

"I'm glad you came."

"Me too."

"Maybe when we get back, we should go shopping or have lunch. I know this great vegan place. You are vegetarian, right?"

"Yes, I am a verdure enthusiast. How'd you know?"

"I may have read your bio on your website."

"Stalking me, Alexandria?" Cari chuckled.

"No." Alexandria's cheeks flushed red. "I think you're nice. I don't have many friends, and I like you."

"I like you too, Alexandria. A little more than I should, I think."

"I'm married, Cari."

"I'm shitting you. Duh. I got you again." She sipped from the mug.

"You really must stop doing that, jerk."

"Okay, I promise."

"Pinky promise."

"Pinky promise." Cari intertwined her finger between Alexandria's. Alexandria felt a chill run down her spine as their fingers touched. Her body quivered as if trying to shake off the feeling. But deep down, she knew that she and Cari had a connection. The connection the two women had would remain dormant.

CHAPTER 28

Darkness Falls

Georgia faxed Alexandria several papers to review before finalizing their expansion to Los Angeles, New York City, and Georgia. Now that Alexandria's marketing plan had unfolded, the board members were ecstatic about the firm's high numbers. Crusade Marketing & Consulting Firm was becoming an elite business due to Alexandria's skillful tactics. She sorted through hundreds of files as she contemplated which task to tackle next when her secretary buzzed her phone. "Georgia's on the line, Alex."

"Thanks, Ivan, send it through." Alexandria scrolled through her text messages from Cari while listening to Georgia.

"Alex! Do you have the copies for the New York office?"

"Yes, Georgia, I'm sending the files to you now. The pamphlets are also done."

"There's no rush. Would you like to grab lunch?"

"I'm not hungry."

"Well, I'm off to lunch. Give those pamphlets to my assistant before you leave."

"Okay, Georgia."

Alexandria lay across her couch, staring at the high ceilings until she drifted off to sleep. Instantly she heard a knock at her office door. She jumped up, pulled her skirt down, and opened the door. Ivan stood with a box in his hand.

"Sign here, Alex." He gave her the pen, and she signed off, watching Ivan pass the electronic clipboard back to the courier. Ivan bit his lip as he stared at the courier until she had disappeared.

"You should've asked for her number." Alexandria grinned, clutching the box under her arm. She placed the box down beside her before rushing past Ivan and a few coworkers that stood nearby, gossiping when she realized she had forgotten the package beside her desk. She fled back inside the office, grabbed the box, and caught the elevator to her Porsche.

She met Lea and the twins at the estate and kissed them goodbye before their gymnastics meet. After taking a soak in the bath, she sat in the theater room with the box beside her. She stared at the TV and placed her laptop aside, holding a pen from the penholder to slice the tape from around the tightly sealed package. The box smelled unusual; it was a strange but familiar scent. The bag was orange and appeared to be burned on the edges, and there was no return address. A pack of folders, a flash drive, and a large envelope filled the box. Alexandria pulled the thumb drive out and placed it on the ottoman by her foot as she sliced open the three-page letter. Pink and purple feathers fell out. She brushed the feathers aside, flipping the message open, and read silently. Her eyes went from small to broad in the blink of an eye. Throwing the letter to the floor as if it had shocked her fingertips, she fumbled through the rest of the belongings inside the box. The more items emerged, the knots in her abdomen squeezed tighter and she puked. Her eyes filled with water as vomit hung from her bottom lip, leaving a mess. "Oh my god!" Trembling, she spilled her tea. The glass hit the floor, breaking into tiny pieces. Her chest tightened. It felt like that day her parents left her at the airport years ago.

Hyperventilating, snot dripped from her nose onto the papers. She grabbed the feathers and ran into a room filled with designer clothes. Tearing through the closet space, she found a fur coat. She balled it up and threw it inside their bathtub, lit a match, and watched it burn, peering into the fire as if her pupils would strengthen the blaze. The flames were almost as hot as the steam emitting from her flesh. She lit a cigarette, waiting for the fur to disintegrate before running water over it.

Next, she went back into the theater room, sitting down, zombified. Finally, she got up, paced the floor back and forth, then sat again. Her eyes had to be playing tricks on her, she thought. She wanted to call Nial but could not manage to pick up the phone. Her eyes blurry, she reached for what looked like two flash drives instead of one as she scooped it up and stuck it into her laptop. A video showed. The laptop hit the floor, breaking in two. Looking around at the pieces of artwork on the wall, the furniture, the vases, and the thousand-dollar floors, countertops, appliances, their clothes inside the bedroom closet. The bed kept her for the rest of the day. Lea and the twins had come and gone the entire evening.

That night, the twins lay in bed beside her and fell fast asleep. Her thoughts swirled inside her head as if she was on a roller-coaster ride that would not stop. The twins resembled sleeping puppies as they huddled close to her.

The following day, she woke up late. Lea and the twins had already left for school. Abella Rose left a note beside the bed written in crayon:

> Mummy luk tire. I LUV u.
> Ella bunny.

The note had yogurt stains and fruit juice covering it, which made Alexandria smile a little. She muscled the strength to jump in the shower when she heard the garage door open. It was Nial. Alexandria could hear her stilettos colliding with the hardwood floors.

"Bébé!" She crept into the kitchen with a hand full of bags, throwing her things on the floor. Alexandria's hair was still wet as she sat in the corner of the room in silence, breathing profoundly, watching Nial's every move. "I slept at the office. The business ran over last night." The room was quiet. It had no passion, no sense of pleasantry.

"You're home?" Alexandria drank from the bottle of red whiskey.

"Alex...what is going on? It's a little early for the bottle, isn't it?"

"Lea will take the twins to Joan's Art Camp today after school."

"Give me luff." Nial attempted to kiss Alexandria, but she turned her head away.

She handed Nial the letter she'd read repeatedly. "READ IT!" Alexandria shouted. "The box belongs to you as well." She gulped more whiskey from the bottle.

"What is this?" Nial kneeled in front of Alexandria. Alexandria shoved her to the floor.

"READ IT!" Alexandria sat back in the chair, waiting.

Nial flipped through the letter, reading it aloud.

> This may come as a shock to you, Alexandria, but I am an investigator hired by Agatone before he went missing. The box's contents contain information from the past and Nial Paul's present, pictured with several women callers in the photos.

Nial stopped reading the letter as her eyeballs widened. "READ!" Alexandria screamed.

> Warning: graphic images. Nial has been involved in many criminal acts that can cause you and your family much harm. She is a member of the Colombian Cartel, wanted for the murder of Rebecca Weinberg, and sex trafficking is only the tip of the iceberg. Taiyo Chao, you may learn that she is an undercover agent assigned to investigate Nial after authorities in the United Kingdom discovered Nial committed fraud and extortion, taking and accepting millions from offshore accounts. Taiyo has gone missing, and the evidence is inadmissible in court without her. Your wife is not who she says she is, Alexandria. Beware. The evidence that has been provided is

for you, Alexandria, to follow up as you see fit.
The videos will explain more.

Nial threw the letter down as tears rushed down her face. "Is this a joke?" Nial laughed.

"Yes, the world's fucking funniest." Teary-eyed, Alexandria gritted her teeth like the joker and gulped from the whiskey bottle.

"I can explain."

"You are a true protean," Alexandria scoffed as tears continued to run down her face.

"That letter…Alexandria." Nial paced the floor, sniffling. "It is filled with misconceptions and lies." Her hands shook. It was as though rage had taken over. "How do you think we live like this? Mary Poppins could never."

"Why do I keep ending up with psychos and sociopaths? You disgust me!" Alexandria picked up the box and threw the contents at Nial's face, but she blocked it with her hand, knocking the items to the floor—several images of Nial in bed lying between Francesca's legs with whip cream all over their bodies. She snorted cocaine from the bodies of unknown women Alexandria had never seen before—inside bathroom stalls, lying on beaches, by the poolside outside their guest home, Josephine on a beach in Santa Monica, and several models that Alexandria ceased to know existed. Nial and Elizabeth were practically naked inside Club Exotica. Elizabeth wore a fur coat with similar feathers, which Alexandria burned inside the bathtub.

"Agatone was right. Oh my god, I fell in love with a monster! What planet are you from? I don't know you!" Alexandria screamed. "Francesca was right. *You fuck* anything with legs. You make me look like a fool. You fucked Elizabeth in Russia, then you come home to kiss me, MAKE LOVE TO ME?" Tears continued to race down Alexandria's face as she fell to the floor. "How could you do this to me? You gave my love away, Nial. I would do anything for you. *Why…*" Alexandria's words slurred.

Tears trickled down Nial's face. "Bébé? I did not have a choice."

"Everyone has a choice. I want you to leave." Alexandria pointed to the door.

"Alex, I luff you. I am addicted to you. You are my life."

"I don't care! I loved you with all of me!" she yelled until she could not scream anymore. Her throat was dry, hoarse, and sore.

Nial did not blink as she blocked the doorway. "Alex…I cannot leave. I luff you. Do you hear me? You are my wife. I know this looks bad. It is true. I murdered for you, for us. I did sleep with those women. I did all those things, but I can make this up to you." Nial reached for Alexandria's hand, but she snatched it away.

"I said leave!"

Nial cried irrepressibly. "I cannot leave, Alex. I will not leave! You and the twins are everything to me."

"I can't trust you anymore. I asked you several times, 'Are you cheating on me?' You said no! I trusted you, Nial!" Alexandria shouted. "I loved you!"

"Luffed me? No! You luff me, Alex. You luff me. We can get through this. I promise!" Nial's phone rang.

"Who is calling you?"

Nial looked down at her phone. "It does not matter. I'm here with you."

"Answer the fucking phone!" Alexandria demanded.

"Hello." Nial pressed the speaker on her cellular so that Alexandria could hear the person.

"Did your wife receive our lovely gift? I figured by now she should have received it," the voice revealed.

"Francesca? Why the fuck are you calling my phone?"

"Upset are we? Well, you see, it is obvious I was not the only person you were sleeping with. It is a shame your wife had to find out this way. You deserve everything you get."

"Francesca?" Alexandria pushed Nial against the wall. Nial jumped up, threw her phone down, and followed behind her wife.

"What are you doing, Alex? Where are you going?" Nial stumbled out of her heels.

"Francesca is the woman in the pictures."

"Bébé…please…I am begging you. I never beg!"

"I can't do this with you. If you do not leave, I will!" Alexandria pulled off her pajamas as she scurried down the hallway naked. Nial snatched her by the waist, and Alexandria fell against one of the French montages on the wall. It broke into tiny pieces. Nial stepped on the glass, slicing the bottom of her foot until the white meat seeped through the cut. She yelped, ignoring the pain as her blooded footsteps marked every room they entered.

Alexandria ran into the kitchen, snatching a knife from the drawer. Nial stopped in her tracks before charging like a raging bull. Scared, Alexandria threw the blade to the floor before bolting to the bedroom—Nial fast behind her. The door locked as it slammed shut. Alexandria gasped for breaths.

Nial beat her fist on the door. But she could not get inside. She rushed back to the kitchen to retrieve the knife from the floor, sticking the point in the seam of the door to pry it open. Alexandria paused as Nial hopped over the bed, where she sat with tears in her eyes. Her hand trembled as she held the knife to Alexandria's throat.

"Do it. Get it over with." Alexandria plummeted to that level, taking deep breaths.

"Please! Bébé, please let me explain." Nial attempted to grab Alexandria again. Her eyes filled with tears as she threw the knife across the floor. The fear in her wife's eyes made her heart heavy.

Alexandria, scared, struggled for breaths. "Explain."

Nial stared at Alexandria momentarily. Then her words were stuck inside her mouth.

"Fuck it! You stand there with that dumb look on your face like you are the hurt one. You do not get to be that person! I am broken. My heart…my heart has fallen to my feet, and I cannot find the strength to lift it."

"You promised you'd never leave me. You said if you knew the real me, you would not leave. Well, this is the real me, and you are leaving!" Nial screamed. "Alex, please! Do not do this!"

"I do not want you in my life anymore. No part of you. The real you. The fake you. Fuck every part of you."

"Alexandria, please do not do this. Please, Bébé, please."

"From this day forward, I am no longer your baby."

"Are you crazy? We are not getting a divorce. I will kill you first."

"Great, now you're going to murder me just like Agatone tried to? What a fucking cosmic joke!"

"No, no, I am sorry. I did not mean that. I would never harm you. I luff you."

"Tuh, right. Says the woman that held a knife to my neck," Alexandria scoffed as she sat on their bed in silence.

Nial surrendered. "Okay, Alex, if you really want me to leave, I will leave. But I will not divorce you. I want to see my bébés."

"I will be in my office. Lea will have them home shortly. And don't notify me when you're gone. Just fucking leave!"

Nial began packing her garments when she heard the twins running through their home.

"Mommy!" the twins screamed for Alexandria as they searched throughout the house.

"Mommy? Mommy. Oh, Mama?" They stopped instantly. "We didn't know you were home." Abella Rose placed her bag down on the floor, running toward Nial.

"Yay! I'm glad you are home, Mama. I have so many things to show you. We did a lot while you were away. We painted da playroom for you again," Nathaniel said. He tugged at Nial's skirt. "Mama, what's wrong?" he asked when he noticed Nial did not smile when she saw him.

"I'm sorry, my bébés. I am emotional today. Mama would luff to see the playroom. I want to hear all about your artwork. Lea told me you guys did a wonderful job." She held both of their tiny hands, and they led the way.

While Nial and the twins admired their color schemes, Lea gave Alexandria a full report on their day at camp before saying her good-byes. Afterward, Alexandria walked downstairs to see if Nial had left yet. She overheard the twins talking as she sat beside the playroom wall, listening. The twins showed off their paintings and new desk chairs that resembled the big office upstairs.

Nathaniel turned around to see Alexandria crying. "Mommy, are you feeling emotional today too?" he asked.

Alexandria wiped her face as she walked closer. "Yes, Mommy's feeling emotional today, bunny. But I don't want Mommy's emotions to spoil your and Ella's day. So do me a favor and ignore Mommy because I may feel emotional for a little while longer. So if I'm acting a little strange, forgive me. *Muah.*" Alexandria kissed him while staring into his eyes.

Abella Rose grabbed Nial's hand, tugging at it. "Mama?" Why don't you give Mommy a hug? That way, you can both hug your sad faces away."

"Ella, Mama needs to speak with you and Nate, okay? Come sit with me. Let's talk inside your and Nate's office." Nial attempted a smile.

Alexandria continued to stand in the doorway next to the glass wall. The twins sat at their tiny desks with complete focus on Nial as she sat between them. "I luff you so very, very much. And I want you to always remember that."

"Why? You are acting weird," Nathaniel asked.

"Mama, what's going on?" Abella Rose asked.

Nial gently grabbed her face. "I must leave for a while. I hurt Mummy. We are both emotional."

"What did you do?" Abella Rose asked.

"Did you hit Mommy?" Nathaniel asked.

"What? Nate, nooo...I would never hit Mummy. Let's not get into what I did. As long as you know I luff you and your Mummy so much—"

Alexandria interrupted, "We love you very, very much. And just because your mama is leaving doesn't mean you can't see her. Right, Nial?"

"Yes, you guys can see me whenever you like. I will secure an apartment close by, so anytime you need me, I'll be near."

"Noooooooooooo, Mama! You can't leave." Nathaniel jumped into Nial's arms, throwing a fit, kicking, and screaming. Nial held him tight until he became calm.

"You did this," Alexandria said before leaving the room.

"Why can't you work it out?" Nathaniel whispered in Nial's ear.

"That is what people do when they love each other." Abella Rose climbed onto her lap.

"You cannot leave!" the twins said at once.

"Mommy will forgive you. I know she will. She always forgives you." Tears rolled down Abella Rose's face. "I hate you!" she screamed at Nial before leaping from her lap and out the playroom directly into Alexandria's waiting arms.

"Bunny, it's okay. Everything is going to be okay. But Mama and I need some space apart to sort things out." Alexandria wiped her tears away.

"But…this house is big enough for both of you to get a lot of space." Abella Rose sniffled. She buried her face into Alexandria's chest. "I hate Mama."

"No, bunny, your mama loves you and your brother very much. I know this is hard for you and Nate. You don't understand now, but later you will."

Abella Rose ran into the master suite where Nial and Alexandria slept. She climbed in bed, lying there, curled up into a ball. Alexandria covered her with a blanket and placed her favorite stuffed monkey beside her. Then she went back into the playroom to check on Nathaniel after Nial left out of the room.

"Nate, honey," Alexandria called his name, but he sat in a corner, ignoring her.

Then finally, Nial took her suitcase to the door. When Nathaniel heard the door open, he got up to run behind her, crying, pulling her coattail. "Mama, don't leave, please. I'll be a good boy. I'll help you and Mommy be happy. I can do it. I know I can. I'll do anything you want me to. I'll wash my feet when I take a bath. I promise. I'll wash my hands and face every day. So you don't have to make me do it anymore." He held on to Nial's legs tight.

She picked him up, holding him close to her heart; walked him into their bedroom; and lay in bed beside him and Abella Rose until they dozed off fast asleep.

CHAPTER 29

Checkmate

It was Alexandria's first day back to work since the private investigator revealed Nial's affairs. The twins had become sick with sadness, but Lea managed to talk them into going back to school. Nathaniel had a cough, so Alexandria gave him a cup of herbal tea with a drop of lemon juice to soothe his sore throat. Abella Rose drank tea for precaution since she slept in bed with Nathaniel after Nial left. Alexandria dropped the twins off at school after calling to remind Lea to pick them up after her last class.

The day was long, and Alexandria was tired, thinking about all the work she needed to complete when she received a phone call from the twins' school. "Hello, this is Alex." She answered her cell phone quickly.

"Yes, this is Maylene, the nurse at Upperhan Private Institute. Can you send someone to pick up Nate and Ella? They have been vomiting since this morning."

"Vomiting since this morning?" Alexandria questioned. "Why didn't you call me sooner?" she asked, angrily staring at the clock on her wall.

"We'd hope it would stop, but it has not. So just send someone, Mrs. Paul."

Alexandria paused before speaking. "Someone will be there shortly, Maylene. Thanks." She hung up the phone, quickly dialing

Nial's mobile. She had not heard Nial's voice since she left the estate a month ago, dreading hearing her accent that she once loved so much.

"This is Nial," she answered quickly.

"I need you to pick the twins up from school. I'm swamped and cannot leave. Lea's in class. I think they may have a virus," Alexandria spoke dryly.

"Alex, yes, I will go get my bébés."

"Great, let me know when you have them." Alexandria hung up quickly before Nial could get another word in.

* * *

Nial called the pediatrician on her way back to the department store after getting the twins from school. Their physician met her at the office to provide a thorough examination. After the doctor left, Nathaniel and Abella Rose lay down on Nial's sofa while she worked.

Nial waited for her assistant to contact her when a vital client arrived in the building. A multicolored patched jacket worth one hundred thousand dollars was ready to be worn by one of San Francisco's most influential people, a well-connected lobbyist that Nial did not want to disappoint. Nial checked the children's forehead to ensure their fever had subsided before leaving her office to get the jacket from the vault. "Nate and Ella are sleeping. Keep an eye on them. I will be right back," Nial said to her secretary, Bethany.

She waited for the elevator to arrive. "Hmm." She sighed. "We must do something about this elevator," she mumbled right before it appeared. She stepped on quickly as it opened. A woman stood there with two boys as a man rushed out the elevator, bumping into Nial's shoulder. She could not stop thinking about the jacket that came from her new collection that she'd named *Alexandria*. Nial pondered as she continued to press the button to take her to the ground floor, but it did not budge. She hit the button several times until her finger turned red.

The elevator slipped, and the doors opened halfway. Burning fumes filled the air. Nial attempted to pry the doors open to see where the smell came from and noticed thick wires dangling above.

She looked down. They were ten floors up from the ground, stuck between floors. Nial immediately turned to the panicking mother. "Calm the fuck down!" she yelled at the terrified woman. "I am sorry, please. I must think."

The elevator clattered as it jerked. Nial fell backward. She reached for her cell phone but had left it inside her office. "Merde!" She pressed the emergency button when a loud explosion rang through the elevator as it went crashing down underground.

"We are going to die!" The woman and her boys screamed uncontrollably.

Moments later, there was smut and smoke everywhere. The woman and her boys did not move a muscle. Ignoring them, Nial slowly crawled from underneath the debris when suddenly another explosion sounded nearby. She pushed the woman off her leg, attempting to climb onto the rails. The department store was blazing orange and red. The miasma left behind by the fire made the bystanders cover their mouths and noses. It looked like a monster's face had formed inside the thick smoke, hovering above the severed pieces. The jacket was a mere thought at this point. The only thing on Nial's mind was the twins sleeping on the sofa inside her office. Finally, she belted out a scream so loud the firemen could hear her from afar.

The firemen and an ambulance bulldozed in her direction. The men struggled to pull Nial, the woman, and her children out at once before the explosion caused any more damage.

"My bébés!" As soon as Nial was on level ground, she trampled in the direction of the smoke, but her ankle would not let her get far. "My bébés!" she cried. "They are up there!" she repeated.

"I'm sorry, ma'am, but there is too much smoke. They are trying to contain the fire," the fireman said while placing a mask on Nial's face. She pushed it away as she continued to squirm.

One of the clerks that worked inside Nial's building came running out, screaming. "There are bodies everywhere!" he screeched.

"No! My bébés…are up there." Nial fell to the ground, attempting to creep up the stairs that led to her office. Her ankle had swollen, keeping her from standing upright. Smoke filled her lungs. She became delusional. She tried to inhale when visions of Rebecca tormented her as she remembered watching Rebecca from a hotel closet having sex with one of her models.

The model scuffled as she attempted to stick Rebecca with a contaminated needle. The thick green substance poured into Rebecca's neck vein from the syringe, and soon after, a seizure followed. Rebecca's body vibrated so hard it shook the entire bed. Foam erupted from her mouth as she fell to the floor. The model grabbed her things, ran out of the room as fast as possible, and called Nial. Nial's cell phone rang as she crept out of the closet, tipping past Rebecca's fragmented body.

"It is done, boss," the model said.

"Boss, it is done. The entire building is destroyed. There is no sign of the twins anywhere," the department store clerk frantically blurted out as the emergency technician picked Nial up, carrying her to the ambulance.

"Ma'am? Ma'am, we are going to give you something for the pain." The medic scanned her body. "It looks like you may have broken your foot." The emergency technician stuck Nial's arm.

The door on the emergency van swung open. Nial yelled out, hallucinating the figments of a tall slender man walking near her, wearing an oversize fireman coat. The bottom half of his face was disfigured. He leaned over her as if he were about to kiss her. Her eyes closed tight. She muttered, "No, no!" moving her head side to side, attempting to avoid his breath and his horrendous face. "My bébés? You killed my bébés, you son of a bitch!" Nial squirmed, trying to get up from the stretcher. The man tied her hands to the rail.

"Checkmate, bitch!" the man whispered in her ear, and she passed out.

Days later, after Nial's department store had burned to the ground, she woke up inside a hospital room. The room was filled with blinding lights that bounced off the ceiling, her eyes blurry as she gazed around the room. Alexandria lay asleep in a recliner nearby. "Alexandria?" Nial called. "Alex." She picked up the remote control beside her and threw it.

Alexandria raised up quickly when the remote hit her stomach. Her eyes resembled raccoons. She hopped from the chair. "What happened to my bunnies, Nial?" Her mouth trembled as she stood over Nial's bed with tears in her eyes. "I want my bunnies, and I want them now!" she screamed as she hopped on top of Nial's stomach, punching her in the face several times before the nurses intervened. Scuffling to inflict more pain on Nial, needing her to feel worse.

Nial cried and moaned in the same breath. "Alex? I do not know what happened, bébé." Her face was swollen and solemn. It was no longer bright and filled with life.

Alexandria had an enduring scowl on her face. "How could you do this to me? You killed my bunnies. How could you?" She blamed Nial. "I will never forgive you." She hurried out of the room, leaving a trail of tears behind.

* * *

After the explosion, Nial had begun to spiral out of control. Night after night, she threw parties that lasted for days. She never grew tired of the escapades, sleeping with one of her neighbors, parading around town with models and actresses. "What do you want, Jonah?" Nial stumbled through her place with no direction. She placed little emphasis on her next move. The Los Angeles and Russian department stores continued to thrive even though she had little input. Her assistants and department managers took sales as they designed their own fashion line and stuck NPD labels on them without Nial's permission. The twins' death was a breaking point for her. Nothing mattered anymore. It was as if she had fallen to pieces without the will to put herself back together again.

"Watching you." Jonah gulped a can of beer and tossed it into the trash beside him.

"It's not polite to stare." Nial sniffed a line of cocaine, one line after the other.

"What is it with you? Why do you need to use drugs to ease your pain?" Jonah stepped into his skinny jeans. His ribs seeped through his skin along his muscular chest. He rubbed his neatly shaved head, reaching for a pack of cigarettes on the bar next to the kitchen.

"You act as if I'm on heroin or something."

"Cocaine is bad enough, don't you think?"

"No, I do not think!"

"You're so beautiful!" Jonah walked near her and wrapped his large hand around her neck, squeezing as he kissed her powdered lips.

"Are you going to fuck me or tell me how pretty I am?" She stared up at him as her face began to turn red. He let go. She grabbed a glass filled with whiskey while rubbing the imprint he had left on her skin. She got up, leaving him sitting in the great room among complete strangers.

"I don't think she's interested in you." A woman lying on the fluffy white rug laughed as she inhaled, then exhaled, blowing a cloud of smoke from her mouth.

"Why are you still here?" Jonah frowned at the woman.

"She wants me here." The woman got up swiftly and followed Nial.

"Yes, Jonah, I want Lexi here." Nial's shadow appeared in the hallway as the woman hung off her shoulder like a shawl.

"What kind of doctor are you? A gynecologist because you're acting like a pussy." Another woman walked from the back and sat on the sofa next to Jonah. You have one of the sexiest women in the world standing in front of you naked, and you want to talk. Fuck that! I'll do whatever you want me to do, baby." The woman crawled on her knees toward Nial.

"Jonah, you may leave." Nial opened her legs wide as the woman kneeled in front of her.

"I'll leave." Jonah scooped his shoes up off the floor, grabbed his jacket, and slammed the door behind him.

"Yes, you do that," Nial said as the door closed. "I'm tired of everyone telling me what to do! Wait…" She paused. "What am I saying? No one tells me what to do!" She laughed so hard she began to cough when there was a knock at the door.

The three women looked at one another and laughed. "I guess he is coming back to beg." The woman lying between Nial's legs giggled. The knocks became louder, and Nial jumped out of her drugged-out stupor.

"Open up!" a loud voice yelled.

Nial pushed the girl over onto the floor. She answered the door. "WHAT?" Her eyes glazed over.

"Nial Paul?" the person asked.

"Yes, what the fuck do you want?" Nial's words smeared.

"You are under arrest for fraud, conspiracy to murder, and kidnapping in the first degree. Anything you say will be held against you. If you don't have an attorney, you will be appointed one." The man grabbed Nial's arms, placing her in handcuffs.

"She's fucking naked. At least let her put on clothes. Have you no decency?" Lexi grabbed a long jacket from the coatrack and drenched it around Nial's shoulders.

Nial did not say a word. Instead, she allowed the officer to handcuff her. Then she blew a kiss at the ladies before the officers took her away.

CHAPTER 30

Win or Lose

Bryn wrote in her writing room for hours until she realized Aamir's final cup race for the season was showing live. She ran into her entertainment room and turned the television volume up. "Just in time!" She eyed the television. "The red and yellow sports logo. Okay, there's my king." Sitting on the edge of her seat, she zoomed in on her fiancé. "Come on, king. You got this. I know you can do it. Sam the Ghost Rider, he has nothing on you, baby!" During the commercial break, she hopped up, ran to the pantry inside the kitchen, and grabbed a bag of popcorn. Then she scurried back to the TV and sat on the sofa, staring at the screen.

The broadcaster came back on to make an announcement. Bryn dropped her popcorn on the plush carpet, trembling with fear. Her hands unsteady, she picked up her phone to call Mimi, but there was no answer. "Damn it! Answer the phone!" She threw her cell phone down, grabbed an overnight bag, and fled out the door. She drove maximum speed on the freeway, arriving at the airport fifteen minutes later. Instantly a text chimed on her phone.

"Hi, Bryn, it's Mimi. Aamir was in a terrible accident. Meet me at the airport ASAP. Call me when you get here."

"On my way."

Bryn walked swiftly through the security gate, stated her name, and provided identification before snatching her ticket from the service agent. Nervous sweat saturated her forehead as she came upon Mimi standing in the distance.

* * *

Aamir was laid out on a stretcher, unresponsive. The paramedics tried to do all they could to resuscitate him. His agent, Martha, was right beside him with her hands in the praying position, waiting on Aamir to make a noise, sarcastic joke, or something that gave her hope that he was alive.

"It's okay, Mr. Bahar. You are at Tampa Memorial." The nurse watched his eyes roll in the back of his head. "You were in an accident. We are going to sedate you and give you something for the pain. Let us take care of you."

The medical team rushed him to the back of the hallway as blood covered his uniform. Martha waited in the waiting area for the doctor to give her an update. Several hours passed; and the doctor, along with his nurse, joined Martha in the lobby.

"Mr. Bahar has suffered severely. His left leg is broken. He has an abrasion to his forehead. In addition, his left arm was wounded severely."

"Okay, fix it." Martha panicked.

"He lost a lot of blood, and the tendons and the muscles are severed. So the plan is to save it," the doctor explained.

"HIS ARM? YES, SAVE IT!" Martha screamed. "You're supposed to be a professional—the best!" Martha held her chest.

"I am so sorry, ma'am. I am a huge fan of Mr. Bahar, and we are trying everything. If you will allow me to give you the full report."

"Sure." Martha sat down.

"His pelvic area is bruised, and his ribs are crushed."

Martha listened to every word. "Will he ever race again?" She quivered.

"Ma'am, we will notify you of any changes that may occur, but we must continue to monitor Mr. Bahar carefully."

"I'll be right here." Martha paced the floor. "This can't be happening..." she mumbled under her breath right before her phone rang. "Hello."

"Martha, this is Mimi calling. I am on my way to you. Where are you?"

"Tampa Memorial, the private sector. Give me a call when you've reached the facility, and I'll come to meet you downstairs." As time passed, Martha waited impatiently for the surgery to end. She rotated cigarettes until she had no more left in the pack.

The doctor walked inside the room, where Martha sat waiting. "Miss? Can I speak with you for a moment in private?"

"Yes, Doctor, I've been waiting to hear from you."

"Mr. Bahar is not in a great state. We are doing everything we can to keep him alive. He may need more surgeries performed. We must keep him on a ventilator for now because his lungs are damaged."

"I'm sorry, Doctor, but I'm still waiting for the good news. You've told me everything wrong. I need to know what's right."

"I'm sorry, but for now, this is as good as it gets. Until further notice—"

"Just wonderful." Martha sat down on the arm of the chair with her head down.

"One more thing, traces of alcohol were found in Aamir's bloodstream—a considerable amount. Ethically, we report this sort of thing."

"There must be some mistake. Aamir would never—"

"Tests don't lie, ma'am. It is a strong possibility that his inebriation caused the accident."

"You cannot report this. Aamir's career will be over."

"His career is already over. It is possible Aamir will not race again with that arm."

"No, his endorsements, they'd be taken away. You can't, Doctor. You just can't." Martha squeezed the doctor's hand until it turned purple. "I will give you anything, just name it."

"It is illegal to bribe."

"Anything you want, I will make it happen." She stared into his eyes.

"I'll keep in touch." He walked away.

Martha and her boyfriend, Gary, were inside a private room near the critical intensive care unit. Pain and sadness wander the hospital unit with no remorse as family and friends awaited their loved one's medical prognosis. After a while, Gary went downstairs to get Martha a coffee and a few magazines while waiting. Suddenly Mimi rushed through the revolving doors with Bryn running beside her. Mimi ran over to Martha and her boyfriend. "Who is this you have with you, Mimi?" Martha asked.

"This is Bryn, Aamir's girlfriend, remember?"

"His fiancé," Bryn corrected her.

"You're gorgeous…" Martha ogled.

"Thank you, how is he?"

"I may as well get to it…Aamir isn't doing well. He's on the ventilator machine."

"The ventilator!" Bryn sobbed instantly. Mimi rubbed her shoulders, passing her a tissue.

Martha continued to speak, "The doctor said he should be coming off the ventilator, but since his lungs are injured, it's hard for him to breathe on his own. But—"

"But what?" Mimi asked.

"His left arm is poorly damaged." Martha hesitated.

"What about his left arm?" Bryn moved closer to Martha as she continued to speak.

"They are trying to save it." Martha held her head down.

They walked to the hallway that would lead them to the nurse station. Bryn detoured away in the opposite direction. As soon as she reached the door, she saw a sign that read Private Intensive Care Unit while searching for Aamir's room. She noticed the unit's security standing nearby. "Excuse me, sir. Can you direct me to Aamir Bahar room, please?"

"I'm sorry, miss, but that room is off-limits." One of the nurses overheard Bryn and blocked the entranceway to Aamir's room, but Bryn pushed past her.

The sight of Aamir blindsided her. Standing in a pool of tears, empathetic to the hurt and pain he endured, she released her feelings all at once. He was bandaged from head to toe with tubes extending and intercepting as they ran through his nose and mouth. Every area on his body was bruised, and his left arm was missing. Bryn took a long hard look, scanning over his entire frame. "Oh, baby," she mumbled, stuck in a daze.

"Miss? You cannot be up here. We must escort you out." The security officer tapped Bryn's shoulder, and she backed away.

"No! I must let him know that I'm here! I can't just do nothing!" Bryn's behavior became erratic, and the security officer picked her up, removing her immediately.

"No crazy fans on this floor," the lead nurse ordered.

CHAPTER 31

Fallen

Months had passed since Alexandria spoke with anyone. The detriment and betrayal she endured brought upon an anatomical depressive state seduced by drugs and alcohol. Luckily, her partnership with Georgia allowed her the luxury to work from home for as long as she needed. Alexandria jumped out of bed, hitting the floor. A bottle of pills had spilled on the table beside her. A line of cocaine sat next to a bottle of whiskey. Her pajamas were drenched in sweat as she panicked. "Shit!" she mumbled, barely keeping her eyes open. *If only time capsules existed*, she thought of the twins. The cell phone rang repeatedly. "Yes," she answered quickly.

"Alex," a voice calmly spoke.

"Cari?" Alexandria questioned.

"Yes, I've been trying to contact you. Can we meet? I have something important to tell you." Cari waited for a reply.

"No." Alexandria threw the phone across the room, knocking over a vase as she popped more pills into her mouth, staring out the large bay window like a zombie.

* * *

Alexandria accepted Detective Hallow's invite for dinner and drinks. The narcotics numbed her as she drove to Detective Hallow's apartment. Oblivious to the approaching traffic, swerving in and out of lanes, vehicles dodged out of her way. She placed a bottle of whiskey underneath the passenger seat as she entered Detective Hallow's garage unscathed. She got out and rang the doorbell. Detective Hallow greeted Alexandria with a warm hug. "Hi Jennifer. Smells delicious in here. What's on the menu?" Alexandria asked.

"It's a special dish I learned to cook in Beijing." Detective Hallow passed her a glass of wine.

"So you cook dinner for all your special ladies?"

"Yes, I do, if I'm honest."

"Honesty is the best policy." Alexandria paused shortly after, gazing into space. Her mind drifted as she replayed moments of Agatone. At first, he gave her butterflies and anticipating moments. Then after a while, everything calmed down. She felt safe and secure until he relinquished his wrath upon her.

"Alex, I need to tell you something. I know that you no longer want to be associated with your parents in any way."

"You are right."

"You will want to know that your mother murdered your father and that she's apparently hiding in another country."

"Wow. Can my life get any better?"

"No. Before finalizing the investigation, we found your mother's DNA and traces of ricin. I'd hoped that you could share your mother's location with me."

"So this is why you invited me over? No, I have not spoken to my mom since that day at the police station. They disowned me. I have no idea where she could be, and if I did, I would not tell you." Alexandria began to hyperventilate when suddenly the front door flew open. Startling her, she jumped from her seat. She breathed in intervals, producing the deep-breathing exercises Dr. Winters taught her. A tall man wearing steel-toe boots overshadowed Alexandria.

"Hello." His voice was deep.

"Hi." Alexandria continued to breathe, silently staring at the man from head to toe.

"Jenni?" He spoke.

"William? What are you doing here so soon?" Detective Hallow's eyes widened.

"Introduce me to your friend." William grabbed a beer from the fridge, chugging it.

"This is Alex. Alex, this is William, my husband."

"Nice." Alexandria's voice squeaked. "It's nice to meet you, William, the husband. I must get going. It's getting late."

"You don't have to leave. Maybe you can join my lovely wife and me in some extracurricular activities. I see why my wife wants to fuck you."

"I'm not interested, but thanks."

"Alex, can we have a chat, please?" Detective Hallow led Alexandria to the balcony.

"Jennifer, I'm not sure what's going on here, but I'm not interested."

"That's probably why your wife cheated on you. Live a little!"

"You have no idea what happened between my wife and me."

"Then tell me."

"No, I will not discuss my wife—her—with you. It doesn't matter. Besides, it's over now." *I miss laying my back against her soft breast, her deep breaths comforting me as I feel her heartbeat. She was my home as we curled up in each other's arms. No more roller-coaster rides and slippery slides. Our legs no longer intertwine where hers begin and mine end. No more sweet smells aroused from her body and no more lasting orgasms to take over my entire existence. No more bunnies interrupting us as we experience a piece of heaven while cumulating together.*

"Alex? Alexandria?" Detective Hallow snapped her finger in front of Alexandria's face until she gained composure. "How about you and I go inside, have a few more drinks, and let's see what happens? No pressure."

"Fine."

"I apologize for not telling you about William. I promise you we'll enjoy tonight if you trust me."

"What do you have in mind?"

Detective Hallow grabbed Alexandria's hand, leading her back inside, pulling her close when Alexandria's phone rang.

"I'm…I'm sorry. I have to get this." She traipsed toward her bag, grabbing her cell phone. "Hello, hello, this is Alex." She listened attentively, stumbling into her heels, reaching for the doorknob. "I have to go." Her voice quivered.

"Call me!" Detective Hallow yelled. William grabbed Detective Hallow and swung her over his shoulder. She laughed as he carried her to the bedroom and threw her down on the bed, ripping her panties off. He shoved himself inside of her, fucking her aggressively. She let out a disturbing moan, perplexing the neighbors.

Alexandria pulled onto the estate. A silver SUV was parked outside with a shadow of a person in the driver's seat with dark shades. She ambled near and knocked on the tinted window. The glass streaked down, and Taiyo unlocked the door.

"Get in," she said to Alexandria.

"Come inside," Alexandria suggested.

"I rather not. I'm going to make this short. Your wife is in jail."

"I'm not surprised." Alexandria lit a cigarette.

"You put her there, didn't you?" Taiyo smirked.

"Why would I do that?"

"We need you to divorce her, so you can testify against her in court. Some of the charges will not stick. We need them to stick so justice can be served."

Alexandria burst into uncontrollable laughter. "You need me? I don't know anything. Nial kept me in the dark." As she spoke, she realized why Nial kept the dark secrets to herself. As a result, Alexandria could not testify against her, and if given a polygraph test, she'd pass. *Slick bitch.*

"I don't believe you."

"I cannot help you." Alexandria blew smoke in Taiyo's face. "Unlock my fucking door!" She jumped out as soon as Taiyo released the lock.

* * *

The following day, Alexandria grabbed the remote to the television, attempting to turn it on. Nothing happened, so she checked the batteries and replaced them with new ones. The TV still did not work. Frustrated, she ran to the bathroom to drain the bubble when she noticed the motion sensors did not detect her movement, and the lights did not fade on. "Shit!" she screamed. "None of the fucking bills have been paid."

The electricity had been shut off. Usually payments were automatically drafted from her business account, yet they hadn't been. Afterward, she checked the joint bank account and logged into her personal accounts but was unsuccessful. Then, she contacted the branch where she and Nial still kept their stocks, bonds, and extravagant jewelry. After speaking with the bank managers and receiving no help, she called Aamir, but there was no answer.

Her Bible lay on the bedside table. She picked it up, reading through pages, and then threw it against the wall as if the words had pissed her off. A key fell out of the Bible. She examined its unusual shape; it was flat with three sharp edges and a human skull in its center. Her finger traced across the skull head before she placed it in a jewelry box inside a safe next to the dresser. Calling Bryn, her phone went directly to voice mail. She fumbled with the phone before putting on clothes and darting out the door.

Moments later, she reached Aamir's beach house. Cari's motorcycle was parked next to Bryn's BMW out front. A man and a woman in white jackets exited a large van and quickly entered his home. Alexandria stepped out of her Porsche, lurking toward the front entrance. She peeked inside and saw no one. She used the spare key that Aamir gave her years ago when he purchased the estate.

"Aamir? Bryn?" she called, but no one responded. "Cari?" The hallway was silent as she treaded toward Aamir's bedroom. She gasped when someone covered her mouth and pulled her into one of the guest rooms.

"Shh, it's only me," Cari whispered.

"What the fuck, Cari?" Alexandria snatched away. "I almost peed my fucking pants. Why are you so cryptic?" She squeezed her legs tight, running to the bathroom in the squatting position. It had been a while since Alexandria saw Cari as she watched her from the commode. The crack in the door gave her a different perspective of

Cari. At that moment, she was drawn to her. Alexandria thought it may be the thick blond disorderly dreadlocks hanging underneath the backward baseball cap or the crisp white sneakers complementing her black, khaki pants and a white polo shirt.

"Are you okay, Alex?" Cari peeped through the door, and their eyes met as if imprinting on each other.

"Yes, yes, I'm coming out."

Cari walked up to Alexandria, pushed her hair behind her ear, whispering so that no one could hear. Alexandria closed her eyes, absorbing the information that Cari provided. Tears ran down her face, and Cari held her tight. "I'm so sorry, Alex. I tried to contact you."

"Take me to him. No, don't take me. Yes, take me to him."

"Come with me." Cari grabbed her hand and led the way.

* * *

Everything is different now. Aamir's life had changed in the blink of an eye, and my life changed from one day to the next. How can I face him? How can I tell him my babies are not alive? How can I reveal such heartbreak when he is in so much pain—emotionally, physically, and mentally? Is this the result of my relationship with Nial? Am I doomed to be cursed *because of my love for a woman? If so, my mom was right, and I will never be with another woman ever again,* Alexandria thought as she closed her eyes tight. She took deep breaths before she and Cari entered the large bedroom.

Aamir sat on the sofa near his patio, wearing a black-and-yellow tracksuit. His eyes were gloomy, staring at the physical therapist and nurse aides as they prepped him for the day. The nurse scooped a sizeable red bag filled with bloody bandages out of the trash. The physical therapist grabbed her items from beside him, wiped them off, and placed them in her medical bag.

Alexandria could not believe her eyes. Squinting, she rubbed them as if trying to rub the sight of Aamir's missing arm away. A part of him that once worked was no longer attached to his body—the component that drove a race car like he was floating on air; created blueprints and layouts of buildings, homes, and landscapes; and gave hugs and foot rubs that melted your pain away. The arm that made him a billionaire. Alexandria stared without blinking when a tap pounced her shoulder. She damn near jumped out of her skin.

"Alex?" Bryn spoke softly as if the life had been sucked out her lungs. She looked different as her hazel eyes sank underneath puffy bags and dark circles, with a frail, quiet voice—a live walking, talking corpse.

"Bryn?" Alexandria cried.

Cari stood in the doorway as the therapist and nurses exited the room. "I'll see them out," she said, following behind the team of men and women.

"And you thought I had an entourage before." Aamir wiped sweat pebbles from his forehead. "What are you doing here?" he asked Alexandria snidely.

"Aamir! What the *fuck* is going on?" Alexandria screamed as her staggering glare caught Aamir's scrupling eyes.

Aamir repositioned his electric wheelchair, aiming it in Alexandria's direction. "Like my new wheels? I was sort of going for Professor X's look, minus the bald head and crippled legs." He sped past her, heading outside to the terrace. "How great is my fucking life? Just look at all this shit that doesn't mean anything to me anymore." He looked around out at the beach.

Alexandria scurried to keep up with him. "Oh, Aamir." Her eyes saddened even more. "I'm sorry this happened to you." She threw her arms around him, hugging him without letting go.

"Who would've thought?" He threw a few pills back and sipped from a glass filled with water. "What's up? Where ya been, dude?" He glared at Alexandria. "You fell off the face of the fucking earth. Did Nial hold you hostage in her sex dungeon?" He readjusted his arm in the comfort strap. "Did you touch the stones and go back to the eighteenth century?"

"Aamir." Alexandria's head sank into her chest. "I'm so sorry. There's been so much going on. I don't know where to begin."

"How about the beginning?" He looked out onto the sandy beach.

"The twins…umm…they…Aamir." Alexandria dropped down to her knees, crying. "My bunnies, THEY'RE GONE!" she screamed.

"Gone where?" Aamir was puzzled. Bryn walked near Alexandria and stooped beside her, wrapping her arms around her.

"Where are they, Alexandria?" Bryn asked.

"They're…they're dead." Tears and mucus covered Alexandria's face.

Aamir turned his chair around quickly. "What did you say?" Tears filled his eyes. His lips quivered with every word that he uttered, watching Alexandria balled up like a fetus in front of him. There was nothing he could do to ease Alexandria's broken heart. Aamir cried. "Where's Nial?" Stunned, he went to the wine bar and pulled a whiskey bottle from under the sink. He grabbed two half-pint glasses, placed one in his mouth, one under his chin, and the other in his lap. He put the glasses down one by one, filling them to the rim.

"Nial." Alexandria continued to bawl. Mumbling, her mouth barely moved as she attempted to reveal the tragic events that had recently occurred. "Nial's in prison. I don't know where or what prison. It's like she disappeared."

"Damn! God, help us!" Aamir yelled out.

Alexandria muscled up from the floor and grabbed a box of tissue from behind the wine bar. She gently placed it against Aamir's nose.

"I'm so sorry, Alex." His congested nose dripped snot. "I'm sorry this happened." He blew his nose so hard it resembled a trumpet.

Alexandria had never heard Aamir call out to God. "I couldn't face you, Aamir. I'm so hurt. There is so much going on. I need a lawyer. I need help finding Nial, and all our bank accounts are frozen because of her. The police are trying to make me testify against her."

Bryn stood by, listening. "Jane can help, Alex." Bryn calmly laid her hand on Alexandria's shoulder. "We will get through this—together."

"And I'm here for you, Alex—for all of you. I want to be here for you all, anything you need," Cari chimed, throwing a shot of whiskey back. "Just let me in." She stared at Alexandria, longing for her approval.

"I hear you. Okay." A slight smile crept across Alexandria's face.

"The darkness will not win. We will not be defeated." Bryn turned on the radio, and the speakers blasted one of her favorite songs, "Never Give Up." She sang, dancing around, swaying her hips to the hypnotic music, screaming the lyrics until her voice cracked.

Alexandria stared at her in wonder and danced along beside her. Aamir pressed a button on his chair, instantly twirling around in circles. Skids marked the terrace floor and lifted his right arm, slowly pumping his fist in the air.

CHAPTER 32

Marley

A profound odor pervaded the everglades. A massive mudslide washed across the wetlands, drowning most of the aquatic animals. In the center of it stood a building tucked behind what used to be evergreen trees. The building had many shapes and dimensions to it, with the prickling of barbed wire surrounding it. It was sort of like an awkward-standing Rubik's Cube. The stair configuration had a large radius circling the building above the courtyard. No one could get in, and no person could get out.

In between the cold steel walls, women shivered in their blue, white, and black jumpsuits. Murderers wore the blue jumpers. Those who'd committed environmental endangerment such as bombings, members of the cartel, and mafia members wore the white jumpsuits. The black jumpers were for those who committed embezzlement crimes, robbery of high-end organizations, conspiracy, and fraud.

A blindfold had been placed on Nial's eyes. She had no idea where the detectives had taken her, but she was determined to escape somehow, someway. When she entered through the double doors, guards and inmates stared at her from head to toe. The guards held on to their guns. The floors peeled, and the cracks held mildew in the crevice. There were whispers of asbestos in the food and water but no solid proof. Nial bypassed lunch in the dining hall daily. She'd learned the janitor's closet was a great hiding place near the laundry room. None of the inmates fancied laundry, so they stayed away unless they worked there. The laundry workers were too busy smuggling anything they could get their hands on.

Within Nial's first week at the prison, her roommate, Coffee, spat in her face. She bullied Nial regularly, urging Nial to join her gang for sexual favors. For every refusal that Nial gave, Coffee's behavior became worse. Finally, she began beating Nial in her sleep, hoping to break her. Nial was furious, so she plotted and waited for the perfect time to get revenge. It was like fate when she came across a bottle of rat poison in the janitor's closet. She sacrificed her tube of toothpaste so that she could stuff the rat poison inside of it.

Night after night, she anticipated the killing when the night would come. Finally, Coffee was exhausted from honoring the warden's demands. She slept with her mouth wide open, making it easier for Nial to squeeze the tube of poison into her mouth. She watched as the poison drained down Coffee's throat. By the time Coffee realized what had happened, it was too late. She had fallen on the floor, scuffling and gagging; but Nial held her down, covering her mouth, pushing the vomit back down her throat until she passed out dead. Nial struggled to put Coffee back in her bunk before early morning checks. Just in time, she jumped back in her cot before anyone noticed what she had done.

The next morning as the sun peeked, Coffee lay stiff as a board with foam spewing from her mouth. Her body began to decompose from the inside out. The smell stifled the room, almost suffocating Nial when the guards came rushing into the mephitis-stricken cell. The guards questioned Nial about Coffee's passing, but she knew that it was a façade. Instead, the warden chose another of Coffee's crew members to do her dirty work and pretended to write a letter explaining the unfortunate occurrence to the family. Soon after, it was like nothing had ever happened, the same way she'd done to all the other inmates that mysteriously disappeared.

Nial had the room all to herself, but sleep was the last thing on her mind. She lay awake for almost a month as dark rings ran circles around her eyes. The mattress was uncomfortably hard. The rain was the only thing that gave her a sense of peace, listening to the water rise, coercing the waves against the building. It reminded her of San Francisco, early mornings, making love to Alexandria. She reminisced.

Little did she know upstairs on the other end of the hallway, she had enemies awaiting her demise. Coffee's crew wasn't happy about her death. Whether Nial had something to do with it or not, they blamed her. Nial would show her face in only a few places because the gang of ladies was always around. The dining hall and the courtyard were off-limits until Nial met an older Dominican woman named Junebug. Junebug had befriended her after Nial gave her a banana one evening when she passed out. Nial remembered that Alexandria would give Goether orange juice when she became hypoglycemic and assumed that that was what Junebug needed. Junebug had a click of her own. It was five of them: Junebug, Pickle, Swan, Bosh, and Tiptoe. They were all Dominican and stayed close to one another as much as they possibly could. Nial met the women during a spades game when they needed more people to play. Even though gambling was forbidden in prison, the ladies found a way to camouflage the game. They'd play for food, drugs, medications, cigarettes—anything they could get their hands on as leverage if necessary.

"What'd you do, Mami?" Swan asked Nial as she slammed a deck of cards down on the table.

"Where are we?" Nial asked. "Are we in California? San Francisco?"

The ladies laughed hysterically. "No, fefe. Why are you here? You don't look like a murderer." Swan picked her nose.

"I need to know about our location. If you help me, I will help you when we get out," Nial assured the women.

"Get out? Yuh, baby girl, we ain't going nowhere. We're surrounded by swamp creatures and muddy waters." Junebug slapped a card down on the table.

"There is always a way." Nial leaned back in her chair with her legs crossed.

"We're inside the new Alcatraz, darling," Bosh answered. "Haven't you heard?"

Suddenly one of Coffee's girls walked up to their table, making demands. "You owe us, bitch." A tall buff woman with knife tattoos across her arms and neck pointed at Nial.

"I do not know you." Nial ignored the woman. "Alcatraz?" she questioned as the name resonated.

"What does she owe you?" Tiptoe asked.

"Her life, she killed Coffee."

"No, her debt is our debt now." Junebug stood up, and all the Dominican women on the courtyard surrounded Coffee's crew. About one hundred Dominicans were standing around them. Some of them folded their arms, while others rubbed their hands together. Coffee's team didn't utter a word. They knew there was no chance of getting Nial with Junebug and her girls around. They'd have to catch Nial alone. So they stood in silence until the security guards came running their way.

"We'll get you, bitch!" one of Coffee's crew members yelled out as she backed away.

Nial smirked as the guards took them off the yard. The fatuous women were no match for what she had planned for their demise even if it took prevarication to succeed.

The closet space had become Nial's sanctuary, so she thought. She had made a flashlight out of wires, two plastic bottles, popsicle sticks, two batteries, some glue, one LED, and a cap. She remembered watching a video with Nathaniel when he had a class project on famous inventors, and he chose the inventor of the flashlight. She and Alexandria had a considerable debate about the Russian guy rumored to manufacture and market the product and the British immigrant that supposedly patented the idea.

She collected the items needed by doing favors for Tiptoe and Pickle on the side. She was also a runner for the Dominicans. She'd run drugs, cigarettes, fruits and pass them off without being noticed by the prison guards. It was her specialty, and she was utilized for her talents. She had to play her part to keep their protection.

As she sat plotting inside the closet space, nibbling on an apple, someone burst into the room, quickly locking the door behind them.

"Who the fuck are you?" Nial shone her flashlight.

"Marley." The woman sat down on the floor. "Marley." She held her hand out for Nial to shake. "Inmate 456654, if we're technical." She rolled her eyes, and Nial smiled slightly.

Marley was beautiful, with a smile that lit up the closet like a candle. Her hair was white as snow. And she smelled like lavender and frankincense, Nial thought. The woman reminded her of Alexandria—warm, innocent, and uniquely gorgeous. A tear fell from her eye, but she swiped it away quickly. "What do you want? How did you know I was in here?" she questioned.

"I've been watching you. You're beautiful." Marley moved closer to Nial.

"Who sent you?" Nial was skeptical. She stood up, shining the light down on Marley.

"Nobody sent me." Marley reached up and untied Nial's blue pants, allowing them to fall to the floor. She placed her hand inside her panties. Nial tried to resist, but she had been sexless for over ten months and needed to release some tension. Marley kissed her thighs and legs. Nial grabbed her up by the throat, kissing her, throwing her against the wall. The mop bucket fell over, causing a loud thud, scaring them both. They jumped, giggling at the same time.

"I hear you need a roommate. It should be me," Marley whispered in Nial's ear.

"I'd like to see you pull that off." Nial laughed.

"It's done. I made sure of it."

"What did you do, fuck one of the guards?"

"I made someone else do it." Marley laughed, pulled up Nial's pants, and opened the door. "See you soon, roomie." She winked, licking her lips at the same time.

One year had passed, Nial and Marley had become closer than Nial expected them to. The closer they became, the more details Marley shared about her life. After Nial realized Marley's value, she committed herself to Marley. Of course, it didn't hurt that Marley was beautiful, charming, and chatty. *When people talk more than they should, they're bound to provide more information than they need to,* Nial thought as she leaned in carefully during late-night conversations, listening to the waves crash against the building. Marley did most of the talking, while Nial paid close attention.

"How long have you been here?"

"Over eight years, I think." Marley played with Nial's navel.

"What did you do?"

"I'm innocent."

"Says everyone that has ever been caught."

"Seriously, my sister did the crimes, and I'm doing time."

"Your sister?"

"Yes, you may have heard of her, Rebecca Weinberg."

"Hmm…Weinberg? Weinberg? No."

"She was a snake. She's always been that way since we were kids. Then after a while, my mother said she suffered from a mental illness and tried to get her help. When Becca found out, my mother came up dead, and I know Becca had something to do with it."

"Where is Rebecca now?"

"The bitch of the wicked is dead."

"Dead?"

"A disease took her out."

"That is heavy."

"My mother was an angel who birthed the spawn of hell. Becca made lives hell. She was so manipulative. She manipulated her own husband. Well, something happened to him overseas, and he ended up being just as crazy as Becca."

"Heavy."

"Yesss, the worse thing about it is…her husband kidnapped some kids. I think they are twins. I'm not sure of the details, but I heard from the streets…allegedly. Crazy shit, right?"

Nial stood up quickly, grabbing bottled water she had taken from the Dominicans, splashing it on her face. "Are you sure he kidnapped the kids? He has the kids now?" Her thoughts and emotions were wrecked. It was confirmed that her children were still alive. Joy and utter hate took over at the same time. The need to escape the hell she had been placed in was no longer a question mark.

"Yes, babe."

Nial kissed Marley and instantly began doing push-ups and sit-ups. Excitement had taken over and pure determination to get her family back. How would she get off the prison ship surrounded by water? She contemplated *the new Alcatraz*. She had to find out more.

CHAPTER 33

Katherine Dumont

Two individuals rushed into Nial's prison cell and snatched her from the bunk as she lay next to Marley. They blindfolded, handcuffed, and took her away. For two days, she was locked inside an unknown place without food or water. She was transported from place to place but had no idea where to. Thunderous propellers hurt her ears as she found herself aboard a plane. Hours later, a vehicle hit every bump and hump on a winding road.

She woke up, confused at first until she realized the familiar environment. She lay inside a huge gazebo surrounded by flowers, sand, and a body of water that stretched for miles. It was like someone had meticulously placed her in position—her hair, her clothes, the way her neck lay across the satin pillow, her arms and legs underneath the lilac satin sheets. There were no other homes nearby for miles. She wasn't in the United States anymore.

A woman walked near with two Dobermans by her side. The dogs stood high above her hip. Her jeans hugged her frame, and her white tank top followed suit. "It took me a while to find you. How could you allow this to happen? I taught you better." The woman released the dogs from their leash and sat down beside Nial.

"I cannot be here. Why are we in Milan? Your father's old hideout."

"You are here, and you will stay. What the hell happened, Kitty Kat?"

"Don't."

"What...call you that? You used to like it."

"I need to get my bébés. I cannot do this right now, Lina."

"After all I've done, favors I've used, and this is how you repay me?"

"You have my deepest gratitude, but I need to locate my bébés. I think I know where they are."

"Alexandria?"

"No, my bébés."

"I'm going with you."

"No."

"You are mine, Kitty Kat. I let you have your fun. Now it's time to come back home."

"I must get Nathaniel and Abella Rose."

"I am going with you."

"No."

"Yes, did you not miss me?"

"Yes, always, Lina.

"I am yours, and you belong to me always."

"I need my things. Is my account obtainable to me?"

"Yes, of course, where are you going? Do you have a plan?"

"I will make one as I go."

"No, no more reacting without a plan. We will do this right. I got you out that prison, and I will not do it again if you get caught in more bullshit. You are lucky some people owe me favors."

"Lili." Nial got down on her knees.

"The last time you called me Lili, we were kids. Alexandria has made you soft. Get up." She lifted Nial from the ground by her hands and dusted the sand from her knees.

"Agatone is alive. He has the twins."

"Why is he still alive? Damn it! Must I do everything? I want him dead." She picked up her cell phone and instantly began to make demands. "Are the children chipped?"

"Yes, but I must go back to San Francisco to access the chips, the estate where Alex is—"

"Great. Just fucking great. I suspect Alexandria does not know about me? About us?"

"We need to keep it that way."

* * *

Back at the estate, Nial stood at the door, hesitant to go inside. She looked around at the bushes and trees that had grown over the windows and the rooftop. Everything else still looked the same on the outside but a mystery inside. Alexandria's car was parked out front. Nial crossed the threshold. Alexandria came rushing toward the door as if in a hurry and instantly paused at Nial standing there. The women did not utter a sound. It was as though they could not find the words to create a sentence. Nial reached for Alexandria's face, but she slapped her hand away. Nial walked past Alexandria, leaving her standing at the door. Cigarette butts and wine bottles had taken the place of vases and statues. The eclectic art that Nial had bought no longer filled the open space.

"We must talk."

"It's been three years, Nial." Alexandria sat on the chair inside the foyer with her legs crossed and a cigarette between her fingers. "Talk about what?"

"Our bébés."

"What about them?"

"Alexandria, they are alive." Nial eyes squinted in happiness and sadness all at once.

"Alive!" Tears instantly filled Alexandria's eyes. "What? Where are they? Wait. What?" *Three birthdays would make them eight years old. What if they do not remember me? What if they've been hurt, or mistreated, abused?*

"I have a plan." Nial grabbed Alexandria's hand and pulled her along. "Come."

They walked inside the bedroom that looked as if no one had slept in for years. Nial searched the room for something, and Alexandria stared confused. "What are you looking for?"

"A key. Where is the damn thing?"

"A skeleton key?"

"Yes, do you have it?"

Alexandria went to her jewelry box inside the safe and swiped the key. Nial snatched it and took off instantly through the home. Alexandria ran behind her. Nial stood in front of the middle closet inside the long hallway. The closet door opened when she placed her hand on the top glass. An elevator was there. "What the fuck, Nial?"

"Come." Nial pulled Alexandria onto the elevator with her, and they went underground.

"What is all this?" Alexandria pointed at the pictures plastered against the wall of an unfamiliar woman. "Who is this woman? She looks like you."

"My mother." Nial stared briefly at Alexandria.

Alexandria continued to examine the room and the gallons of water in every corner. There were computers, monitors, phones, and other unknown machines that Alexandria was not familiar with. It looked like they were inside a secret agent's office with all the different gadgets and doohickeys. It was as though they were inside another place instead of their loving family home.

"I chipped the twins. I can access the chip from here."

"Chipped? When?"

"When they were born." Nial sat down at a screen that looked like a computer, but it wasn't. It was something else. She stuck the key inside a funny-shaped hole that fit perfectly and turned it as she typed a code on the keyboard. "I did not want anyone to know."

"Not even me…I am their mother." Alexandria could not believe what she was seeing. All this time, she had been living inside a home with a secret passage.

"I couldn't risk it. Got it. It looks like…" Nial hesitated.

"Looks like what?" Alexandria stretched her neck, trying to see what Nial saw.

Nial picked up the phone and began speaking in Spanish. "I have to go. We will speak later. There's more to discuss."

"No, you cannot barge in here, then leave. What the hell! Who were you talking to? What is going on?" Alexandria screamed in frustration. Nial stopped in her tracks.

"I am *so* sorry for everything I put you through, Alex. I luff you with everything in me. I will never stop luffing you, but now I need to get Ella and Nate back."

* * *

Alexandria anticipated Nial's phone call for several weeks when suddenly she received a mysterious package at the front gate with detailed instructions. On the same day, she caught a private jet to a secret location. A black SUV waited for her when she arrived. Alexandria rolled her overnight bag toward the truck. Nial reached for her hand when the driver opened the door.

"Thank you for coming, Alex. However, I must tell you."

"Tell me where my bunnies are."

"We will get to that. I have found a location, but we must be strategic." As Nial spoke, her phone rang, and she began speaking in Spanish. She watched as Alexandria's facial expression changed.

Alexandria snapped the phone from Nial's hand and threw it out the window. "Where the hell are my bunnies?"

"Calm down. Listen. We are going into dangerous territory. The woman you are about to meet is the potentate of this country."

"So she's more dangerous than you?" Alexandria scoffed.

"I am not...Alex, please listen to me. These people...we cannot play with. Please do as I say, and we will get Nate and Ella back."

Alexandria sat back in the seat quietly and lit a cigarette. "Tuh, do as you say," she mouthed. Nial side-eyed her as she placed her hand on Alexandria's thigh.

Moments later, they pulled into a compound surrounded by guards. Nial rolled down the window, holding two fingers up, and the gate opened. Alexandria sat up in her seat. More men were standing by, holding big guns, protecting a woman staring down at them from the mansion's top floor. Another gate opened, and the driver drove into a garage under the manor. Nial and Alexandria hopped out, and Nial led the way up a flight of stairs. They walked a long hallway until they came upon a room where a woman stood wearing an erubescent suit.

The woman continued to stare out the window as if they were not standing behind her. A large dining table that could fit about twenty people sat in the floor's center with multiple computer monitors and tiny cell phones beside them. Behind the woman was another table. It was round, covered with framed photographs of an older man with white hair, familiar dignitaries, and a signed autograph of Colombia's president. The woman turned around, and Alexandria stared at her from head to toe.

"Finally." The woman sauntered toward Nial, grabbed her waist, and kissed her on the lips.

"Alex, this is Lina. Lina, Alex."

"Catalina to strangers. I see what you saw in her." Catalina walked circles around Alexandria as she towered above her. "She smells sweet." She twiddled the ends of Alexandria's hair, sniffing her tresses.

Nial pulled Alexandria back from her. "Lina, stop. We are here to find the twins, nothing more."

"What is this? Who is this woman, Nial?" Alexandria scowled.

Catalina sat down at the roundtable and pulled a Cuban cigar from her jacket pocket. "I am the person that made Nial, Nial. I do not know why she plays these games with you girls." She smirked.

"Do you have my twins? Does she have our babies, Nial?"

"Do you have my twins? No. Why would I have your little rug rats?" Catalina mocked Alexandria, blowing smoke from her mouth.

"Lina?" Nial eyebrows contracted.

Alexandria began to hyperventilate. The room started to spin, and everything went dark.

CHAPTER 34

Nicoll

Far from Bogotá, Bryn was singing on the balcony when Aamir's physical therapist, Nicoll, interrupted her. She had replaced the first therapist after she left for another position within the organization. "What's wrong, Nicoll?" Bryn laid her guitar aside.

"I have good news. Aamir's arm is back. He just received it. He wants you to do the honors and put it on for him."

Bryn placed the microphone on the chair and ran into Aamir's man cave. He ripped through the box like a child on Christmas morning. "Slow down. You do not want to damage it." Nicoll assisted him.

"Wow, it's beautiful. It looks real!"

"It took a lot of cell mapping. The color will eventually change, so don't be alarmed when it's adapting to Aamir's skin tone."

"You never answered me…will you two be in attendance tonight?" Bryn asked as she read the instruction manual.

"Wait. Wait. First, you must apply the gel, so it slides on perfectly." Nicoll took the tube of lube from its pack and rubbed it along Aamir's stub. "The prosthetic arm was developed by the AB-Bionics Institute in Italy. Its estimated cost is twenty-two million dollars. The arm can detect any surface, skin, wood, metal, hot, or cold temperatures. When you and Aamir make love, Bryn, the hand will adapt to the temperature when he lays his hand next to any surface. He will be able to utilize his hand better than ever, and wait for it. It will start to attach itself to Aamir's body. It is designed so the blood vessels and veins will connect to it, and he will never have to take it off. Our doctors and scientists have been working on this for a decade. Aamir is one of the firsts to receive it," Nicoll explained as she read the label.

"Never take it off? What about the stitches? Is that painful?" Bryn's mouth flew open. "But isn't that dangerous? It looks like a superhero's arm. It's…wait. When I touch it, the texture changes. How?"

"No, there is a numbing agent inside the pocket, so when it's clasped, he doesn't feel it. Also, the doctors have rerouted the stitching so the arm will attach to the vessels. So what can I say? Technology." Nicoll winked.

"Fucking *fire*! Right, babe?" Aamir made a fist, then opened and closed his hand. He grabbed Bryn's face with both hands and kissed her lips before he took off into his gym downstairs. He began hitting the punching bag until it detached and went flying across the room.

"My king? Be careful." Bryn watched as he punched the air and clapped his hands together and pumped his fist.

"Bryn, Aamir is familiar with the arm. He wanted to surprise you. This is what we have been working on at the facility. This is why he came home with bloody bandages because they rewired his blood vessels."

Bryn was speechless, excited, and ready for Aamir to hold her the way he used to. She had never seen anything like it. Seary ran into the room where they all stood. He stopped and stared at Aamir's arm. "What the fuck is this!" he yelled. "Bionic man?" He laughed. "Damn. Cool!"

"Watch your mouth. Go do your schoolwork!" Bryn yelled as he ran out the room and out to the side yard where he kept his puppies. He rolled around on the grass with the three pups as they licked and tugged on his shoestrings.

Bryn contacted Alexandria to see if she would attend her live singing party. The voice mail answered as usual. They suspected she was on a work trip, so neither she nor Aamir bothered to follow up. Millions of people were attending online from around the world.

Celebrities and other famous people attended in person as the event streamed live on the beach outside their home.

After Aamir began posting videos of him and Bryn online, the couple went viral. Bryn's fans searched through them, finding a video of Bryn singing to Aamir during his recovery. She motivated him with her singing while the masseuse massaged the sensitive parts of his body. Her fans supported them, provided encouraging words and get-well wishes. Their support was unwavering.

She promised her fans a live performance for them after releasing her latest book, *How We Survived the Crash*. The story entailed Aamir's car crash, alcohol addiction, and the loss of their unborn child. The nonfiction topped the best seller lists for several months. Bryn wrote five songs as an extended addition to the book and gifted the pieces to supporters.

There were lights and candles and tent canopies stretched across the beach. A camera crew was also there to film the entire event. The live event would also be captured on network television for the world to see in days to come.

"Nicoll." Cari had been eyeing Nicoll all night. She held two beers in her hand.

"Yes, Cari." Nicoll took one of the beers and sipped from it.

"I want to fuck you right now." Cari grabbed Nicoll, pulling her inside one of the canopies tucked away from the crowd of people. Nicoll slid out of her embrace as her shirt hung from her shoulder. Cari snatched her closer, ripping the shirt completely off, and threw Nicoll on the mattress. She wrapped her hand around Cari's neck, squeezing as Cari's hands fondled her breast. Next, Cari kissed underneath her belly button before wrapping her tongue around Nicoll's pearl before easing her dildo from her pants and inside Nicoll's hot spot. She slipped in and out of Nicoll, stroking her insides as if it were their last night together. Nicoll flipped Cari over and climbed on top of her, riding her, nibbling her neck and chest. They screamed out in lust.

They didn't realize someone was watching them the entire time, recording their every move. There was a glare that shone from the camera light through to the canopy. It almost blinded Nicoll as she continued to embrace Cari's thrusts. She swiftly hopped up and somersaulted toward the glaring light quietly without alarming the guests. She kicked the camera phone from the guy's hand, picked the phone up, and knocked him down to the ground with her fist. The guy screamed as she held him down. "I will kill you." The look in Nicoll's eye terrified the man. Her pupils turned black as the raven eye in that moment of anger.

"This bitch is crazy, man!" the man yelled as he trampled away, falling over his feet in fear.

Cari stood watching from afar as Nicoll walked back toward her. "What was that? That was some ninja shit." She pulled her dreads back up into a ball.

"No worries. Shall we continue this at my place?" Nicoll pulled Cari by the front of her pants, leading the way.

A few weeks later, Nicoll and Cari had begun seeing each other regularly. They went on dates with Aamir and Bryn to exotic museums, fishing, and excursions to Nigeria and Belize. On one of the many nights Cari and Nicoll spent alone ordering takeout, Nicoll waited inside Cari's truck while she paid for dinner. Cari ran back to her Pagani, attempting to dodge the drizzling rain. The door was raised as she slid into the seat. "Who is that?" she asked as she drove off into the streetlights.

"It's you." Nicoll pointed to Cari's chest. "And me." She smirked. "I want you." She slid her panties down and began to play with herself, stimulating her lady parts. Cari pulled alongside the road onto gravel, laid her seat back, unbuckled Nicoll's seat belt, and pulled her on top of her.

"I got it from that creep, remember?" Nicoll began to moan as Cari pulled her deeper into her mouth. "Recording us!" she screamed as she creamed all over Cari's face.

"You turn me on."

Thick fog smothered the windows as the heat rose from their body. Nicoll slid to the floor under the steering wheel, returning the favor until Cari climaxed all over her seat.

On their drive back to Cari's place, Nicoll revealed that she'd been called back to her country and needed to leave. Cari pulled up to her residence and sat quietly. "How long have you known this?" She tucked her hair behind her ears.

"Just got the text. I'm so sorry. I'll be back soon, but I must leave tonight." Nicoll kissed Cari's cheek.

"If you have to leave…I'll see you when you return. How long will you be away? Does Aamir know you're leaving?"

"Yes, I will no longer work with Aamir, but he has my number in case he needs me. He invited me to the wedding they've put off for far too long." Nicoll placed Cari's arm around her shoulders and lay on her chest. "I'm so sorry to spring this on you like this, but I have no choice."

"I'll see you when I see you, right?"

Nicoll looked at Cari strangely. "Sure."

* * *

Back in Bogotá, Alexandria and Nial waited inside a private room. The room was set up like the secret room inside their estate back in San Francisco, minus the gallons of water. Alexandria sipped from a teacup while Nial sniffed a few lines of cocaine.

"Still on the booger sugar?" A man wearing a three-piece suit entered the room. He was neatly dressed, and there was not a single strand of hair out of place. A gun sat on both sides of his hip. Nial rose and hugged the man.

"Where is your dumbass brother, Rico? We need to hurry and get this done. We have not slept in months scouting this place." Nial leaned over and rubbed the top of Alexandria's hand.

"Pipe down, *chachita*. Rico and Catalina are on their way."

"Thanks for making it on time." Alexandria smiled at him.

"Anything for you, mami." He grabbed her hand, attempting to kiss the back of it when Nial intervened.

"Don't get too comfortable, Ronaldo." Nial's perpetual scowl was on the brink of rage.

"I see everyone made it. Thank you, uncles, for coming." Catalina rushed through the door. "See, I have my white cape on. I come to save the day." Her hands on her hips, she paused, glaring at every person in the room. "Kitty Kat, it is always a pleasure." She winked at Nial.

"Kitty Kat?" Alexandria repeated.

"Yes, did Nial not tell you her real name? Katherine. Katherine Dumont. Sexy, yes? I do not know why she hates her name. But she will always be my Kitty Kat."

"Don't listen to her," Nial said right before a familiar face entered the room. "Nico? I thought you were at that scientist lab you own." Nial fixated on Nico as she took her seat beside Rico in a hurry.

"No, what is the plan?" Nico asked.

"Nice of you to finally join us, Nico," Catalina spoke calmly. "Now, if everyone would shut the fuck up, we can get started!" she yelled.

A few unfamiliar faces joined the meeting as they sat around the giant screen, listening to Nial and Catalina speak in accordance. One would lead, then the other followed. The screen captured images of five warm bodies.

"What is the plan? I'm tired of waiting." Alexandria was unsure if she should voice how she felt, but it was now or never. Uncertainty showed its face when dealing with Catalina and her uncles. But she trusted Nial to handle business as usual. She fiddled her thumbs when thinking of what her children must've endured all these years without them.

"Spicy," Catalina mocked. "If you look closely, you will see my men guarding the perimeter." She aimed the stick to the different areas on the screen, following the highlighted fields. "The yellow here"—she smacked the screen—"these are my men in the trees and under the dirt, camouflaging themselves. Nial and I have been working on this for a while. These are your children with Agatone, the two purple dots here." She smacked the monitor with the end of the stick once more. "Your twins are with Agatone, and the woman is Bethany Stone. There are others with them, but as of now, we do not know who they are."

"Bethany Stone? Nial's secretary Bethany?" Alexandria interrupted. "Where are they?"

"They are in the Philippines. And yes, Alex, Bethany helped him kidnap the twins." Nial tried to keep her composure, but her face turned beet red.

"Now!" Catalina yelled, hitting the monitor. "If I may finish. I will get the kids. Nico will distract Agatone."

"Why can't Nial or I go?" Alexandria asked. "They're our children." She got up, pacing the floor.

"Agatone is familiar with you, and so is Bethany. You will be here monitoring the screen." Catalina continued to explain how things would go as everyone listened. "Kitty Kat is familiar with what happens next."

* * *

Nico wore a disguise in case Agatone remembered her. She walked up to the house, pretending to be hurt, stumbling up the steps where Agatone held the twins captive. She knocked on the door until someone answered. An overweight woman with blond hair and a mole the size of a dime on her chin answered, "Whattaya want?" It was as though she strained to speak. Her vocal cords sounded like they had been damaged. She smelled like old mop water.

"I was hiking with my boyfriend, and now I can't find him. Can I please use your phone? My battery died." Nico held up her cell phone. Fake scratches and blood ran down her leg. "Can you help me, please?"

The woman closed the door in her face and went back inside. A few minutes later, Agatone came to the door and spotted Nico laid out on the porch. He stared at her, and then he scoped out their surroundings. "We do not have a landline. Who do you need to call?" he asked.

"I need to call the police to help me find my boyfriend. My battery died." Nico held her phone up, and Agatone snatched it from her.

"No, there's no need for the cops to come search. I will help you. I know this forest inside out." Agatone grabbed his keys, and they got in his Jeep Wrangler that was parked on the side of the house, where no one could see it.

While Agatone was out searching for Nico's boyfriend, Catalina crept through the back window with her gun on her hip when she heard voices coming from a back room. She signaled her uncles, Rico and Ronaldo. Rico took the front of the house, and Ronaldo guarded the back. They captured the older woman, but Bethany was nowhere in sight. Nevertheless, the woman screamed, crying, "Agatone will be back soon! He has eyes on this place."

Ronaldo gagged the woman. Catalina entered each room, her pistol leading. Suddenly she came upon a place with locks on the door. She called out, "Is anyone here?" But there was no answer. There was faint whimpering, so she burst through the door. But no one was inside. She looked at the tiny monitor on her wrist that showed the purple dots that had appeared on the screen. She couldn't figure out why the dots were showing because there was no sign of the twins. The room had three twin-size beds, a small television, and a rocking chair. Mold covered the windowsill. The floor was weary, and insulation spewed from the cracks in the wall. A ridged rug was underneath one of the beds. She slid the bed away from the wall, and there was a large hole underneath. Catalina was small enough to jump inside the cave.

"Hello."

No one answered.

"Nathaniel? Abella?"

The kids had not heard their names called in a long time. Agatone didn't know their names because they refused to tell him. The words *Him* and *She* had become their names for the last three years. Nathaniel and Abella Rose were scared. They hid underneath the house. The house was old, and the wood was soft. Termites and bugs were crawling and flying everywhere when suddenly Catalina saw a set of young frightened eyes.

She aimed the light from her gun in their direction. The closer she became, a smell that wreaked havoc filled her nostrils. "Hi, I come to get you for your parents." Catalina shone a light on a picture of Alexandria and Nial. The twins shivered like lost stray kittens and did not speak a word. "Come with me. I promise I will take you to them." She held her hand out, and Abella Rose bit it. "No wonder he's keeping you down here. You're like wild wolves." She pressed numbers on her watch, attempting to call Nial and Alexandria's location when a loud noise chimed through the room. The sound came from above. She snatched the twins in her arms as they kicked and screamed.

"No, no...you're leaving the boy!" Abella Rose shouted and kicked.

"What is happening, Lina?" Nial yelled.

The twins continued to kick and scream as Catalina pushed them up through the hole in the floor. She continued to hold on to them as she ran toward the back of the house. Finally, she tossed the twins out the window to the soldiers. Nial's voice continued to sound through Catalina's watch, and Nathaniel recognized her voice. "Mama?"

"Yes, Nate, it's mama, my sweet boy. Listen to the lady, sweetie. She will bring you home to me safely."

Catalina jumped out the window.

As soon as her feet plummeted to the ground there, Agatone stood in front of her with a knife to Nico's throat. "These are my kids. You can't take them from me."

Catalina was torn between shooting him right there and not wanting the kids to see him. Her men also had their guns pointed at him.

Somehow, Nico swung herself around and jumped on the back of Agatone's neck, choking him with her legs. She squeezed so tight blood oozed down his nose. What they didn't know was that Bethany stood behind Catalina with a rifle aimed at her head.

"You better kill me," Catalina snarled when she heard the gun cock. Blood splashed on the back of her neck as one of the lead snipers shot Bethany in the back of her head. She fell to the ground, dead on sight. The rest of the men came running behind them. One of them held the overweight woman in handcuffs.

"My daughter!" the woman screamed. "You killed my Bethany!" she sobbed.

"Shut up, bitch, before you're next. As a matter of fact..." Catalina pulled a small gun from her inner jacket pocket, pointed at the woman, and released the trigger. Blood splattered. The woman fell to the ground. The twins screamed, and the guards took them away to a helicopter nearby as Catalina requested.

Nico released Agatone's neck. He heaved and coughed, spitting blood from his mouth. There were about ten infrared beams aimed at his head. "Kill me, you bitch! You took away everything that matters to me."

"What? Your kids? You held them hostage in a back room, you imbecile!"

Suddenly they heard crying and sniffing. Catalina turned around, and a little boy was hiding behind a bush. He appeared to be approximately ten years old. "Please don't kill me too," the boy cried.

"Great. Fucking great." Catalina nodded for Nico to go get the boy.

"What are we going to do with him?" Nico asked.

"Who are you? Who do you belong to?" Catalina asked.

"My son, he is my son," Agatone revealed as blood dripped from his nose.

"Let's go! Bring Agatone!" Catalina shouted to her men. "And the kid."

CHAPTER 35

The Wait Is Over

Nial and Alexandria waited in northern Bogotá for Catalina and Nico to return with the twins. They stayed in the same home that Catalina and Nial lived in for many years before Nial left Colombia. Alexandria placed her bags down on the floor, admiring the house that was tucked behind the hills. Nial reminisced, gliding her fingers across old photographs of them when they were teenagers that Catalina kept.

"What's going on with you and Catalina?" Alexandria asked. "Is she your new woman, old woman? And why does she know so much about you, Katherine Dumont?" She laughed sarcastically. "You are filled with surprises, Kitty Kat."

"Don't ever call me that." Nial snapped.

"Oh, so only Catalina can call you that?"

"Yes, yes, she can."

"Fucking asshole. Who are you?"

"I am Nial, the person you fell in love with and married, the person you promised you'd never leave."

"Don't you dare throw that psycho-blah-blah bullshit on me."

As the ladies argued, Catalina came whistling through the door. The ladies turned around and stared, waiting. "Carry on." She smirked. "Don't stop on my account."

"Where are my children?" Alexandria walked toward Catalina, huffing mad.

"Kitttyyy?" Catalina called Nial's name as if warning her to stop Alexandria. Her forehead wrinkled, and she reached in her inner jacket pocket.

"Alex, please calm down." Nial grabbed her hand, and she snatched it away.

"Where are my fucking children?" Alexandria asked again when suddenly Nico came through the door, holding Abella Rose and Nathaniel's hand.

Alexandria dropped to her knees, crying. Nial stared at them without a word. The twins' faces were solemn as if life had been sucked out of them. They didn't smile or shout or anything. It was as though they didn't know who Alexandria and Nial were. Instead, they continued to hold on to Nico's hand without letting go.

"Nico has a way with kids," Catalina scoffed.

"Nate, my sweet boy, come to Mama, sweetie." Nial held her hand out as she strolled toward him.

Nathanial's eyes brightened a little as he focused on Nial, and then he looked at Alexandria on her knees and then back at Catalina and took a step back behind Nico's legs, peeking around her thigh. "Mama?" Nathaniel said softly.

"Yes, sweetie, it's your mama Nial. I luff you so much, my sweet boy."

"Mama? Mama!" Nathanial took off, running directly into Nial's arms. He held on to her so tight she could barely breathe. "Mama! Mama!" he screamed and cried.

Nial wondered what went on all those years. Nathaniel spoke as though he were still five years old, like he had not grown mentally or intellectually. *Had the children been to school or eaten a healthy meal? Had they learned anything aside from what I and Alexandria taught them three years ago?*

Yet he continued to hold on to her tightly. His legs were longer, but his body was thin and frail.

Abella Rose watched her brother, as well as everyone in the room. Then she slowly let go of Nico's hand and walked toward Alexandria. "Are you my mommy?" she asked Alexandria.

Alexandria looked up with a stoned face of tears. "Yes, bunny, I am. I am your mommy. Do you remember me?" She stretched her hand out, hoping, waiting for Abella Rose to latch on.

"A little." Abella Rose hesitated to place her hand inside Alexandria's.

The look in her eyes was unlike anything Alexandria had ever seen. She moved closer to Abella Rose and placed her arms around her, hugging her gently. "I'm never letting you out of my eyesight again," Alexandria whispered in her ear.

Catalina and Nico left the room, leaving Nial and Alexandria with the twins. Nial led Nathaniel near Alexandria and Abella Rose. They huddled together, holding on to one another, crying.

That night, Nial, Alexandria, and the twins stayed in the king suite. The twins stayed close holding each other, trembling in their sleep. Their eyes mirrored raccoons as they dozed off simultaneously, keeping one eye closed and the other on their surroundings until their eyelids collapsed at once. Alexandria lay on one side of the bed as Nial sat up on the other side.

"What now?" Alexandria whispered as she rubbed Abella Rose's long hair. Her hair had grown down to her bottom.

"Cut their hair."

"It's not a joke. I'm worried. I don't trust these doctors. I want them to see our doctor, their doctor."

"They had x-rays, scans. The necessary procedures have been completed. Cotton-swabbed. They'll see a therapist soon when they are up to it. We are lucky to have them back."

"I want to go home, and not the estate where all the secrets stare me in my face, laughing."

"No, we must stay here for a while until we figure out what to do with him."

"Him? Him who?"

"Agatone."

"What? He's here?"

"Yes, behind bars. He will not escape. I promise."

Alexandria stayed awake all night, keeping her eyes on the twins. *They don't talk much. All they do is stay close to each other, whimpering like puppies.* As her thoughts interwove with insomnia, the sunlight seeped through the window cracks. As Nial and the twins slept, she tiptoed into the next room, locking the bedroom door behind her. She didn't notice Catalina sitting with a coffee mug in one hand and a cigar in the other as she walked outside to talk on the phone. Catalina snuck behind her.

"Nial doesn't want you."

"What?" Alexandria hung up the phone and turned facing Catalina.

"You are not meant to be together. You have no idea who she is…who we are."

"You are a lonely bitch. You have all these people around so that you can feel superior. But you are nobody. That's why Nial left you."

"You have no idea who I am. If you say one more word, I will release Agatone and feed your rug rats to him." Catalina laughed in between puffs of smoke.

"One day, you will die, and your people will sing praise at your burial site, grateful that the wicked witch is dead." Alexandria walked farther away from Catalina.

Catalina stepped three feet closer to Alexandria and slapped her with the back of her hand. "Watch your mouth. You are in my home. I own this country, and I will not be disrespected by an outsider."

Alexandria spat in her face, daring her to do something, anything. She was not afraid of Catalina anymore. She was tired, tired of it all—the endless disrespect, the murder, the secrets, the lies, the betrayal. Even if it would cost her, her life, she demanded respect. Too much trauma and sadness had occurred during her lifetime. She refused to let this woman belittle her anymore. At that moment, she was ready to fight, fight for her life, her kid's life, and her wife—fight for it all.

But it was as though Catalina was proud, or maybe even shocked, that Alexandria did not appear afraid. Nial was the only person that had stood up to her. She was slightly turned on by Alexandria's fierceness. She wiped the glob of spit from her face and rubbed it across Alexandria's shoulder, lit fire to her cigar, and walked away.

Alexandria did not reveal what had transpired between her and Catalina. Instead, she spent the rest of that week in Colombia reading, cooking for the twins, keeping her distance from Nial and Catalina.

Months rushed by, and Nial woke up horny and more hungry on one cloudy morning than ever. She searched the compound for Alexandria and the twins, but they were not inside the mansion. She waited for hours for them to return. Finally, she cooked brunch for them, assuming they had gone to the market or the green pastured fields as they always had. The grounds were a calming place that Alexandria had found for the twins. They were fond of the sunlight that beamed on the hills as they sat in the grass. Nathaniel played and tumbled down the slope, but Abella Rose would only sit under a tree with a book in her hand as though lost in her thoughts most days.

Each room was vacant. Nico remained asleep. From the sounds that came from her bedroom, she had a long night. As the sun began to fade, Nial decided to check the vicinity before rushing to Catalina's mansion. She phoned her, but there was no answer. Once she reached Catalina's place, she jumped out the vehicle, leaving the engine running. The gate was locked, so she stood out front, waving at the camera. Then the gate was released, and she scurried inside. Catalina waited at the entrance in wonder.

"Wha-what are you doing? Why are you dressed like that?"

Nial shoved her way inside past Catalina. "Where are they?"

"Who, Kitty?"

"My bébés, Alex, where are they?"

"I left her there with you. What is this foolishness?" Catalina whipped her hair back as she followed Nial around her home. "No one is here."

"What have you done? I can't find them anywhere. Where is my family?"

"Your family? I thought I was your family…hmm."

Nial raged toward Catalina and knocked her to the floor. "Where are my wife and twins?" She placed her hands around her throat, squeezing until her hands turned purple.

"The last time you held a knife to my neck, I released you. This time you'd better kill me." Catalina's words were unclear as she tried to pry Nial's hands away.

"I am going to ask you once more. Where is my fucking family?" Nial held Catalina down as she sat on top of her stomach.

"If I was going to kill them, don't you think I would've done it by now. I am Catalina Ceron, or have you forgotten? Hurting them would hurt you, and you know I will not do anything to hurt you, Kitty."

Nial eased up and released Catalina. "Then where are they?" She began to pace the floor when she noticed a shadow walking down the hallway.

"May I have some water, please?" A young boy appeared with sad eyes, staring at them without blinking.

"You kept Agatone's son?" Nial's eyebrows raised in suspicion as she got up and walked to the vestibule. "If I find out you had something to do with Alexandria and the twins, you will never see me again." She left, leaving Catalina standing beside the boy.

CHAPTER 36

Matrimony

A year had passed since Alexandria and the twins had gone missing and could not be tracked. Nial had moved back to San Francisco to search for them. Her hope was that they'd return to her back to California. Aamir, Bryn, and Cari searched every place imaginable for them, but it was as though they had disappeared from the face of the earth. Nial believed Catalina had nothing to do with their disappearance, but she was still unsure of the Colombian queen's intentions.

Nial sold their estate, vehicles, and jewelry and purchased a home outside the city limits on farmland. The countryside reminded her of her time in France when she was younger, except for the surplus trees, tractors, chickens, goats, and horses. Her farmhand helped her run the land, seeing as she had never been a boonies type of girl. She needed a familiar space to help her cope with the disappearance of Alexandria and the twins. Her business continued to flourish after everything she had endured. Yet her heart was hurt by the unknown. Will she ever see them again? Where were they? Were Alexandria and the twins alive? There were so many unanswered questions.

While Nial prepared for the special occasion, there was a knock at the door. She unlocked the latch, and Elizabeth shoved her way inside. "I thought we agreed you'd never come by?"

"The wedding is today?" Elizabeth tossed her handbag across a tall statue that resembled Alexandria.

"I do not want any drama." Nial walked into her bedroom.

"Why would there be a conflict? You know that I'm nonconfrontational. Besides, everyone who is somebody will be there."

"Except you."

"You're still in love with her? Why are you with me? If I am your woman, why does it matter if she shows up or not? You act as though she's still your wife!"

"She is my wife. And yes, I am still in luff with her. She is the mummy of my twins."

"You are a fool! Alexandria left you! Can't you see? She's never coming back. Don't you get it?"

"Get out. Get out. Get out!" she yelled so loud the glass vase shattered on the table. She continued to yell, "Get out!" until Elizabeth was out of her sight.

* * *

The wedding was extravagant—the banisters filled with tulips and yellow orchids that complemented the bride's yellow-and-white attire. There were white doves alongside the first set of pews. Bryn and Aamir chose not to have a traditional ceremony, so they walked down the aisle together instead of separately. The guests were enamored as they stood when Aamir and Bryn's favorite musicians began to play their hit song, "Love of My Life."

Walking down the aisle, Bryn wore a beautiful sleeveless soft shimmer satin gown artfully draped with an asymmetrical bodice, along with a yellow gold, diamond bracelet. Yellow diamond teardrop earrings hung gracefully from her earlobes. The Swarovski crystal heels complemented the ensemble.

Aamir wore a gorgeous white satin suit, a yellow vest, a white bowtie, yellow diamond studs in his ears, and white patent dress oxfords with yellow striped satin. They glistened and sparkled as the sun beamed on them from the vast stone windows.

Security surrounded the park on the outside so no photographers or unwanted guests could enter.

Standing in front of the minister, Aamir began his vows first. "I, Aamir Bahar, take you, Bryn, to be my stunning wife. I will cherish every day for the rest of our lives. You are everything, and I will never forget my vows to you on this day." His eyes filled with tears. He took the ring from Cari and placed it on Bryn's finger.

"I, Bryn Michaels, take you, Aamir, as my husband, my soul mate, and my best friend. I will love you and care for you through good times and bad. If we have disagreements, I promise to work them out with you. I love you, Aamir." Bryn waited for Seary to pass her the ring, but the doves alongside the pews had his undivided attention. "Psst…pssst…Seary!" she shouted.

He looked around.

"Ring, please?" Her voice was high-pitched.

The guest chuckled as Seary passed Bryn the ring. She placed it on Aamir's finger.

"You may kiss," the minister said.

After their long passionate kiss, the couple walked down the aisle. Everyone stood to acknowledge them. The guests met the bride and groom next door inside the garden pavilion.

As the guests poured into the garden area, they noticed a six-foot-tall black-and-gold wedding cake in the center of the room. Yellow and white roses filled the space, and a massive number of tulips and life-size ice sculptures were in every corner of the room. Aamir changed into a yellow-and-gold Oui suit by one of his favorite French designers, while Bryn wore Valant's black-and-gold sequenced gown, an upcoming local designer. They held hands as they entered the pavilion halls. Everyone danced, laughed, enjoying themselves—every person except Nial, who was sitting across the room, drinking one of many glasses of champagne.

She stared into the crystal flute. Her body was there, but her mind was not. It was as though her brain had fallen into the glass and attached itself to the bubbles tickling her nose. Instantly she got up from her chair and sped into the hallway, bypassing Nicoll as she entered the double doors.

DANG

The children's pavilion was packed to capacity as they were being entertained by clowns, go-karts, slides, swings, bouncers, and other fun activities the ample space had to offer. She couldn't help but imagine Nathaniel and Abella Rose playing alongside the other kids. They would be more prominent now, and Abella Rose would most likely be dancing with Alexandria or holding on to one of her favorite reads. Nathaniel would be next to her, begging to leave so that he could go home and play his game console. But they weren't there, and she was alone now. Now nothing else mattered, not the women, the money, the cars, the clothes—none of it. This was the first time in her life she'd felt helpless and alone. The love of her life was gone.

Seary sat with his sister and Aamir. He tapped his glass of sparkling water so he could gain everyone's attention. "Ummm…hello, everyone, I am not good at giving speeches, but I want to thank Aamir for coming into my sister's life. He has made a huge impact on Bryn's life and mine. I wish Aamir and my sister lifelong happiness and health. To the bride and groom." Seary chuckled. "I always wanted to say that." He leaned over to kiss his sister's cheek, hugged Aamir, and quickly exited the room.

Next, Nial entered the room as she stood in between the threshold. "Excuse me. Excuse me."

Everyone turned their chairs and heads toward Nial, waiting to hear. She paused, thinking about Alexandria, what she would say, how she might feel at that moment, and, most of all, wishing she was there.

What must the crowd-filled room be thinking? *Is she about to give an announcement about Alexandria? Maybe she's been found.* They'd seen Alexandria and the twins' face plastered across their screens and other news outlets and social media. Everyone knew they were missing or dead.

Her eyes teary, she spoke, "I am so happy for you, Aamir and Bryn. You remind me of what luff is, should be, and what we strive for. Wishing you the best on your journey of luff. Just remember what it is all for, even when the times get tough. I want you to look back on this day and remember why you are so perfect together. To

Mr. and Mrs. Aamir, Bryn Bahar. You are as one now," Nial said in tears, raising her glass.

As people cheered and clapped, Nial dashed out of the room and into the powder room. She powdered her nose with her favorite substance. As she investigated the mirror, a face appeared. "Alex? Alex, is it really you? I miss you. Please take me back. I will never hurt you again." Nial kneeled on the floor.

"What are you doing?"

"I want you so bad, please!" Nial slid her hands up her dress and pulled her panties down. She held on to her ass, pulling her body toward her face, sucking from her asshole to her pussy.

"I am not Alexandria. Get the fuck off me!" Nicoll enjoyed the feeling, but she was confused as hell. "Nial!" She pushed Nial to the tile.

"Alex?"

"Nico! What is wrong with you?" Nico grabbed her panties and slid them back on when Cari entered the powder room staring at them.

Nial stayed on her knees, crying. Mucus ran down her mouth as Cari helped her up. "She's gone. Alex is gone."

"You need help, dude." Cari frowned. "You are seriously losing it."

Nial's makeup smeared. Her eyes had noticeable dark circles she had been covering with makeup. She shoved Cari out of the way. Then, stumbling out of her heels, she walked down the hallway barefoot.

Cari stared at Nicoll. "I've been looking all over for you."

"I've been in here. Nial is behaving like a mad person."

"How do you know Nial? They were not in town when you came to work for Aamir," Cari asked. "Nicoll?"

"Nico, Nicoll, they are the same person. I am the same person. Nicoll Ceron is my given name."

The more Nicoll talked, the less Cari believed her. She was astonished and saddened by the blatant lies that fell from Nicoll's lips. Then she left the room, leaving Nicoll standing in a puddle of explanations.

As the evening streamed, the guest began to leave. Seary said his goodbyes and left the pavilion with two of his closest friends. Aamir and Bryn danced the night away. After all the guests had left, they remained on the dance floor in each other's arms.

"Did you see Nial? She was wrecked." Bryn laid her head on Aamir. She was so short her head rested right below his chest with heels on.

"Yes, I spoke with her briefly on her way out."

"I know this is tough, Alexandria not being here."

"It's not tough. It's heartbreaking, Bryn. But I want to enjoy this moment with you. So come on. Let's get out of here." He grabbed Bryn's hand and led her to a helicopter out back.

"Where are we going?"

"Anywhere we want." He kissed her lips and placed the headphones on her head. The helicopter took off into the night. The grass blew, and the trees swayed. The future was in their presence. San Francisco was in the distance, and so was their past.

*You never know where you are going
unless you dreamed it first.*

—Rei BiLLi

ACKNOWLEDGMENTS

I would like to thank God, the source of my creativity. My mom, your love and witnessing your strength motivates me daily. Thank you, Skylar. Your unwavering support is unmatched, my love. Shenna, Dorcas, and Shavonne, you've read and reread and listened to my endless story ideas. You are appreciated more than you know. Last but certainly not least, thank you to the editor, illustrator, and publisher for helping to make my dream a reality.

Rei BiLLi is the author of the children's science fiction, *In Chadwick's Eyes* under the pseudonym, Rae Yung. Billi enjoys writing children's sci-fi, fantasy, poetry, fiction, and young adult. The author's second upcoming publication, *Dang*, is an exhilarating women's fiction, crime story meant for open-minded adults and poses to open the minds of those who enjoy diversity.

Dang Divulgence coming soon.

If you are in a crisis, please contact the crisis text line.

United States and Canada: Text NAMI to 741741 or call the NAMI Helpline, 800-950-6264, to connect to a crisis counselor.
United Kingdom: Text SHOUT to 85258.
Ireland: Text HOME to 50808.